W9-BPM-037

*Praise for Dan Fesperman and*

# THE LETTER WRITER

"Stunning. . . . Danger, intrigue, politics, and spies are all masterfully woven for the reader's entertainment. . . . Addictive, fast-paced, and thrilling."  —*San Francisco Book Review*

"The WWII alliance between the Mafia and the U.S. government has been explored in crime fiction before . . . but never in such compelling fashion as Fesperman does here. . . . What makes this novel shine is the way Fesperman combines it with the mobsters-as-patriots angle and with the rich character of the letter writer. A multifaceted mix of mystery and historical fiction."  —*Booklist*

"Fesperman is a skilled, unpretentious writer who deftly incorporates his extensive knowledge of the period."  —*The Boston Globe*

"Intelligent. . . . Fesperman shows a skilled hand at creating the detail of wartime New York. . . . [T]he likable and well-drawn [protagonist] will go over well with readers, especially those fond of historicals."  —*Publishers Weekly*

"[T]he brilliant Dan Fesperman takes us into a world of intrigue. . . . Don't miss this one—it's sure to be on my list of the year's best books."  —Margaret Cannon, *The Globe and Mail* (Toronto)

"*The Letter Writer* is a unique blend of a scholarly sleuth teamed with a Sherlock Holmes–like chameleon in a time of history ripe for building stories of suspense around. . . . The combination is pure chemistry, and pure entertainment." —*Bookreporter*

"You come away from a Fesperman novel not only abuzz with the exhilaration of the chase but also aware that you've absorbed something of the complexity of the world's conflicts." —*San Francisco Chronicle*

*Dan Fesperman*

# THE LETTER WRITER

Dan Fesperman's travels as a journalist and novelist have taken him to thirty countries and three war zones. *Lie in the Dark* won the Crime Writers' Association of Britain's John Creasey New Blood Dagger Award for best first crime novel, *The Small Boat of Great Sorrows* won their Ian Fleming Steel Dagger Award for best thriller, and *The Prisoner of Guantánamo* won the Hammett Prize from the International Association of Crime Writers. He lives in Baltimore.

www.danfesperman.com

ALSO BY DAN FESPERMAN

*Unmanned*
*The Double Game*
*Layover in Dubai*
*The Arms Maker of Berlin*
*The Amateur Spy*
*The Prisoner of Guantánamo*
*The Warlord's Son*
*The Small Boat of Great Sorrows*
*Lie in the Dark*

# THE LETTER WRITER

# THE LETTER WRITER

# WRITER

*Dan Fesperman*

VINTAGE CRIME/BLACK LIZARD
VINTAGE BOOKS
*A Division of Penguin Random House LLC*
*New York*

FIRST VINTAGE CRIME/BLACK LIZARD EDITION, MARCH 2017

Copyright © 2016 by Dan Fesperman

All rights reserved. Published in the United States by Vintage Books, a division of
Penguin Random House LLC, New York, and distributed in Canada by Random
House of Canada, a division of Penguin Random House Canada Limited, Toronto.
Originally published in hardcover in the United States by Alfred A. Knopf, a
division of Penguin Random House LLC, New York, in 2016.

Vintage is a registered trademark and Vintage Crime/Black Lizard and colophon
are trademarks of Penguin Random House LLC.

This is a work of fiction. Names, characters, places, and incidents either are the
product of the author's imagination or are used fictitiously. Any resemblance to
actual persons, living or dead, events, or locales is entirely coincidental.

The Library of Congress has cataloged the Knopf edition as follows:
Names: Fesperman, Dan.
Title: The letter writer : a novel / Dan Fesperman.
Description: First edition. | New York : Alfred A. Knopf, 2016.
Identifiers: LCCN 2015037235
Subjects: LCSH: Police—New York (State)—New York—Fiction. | Murder—
Investigation—Fiction. | Conspiracies—Fiction. | BISAC: FICTION / Mystery
& Detective / General. | FICTION / Suspense. | GSAFD: Mystery fiction. |
Suspense fiction.
Classification: LCC PS3556.E778 L48 2016 | DDC 813/.54—dc23
LC record available at https://protect-us.mimecast.com/s/NV8GB7CY7RpKTx

Vintage Books Trade Paperback ISBN: 978-1-101-87399-1
eBook ISBN: 978-1-101-87507-0

Book design by M. Kristen Bearse

www.blacklizardcrime.com

Printed in the United States of America
10  9  8  7  6  5  4  3  2  1

# THE LETTER WRITER

# PROLOGUE

......................

HIS WAS AN ARRIVAL of dark portents: Black smoke on the Manhattan skyline. Hushed crowds gazing toward a crosstown calamity. Whispers of a ruthless enemy, willing to do anything.

Clearly, something terrible had just happened. But what? Woodrow Cain, groggy from a long passage out of the South, eyed the worried faces outside of Penn Station and tried to come up with an answer.

It was just him now. Wife gone, daughter abandoned. He'd forsaken all he held dear for a fresh start, only to be greeted by symptoms of mass hysteria. Suitcase in hand, he turned to a man in a fedora.

"What is it?" he asked. "What's going on?"

"The *Normandie*," the man said. "She's on fire at Pier 88."

"The *Normandie*?"

"The big luxury liner, the one they're turning into a troop ship. Guy I talked to says the Germans did it. She's rolled over on her side, gonna sink any minute. Thousands of people down there, even the mayor."

"La Guardia?" Cain was still learning who was important up here.

"In a black raincoat, soaking wet from the hoses. Heard it on the radio. Walking the fire lines like he owns the joint."

"He better be ready for more of the same," another man said. "If they can do this, who says they can't fly a bunch of planes in? Bomb us to smithereens, just like the Japs at Pearl."

Others nodded, but the first guy shook his head.

"The waterfront. That's where they'll come for us, just like today. The longshoremen, the shipbuilders, even the goddamn fishermen— half of 'em's either kraut or dago, and who you think they're rooting for? You watch. This is only the beginning."

Cain looked up at the sky. The smoke was spreading, an inky smudge blowing east from the Hudson. He shook his head in angry disbelief. Ten lousy minutes in New York, and already his new life felt as full of loss and betrayal as the one he'd left behind.


A revealing account, don't you think? It came to me secondhand, but my source is trustworthy, and I will vouch for its accuracy as if I had witnessed it myself.

The day in question occurred two months ago, on the ninth of February in this tumultuous year of 1942. I wish I could report that conditions have improved in the interim, but if anything the city's fortunes have become even more unsettling. U-boats prowl the mouth of our harbor, sinking ships whenever they please. Residents of penthouse apartments—yes, I still know a few, despite my reduced circumstances—say the offshore glow of flames is visible in the night sky. My more numerous acquaintances from tenements and flophouses swear that fishing trawlers from our own docks are secretly refueling these underwater killers. If that sounds far-fetched, then what are we to make of the thirty-three German spies who were just sentenced to prison at the federal courthouse in Brooklyn? And if it was so easy to round up that many, how many more must yet lurk in our midst, relaying vital information by shortwave radio, or by handwritten messages in invisible ink?

In Yorkville, our very own Little Deutschland of the Upper East Side, the streets have gone eerily silent since war was declared, but only last summer its inhabitants were packing the movie houses for Nazi propaganda films. They marched by the thousands down 86th Street, the German Broadway, wearing brown shirts and swastikas and singing the Horst Wessel song. And who can forget how the Italians of East Harlem celebrated the conquest of Ethiopia, by raising tricolor flags from every window and cheering Mussolini's name? That fellow in the fedora, the one who spoke to Mr. Cain so direly of our future, may be an alarmist, but he was right about the abundance of enemy nationals. Three-quarters of the seven and a half million people of this city are first- or second-generation immigrants. Me included, I should add, and practically all of my neighbors, plus just about everyone I've ever known or met since I first arrived here so long ago, at the age of eleven.

Who are we to trust, then? And when events inevitably turn for the worse, who are we to blame? When you are born in one homeland, and then move to another, and the two become mortal enemies, who can say for sure where your loyalties will reside? Those are the questions which press upon our souls.

By day, New Yorkers go about their business in a sort of concealed dread, wondering when the worst of the war will reach our shores. Not long after sunset we begin dousing our lights as a precaution against air raids, even on the Great White Way, where the only illumination comes from a scatter of low-wattage bulbs beneath the marquees. A dim-out, they call it, so that the silhouettes of the merchant ships offshore will not be so easy to see against the bright backdrop of the skyline. Although, as with most calls for austerity, I have noticed that the wealthy do not always participate.

A few weeks ago, soldiers began entrenching anti-aircraft guns in the parks and along the rivers. One went off by accident at the foot of Grand Street, and the errant 37-millimeter shell blew a chunk out of the thirty-eighth floor of the Equitable Building, two miles away in the financial district. The stock market wavered, and moved on.

Yet, when the sirens wail for air raid drills most New Yorkers react slowly, if at all, especially now that spring has arrived. They mill and laugh on the street until the all-clear, as if refusing to accept that the revelry of our previous lives has ended. I sense a looming disaster.

As for Woodrow Cain, one can only imagine his bewilderment. Even at the best of times this city takes a smug pleasure in overwhelming new arrivals from the provinces, especially those who come by necessity. He came for a job, from the small town of Horton, North Carolina, where he was a senior detective on a small police force. As of late last week he is now a detective sergeant with the New York City Police Department, posted to district level in the 14th precinct house on West 30th Street, the building that looks like a bleak old castle, turrets and all. He is thirty-four years of age, and he has a young daughter, Olivia, who he left behind in the care of his sister. If he is able to make a home here, she will join him at the end of the school year.

I am told that he departed his previous employment under dubious circumstances, but if experience has taught me one thing, it is that everyone has a past. The trick is in learning to manage it. It is said that well-placed connections led to his hiring here. I suppose it also didn't hurt that the police department has lost so many men to the armed services. Due to wartime shortages, the newest officers—Mr. Cain among them—were rushed through their training in half the normal time, or else he would still be in a classroom.

Supposedly he is the sort of man whose demeanor warns you to keep your distance, although those who make an effort are sometimes rewarded with easy laughter and quick confidences. A hard shell with a soft center, if you will, unless he is one of those quiet men whose center lies even deeper within—a shell within a shell, impenetrable. Perhaps I say this because from my one glance at him I sensed an inner darkness, a tendency toward undue risk. Something in the eyes, I think.

Mr. Cain's life is in some ways a study in contradiction. He is well educated, holding a degree in the humanities from a respected state university. Not what you'd expect from a policeman, perhaps, but the Depression has pushed many a promising young man into careers they might once have sneered at. For all his bookish enlightenment, I am told he killed a man in cold blood. He is a lifelong Southerner, supposedly full of affection for the place, yet he speaks poorly of the region to almost all who ask. He is in fine health, but he sometimes walks with a limp. Its origins are the subject of rumor.

To this point, none of what I have revealed to you came to me in confidence. Indeed, if this were the extent of my knowledge about Mr. Cain, I would probably not give his affairs a further thought. But in the course of my daily duties I quite recently came across several disturbing items which made me fear for Mr. Cain's safety. That is why I have taken such a keen interest in learning more about him, although I will admit that I am also fascinated by the nature of his profession, partly because of its similarity to my own.

Both of us, you see, trade in secrets, even though we handle this commodity in radically different ways. Detective Cain's success often depends on making his findings public—airing them in a court of law, or leaking them to newspapers. I, on the other hand, am a steadfast practitioner of concealing and forgetting. Almost from the moment an item of confidential information comes into my possession, I begin working assiduously to set it aside, bury it, forget it—even as I begin dispensing its particulars with the greatest possible precision as instructed by my customers. It is a policy geared toward protecting not only the privacy of my clients, but my own peace of mind. For me there is never any "tracking of clues" or "adding up of the facts." When it comes to the secrets of others, I am a bit like a farmer who is forever plowing under his sprouting crops, lest they grow into something larger and more noticeable to the neighbors.

You may call me by my professional name, Danziger. Mention it in a certain sixteen-block area near Rivington Street and almost anyone will be able to direct you to my door. My product, as my business card plainly states, is information, although the duty I am best known for is the translation and writing of other people's letters. I handle written correspondence of all manifestations, from personal pleas and job queries to requests for help from municipal, state, or federal officials, or letters of explanation to bankers and creditors. My clientele comes mostly from the illiterate portion of the city's immigrants of four different tongues—German, Russian, Yiddish, and Italian (the latter, an obvious outlier, is explainable by an episode of youthful folly, the details of which are not relevant to our discussion).

My working methods are straightforward and simple: Customers come to my place of business, say what they wish to say, and then wait while I polish their words into more serviceable syntax, writing it down for them either in English or in their native tongue, depending on their needs. For those who have received mail, in whatever language, I read it back to them, translating when necessary.

I dispense these services from the ground floor of a tenement house, in a drafty sprawling room of pigeonholes and sagging bookshelves, a dim chamber which serves as both post office and nerve center for a needful clientele. I live in the same building, in a small room upstairs with a cookstove and a cold-water sink.

As you might guess, my line of work brings me into contact with a wide variety of people. My life fairly abounds with eccentrics. Abounds. What a fine word of your marvelous language, a tongue that borrows and then keeps, promiscuous in its adoptions. Not the English of the king, but of his subjects, his colonists, which is one of the things I have always liked best about your country. Your people, with all their different beginnings and backgrounds, have hammered and buttressed this language into an international emporium of wonders, a hall of mirrors in which I can roam happily for hours at a time, especially when I am accompanied by the massive two-volume collegiate dictionary which holds pride of place on my shelves.

My guilty secret is that as a *speaker* of English I am not always quite so comfortable or confident. Orally, my tendency is to move a little slower, more deliberately. Now and then I grope for the correct grammar, a more precise meaning. As a result, when I speak it is often in a mannered fashion, like some upright fellow being served tea in her ladyship's parlor.

On paper it is a different story. I am as fluent as a Founding Father, at ease among various locutions and in almost all thickets of foreign influence. I am even comfortable bushwhacking my way through swamps of idiom and slang, although I confess that some coinages of the South and Midwest still elude me, Southerners and Midwesterners not exactly being common to the environs of Rivington Street.

And so, while writing I sometimes find myself thinking in many voices at once, a ventriloquist of the open page, neatly setting down locutions in varying tones to suit the needs of different tasks and personalities.

My rates are reasonable. Fifty cents to read a letter, fifty cents to write one, provided you keep things brief and to the point. The long-winded pay extra. On an average day I handle about ten correspondences, and whenever possible I avoid the drafting of love letters. Such material is too chancy, too wrapped up in a client's deepest hopes and anxieties. Only for a surcharge will I relent, and even then I accept no blame for any ensuing failure or recrimination. My own status as a confirmed bachelor with a narrow bed would seem to be advertisement enough to not entrust me with such correspondence. Yet, customers continue to ask, often in tones of deepest desperation.

Thus has my home become a place where clients often learn important news, for better and for worse. It is also where they frequently begin framing reactions and replies in the first flush of revelation. With my able assistance, they give joy of their good fortune, or regrets of their tragedies. At each important turn of their lives I am their mouthpiece, their amanuensis, the intermediary entrusted with relaying their most vitally important news to loved ones and enemies alike.

I doubt that I shall be lacking for business anytime soon. Despite a recent profusion of schools and academies offering instruction in English, my corner of Manhattan seems to hold an unlimited supply of clients, young and old. Indeed, my neighborhood teems with more life than I once could have imagined. Teems. Now there is another fine word, bringing to mind the sight of tiny organisms aswarm on the slide of a microscope, multiplying, dividing, jitterbugging their way toward the edges.

So often in this quarter of the city, life teems to the point of peril, with some specimens falling entirely from sight. Or perhaps I say that because, in recent months, I have become ever more conscious of the gathering peril that looms over so much of my clientele. Although I still write many letters for the domestic mails, much of my current work involves correspondences abroad—chiefly to and from Europe, more particularly those countries which for the past three years have been at war. As the months have passed, my clients' secrets have grown darker and more sorrowful, placing an ever greater weight upon their souls, and upon mine. More and more, letters to that benighted landscape go unanswered. Voices once full of life and whimsy fall silent. The tears of many stain my blotter.

All the more reason for me to work actively to scour these accumulated items from my conscious mind. As I said before, I do not hoard, I do not gather, I do not analyze. Almost from the moment I have committed a client's thoughts or wishes to the printed page, I begin rolling them into a ball, figuratively speaking, before tossing them onto the mental waste heap of the hazy and the forgotten, where they may no longer trouble my thoughts.

Or so I thought until a few days ago, when a small item in the pages of the *Daily News* made me realize that some of those discarded secrets apparently remain adrift, just beneath the surface. They are, to use a disturbing modern analogy, like those U-boats which lurk offshore, awaiting their moment. As I scanned the newspaper story it felt as if a submerged memory had fired a torpedo, which then exploded to reveal other thoughts, many of them fearful. Alarming, even, because this has always been my greatest worry about the nature of my work—an anxious dread that, someday, some long-buried item would find its way back to the light and take on a life of its own, malignant, redoubled in strength, capable of harm.

A few hours ago that dread was realized in the most terrible of ways, and I was an eyewitness to its grisly aftermath. That event moved me to take action, or at least to contemplate the possibility. It is also why I quickly began learning as much as I could about Mr. Cain, because I have reached the crucial moment when I must decide what, if anything, to do next. It is now Friday, with the hands on the clock approaching midnight. By Monday morning I must either drop this matter or seek the assistance of Mr. Cain, the newly employed detective, the bringer of portents.

My only hesitation is that he, too, is likely to be threatened by the potency of what I know. Is this not often the nature of a dark secret, once illuminated? I am reminded of the advice of a wise and powerful man I once knew, who said, "If one man knows something, it's a secret. If two know it, eleven know it. When three know it, a hundred and eleven know it." He called this the mathematics of danger, may he rest in peace.

But here is my dilemma: Mr. Cain might also be at risk if I choose *not* to act. Even from my remote vantage point I sense that he may have already slipped into currents of influence which he neither knows nor understands, dangerously adrift among hazards he cannot see. By seeking his assistance, I might also be able to save him.

It would be incorrect to leave you with the impression that my motives are entirely selfless. They are not. A name has surfaced in this affair which leads me to believe that, unless actions are soon taken, then I, too, may be vulnerable. So perhaps my decision is already made. If so, then on Monday I will journey to the precinct building on 30th Street, where I will tell Mr. Cain what I know, offer my help, and hope for the best.

Wish me well, then. Wish us all well.

# 1

.....................

FIRST DAY ON THE JOB, half an hour left on his shift, when the call came in. There was a body in the Hudson, down by the docks at the end of 30th. Captain Mulhearn wore a big crooked smile as he carried the sheet over to Woodrow Cain's desk, like he was delivering a housewarming gift to a neighbor he didn't particularly like.

"All yours, Southern Boy. Welcome to the third district, and enjoy your night on the town."

Twenty minutes later, his left thigh stiff after sitting all day, Cain limped carefully through the dark, crossing railroad ties and wet cobbles, and then stepping beneath the trestled gloom of Twelfth Avenue as he approached the muted shimmer of the waterfront.

Just ahead were two uniformed cops in silhouette, illuminated dimly by the twinkle of Hoboken on the far shore. They were talking, hands in motion, not yet aware of his presence.

Cain stopped to listen.

"I say we poke him."

"Poke him?"

"Toward downtown, with a stick. One of those things with a crook on it, like the swabbies use."

"A boat hook? Where we gonna find a boat hook?"

"Okay, so maybe we throw something. Make enough waves so he

gets pushed back into the current at the end of the pier. Presto, he floats on down to the tenth. Then he's their problem."

"It don't work that way. Besides, what if the tide's coming in? Then he floats uptown a couple blocks and we've turned a one-hour job into a whole night's headache, and I'm freezing my ass off as it is."

"Whadda you mean, 'tide'? It's a fucking river. It's upstream or downstream, and the tenth is downstream."

"With a tide, numbnuts. Besides, he's bumping the wharf, so he's already ours. It's in the *Manual of Procedure*. 'Cases Occurring on Piers, Boats, and Navigable Waters.' Jurisdiction depends on which bulkhead or pier the body comes to rest on."

Cain stepped forward, looming up out of the shadows like a ghost. The cop advocating the boat hook strategy jumped like he'd been goosed, while the one on the right reached for his sidearm.

"At ease, gentlemen." Cain flashed his brand new shield. He recognized the patrolman on the right from the station house. "Officer Petrowski is correct. Article 7 from the manual. It was a question on the sergeant's exam."

"They made you take that? I heard you was a charity hire."

"Made me take all kinds of tests. So what have we got?"

"Floater. Have a look."

Cain peered down from the bulkhead. Bottles and trash formed an atoll around a man's body, facedown in the dark water. Fully clothed, but bloated tightly in a T-shirt and work pants, like a roasting sausage ready to burst its casing with a pop and a sizzle. The smell of dead fish, boat fuel, and putrefaction wafted up to him in the gloom. Something rippled the water from just beneath the surface, a carp or a swimming rodent, nosing around the body. Bile surged to the base of his throat. He swallowed to keep it down, leaving a sour burn. Then he stepped back, took a deep breath. Petrowski and the other cop were talking again.

"You gettin' that smell?" the first one asked.

"What'd you expect?"

"No. Like something burning. You smell that?"

"It's the *Normandie*."

"Can't be. That was, what, two months ago?"

"But she's still there, laying on her side. Burnt stuff really holds its stink, and it's less than twenty blocks away. So when the wind's right . . ."

"See? It's blowing south. If we'd just pushed him out far enough—"

Cain interrupted. "Did y'all call the morgue?"

"Fifteen minutes ago," Petrowski said. "Said they were on their way."

"Then I need y'all to secure the area."

"Nothing down here this time of night but bums and railroad bulls."

"Then keep the bums and bulls away. Split up, one to either side."

"Yes, sir."

They headed off in the same direction, Cain shaking his head at the insolence. He began counting to ten under his breath while they resumed their conversation in lowered tones.

" 'Y'all.' You get that? Said it twice, like he's from Dogpatch in the funny papers. So what did the krauts put in it to make it burn like that?"

"The *Normandie*? That wasn't the krauts. It was a dumb fuck welder with an acetylene torch. Threw a spark on some packing straw."

"Likely story."

"It was in the papers."

"Like I said. If—"

"*Hey!*" Cain shouted.

The cops froze.

"You guys forget how to secure a scene? One to either side. Now split up and get moving!"

"Yes, sir," Petrowski answered.

"New guy who don't know shit," the other one grumbled. "Already throwing his weight around."

"He's got a rabbi."

"Figures."

"His father-in-law is what I hear. Some white-shoe asshole on Wall Street."

Second time today he'd overheard a cop muttering about his rabbi. Cain was Baptist, and his father-in-law was Episcopal, but the meaning was obvious enough. A ward heeler, a political hack. A guy who called in favors from the powers that be. Obviously his new colleagues had found out that Cain's father-in-law, Harris Euston, a partner with a patrician law firm on Wall Street, had put in a word for him.

True enough, but it rankled all the same. Probably explained why everyone at the station house had been so standoffish. A few nods and hellos, not a whole lot more. He supposed he understood. Half the cops on the force seemed to be studying for the sergeant's exam, trying to climb the next rung on the ladder, to the level he'd already reached. He'd heard them firing questions back and forth in the break room while he ate his lunch alone, a ham sandwich with a Lucky for dessert, everyone acting like he was invisible. Although later Captain Mulhearn had said something about going out for beers next week, first round on him, like it was a rite of passage. So there was that to look forward to, he supposed.

The dimmed headlights of the meat wagon crept toward Cain down 30th, past the high brick walls of the Stanley Soap Works. Two men hopped out, equipped with netting and what looked like a pair of giant tongs. They got to work like it was no big deal, an everyday occurrence. Maybe it was.

For Cain it was a milestone—his first corpse in New York. He'd come across only one other floater, years ago, similarly bloated. A poor soul who'd snagged on a fallen tree in the Neuse River. Presumed drowned, until they rolled him over and saw the damage from a shotgun blast. Pellets of lead had remained lodged in his skin even as his chest wheezed out the sump of the river like a broken accordion. It took a week to make an ID, but Cain never solved it, and so far this one looked equally promising.

Cain had never grown accustomed to the gore and grief of homicides, but he was passionate about working them. Unsolved cases never faded over time. Like debts, they accrued interest and weighed on his mind. He was not particularly religious, but whenever he contemplated an afterlife he imagined being accosted from the moment he arrived by everyone whose murder he'd never closed, and who wanted to begin eternity like that?

Within minutes the guys from the morgue had maneuvered the body onto the dock next to a giant pile of coal. They flipped him onto his back, which made a slapping noise like a landed fish. The eye sockets were empty. Foul gases erupted from the open mouth along with a gray stream of water that rolled down his cheeks like spilled gravy.

Cain swallowed fast and breathed through his mouth. He stepped forward for a closer look.

A pink scar ran diagonally across the man's forehead toward a big dent in the cranium. Someone had bashed him hard enough to either kill him or knock him cold. Cain wondered if the man had still been alive when he hit the water. He imagined a body falling from way up on the George Washington Bridge, miles north of here, an impact which surely would've finished the job. But that seemed like a dumb place to dispose of a body—too showy, nothing that a professional would do. They'd use a boat, although a thorough practitioner would've also weighted the body to make it sink. Unless he was in too much of a hurry. Perhaps he—or they—had been interrupted, or were new to the business. Not that Cain knew much about how the murder business worked up here.

He reached into an overcoat pocket and withdrew a dog-eared steno pad, the latest in a series dating to his first days on the job back in Horton. The NYPD had given him an official one—a memo book, Mulhearn called it—but Cain preferred his old one, maybe because he used them for more than just work. Scribbled on pages between the case notes were grocery lists, nature sketches, birthday reminders, a bad poem or two. Having all those things in the same place made his life feel more stitched together, which seemed more important than ever now that almost everything else had fallen apart. Although he'd always wondered what the consequences would be if his notebook ever got entered into evidence—all those private musings and observations, laid out for judge and jury. His life in miniature, scarred by bullet points, cross-outs, and erasures. Cain on the page was a mess, barely legible.

"Anything in his back pockets?"

They shrugged.

"Heave him back over."

They looked at each other for a second, then did as he asked, uncorking more gases, a cold smell of mud, the sediment of centuries from the bottom of the Hudson. Cain crouched and slid his hand into the man's front right trouser pocket, wet and tight.

"Hey," one of the morgue guys said. "You shouldn't be doin' that."

Cain pried loose a stick of gum, still in its wrapper. Stuck to it was a sodden ticket stub from a movie theater, the print faintly legible. Nothing else. He stood and wrote down the details.

"Pull up his shirt."

They hesitated, gave him a look.

"C'mon. The sleeves, too."

On the man's chest there was a scatter of a dozen or so small black circles—cigarette burns? Cain had once seen them on the body of a child, a memory that made him pause in his writing. On the man's right shoulder was a small, crude tattoo of a woman's name in cursive, "Sabine." Otherwise, there was nothing that might identify him. Someone at the morgue would take his fingerprints, but without a name to go on there would be no way to make a match with the thousands upon thousands that were on file.

"Not carrying any ID, huh?" one of the morgue guys asked.

Cain shook his head.

"Another John Doe, then."

"You get a lot of those?"

"Ninth this week. Maybe seven hundred a year."

"*Seven hundred?*" Cain shifted his weight to keep his bad leg from stiffening. "What happens to them?"

"With most of 'em, some friend or relative comes by in a week or two, stakes a claim, gives 'em a decent burial. If not, we keep 'em three months. Then it's off to City Island, up in the Bronx."

"A potter's field?"

The guy nodded. "Big damn place. More than a hundred thousand. Stinks to high heaven."

Cain shook his head in amazement. That was more populous than any city in his home state. He took out a handkerchief and blew his nose, the gases lingering in his nostrils. He knew from experience that his overcoat would smell this way in the morning. To him, at least.

"We'll take it from here unless you need to see more. Our pencil pusher will be around with some papers to sign."

Cain nodded and stepped toward the bulkhead, where he cleared his throat and spit into the water, which again rippled from below, some creature rising to inspect the latest contribution. He pulled out his pack of Luckies, the flare of the match flashing on the river as he inhaled deeply, a small moment of tribute to his home state. Bright leaf tobacco, like his dad used to grow. Cain had once helped hang it, leaf by leaf, in big barns in the fields east of Horton, where the smell of curing fires had been as much a part of fall as carved pumpkins and college football.

A guy walked up out of the darkness, notebook in hand.

"You handling this?"

Cain nodded.

"Got an ID yet?"

"No. Nothing in his pockets but a gum wrapper and a ticket stub."

"Beemans?"

"Huh?"

"The gum wrapper."

He consulted his notebook. "Blackjack."

"Anything else?"

"Big blow to the head, looked like. A bunch of small marks on his chest, you'll see 'em. Cigarette burns, if I had to guess. A small tattoo on his right shoulder with a name, Sabine."

He asked Cain to spell it, so he did.

"Cause of death?"

"Thought that was your department?"

The guy smiled, kept scribbling.

"What about the stub? Ballgame?"

"Some movie theater on 96th."

"The one up in Yorkville?"

"Don't know. Maybe."

"Then he's either been in the drink a while, or never did his laundry. That joint's been closed since December. Kraut hangout. Shut down right after Pearl. The whole neighborhood's kraut."

The guy scribbled for a few seconds more, then asked another question.

"And your name is?"

"Woodrow Cain. Detective sergeant, third division."

"Kane with a K, like the movie?"

"With a C."

"Like Cain and Abel?"

"In name only. Woodrow as in Wilson."

Officer Petrowski ambled up.

"Hey, Cain. The morgue guy is here."

"I got it covered."

"No, dunce, back over by the body. You ain't talking to this jackal, I hope?" He scowled and drifted back into the night.

"Who the hell are you?"

"Sam Willett, *Daily News.*"

"Fuck."

"Is that official?"

Cain frowned and gave him a pleading look that said *Go easy.* In return he got a look that said *Fat chance.*

"New, huh? And not from around here."

"Scram, will you? Before I get in any deeper."

"Okay by me. Got all I need." Willett shut his notebook. "Good stuff on the cigarette burns. Sounds like somebody really worked him over. Decent bet he's German, which should get me a few column inches. Be seeing you."

Cain tossed his cigarette toward the water and went off to find the morgue guy, a tall fellow as pale as a cadaver with a personality to match. He looked up from a clipboard and gave Cain a fisheye, head to toe.

"Word to the wise, Bud. Never, repeat *never,* have my people rearrange clothing or go fishing around in pockets."

"My name's Cain, *Bud.* And I did the pockets myself."

"Even worse."

"Duly noted. Will you be doing the autopsy?"

"I'm not a cutter. This'll be Doc Bolton's."

"How 'bout a favor, then? Tell Bolton that in addition to the usual items I'd like an estimate on how old the tattoo is. The one on the right shoulder that says Sabine."

"*Duly noted.* But put it in writing, then sign these. Plus your initials on that box down at the bottom that says you disturbed the corpse. Bud."

Cain wrote his request and signed what he had to. He sent Petrowski and the other cop home, and lit another smoke as the meat wagon pulled away. By then the reporter was gone, and things got quiet in a hurry. Nothing but the slap of the river against the bulkheads, the low roar of passing traffic up on the viaduct. Further down the waterfront you could hear hammering, a twinkle of industry, the war effort still lumbering to its feet. He stared into the murk. If his name ended up in the papers they'd probably think he was grandstanding, already playing to the crowd. Too late now.

For all his zeal in murder cases, they'd never been a big part of the job in Horton—three or four per year, six at the most. Maybe that's why they stayed with him. Back in February, during his train ride north, Cain had taken out the same notebook he was using tonight. It was three a.m., with a half-moon rising over a tidewater landscape, bare trees wild against the sky as the train clattered through the night. The other five passengers in the compartment were asleep, including, mercifully, a nosy old woman to his left who'd already asked a zillion questions. *Where's your family? Where do you go to church? How old's your daughter? Why isn't she traveling with you? Where'd you say your wife went?*

The only wakeful company was his reflection on the window. He began writing in the notebook, and before long he'd filled an entire page with names, forty in all, a list of victims from every homicide he'd ever worked—in flawless chronological order, no less, complete with race, age, and cause of death.

Now, standing by the Hudson, he flipped back a few pages, and there was the list. Number eleven was his unsolved floater: *Eldridge Warren, Negro, 53, shotgun.* The other two unsolved cases were at numbers nineteen and twenty-two. *Jake Tarn, White, 37, stabbing; Janelle Ellerbe, White, 24, strangled.* Cain scanned the page. Shootings, stabbings, a drowning in a bathtub that had splashed blood and water all over the floor tiles. Three beatings—one with a crowbar, one with a shovel, one with a stone pried loose from the wall of a cemetery. A single poisoning—rat powder baked into a damson pie, the victim's favorite.

So vivid, all of them. Gaze long enough at any one name and other faces swam into view—grieving mothers and children, a father whose loud sobs had sounded like the shrieks of an elephant, right there in the middle of the police station, everyone giving him a wide berth.

Cain remembered that the nosy old woman on the train had awakened without him noticing.

"What are all the names?" she'd asked. "Friends of yours?"

"Work stuff," he'd said irritably. *None of your damn business.*

Now he wondered exactly what he'd been up to. Taking a final inventory, perhaps, like a shopkeeper listing all his merchandise before he sold the store. Did these names represent items he'd hoped to leave behind, entrusted to others? If so, did that apply even to the most memorable one?

*Rob Vance, White, 34, gunshot.*

Rob's name was last on the list, as if the others had been part of a process, a mechanism, that inevitably led to his death. Cain didn't even need to close his eyes to see Rob's face the way it had looked at the end, pale and drained, or the huge bloodstain soaking wet across Rob's chest, like someone had just hit him with a water balloon—a campus prank, maybe, from their days in Chapel Hill, or from their first years as cops, young detectives learning together in a job they hadn't really wanted but had taken anyway because in 1930 no one else seemed to be hiring college graduates in that part of the state. He couldn't shake that final image of his friend, dead on the floor, the shots still ringing in his ears and Rob's mouth thrown open in surprise, his eyes already too glazed to be accusing.

No problem solving that one. Cain had witnessed it from start to finish. But questions had remained, for him and for everyone else in Horton: Could Cain have done more to stop it? Had he been complicit in some way? And what about the role played by Cain's wife, Clovis? In that sense, at least, it *was* unsolved. Number four on his list. And here he was now, same notebook in hand, with a new and nameless body to go at the top of a clean page.

Cain edged closer to the water. Looming just down the Hudson were the tall, spectral silhouettes of docked ships from the cruise lines he had read about but had never sailed on—Cunard, Panama, and

Munson. They'd been a part of Clovis's world, or at least the world she'd grown up in. Clovis, the Manhattan girl who traveled south for college, exiled by an overprotective father. Harris Euston's intent had been to sever her ties to the fast crowd—swank boys who plied her with drink, social-climbing girls who egged her on. Let her settle down in the provinces for a few years, he reasoned, while everyone else headed for the Ivies and the Seven Sisters. Break free from the glut of easy money, and return home with a fresh outlook.

Her father got more than he'd bargained for when she also found a husband and a whole new way of life—culturally barren, to Euston's way of thinking, since it was an existence in which she almost never set foot in New York. Since his arrival Cain had hardly been able to turn a corner without feeling her presence. He was confronted daily by all the places she used to talk about—Macy's, Fifth Avenue, Central Park, Carnegie Hall, and now the cruise lines from her long ago vacations, lush trips to Europe and the Caribbean. Everything marked by energy and glamor, her trademarks, the very things that had first caught his eye. Rob's too, probably.

He tossed his cigarette, lit a new one and turned away from the water, crossing a rail line and then pausing. The tracks down here were from all across the country—the Lackawanna, the Erie, and the B&O—all roads leading to Gotham, city of voyagers, with Cain still feeling very much like he had just landed. Then he realized something. Try as he might, all forty of those victims from Horton had somehow made it here with him. Crafty stowaways, forever his companions. Clovis, too, a spirit whispering his name from over his shoulder. The past wasn't something you left behind. It was a parasite in the bloodstream, a congenital disorder. You could only hope that others wouldn't spot the symptoms.

The only way to respond, then, was to work this case, and work it hard. Cain inspected the glowing end of his cigarette and wondered how long you'd have to press it against human skin to produce those angry black dots. Five seconds? Twenty? A full minute, perhaps? Another question for Doc Bolton at the morgue.

He was about to leave when a bright wash of headlights caught him in profile, a big car coming straight toward him as it bumped across the cobbles. No cloaking at all on the headlights. Didn't they know there was a war on?

The car stopped twenty yards out, idling, as if whoever was inside was deciding what to do next. Cain slowly reached inside his overcoat for the .32 caliber Colt revolver holstered beneath his shoulder. The cross-hatched walnut stock felt rough and chilly. Way too soon for this, no stomach for it. As he slid the gun free from the holster he felt its life-taking power, coursing up his arm like an electrical impulse.

A car door opened. A big body emerged and moved in front of the headlights. Wide-brimmed hat, bulky overcoat. No face visible, but certainly an easy target if it came to that.

"Detective Cain?"

"Who's asking?"

"Headquarters."

"The fourteenth?"

"Downtown."

*The* headquarters, in other words, the one for the whole department down on Centre Street. A place Cain had seen, but hadn't yet visited. He'd been sworn in a week ago during an outdoor ceremony while standing in formation with more than a hundred new recruits on a windblown park square.

"Your attendance is required tomorrow at twelve thirty. Room 114-B."

"Says who?"

"Come on your lunch break, and keep it to yourself. Not a word to Captain Mulhearn or any of your asshole buddies in the station house."

"Says *who*?"

"Twelve thirty sharp. 114-B. You'll be expected."

The engine revved as the guy stepped out of the beams and climbed back in. The car made a slow U-turn, leaving Cain in darkness as he watched the tail lights wink around the corner at Tenth.

What the hell could they want with him at headquarters? And why all the secrecy? Was he already in trouble? Fired, even? Then a mud-smelling breeze off the water reminded him of what they'd just fished out of the river. He shivered, and set out for the station house.

He moved slowly at first, his leg stiff from all the standing around. The cold wind made him crave a warm bed, which in turn made him think again of Clovis, his wife, on silken sheets in some posh uptown hotel, the Plaza or the Astor, waiting for him in some other life where he'd never been a cop and she'd never traveled south. Plenty of blame for both sides, he supposed. Then the image was gone, and with each step afterward he felt the pressure of a hidden presence to his rear. Something creeping toward him from the river, building like a wave. He stopped, pivoting to face the shadows.

Nothing.

He resumed his journey. Muscles loosening, he quickened his pace, and did not look back.

No choice now but to keep moving forward.

# 2

.....................

IN THE MORNING CAIN DECIDED it was time to stop living like a vagabond hermit. Two months in the city and he was still taking his clothes from a suitcase and keeping to himself.

He looked around the apartment, a modest one-bedroom flat in Chelsea, where he lived among garment workers, furriers, and butchers. The building was stout and modern, wedged between tenement houses with their clotheslines and chaos, the black zigzags of the fire escapes. Best address in the neighborhood, according to his father-in-law, although Harris Euston had made it clear he was providing it on behalf of his granddaughter Olivia, who'd be arriving later.

By Manhattan standards it was about as clean and roomy as you could get for $60 a month. The building had an elevator, hot water, a doorman. But the way Cain had been using it so far was more befitting of a flophouse. The dresser drawers remained empty. His mattress lay on the floor, which was as bare as the walls. In the icebox was a bottle of milk, nothing more. The tiny eat-in kitchen, hardly used, was as spotless as the day he moved in. He ate instead in cheap diners and luncheonettes, some of them barely wide enough for a counter.

Once he'd splurged on dinner at a Horn & Hardart automat. Now there was a place perfectly designed to make you feel alone. No one to take your order or bring your food. All you needed was a few nickels to open the tiny windows—a bowl of stew from this one, a slice of pie from that one, with the empty slots refilled before you took your first bite. You came and went without speaking to a soul. If this was the future of American dining, he wanted no part of it.

The only visible sign that Cain was still part of polite society was the pile of letters on the kitchen table. He corresponded daily with Olivia, reading her letters the moment he got home and scribbling replies until well after midnight. She kept him apprised of the doings at his sister's house in Raleigh in a tone that was newsy, chirpy, although he sensed she was not all that happy. Sue, Cain's sister, wasn't known for a light touch, and Olivia's stories implied that an unaccustomed strictness prevailed. No more freewheeling mom who mixed a nightcap—or two or three—after the dinner dishes were put away. No more flashlight searches with Dad for owls hooting in the longleaf pines out front. No more reading in bed once the call for lights-out was issued promptly at nine.

But it wasn't so easy to read his daughter's moods anymore, even between the lines of a five-page letter. She was now twelve going on thirteen—the beginning of the age of concealment, as Cain knew from his own youth. Considering all the upheaval that had preceded his departure, he supposed he should be happy she was writing him at all. So, rather than press her for more details, Cain tried to prepare her for New York's wonders without hinting at its terrors and indignities, or its noises, or the exhausting way so many faces came at you on the street and in the subway. On his first few nights in the apartment he'd barely been able to sleep because he'd been so overwhelmed by the sense of so many people living above, below, and to every side of him—people who spoke other languages, dressed differently, and were neither still nor silent. He'd felt hemmed in by their calls and cries, the scrape of their chairs, the slam of their doors, the groan of their windows in the sash. For a day or two it had almost been difficult to breathe.

But, now, with a fresh case, new colleagues, a daily routine, a desk to call his own and even a shitty new boss to complain about, maybe he should work a little harder to settle in.

It also didn't hurt that spring had arrived. Until recently his outlook had remained frozen in the images of February—curbside banks of gray slush, towering aisles of dirty wet buildings, looming like mega-liths. Then, almost overnight, sprigs of green had burst from every urban fissure like a long-held breath. In the parks, blossoms fluttered to the ground. Kids raced down his street at all hours in games of tag and stickball while, from open windows, radios blared the first games of the baseball season—Red Barber calling it for the Dodgers, Mel Allen for the home-standing Yankees and Giants.

So that morning Cain moved his clothes into the dresser drawers. He set up the cheap bed frame he'd gotten at a secondhand shop. He bought fruit from a street vendor's horse-drawn wagon. He picked up three newspapers, a loaf of bread, a carton of eggs, a slab of bacon, and a pound of coffee. Then, with coffee perking and bacon popping in the skillet, he unfolded his map of the city to begin plotting the day's movements: first stop, Yorkville, the neighborhood supposedly filled with krauts.

A car would've made the trip even more of an expedition. But between his junior status and the department's wartime rationing, cars were now exclusively for big bosses and radio patrol officers. Even Mulhearn had lost his eight-cylinder Hudson, and Cain was only authorized to hail a cab on the city's dime in an emergency. That meant he was truly a flatfoot, a gumshoe. He traced his finger along a map, following the colorful spaghetti threads for the subways and omnibus lines. A crosstown walk would take him from the station house to the IRT stop for the Lexington line at 33rd. From there, six stops north to 86th, the so-called German Broadway, where he'd poke around until it was time for his appointment at headquarters.

He threw open a window. Cold and gray this morning, but he could live with that now. He stuffed his notebook in his overcoat pocket and headed for the streets.

After what the reporter had said, Cain half expected Yorkville to feel more like Berlin than Manhattan. The reality was more complicated. Initially it didn't look all that different from the rest of the city. There was even an Automat and a Woolworth's, plus a Thom McAn shoe store just like the one he'd taken Olivia to in downtown Raleigh.

It was the sounds that first told Cain the place was different. After he climbed the stairs from the subway the first conversation he heard was in German—two older men arguing, gesturing theatrically, cigarettes bobbing on their lips. The only other times he'd heard German spoken recently were in newsreels of Hitler and Goebbels. Back home a cop's first instinct would have been to lock these fellows up, or at least ask what they were up to. If there had been even a single German family in Horton, everyone would have watched their every move. Here there seemed to be thousands, stretched out for blocks in tenements beneath the Third Avenue El.

Cain headed east on 86th. He passed a travel agency that called itself a Reiseburo, with gold lettering on the storefront touting the availability of "Schiffskarten und Reisechecks." There were so many beer halls, or *brauhausen*, that Cain soon lost count—Platzl, Rudi & Maxl's, Geiger's, Willy's Weindiele, Café Hindenberg, Kaiser's, Martin's Rathskeller, Kreutzer Hall, and more. Yet, in the middle of everything there was also an Irish pub called the Shamrock Bar, and other places, like the Eatmore Delicatessen Deutsche, that seemed to straddle several cultures at once. A joint called the Lorelei was already doing a rollicking trade at eleven a.m., and Cain's stomach grumbled as he smelled the smoky sizzle of wurst, the yeasty tang of beer. But even there he saw signs of change to accommodate anti-German sentiment. A sign in one window with a drawing of sauerkraut billed it instead as "Liberty Cabbage."

A colleague at the station house had told him that before Pearl Harbor quite a few businesses here had displayed swastikas in their windows, or portraits of Hitler. Yorkville had been a hotbed for the Nazi organization known as the American Bund, and as recently as a few months ago beefy fellows had brazenly gone door to door collecting money for the Reich. One bunch claimed to be taking donations for the Fatherland's wounded soldiers. Another supposedly peddled Reichsmarks for dollars, a shady currency scheme designed to pump cash into Hitler's war machine. Both groups pressured potential donors by tracking down names and addresses of their relatives back in Germany: *Please give unless you want things to go badly for Uncle Hans in Dusseldorf!* Nice fellows. No swastikas or roaming bands of thugs now, of course, but Cain doubted everyone's political views had changed overnight.

Then again, some of the Germans here—maybe even a lot of them—had come to Yorkville to escape Hitler. So had other newcomers from Hungary and Czechoslovakia. As if that dynamic wasn't volatile enough, Cain noticed several storefronts with Hebrew lettering. If any had been previously defaced by Bundist thugs, the damage had long since been repaired. Maybe for now they'd earned some peace.

Cain breezed by Herrlich's Funeral Home and the Vaterland Café and Restaurant as he finally reached the upper end of Yorkville. He made his way over to Third Avenue and 96th, where he found the movie theater, a two-story building that had seen better days. It was closed, just as the reporter had said, with a big padlock on the front door. Posters in the display cases were already fading. A set of double windows on the second floor had been covered from the inside with bed sheets. It looked like the place was empty. He nonetheless rattled the big lock, then pounded on the whitewashed glass door. No response.

He stepped over to a display case for a closer look at a poster for a propaganda film, *Sieg im Westen*, which touted Germany's conquest of Belgium and the Netherlands. Someone had painted anti-Nazi graffiti on the glass.

A tapping noise startled him from behind. He turned to see a young woman in the ticket booth. She had apparently just entered from the theater, yet was already enshrouded by cigarette smoke. More astonishing was the way she was dressed, or not dressed. Temperatures were in the forties on this chilly spring morning, yet she wore a gauzy black negligee, open in the front, with only a lacy black bra underneath. Her face was striking for its lack of color, all whites and blacks like in a publicity still, except for her lips, lacquered a deep red. Her dark eyes were heavily lined, lashes full. Pale pancake makeup coated her face, or maybe that was her natural complexion, practically drained of blood. Her hair, as glossy as the feathers of a raven, was bobbed in a pageboy that left her long white neck exposed.

She tapped again on the glass and spoke in a voice muffled by the compartment.

"Alles geschlossen. Acht uhr."

"What?"

"We are all closed. Until eight. Then showtime."

"Eight? This place is still open?" She nodded. He opened his over-coat to show his detective's shield, feeling like a flasher—probably because of how he was reacting to all that bare flesh. The oddest part was that her skin didn't show a single goose bump.

She frowned.

"So you are not come for the show?"

"I have a few questions about one of your customers."

She considered this a moment, then nodded wearily. "Um die ecke. Around the corner, then to the back. There is a door in the alley."

Cain made his way around to a black steel door in a rear alley where the cobbles reeked of stale beer, with broken bottles underfoot. He hammered at the door, which groaned on rusted hinges to reveal a dark hallway. She began walking away before he was even inside. High heels and black hose, with a ladder-back run down the left thigh. Still no sign that she was the least bit cold. She led him behind what looked like the back of a movie screen before turning left at the end. They emerged into a vast theater, cold and dim, at least fifty rows leading up into complete darkness. Pigeons fluttered above, cooing and reset-tling. The dusty air was nearly as chilly as outside. The soles of Cain's shoes stuck to the floor with every step, with a sound like he was tear-ing pages out of a magazine.

A skittering noise from behind made him jump.

"Rat," she said blandly. "Not to worry. You will find many here. Even among the ownership."

"And who does own this place now?"

She took a seat in the front row, her stockings making a zipping noise as she crossed her legs. Looking as comfortable as if she were settling in for a double feature, she poked out her lower lip and exhaled smoke toward the ceiling.

"Albie Schreiber and Joel Feinman. Two Jewish boys."

Cain was too surprised to answer.

"Yes. No one expects that. Especially the Bundists, who become outraged to learn they have paid money to a Jew."

"But the place is still running?"

"Not for kino, or cinema. Distributor of German films, he is kaput. So a floor show now. Live act."

"You?"

"And other girls. A revue, I think it is called. With piano." She pointed toward the corner. "Plinky plink. Sometimes a singer. And still with popcorn."

So maybe the dead man had been here recently, after all, to watch a floor show instead of a movie. Just the sort of seedy place you'd expect to be frequented by someone who ended up with cigarette burns on his chest.

"What's your name?"

"Angela." She pronounced it with a hard *g*, the German way. Her breath vapored as she spoke. "Tell me, is it warm in here to you?"

"Not especially. Not at all, in fact."

"No. I suspected not."

He wondered what she was on. Pills? A needle?

"Are there other girls in the revue?"

"Three. Sometimes four."

"Any of them named Sabine?"

She stared at him a moment, then slowly shook her head. A quicker no would've been more convincing.

"Is that why you are here? Looking for this Sabine?"

"I'm here about a man with a Sabine tattoo. He had a ticket stub from this theater in his pocket."

"His name?"

Cain shrugged.

"So he is dead man, then?"

"How'd you know?"

"How else would you take ticket from his pocket and not know his name?"

"And you don't know who he might be, this customer with a thing for a Sabine?"

"Many men come. Many have 'a thing,' as you say, for all kinds of girls."

Angela included, no doubt, especially if these were the only clothes she ever wore. Did she live here? His mind flashed on the image of some hidden room with a bare bulb, a cot, a table, a hypodermic syringe. Maybe a few scraps of food, a grimy towel. He felt a stab of weary pity. He got out his notebook.

"Tell me your last name, Angela."

"For your report, or for your black book? That is not official Polizei book, I know that for fact."

"You sound experienced in these things."

"You sound inexperienced. In everything."

He smiled. "Maybe so. I'm new here."

"Feinman," she said, and then spelled it. "That is my last name."

He raised his eyebrows, and she volunteered the answer.

"The owner, he is my brother."

"So how did this place stay open, then, once the Bundists found out who owned it?"

"My brother, he pays a man, Lutz, to make change in his dokumenten, the papers. To show it is now owned by another. This Lutz, he picks out a name from the air, something solid to show it is German and from the goyim. Gerd Schultz, I think."

"What if they ever found out about you?"

She waved her cigarette dismissively.

"Flesh is flesh. Of no matter the origin. It is only my soul that has no worth for them, but one does not fuck a soul. Besides, it is this that really makes them wild for us." She snapped the garter on her thigh. It was banded in red, black, and gold. "The colors of the kaiser's Germany. The new code for them, now that they can no longer fly the flag with the black pretzel."

"And you're okay with this kind of work? Whipping Hitlerites into a frenzy?"

"I do not have to like the customers, so long as they pay at the door." She stood—she was tall, at least five foot ten. "This Sabine you speak of."

"Yes?"

Angela looked him over and exhaled slowly. "You will not find her."

"You say that like you know her."

"I say it as one who knows the way human people act. She is, how you say, a needle of the haystack."

"In. A needle *in* a haystack."

She waved it away.

Cain wrote his name and the phone number for the station house on a blank page in his notebook and tore it out.

"Here. In case you hear anything more about Sabine. Or about any guy gone missing who was carrying a torch for her."

"A torch?"

"In love with." He eyed her legs for a second too long. "Or lust."

She glanced at the paper.

"Cain. The one from the Bible who killed his brother."

He wished people would quit bringing that up. In Horton, where everyone had a Bible, they'd been too embarrassed to mention it, there at the end anyway. She folded the page. For a moment he thought she would toss it onto the floor with the spilled popcorn and rat droppings. Instead she tucked it into the top band of her stocking, next to the garter on her right leg.

"And from your very own not-a-Polizei notebook," she said. "How exciting for me."

She turned and headed up the aisle, speaking over her shoulder as she ascended into darkness.

"The show begins at eight. If you are interested."

Interested in what? he wondered. Under other circumstances, he supposed he might have been *too* interested, given her languid manner, her lack of clothing. But as his eyes adjusted to the dimness Cain had seen the vacancy and despair deep within her eyes. He found himself wishing glumly that she'd put on some clean, sensible clothes and go sleep it off. If he was interested in anything where Angela was concerned, it would be buying her a cup of coffee and a hot meal.

Cain shut his notebook and sighed, his breath clouding the dim air. He supposed Angela was right about one thing. Up here he was inexperienced in just about everything, especially insular little expat communities like Yorkville, where you'd need a local guide to make your way below the surface. Even then you'd probably never penetrate to the deeper workings. But at least now he felt pretty sure that the Sabine on the dead man's tattoo wasn't some girl back in Germany. A new lead, then, however thin.

He checked his watch. Time to get moving if he was going to make that appointment. He let himself out and walked west to the IRT at Lexington, where he took a last glance at Manhattan's Little Deutschland before heading downstairs.

# 3

........................

AN EXPRESS TRAIN SPIT HIM OUT several blocks south of his destination. The short walk uptown turned out to be a primer in the local geography of power.

At the lower end was La Guardia's fiefdom, City Hall, as ornately pretty as a Southern state capitol with its white columns and domed clock tower facing onto a park. From there the buildings got bigger and more imposing. The hulking office tower for the Borough of Manhattan gave way to the federal courthouse, so tall that he stopped to count the floors—twenty-seven? twenty-eight? Then came the colonnaded fortress housing the New York State Supreme Court, followed by a massive, multi-wing criminal justice center where the new DA, Frank Hogan, ruled the roost.

Finally, as Centre Street neared its terminus, there on the right was police headquarters, four stories of classical grandeur with six Corinthian columns across the front. Seated above them on a peaked roof was some sort of Lady Justice on a throne. Stone lions stood guard to either side of the front steps—appropriate, since Cain felt like a gladiator about to enter the coliseum. But he smiled when he noticed a gun shop across the street, Frank Lava's, with a sign in the shape of a giant revolver hanging out front. The six-foot barrel appeared to be aimed right at the space between the lions.

The lobby was more befitting of a grand hotel than a cop shop—

marble floors, a lofty ceiling of gilded florets. Unlike the station house, where you could almost feel the bustle through the soles of your shoes, this place was hushed, giving him the idea that people arrived early and seldom left their desks until quitting time.

A uniform manned the reception desk. He eyed Cain suspiciously.

"You have an appointment?"

"So I'm told." He showed his shield. "Detective Sergeant Cain."

The uniform glanced down at a ledger and shook his head.

"Who you here to see?"

"All they gave me was a number, room 114-B. Is that in the basement?"

The deskman raised his eyebrows at the mention of the number, and he reappraised Cain from head to toe.

"You wait right where you are."

He picked up a black Bakelite phone, dialed a number, and turned away as he spoke: "He's here . . . Yes . . . Of course, sir."

He hung up, looking a little edgy, then spoke sternly.

"He's on his way."

"Who?"

The guy said nothing. But his grave expression said that it must be someone important. Thirty seconds passed in silence while the uniform kept a close watch, as if Cain might try to bolt for the exit. Brisk footsteps echoed off the marble, and Cain turned to see a slim man in a dark suit, no uniform, come to a halt twenty yards out and place his hands on his hips. Cain waited a second, then decided he was supposed to speak first.

"Hi. I'm—"

"I know who you are. This way."

The suit pivoted smartly and headed toward a bank of elevators in the far corner. Cain had to hustle to catch up, stepping aboard just as the doors slid shut. He'd been expecting a trip to the basement, but the button for the second floor was already pushed.

"Room 114-B is upstairs?"

No answer. Maybe the number was part of some code, special appointments only. The attendant out front hadn't even asked him to sign in, which told him no one wanted any record of his visit. The elevator moaned to a halt, and the man stepped off without a word. Cain followed him down a wide hallway to an oak door with gilded lettering: "Commissioner Lewis J. Valentine." Inside, a secretary sat at a desk guarding another door.

"Go right in," she said, without even glancing at him. Cain did as she said.

It took a few seconds for his eyes to adjust to the dimness of the office. In the middle of the room was a huge walnut desk on a dark Oriental rug, so he headed that way. A few papers were stacked atop the desk next to an open file folder with Cain's name on it. There were two telephones. Behind the desk, a wide leather swivel chair, empty. Across the room, a tall, bulky man in a gray double-breasted suit stood in profile by a high window with the curtains pulled back. He was staring down at Centre Street, and he spoke without turning.

"Be seated."

Two ladder-back chairs faced the desk. Cain took the one on the right and sat uncomfortably while keeping an eye on Valentine, who was still gazing out the window. After an awkward pause the commissioner finally made his way toward the desk, moving with the swagger of a beat cop, needing only a night stick to complete the effect. He bypassed the desk and came straight at Cain, leaning low and getting down in his face.

Lewis Valentine had narrow eyes and a small mouth which hinted at sternness, perhaps cruelty. His large ears leaned outward at the top, like they were bearing extra weight. Cain wanted to back away, but was already pressed flat against the chair.

"Before you even open your mouth, let's make one thing crystal clear." Valentine spoke slowly, deliberately. "No matter what you might hear, or what you might think, you didn't get this job due to some political connection. You're not here because some high-hatting buff made a phone call. The day of the rabbi is over. There is no longer any room in this department for parasites and drones. Understood?"

"Understood."

Rabbi. There it was again. Valentine straightened, but didn't back away.

"This father-in-law of yours, Harris what's-his-name."

"Euston."

"He's nothing to me, and nothing to this department. A two-bit Tammany hack in the legal trade, a police buff of the worst order. Throws us a few worthless tips. Kicks in a donation or two to the benevolent fund, then acts like we owe him a favor and thinks he can do whatever he damn well pleases, him and his white-shoe clients. Says 'Jump' and some flunky for the DA says 'How high?' so he probably thinks this department still operates the same way. Hell, he even sent you a copy of the police exam so you could cheat your way in. The sergeant's exam, too."

"*Sir?*"

Valentine closed in again with alarming quickness and pressed a forefinger to Cain's chest.

"Don't act like you don't understand! I saw your test scores. You even knew to miss a few on purpose!"

Cain would have protested, except everything Valentine said was true—right down to the way Euston had advised him to answer a few questions incorrectly in order to avoid raising suspicion. It was a damned hard test, they both were, so Euston had mailed him "study copies" in advance with the correct answers marked. They'd arrived in Horton in a thick manila envelope with the letterhead of Euston's law firm, only a week before Cain moved north. A day later the train ticket and the lease to his apartment had appeared in another large corporate envelope, along with a 475-page blue clothbound volume entitled *Rules and Regulations and Manual of Procedure of the Police Department of the City of New York*. Euston had then telephoned on a scratchy connection to describe the job Cain would be filling, provided he completed the six weeks of instruction and passed the tests. Euston told him not to lose the manual because it would cost a dollar to replace it. His father-in-law had also discussed a few other topics, none of which Cain would dare mention now.

Valentine removed his finger and eased back a step, but remained standing.

"At least you couldn't fake the marksmanship test. At ninety-six you rated out as expert, which was impressive until I reviewed your recent history with firearms."

The remark hit home, and Cain could tell Valentine knew it. He felt the color rising in his cheeks as they stared at each other in silence. The commissioner seemed to be daring him to answer, so Cain waited him out.

"All of this is my way of telling you that you are currently employed on my sufferance alone. I could fire you at any moment."

"Then do it."

"*What?*" Valentine's body went rigid.

"Fire me, then. Get it over with."

Valentine again closed the gap between them.

"If you don't want this job, then that's exactly what I'll do!"

Cain stood, his anger getting the best of him. They were face to face now, inches apart, and he could tell that Valentine could hardly believe it. The commissioner didn't budge, but Cain thought he saw a hint of uncertainty in his eyes, so he seized the advantage and spoke first.

"I haven't worked this job long enough to know if I want it. I *need* it, that's for sure. Without it I don't eat. But frankly, the way I'm feeling I can take it or leave it when it comes to food, drink, and sleep. If I didn't have a bad leg I'd be in the Army by now, someplace where I could forget all about my 'history with firearms,' as you put it. So maybe you should just skip the bullshit and say what it is you want from me. Sir."

Valentine eyed him carefully, the two of them breathing heavily. Cain could smell his aftershave, bringing to mind a barber with a straight razor and the need to stay perfectly still.

"For starters, I want you to back off and sit down."

Cain nodded, their foreheads practically bumping. Then he sat. This time Valentine didn't close the gap.

"Let me tell you something about this department that you, in your towering ignorance and sense of privilege, probably had no idea about. We're an educated force now. The new officers, anyway, and that's the one damn thing you have going for you, your college degree. But don't believe for even a second that you're any smarter than anyone else you came aboard with, understand?"

"Yes, sir."

"This job you took so cavalierly. Do you have any idea how many men took the police exam last time we offered it?"

"No, sir."

"Thirty thousand. Know how many slots those thirty thousand were competing for?"

"No, sir."

"Twelve hundred. And now, even with a war on, these jobs are in such demand that St. John's, Fordham, NYU, and City College—*all* of them!—are offering courses in police procedure. You can be damn sure that every goddamn patrolman in that station house of yours knows one thing about you, and it's that you're a sergeant and they're not, which means you're making six hundred a year more than them. And until they pass the next sergeant's exam they'll hold that over your head like a noose, and unless you demonstrate to me that you can do the job, then I'm all for letting them hang you by that noose for as long as they like. You got that?"

"Loud and clear."

"Then let's get down to business, which starts with the real reason you were hired. *My* reason, not some political parasite's. For one thing, I'm losing men to every goddamn branch of the Armed Forces. I'm more than a thousand officers down from what I'm budgeted for, at a time when order and security matter more than ever. So when a chance arose to hire someone outside the usual channels, I took it. So there's that."

"Okay."

"But mostly I hired you for one assignment. A job for an outsider, someone with no ties to this city or, more to the point, no history of working for the parasitic sons of bitches of the old machine. Which is why any interests of your goddamn father-in-law had better be cleared from your mind from this point forward. Understood?"

"Yes, sir."

"If he ever asks you for a favor—for himself or for any of his goddamn Tammany friends—you're to tell him no and notify me straightaway. Better still, don't speak with him at all. And, by the way, next time one of those bed bugs from the newspapers asks you about a case, you're to refer him to regulation one sixty-one, which you damn well should've known but probably didn't because it wasn't on your copy of the exam. It's *my* rule, and it forbids police officers from speaking in any official capacity to the press."

Cain blushed. Sam Willett must have printed his name in this morning's *Daily News*. Cain hadn't yet had the nerve to check.

"Yes, sir."

"All right, then. Listen up. This assignment is confidential, and you'll be carrying it out in addition to your regular duties."

Cain nodded. Longer hours coming. And by the sound of it, perhaps some danger and aggravation. So be it.

"When Mayor La Guardia put me in charge, my first mission as head of this department was reform. An end to the old ways. No more rabbis, no more bullshit influence from the Tammany rabble or anyone else. No more getting busted down to uniform because you wouldn't do favors for the ward bosses—which happened to me twice, goddamn it! When I took over, the biggest dens of loafers and hacks were the detective division and the goddamn plainclothesmen in vice. I busted more than a hundred of them down or out of the ranks. I also brought back the DD-64, to hold all those bastards accountable for every working hour of every working day."

Cain was already well acquainted with the DD-64—a hated bit of paperwork in which every detective had to keep an account of his daily activities and turn it in at the end of every quarter. It was a pain in the ass, and, for some, an exercise in creative writing. Not that he was about to tell Valentine. Not that he would have been able to. The man was on a roll, pacing back and forth behind his desk and moving his hands like a Baptist in the pulpit.

"In my first six years alone I dismissed three hundred policemen, rebuked four thousand, and otherwise disciplined more than eight thousand. And a goddamn great many of those were either detectives or part of the plainclothes bureau, caught up in all that gambling and vice. But the work of reform is never done. And, right now, whenever I sniff the air around Manhattan the biggest stench always seems to be coming out of the fourteenth precinct. The Tenderloin's part of the problem, of course, or what's left of it. Not to mention the floating crap games. Hell, there's a bookie named Ericson who's been running his racket there for years, completely unimpeded no matter how many times I put out the word to get his ass. Far as I can tell, up in the four-teenth favors are still getting done for all the wrong people, and for all the wrong reasons."

Valentine came back out from behind his desk and again stalked over to Cain, pointing at his chest.

"Arrests are being made, I do know that, and the magistrates are pushing the charges forward like they're supposed to. That end has been cleaned up. But afterward?" He threw up his hands. "Things are falling off the table. Cases are disappearing. I hear of an arrest, or a raid, and then I don't hear a thing more. It started in January, the month after the Japs hit us. Ever since then, nothing. Not from the fourteenth. No results in either vice or gambling, and your job is to find out why."

"So you want me to be your eyes and ears?"

"Hell, if that's all I needed I'd hire a stool pigeon, or a whole room-ful. You're a *detective*, goddamn it! Build a case! Hard facts. Real evi-dence. Something that can stand up before a board of inquiry, or even a grand jury for this new DA, Hogan. Not that all of his people are necessarily on the straight and narrow. Follow any lead, wherever it takes you. But it started in January, so the first thing you should prob-ably do is have a look at the paperwork."

The arrest reports, he meant, plus the reams of other dockets and blotter items and disposition reports that cops had to fill out. All of those items ended up in the Record Room, which for reasons unknown to Cain was referred to as the "95 Room" by everyone at the station house. It was the domain of a handful of officers, the so-called 95 men, who kept the place under lock and key. Meaning that for Cain to "have a look at the paperwork" would be easier said than done.

"I just started," Cain said. "I barely know a soul. And when I do get to know them, I might even like them."

"I didn't say it would be easy. That's why I'm giving you three months."

*"Three months?"*

"As for the question of who you like and don't like, I'm counting on the abilities and talents you exhibited in your previous employment to overcome those sorts of emotions." He tapped the papers on his desk. "If your recent past shows anything, it's that your instinct for self-preservation far exceeds any regard for the health and well-being of your colleagues. While I normally see that as detestable, in this kind of case it's an absolute necessity."

Cain flushed again, this time in anger.

"You've misread the facts of that incident."

"Your file has already spoken for you, and was far more convincing."

Cain stood, furious, but the words backed up in his throat. What could he do, anyway? Complain to headquarters? Valentine continued.

"Your contact here will be Lieutenant Edward Meyer, of my confidential squad. Spring seven, three-one-two-four. Memorize that number. Never try to contact me. Meyer only. If I need to see you, you'll know it."

"You're misreading me, sir, and if you'd let me explain—"

"Just do the job. And if I've misread you, then you'd better start saving your money, because without results you'll be out on your ass three months from now. Archer!"

The door opened. The suit who'd escorted Cain upstairs reappeared. Valentine shut the file on his desk and slid it into a drawer. He didn't say good luck, didn't say goodbye, and didn't look up as Cain left the room.

Cain followed Archer to the elevators. A uniform with all sorts of stripes started to board with them, but Archer shook his head and the guy backed off. As they were reaching the ground floor, Archer pulled a handle and the car shuddered to a stop. He turned to Cain.

"Word to the wise?"

His voice was calm, but with a chilly undertone, like someone you'd hear on the radio at three in the morning and know by his tone that he sat alone in an empty, darkened studio.

"Okay."

"And this stays here. Understood?"

Cain nodded.

"You're not the first mug to draw one of these details, and you won't be the last. But maybe you should know how *not* to do the job. Last September the commish called in a 'tec from up in the two-three.

Good sleuth, clean as a whistle. But lazy, so Valentine figures he needs a kick in the ass. He sends him over to Brooklyn with the same marching orders."

"And?"

Archer shook his head.

"Sat on his ass, mostly. Figured that if the brethren ever found out what he was up to that he'd end up facedown in the East River, or tied up in butcher paper, a piece at a time. And let me tell you, ace, if there's one thing Valentine hates more than a fuckup, it's a do-nothing."

"He lost his job?"

"That's what the commish would tell you. It's probably even what he believes. He never gets involved in the details of the severance arrangements."

"That's your department?"

Archer smiled. "Hey, I figured why just cut a guy loose when he's got those kinds of secrets to spill? So I slipped a word to the brethren about what he'd been up to. Last I heard, he'd retired. To three different boroughs, all at the same time. In butcher paper, you know?"

Archer seemed to get a thrill out of Cain's queasy reaction. Archer threw back the handle, and the jolting elevator resumed its descent. The doors slid open onto the marble lobby, empty as before. Cain stepped off, then turned so they were face to face across the opening.

"Your name's Archer, right?"

"Linwood Archer. You'll be hearing from me."

"Valentine said my contact is supposed to be Lieutenant Meyer."

"Officially, yes. I'm more on the efficiency side of things."

"Efficiency," Cain repeated, pondering the implications.

"You got something to report, you give it to me. Let me worry about Meyer."

"What's your rank and title?"

Archer smiled. The doors slid shut.

When Cain got back to the station house, he opened the departmental phone directory and flipped the pages to the first letter of the alphabet.

There was no listing for Linwood Archer.

# 4

........................

ON THE FOLLOWING MONDAY, Cain managed to arouse the suspicion of his colleagues and get pulled off his one and only murder investigation, all before he'd poured his first cup of coffee. He set those events in motion when Captain Mulhearn caught him rummaging through a tray of arrest reports in the 95 Room, while the two duty officers obliviously compared snapshots from a recent fishing trip.

"Looking for something, Citizen Cain?"

The duty officers looked up abruptly, as if noticing Cain's presence for the first time.

"They, uh, seem to have misfiled my paperwork from the other day," Cain said.

"We did?" one of the 95 men answered, an officer named Steele.

"Well, it won't be in the overnight basket, as you well know," Mulhearn said. "Maybe next time one of you two nimrods will take notice when this fox enters the henhouse."

"Sure, Cap'n." Steele held up one of the snapshots. "Hey, did you get a load of these cods Rose hooked off Long Island? Ten pounders!"

Mulhearn shook his head.

"Sorry," Cain mumbled. "I'm still learning where everything goes around here."

A feeble excuse, although it would have been more convincing if he hadn't blushed a deep red. Mulhearn steered him toward the door. When they were out in the hallway he backed Cain against the wall.

"Listen, Citizen Cain." Cain already disliked the nickname, which Mulhearn had presumably taken from the overblown movie that had come out the previous fall. "Just 'cause you're a detective sergeant with some juice don't mean that I can't assign you to switchboard duty for a month. But maybe that would be right down your alley, answering everybody's calls for them."

Cain tried not to look away. Maybe this was how the doomed cop in Brooklyn got started toward his dismembered "retirement."

"I don't know what you were really looking for in there, Cain, but since you already seem interested in branching out your duties, how 'bout we go make some adjustments to your schedule? Upstairs."

When they reached the second floor, Mulhearn steered Cain by the arm across the floor of the squad room—the wide, shallow chamber where all the detectives worked. He tugged Cain to the board along one side where the duty rosters were posted. By now, every man in the room was watching.

"Here we go," he said, talking loudly enough for all to hear. "This floater of yours, the homicide from the other night." The room was silent as Mulhearn jabbed a finger on the blackboard just beneath Cain's name. Cain hadn't felt this belittled since mean old Miss Vernon had pulled him by his ear up to the blackboard in third grade.

"From what I've seen, you got no leads at all. Hell, you haven't even made an ID. So we're moving it to inactive. Here." He handed Cain an eraser. "You whiffed on that one, Citizen Cain. Strike one."

"But I—"

"If you want it back, give me an ID by the end of the day. Otherwise, I'll be shipping it over to the Borough Homicide Bureau at the close of business. So I don't want to see it showing up on any more of your goddamn DD-64s for even ten minutes' worth of your time. Got it?"

"Yes, sir." Cain sheepishly erased it from the board. Never mind how he was supposed to ID the victim in the next eight hours if he couldn't work the case.

"And remember, tomorrow night you're coming out for choir practice with the rest of us."

"Choir practice?"

"Drinks," someone behind him offered, setting off a few giggles.

"At Caruso's on Eighth, just above 44th," Mulhearn continued. "Right after quitting time." He turned to face the rest of the room. "Everyone else on board for that?"

"Yes, sir," came the replies—some shouted, others mumbled. Mulhearn lowered his voice, as if to pretend the words were meant for him alone, even though he was still loud enough to overhear.

"If I or anyone else ever catches you lurking around the 95 Room again without a good reason, then you'll be busted down to radio patrol faster than water off a duck's ass. Now get the fuck to work, nimrod."

Cain turned toward his desk. His colleagues had their heads down, trying to look busy. There were a few muffled laughs, but this was no time for challenges. The damage was done. And tomorrow night he'd be drinking with all of them. He could hardly wait.

Even on a good day, the squad room could be oppressive. Ten detectives shared floor space in two long rows of battered gray desks, with a row of windows along the back. Hovering above the room was a fog bank of cigarette smoke that rolled and tumbled like it might eventually produce rain. Mulhearn presided from a glass cubicle up front. Six of the detectives formed the squad for the 14th precinct, with their own lieutenant. The four desks closest to Mulhearn's office were posted to district level—Cain, Wat Foley, Bert Simmons, and Yuri Zharkov, which meant technically they were supposed to handle the bigger cases for an area covering four precincts—the 14th, plus the 10th, 18th, and 20th.

Zharkov, a bulky hawk-nosed Russian in his late forties who spoke six languages, was the only one who'd yet made an effort to make Cain feel at home. The previous Friday they'd shared lunch on a park bench, swapping stories and eating from a greasy brown bag of piroshki—fried Slavic treats that Zharkov had picked up from a street vendor. Sort of like hushpuppies, except filled with ground meat and cabbage. Zharkov had come to New York as a boy in 1919 after his family migrated halfway across Russia, fleeing first the tsar and then the Bolsheviks. In his uniform days he had walked a beat in the rough-and-tumble 7th on the Lower East Side, strolling the waterfront from Clinton to Delancey with a Cossack's zeal for the well-thumped cranium.

With their four adjacent precincts, the gumshoes of the third district covered about a sixth of Manhattan, from 14th Street up to 86th, bordered to the west by the Hudson, and to the east by Central Park and, below 59th, by Fifth Avenue. Plenty of interesting territory lay within—the meatpacking and garment districts of Chelsea; the glitz joints of Times Square; the workaday Midtown glories of Herald Square and the Empire State Building; the huge new complex of Rockefeller Center, with its sleek art deco towers that now dominated the Midtown skyline; and, above Columbus Circle, the high rent district along Central Park West over toward the lower end of Riverside Park. Almost as a throw-in you had the fleshpot holdovers of the Tenderloin, which Valentine had griped about even though it was a shadow of its old self, with a few vestiges scattered near Times Square, kept alive by mob money and the remnants of Tammany influence.

Mulhearn began most mornings by standing in his office doorway, browsing a stack of newspapers that were so fresh you could smell the ink. He offered dramatic readings of stories that struck his fancy. Like having their very own Walter Winchell, although the detectives often rolled their eyes when he wasn't looking.

"Hey, here's one for you guys," Mulhearn announced, as Cain settled in. "Says here that some mug got thirty days for mouthing off about the war. Told a sailor he was fighting for a bunch of rich capitalists, and that FDR's no better than Hitler."

"Thirty days for that?" Zharkov sounded shocked.

"Some bum turned him in, and the judge threw the book at him. Said, 'The right of free speech is limited by considerations of public welfare.'"

"Whose public welfare was he endangering?" Wat Foley asked.

"His own, I guess. Judge said if he'd ticked off the sailor enough, 'Violence might easily have ensued.'"

"So this clown got thirty days to save him from getting his ass kicked? Jiminy fucking Christmas."

"Judges, huh?"

Mulhearn put down his *Herald-Tribune* and picked up the *Times*. Cain looked around at his colleagues, wondering who was clean, who was dirty. It was a no-win assignment. At best, he'd end up as the house stool pigeon. At worst, well, why even think about it?

"Hey, Simmons, here's one for you," Mulhearn announced. "Some air ace in the Pacific who bagged six Japs on his last mission? The guys who built his plane out at the Grumman plant on Long Island got together a collection and bought him, get this, *one thousand, one hundred and fifty* cartons of smokes. Shit, that would keep you going at least a month."

"Maybe two," Simmons said. "I been cuttin' back."

Cain, meanwhile, was still so frazzled that he'd forgotten to check his own messages, which he'd scooped up just before Mulhearn had caught him poking around.

The switchboard had taken one call for him, from Harris Euston. That made four calls in the past three days from his father-in-law, none of which Cain had returned. After the meeting with Valentine he felt less inclined than ever, although he supposed he owed Euston big-time. He stared at his phone, glanced at the number, then tossed it in the trash. Less than a week on the job, and he already felt obligated to way too many people.

Cain got so lost in that thought that he didn't notice anyone approaching until Desk Sergeant Romo was practically on top of him. Romo was out of breath, like he'd run upstairs.

"Was going to collar you on your way upstairs," Romo said. "But with Mulhearn right on your ass it didn't look like a good time."

"You got that right. What's up?"

"There's this guy." He gestured over his shoulder. "Been bugging the shit out of everybody at the front desk. Claims he has to see you."

"Me?"

"And nobody else. Been here for three hours."

"*Three hours?*"

"Showed up before sunrise, while the night squad was still on. Won't say what it's about, and won't take no for an answer. Looks too old to hit over the head, so I figured I'd bring him on up, let you sort it out."

"Send him over."

"He's the guy over by Mulhearn. Guess I better grab him before he gets dragged into the show."

Cain took a look, and his spirits sank. Pale thin face, the color of oatmeal, with uncombed white hair sprouting from beneath the sides of a ratty wool cap. Unshaven, with white stubble. The man had supposedly been waiting indoors for hours, yet he was still bundled up against the elements in a scarf and a long mud-spattered overcoat that might have seen duty in the trenches of the First World War. Cain felt a chill just looking at him, as if the old guy had managed to keep winter alive an extra month and carried the remnants around with him. His blinking eyes emanated an air of frailty. Only the stitching of his clothing seemed to be holding him together. Unbutton the coat and he might collapse into a pile of bones.

"Good God. Is he even alive?"

"Like I said. We didn't exactly want to shove him out the door. If he's a crackpot, call downstairs and I'll send Maloney up."

Maloney. Now there was a fate Cain wouldn't wish on anyone. A big, bluff patrolman with scabbed knuckles and a face the color of corned beef.

"I'll handle it."

Romo gently pointed the man toward Cain's desk. The fellow sprang into motion with surprising agility, and with each successive step seemed to shed another year, so that by the time he reached the desk Cain was almost wondering if he was an actor, practicing for a role.

"Have a seat." Cain motioned toward a chair.

The man pulled off his cap, unleashing a gust of boiled cabbage and wet wool. Up close his eyes were cloudless and blue, not frail at all. If his clothing said December, his irises spoke of mid-June, one of those mornings in early summer with bees buzzing and the sense that the day might last forever. He looked alert, intelligent, and, best of all, lucid. Whatever had brought him, he probably wasn't a crank.

"My thanks to you, Detective Cain, for agreeing to see me. I am here to do my duty as a citizen. In fact, I believe that I can assist you in one of your current inquiries."

Cain, just beginning to decipher local accents, couldn't place this one. The man's sentences had started somewhere in Russia, doubled back toward Germany, and had even seemed to detour briefly through Rome before coming to rest in what sounded like Brooklyn, a shout from a clerk in a deli.

"First, tell me your name."

"Ah, yes."

He withdrew a white business card from his overcoat. It was curiously uninformative—raised black lettering on a blank background, with the name DANZIGER on top, all in caps, and the word "Information" underneath. That was all. No address. No phone number.

Cain turned it over. Blank. He took out his notebook.

"I need a *full* name. And your place of residence."

The man frowned, as if this was more than he'd bargained for.

"Maximilian Danziger."

"Do people call you Max?"

"They call me Danziger."

"Of course. And your address?"

"Rivington Street. Number one seventy-four."

The Lower East Side. He'd come a long way, especially for such an early arrival.

"You live in the seventh precinct. What business brings you up here?"

Danziger leaned forward, blue eyes glittering as he turned his cap in his hands.

"I am here to offer my assistance in the case of the corpse found on the sixth of April, at the docks along the Hudson. It was your first day on duty, if I am not mistaken?"

There was no hint of smugness, humor, or triumph in the man's eyes. Just the same solid resolve as before. Cain glanced again at the business card.

"What's your line of work, Mr. Danziger? Are you some kind of private dick?"

"Dick?" Furrowed brow, followed by dawning comprehension. "I see. You mean like in the pictures. A private eye. As with W. C. Fields, *The Bank Dick*." He smiled appreciatively. "No. Not a dick. But I have a name for you, the name of the man you found in the river. I believe I may also have a few ideas as to why he was killed. Leads, as a dick might say."

Cain tried to not get his hopes up. Maybe the fellow was a nut, after all. But for the moment he was Cain's only chance to put his one murder case back on the duty board before Mulhearn shipped it out at the end of the day.

"Let's start with the name."

"Werner Hansch." Danziger spelled it.

Cain flipped open his notebook. Seeing that he had turned to a letter he'd begun writing to Olivia the night before, he flipped to the next page even as he saw Danziger notice.

"What makes you think that the body is Mr. Hansch?"

Danziger again turned his hat in his hand. As before, he spoke slowly, deliberately, picking his way forward through the sentence as if each word was a stepping stone.

"Some of the details published in the newspaper story."

"Such as?"

"The tattoo, with the name Sabine."

"You've seen him when he wasn't wearing a shirt?"

Danziger shook his head.

"He mentioned it once. The girl. Sabine worked in that theater, the one on the ticket stub you found."

Confirming that Angela Feinman had lied to him, Cain thought. To protect Sabine, perhaps.

"Also, Blackjack was his brand of gum, the same as you found in his pocket. He used to leave gobs of it stuck to the bricks outside my door."

"Interesting. But not exactly definitive proof."

"I have other reasons. More definitive, as you say. But I am not yet willing to discuss them."

"May I ask why?"

"I am not yet certain you can be trusted with this information."

Cain put down his notebook.

"Mr. Danziger, I'm a police officer."

"Exactly."

It was an answer Valentine would have enjoyed, given his mistrust of the 14th precinct. Cain decided to overlook it for now.

"If you've got information material to a homicide investigation then it's your duty as a citizen to offer it. But for the moment we'll work around that. This Mr. Hansch, is he a frequent visitor to your home?"

"He was a customer of mine. Of my business."

"Which is what, exactly? I'm afraid that the word 'Information' isn't very, well, informative."

"It suffices for my customers. Mostly what I do is write letters. For those who are unable to write for themselves. It is a common need where I live."

"So Mr. Hansch is illiterate?"

"Illiterate, and he speaks—begging your pardon, *spoke*—very little English. His mother tongue was German. He began employing my services several weeks ago, and I have his letters. All of his correspondence, for the entire period."

Cain picked up his notebook again, pen poised in the air.

"You have Mr. Hansch's letters? His personal mail?"

"As I said."

Cain leaned forward. Now he was hooked.

"I'd very much like to see those letters. Provided, of course, that the body in question is that of Mr. Hansch."

Cain was a bit surprised by his own syntax. He wondered if Danziger's somewhat formal cadences often had this effect on others.

"Of course. Although I do not have them with me at the moment. I presumed that an identification of the body might first be in order, so for the time being I have secreted them in a safe location, outside of my home."

"Perhaps you could take me there."

"Perhaps."

"In the meantime, would you be prepared to accompany me to the morgue?"

"It is the course of action that I expected. It is why I came."

"Glad to hear it, sir."

Danziger reached across the desk and gently placed a bony hand upon Cain's sleeve. Then, with a look of deepest concern, he said,

"But first, sir, please tell me something. How much longer before your daughter arrives in the city?"

Cain, usually a master of the poker face when dealing with witnesses and suspects, couldn't prevent his mouth from dropping open in surprise. A second or two passed before he spoke.

"How do you know about my daughter?"

"Olivia, is it not? Named by her mother. Did she choose it from Shakespeare?"

Cain nodded, transfixed. Had the old man seen the page in his notebook? Even then, how would he have known how Olivia got her name? Impressive, but possibly a trick, like the way fortune-tellers fleeced your wallet and guessed at your life story from the contents. Or, worse, maybe this was all a joke, a nasty prank engineered by his new colleagues. He glanced around him, half expecting to be greeted by a host of smiles and winks, the whole thing a ruse. But no one seemed the slightest bit interested in either him or the old man.

"Good guess," he answered. "It's from *Twelfth Night*."

"An educated guess, of course. Otherwise I would not have ventured it. Perhaps I was only trying to impress you."

"You succeeded."

"I did not ask about your daughter in order to be intrusive, or threatening. I asked because I am hoping her arrival will come as late as possible, preferably after the matter before us has been concluded."

"And why is that?"

"It is one thing for you or me to risk life and limb, quite another to involve a child. So, while we must work carefully, we must also work quickly."

"'We,' Mr. Danziger?"

"Of course. I have rearranged my schedule to make myself available to assist in your inquiries. Provided we come to an understanding, of course. As you said, it is my duty as a citizen, especially considering the dangerous element we are likely to be dealing with."

"That's quite a statement. What makes you so sure about this 'dangerous element'? Apart from a dead body, of course."

"As I said, there are matters I would prefer to discuss only after ensuring that the body is that of Herr Hansch."

"And after being assured that you can trust me."

"Yes, there is also that."

Cain nodded, not sure whether to smile or frown. So he just stared, gaping at Danziger as if he were a spirit that had descended from the cloud of smoke near the ceiling. He shook his head, as if to clear it. Part of him now almost hoped the body *wasn't* Hansch. Better to have an unsolved case, perhaps, than to get entangled with this strange old mystic who seemed to know more than he should. Cain glanced again at the calling card. Information, indeed. He cleared his throat and stood.

"In that case," he said, "we'd better go have a look at the body."

# 5

.....................

IT WAS CAIN'S FIRST TRIP to the city morgue. He told Danziger they'd have to travel by bus, which would require some walking.

"I'd drive you, but, well—"

"Rationing, yes?"

Cain nodded.

"Just as well. I am not accustomed to luxuries. The last time I took a taxi was 1928."

Fourteen years ago. Must have been a grand occasion, or maybe the man had money then. Another casualty of the Depression, perhaps. It stirred Cain's curiosity, but Danziger didn't seem like the type to readily talk about himself. He'd be too busy finding out more about you.

Cain's hopes for morgues were always minimal: freshly mopped floors and strong refrigeration. Some of the ones back in his home state had failed on both counts, and his nose remembered. At least this time there would be no grieving relatives to deal with. Danziger didn't seem the least bit bereaved by the man's demise. Cain wondered if he was that detached from all his customers.

The entrance to the city mortuary, as it was officially known, was on 29th, just off First Avenue in one of the hulking brick buildings at Bellevue Hospital, which was better known for housing nuts and drunks. The dead resided in a building on the south side of the complex, and their quarters were like a lot of the city's housing—cramped and overcrowded, with low ceilings and multiple floors, a tenement of corpses. It was surprisingly noisy, with gurgling pipes, creaking floorboards, and tile walls that echoed every footstep as attendants came and went.

They approached the duty clerk at the front desk. Someone had just parked a gurney off to the side carrying the body of a boy with a livid bruise on his forehead. He was about Olivia's age. His clothes were torn and there was still a touch of color in his cheeks, as if he'd been whisked here straight from a game of stickball. Cain felt a catch in his throat as he announced his name and his business.

"So you're here for one of the John Does, then?" The clerk opened a big clothbound ledger.

"From last Monday night. Fished out of the Hudson. My name should be on the paperwork."

"Here we go. Third floor. Murphy here will take you." He nodded toward a stooped man in white scrubs who'd materialized next to the dead child. "Doc Bolton's report is in, too, if you want to see it."

Cain signed for a copy, which the clerk hammered with a rubber stamp.

"Looks like he didn't get around to the autopsy until Saturday," Cain said.

The clerk shrugged.

"Busy place. And your guy wasn't exactly a Vanderbilt. Who's your guest?" He nodded toward Danziger.

"Possible acquaintance of the deceased. I'm hoping to make an ID."

"You'll have to sign him in."

Paperwork completed, they followed the silent Murphy to the elevator, then trooped past rows of meat locker doorways to the end of the third floor corridor, where Murphy unlatched the door and opened it to a gust of sour, chilly air, smelling muddily of the Hudson. Murphy slid out a stretcher-like tray into the corridor. Cain recognized the body from the scene, except now it was naked, with a row of black stitches down the middle of his chest. Pinkish-blue lips gaped toward the ceiling. Filmy eyes were open to the bright lights.

"That is him," Danziger said calmly. "It is Werner Hansch."

"You're sure?"

"Positive."

Cain nodded to Murphy, who finally spoke. "Everybody got what they need, then?" He gripped the railings, ready to shove it back into cold storage, then flinched as Danziger placed a hand on his arm.

"I would like to inspect him a few seconds more, if it is permitted."

"Hey, he ain't in no rush."

Danziger leaned closer, peering down at Hansch's chest with the concentration of a surgeon.

"The burn marks are from cigarettes, in case you're wondering," Cain offered. "All those black dots. The autopsy confirmed it."

"Except for this one," Danziger said, pointing at Hansch's right breast. "This is what I was looking for. Do you see?"

It was a black semicircle, and at first Cain thought it was another burn. On closer inspection he saw that it was a tiny *L* in black ink.

"Another tattoo?" Cain asked.

"The mark of the Silver Shirts. A group of fascists, or Nazis if you will."

"Like the American Bund?"

"Lesser known. Hansch was with a group of German laborers who went west when they reached this country. Seeking jobs, adventure. I suspect they were all familiar with the tales of Karl May. From the movies probably, since none of them could read. Perhaps they fancied they would become cowboys. Hansch was uneducated and poor, but willing to do hard labor. The Silver Shirts employed them in building a compound in the California hills. Then the war came, and the authorities shut them down. So Hansch and a few others wandered for a while, until they came east, to Yorkville, where I feel quite sure that any Bundists would have welcomed them with open arms."

"How do you know all this?"

"How do you think?"

"His letters?"

"And from things he told me, plus what I already knew, and then putting two and two together. In my part of the city, people talk about these groups quite a lot—the Silver Shirts, the Bundists. Even America First, led by the hero, Lindbergh. When you are a Jew, it is useful to know what sort of person might next come looking for you and your family."

"Then why would Hansch come to you, if, well . . . ?"

"If he knew I was a Jew?"

"Yes."

"I asked myself this same question."

"And?"

"First, allow me to boast that my services are well known among speakers of certain languages, even beyond Rivington Street. I have a reputation for accuracy, and for complete discretion, a vow of privacy which I adhere to as strictly as a priest in a confessional. So there is that. Second, my occupation is not so common anymore. In York-ville it has practically vanished, meaning it is not unheard of for me to receive, how do you call it . . . ?"

He searched the air above him for the right word.

"Referrals?"

"Precisely. Yet, I suspect the greater reason Herr Hansch sought me out is that, Jew or not, he wanted someone who did not move in the same circles as he. Someone who was not at all likely to know his employers or his associates. He assumed it would be safer that way."

"Lot of good that did him."

Murphy, who by now was leaning on the rails of the tray, cleared his throat.

"We stand here much longer and the merchandise starts to stink."

Cain turned to Danziger.

"All done?"

"With him, yes. But there is another body to attend to before we depart."

"*Another* one?"

"The one that made me so certain that this first one would be Herr Hansch." He turned toward Murphy. "So, if you please . . ."

Murphy shook his head. "Unh-uh. It don't work that way. If you gotta second name, you gotta get back in line, down at the desk. I can't be going door to door on your say-so, like you're the mayor or something."

"First, how 'bout an explanation," Cain said, still reeling. "A second body? How long have you known about this?"

"Since late last night, when I went to keep an appointment with another client, and instead came upon his remains."

"You were a witness?"

"Only to the aftermath. Police were present by the time I arrived. There should be paperwork in the appropriate precinct if you would like to check, but I will not be mentioned in it. The body, however . . . Well, if it is here then there is something I need to check while we have the chance."

"I'm going to need more information than that."

"Of course. When the time is right." He glanced at Murphy, then whispered to Cain. "Two men are dead, sir. Information travels quickly, and often by unlikely channels, and I do not wish for either of us to become the third due to a possible indiscretion."

Strangely worded, but Cain supposed it never hurt to be careful. "Then let's go back downstairs. It's your show from here."

Cain expected the duty clerk to raise an eyebrow at Danziger's request. He instead flipped open his ledger with a world-weary sigh, as if requests to view additional bodies happened all the time.

"Going for the daily double, huh? Got a name for this one, or is it another John Doe?"

"Klaus Schaller," Danziger said. "He would have arrived either last night or early this morning."

"Bingo. Just after two a.m. Third floor again, couple doors down from where you just were. Murphy?"

The attendant frowned and took them back upstairs. Cain eyed Danziger the whole way, trying to figure out this strange old fellow—or not so old, who could say for sure? He might be an oracle, might be an accomplice, or even a psychopath who got his jollies by killing people and then viewing the bodies later with a cop. Or maybe, as he claimed, he was simply the guy who opened everyone's mail, and wrote their replies. Although at the rate he seemed to be losing clients, he'd soon be out of a job.

Murphy slid out another tray from the cold. No smell from the river this time. The victim's chest had been blown open by some sort of blast, but once again there was a tiny black *L* tattooed on his right breast.

"Another Silver Shirt?" Cain said.

"It would appear to be so."

"You didn't already know?"

"I was not positive for either man. Certain things they said led me to believe it would be the case. And I know they were friends. Or acquaintances, rather. Traveling companions, from Hansch's time out west." He lowered his voice again. "The rest I will tell you later."

Not that Murphy looked particularly interested. Cain nodded. The attendant slid the body back into the darkness and relatched the door with the same sound the door of Cain's icebox made when he put back the milk.

After they reached the street, he waited for Danziger to speak.

"Well?" he prompted.

"Not here."

"All right, then. We'll go back to the station house."

"Not there, either. In a police station there are too many ways in which your words can reach the wrong ears. Besides, as I told you, I do not have Herr Hansch's letters with me. But now I am willing to show them to you."

"So I passed the test?"

"For the most part."

Cain laughed. "What an honor. But how do I know *you're* reliable?"

"What more do you need to know about me? I am a man of simple means, with nothing to gain from this situation but my honor. Is it my origins that trouble you?"

"Your origins?"

"As a *Mischling*. That is what Herr Hitler would call me. Descended from both Jews and Prussians. The blue of my eyes owes to the latter. West Prussia, city of Danzig. Thus my family name, from my father's side. My mother's people were Jews, a White Russian on one side, Bessarabians on the other, thrown together by pogroms and long rides in ox carts and, later, by transatlantic crossings in leaky, verminous ships. I arrived on these shores when I was eleven. By the time I was fourteen, both my parents were dead. I am fifty-two years old."

Cain was astounded by his age, having pegged him for well over sixty. Then, looking closer, he wasn't. Danziger was a shape-shifter, an apparition in progress—ancient one moment, deceptively youthful the next. The ratty clothes, the pale skin, and the silver hair all made him look ancient. But the moment he moved, or spoke, or squinted in thought, activating the wheels inside his head, the years melted away, and Cain could imagine him as a young man with big ambitions and a full head of lustrous black hair, a glamorous woman on his arm. Something seemed to have aged him prematurely, and something else kept him young, and safe with his secrets. He lived alone. Cain sensed that much already, and he wondered if it was by choice.

People as exotic as Danziger were new to Cain. In Horton you were pretty much either black or white, Baptist or not, rich or poor or of middling income. Go back far enough among your white neighbors and you might find German Lutherans on one side, Scots-Irish on the other. But no one in Horton ever paid much attention to that. The first things anyone ever wanted to know were where you went to church and whether you owned land. In all his years in Horton he'd met only one Jew, Mr. Goodman, who ran a general store. The only New Yorkers he'd come across in recent memory were his wife and his father-in-law, a starchy Episcopalian who fancied himself a "true Knickerbocker," whatever that meant, although it was probably safe to say Harris Euston had never rubbed elbows with the likes of Maximilian Danziger. Not if he could help it.

"You know, the way we're doing this isn't exactly proper procedure. If I wanted, I could run you in right now based on what you've already told me. You're a material witness in two homicides."

"I suggest we meet tomorrow evening," Danziger responded evenly, ignoring Cain's challenge. "By then I may have been able to gather more information. Let us say Caruso's, a saloon on Eighth, just above 44th. There is some drinking ritual you are supposed to attend there, yes?"

"So you know about that, too."

"It was the topic of much discussion in your station house. I could join it in progress."

"By that time I might be too drunk to care."

"You do not strike me as that sort of drinker. Besides, these police events, these rites of . . ." He searched for the word. ". . . of *initiation*. From what I know of them, you may be eager for a pretext to allow for an early exit."

"That bad, huh? As you wish, then. Caruso's it is."

Cain couldn't help but smile. Danziger was running this show, yet somehow he didn't mind. With any luck he might learn something. An old hand from one of the oldest parts of the city. There was probably a lot of knowledge to be tapped from that noggin of his.

"Tell me something. That last time you took a taxi, in 1928. What was the occasion?"

"A funeral."

"Oh." It stopped him for a second. "Family?"

"An employer."

"He must have been a big deal."

"He was."

Cain waited for more, but Danziger nodded in farewell and turned to go. Cain watched until he reached the corner and melted into a crowd that was babbling three languages at once. Everyone crossed the intersection together. Then a bus lumbered by, and they all disappeared.

By the time Cain boarded the subway, the events of the past hour had begun to take on the qualities of a dream, barely believable. But one thing seemed real enough. Now he had a name for the body from the Hudson, plus a second homicide that might be related. The case would go back up on the duty roster, whether that asshole Mulhearn liked it or not.

Cain smiled, already looking forward to his next meeting with this strange old fellow.

# 6

.....................

## DANZIGER

IN THOSE LONG AGO DAYS when I still rode in taxis and dined in restaurants, a valued associate of mine once invited me along to a prize fight at Madison Square Garden. The only pugilist whose name I recall from that night was Kid Lewis, the welterweight champion. My associate had decided that Lewis might interest me because he was a Jew from the tenements of London's East End. He lost in twelve rounds.

While I have since developed a fondness for the so-called "sweet science of bruising," and now follow it closely in the newspapers, at the time I was far more interested in the doings of the spectators. They were a ravening mob of prosperous men, spittle flying with every shout. Most wore straw boaters, with cigars clenched between their teeth. Their eyes gleamed and their blood was up. I have never witnessed a more elemental outpouring of collective heat, before or since, although recent newsreels from Herr Hitler's rallies in Nurem-berg come close.

I mention this because of what I observed only a few hours ago at Caruso's, on this night of my second appointment with Mr. Cain. The barroom tableau included another series of body blows—verbal, this time—and I beheld yet another overheated mob, eager for the kill. No one wore straw boaters, although many in attendance were fitted with the standard-issue hats of the New York City Police Department.

The first punches, so to speak, were thrown shortly after the pouring of the third round of drinks, just when Mr. Cain began picking up the tab.

"So your old lady, I hear she didn't make the move, huh?" This came from a portly man in uniform named Maloney—"as Irish as Paddy's pig," as a former landlady of mine would have said. His mustache was flecked with foam. Laughter was barely hiding behind his eyes. "Something to do with your old partner, wuddn't it? Like how he couldn't keep it in his pants?"

An Officer Petrowski chimed in, followed in short order by cops named Kleinschmidt and Dolan:

"But you took care of it, is what we hear. How many slugs you put in his gut?"

"No, man, wuddn't the gut. Was a head shot. And some lowlife done it for him. Ain't that right, Cain?"

"So is that how the flatfoots do it down on Tobacco Road, laddie? Same way as the mob?"

I watched this unfold from a table in the back, where I was hiding behind the pages of a newspaper. I had arrived earlier rather than later in order to complete my vetting of Mr. Cain. Trust was no longer my primary concern. He seemed genuine enough, and as truthful as any policeman is ever likely to be. What remained was the question of his resilience, his fortitude, and what still troubled me were the rumors I had heard of a possible failure under pressure—the very rumors to which these officers seemed to be alluding. If he had failed then, he would likely fail now, here in this saloon, and I would know he was not sturdy enough for the task at hand. I would have no choice but to limit my part in our collaboration. I'd show him Hansch's letters, as I'd already promised, and then bow out of the matter. So, I watched him closely.

Mr. Cain shook his head, as if dazed by the fury of these first blows. He opened his mouth to reply, but they shouted him down, and aimed for the same tender spots as before. The wife. The partner. The thug. The gunfight.

By then reinforcements were pouring in from the 18th precinct, up on 54th—plainclothesmen and radio patrolmen, a 95 man, a desk sergeant. They took up positions all around him, a semicircle that pinned him to the bar. The hungry looks on their faces said they'd been told to expect a rousing bout with plenty of action, and by the time Mr. Cain slid another row of nickels into place for the next round, fresh jabs were coming at him from every angle. Like Joe Louis going after Schmeling. Not that Mr. Cain would ever be confused for a heavyweight among these slab-faced Irishmen, Italians, Poles, and Germans. They were large men with large voices, some of them barely a step removed from the Old World that I well remembered, yet they were New Yorkers to the core.

Mr. Cain, unsteady on his barstool, swiveled back around just in time to take a figurative shot to the jaw from Dolan.

"So this guy you knew, he was fucking your wife?"

"Which guy's that?" Maloney again. "The partner or the guy he plugged?"

"Thought he plugged 'em both?"

"Then maybe they was both fucking her."

A direct hit, acknowledged by a jubilant roar from the crowd. Mr. Cain wobbled on the barstool, and for a moment I feared he would topple to the floor and be crushed underfoot with the sawdust and the peanut shells. Then he regained his balance and slid off the seat, as if he'd decided to fend them off on foot. He landed stiffly, grimacing as he grabbed at his left thigh. He gripped the bar to steady himself. Careful, I thought. Go to the canvas now and you'll never get up.

"That limp of yours," Kleinschmidt asked. "That for real?"

"Or just a way to duck out on the Army?" Maloney, yet again, joining in another combination. The other cops surged closer, grinning, mugs in motion, hanging on every punch. The door was still swinging open with new arrivals. The noise was at its highest pitch.

"Able-bodied young man like you would be perfect for the infantry if you wuddn't fakin' it."

"But he's got a kid. Can't draft a lone wolf with a kid, can you?"

"A girl, iddn't it?"

"Yeah, but she ain't even here, is she?"

"Her name's Olivia," said Maloney, who was close up in Mr. Cain's face now, leering, almost nose to nose. "Oh-Livia, as in 'Oh, my.' Saw it in his file. Does she take after her mom, Citizen Cain? A little fast and loose? Guess you'll find out when the boys start sniffing round, huh?"

Mr. Cain grabbed Maloney's collar with stunning quickness, and before anyone could react he was twisting and pulling it with both hands, as if breaking bones. He lifted Maloney off his feet, something I wouldn't have guessed was possible for a man so wiry. A button popped loose, then another as Maloney's pink face darkened from medium to rare. Barstools scraped and shoes scuffled in a great rush of movement. A mug shattered, and every voice was in full throat. Maloney spluttered a mouthful of beer onto his chin and uniform, as if he was beginning to choke. Now Mr. Cain was doing all the talking, and at top volume.

"She's twelve years old, asshole! She's my *daughter*, you fucking ignorant mick!"

"Easy man, easy!" It was Detective Yuri Zharkov, materializing from the crowd to grab Mr. Cain from behind, as if to protect him from his own rashness. Others joined in to separate the two brawlers. Mr. Cain bristled, then let go of Maloney's shirt. The officers holding on to Mr. Cain exhibited a certain gentleness, taking their cue from Officer Zharkov. The ones grabbing Maloney were rougher, the first suggestion that maybe some people thought matters had gone too far.

"Who showed you my file?" Mr. Cain shouted. "Who told you all this bullshit?"

Maloney grinned, beer dripping from his chin, while a few men behind him shook their heads and looked away. Maybe the file comment had crossed the line, an admission of official misconduct, something that might get them all in trouble. Maloney threw one last punch.

"You guys heard about his snooping around, didn't you? Down in the 95 Room, like some rat looking for cheese? He's a regular house mouse, our Citizen Cain. Never seen him once out on the streets. Always hiding behind his desk, or some piece of paper."

There were a few grumbles, but they lacked heat or passion. As if sensing that he'd lost his momentum, Maloney raised his hands in a gesture of truce. Mr. Cain went limp, and the men released him, more in the attitude of allies than aggressors. Officer Zharkov acknowledged my presence with a sidelong wink, the only cop who'd yet taken note of me. The gesture reminded me of the way he used to offer a passing hello while walking his old beat, years earlier. We have always shared a certain understanding, especially in tight spots like this one.

But the main focus of my attention was Mr. Cain. And if I sat in admiration of his strength under duress, I approved of his next action even more. He turned toward the bartender and nodded at the taps. Then he lined up a greenback along with a new row of coins and announced to one and all, in a voice steady and clear, "My round, gentlemen."

The bartender began filling the foaming mugs as the men stepped forward, eager to accept his generosity, and I saw Mr. Cain glimpse his own image in a tilted mirror high on the wall behind the bar. I wondered if, at that moment, he saw himself as the rest of us did: thin face, a trifle callow, a tall twig of a man who even after a long winter still had some sun in his cheeks, probably from hours spent in the open fields and country lanes of his home territory. A rube's haircut that marked him indelibly as an arrival from the sticks. In a roomful of people from so many different origins, he was the one true outsider.

But he was learning fast, and he no longer looked spooked, or overwhelmed. They had cornered him. They had given him all they had, but they had never knocked him down. I was satisfied with what I'd seen. Nagging questions remained about what must have really happened down at his old job, but I decided I was ready to move forward, double or nothing, for the task ahead.

# 7

.....................

ZHARKOV TOOK CAIN by the shoulder and steered him toward
the back of the saloon. Cain thought he was about to be subjected
to a lecture—he still couldn't believe he'd been stupid enough to call
Maloney a mick. Instead the burly old Cossack whispered into his ear.
"You have company, there in the back."

The first thing Cain spotted was the gnomish wool cap. Next the
shabby overcoat. Then Danziger's enigmatic face peeped above the
top of a newspaper.

"Y'all know each other?"

"From my old beat down in the seventh," Zharkov said. "We go
back a ways."

Cain made a quick calculation.

"So I take it he's been asking about me. And you've been talking."

"Danziger is a very thorough man." Zharkov smiled and turned
back toward the bar, where the mobbing cops were still happily enjoying the bounty of Cain's latest contribution. Cain himself was still
nursing his second beer. He approached the table.

"My assessment was correct," Danziger said, nodding at the half-
empty mug. "You are not that kind of drinker. Sober or not, I admire
your ability to stay on your feet."

"It was a near thing."

"Yes. I saw. The one named Maloney was particularly troublesome."

"He's a bitter old fuck, pardon my French. I guess that's what happens when they put you back in the bag."

"In the bag?"

"Heard he got demoted from plainclothes, just last year. Pushing forty and he's still a patrolman. How long have you been here?"

"A while."

"How much did you hear?"

"Enough."

Cain pulled up a chair with his back to the policemen. He was still trying to calm down, and he wondered how much he needed to explain. So much had been said—wild accusations, most of them untrue. A terrible event, yes, but they'd twisted it into something far worse. Most disturbing of all was the idea that Maloney had seen his personnel file, perhaps the very one that had been sitting on Commissioner Valentine's desk. Danziger reached across the table and patted his shoulder.

"Everyone has episodes from their past that they would rather forget."

"The *past*? This was six months ago. And what would *you* know about it." His frustration came pouring out. "Your idea of a big foulup is probably the time you misspelled 'schnitzel' in some hausfrau's letter. I'm talking about death—two casualties, three if you count my marriage."

Danziger's hand reached up with stunning speed and dexterity to clutch Cain's shirt front, much in the way Cain had grabbed Maloney's. The man's fingers were bent and bony, smelling of onions, the nails ink-stained, but their strength was undeniable. He spoke in a lowered voice, his eyes flaring.

"You know *nothing* of me. Those kinds of assumptions make you a fool in my eyes, yes?"

Cain, floored, could only nod. Danziger let go. He then frowned and bowed his head, seeming to already regret his actions.

"My apologies, Mr. Cain. An overreaction on my part. But do not presume ever again to speak for me or my interests, for I do not wish to work with a fool."

"Same here."

Danziger watched him for a second, and then nodded.

"So be it. If you wish, we may go now."

"Where?"

"To the place of safekeeping, where the letters await. On Third Avenue, just below 85th."

"That's in Yorkville. Maybe a block from where Klaus Schaller was killed. I pulled the report today."

"Two blocks, in fact. I will take you there as well, if you would like. And then . . ." He spread his arms wide, like an impresario about to announce the featured act. "We will seek out the man who, I believe, will know how and why these deaths are connected. He may even know the names of the next ones."

"*Next ones?*"

"Surely, in these kinds of cases are there not always more? I personally know of at least two likely additional targets. Come." He stood with some difficulty. "Let us go before you are again drawn into the fray."

Cain led Danziger through the mob, and opened the door just as a parting shot flew his way.

"Don't wind up in the gutter, country boy, or you'll land on the shit list in the Commissioner's 'drunk drawer.'"

"Like that asshole Valentine ever turned down a drink!" another cop shouted.

Laughter from one and all.

The door slammed shut behind them. No more voices and clanking mugs. Just the tooting of horns, the hiss of tires on wet pavement, the leather scuffle of the walking hordes. A rain shower had come and gone while Cain was taking his beating, and the April air was invigorating. He could have sworn he even smelled daffodils—from a window box maybe, or on a breeze from Central Park. Or maybe just from yearning.

Soldiers and sailors of all nations were everywhere, roaming the sidewalks on shore leave, or in transit between railcars and troop ships. Most were headed for Times Square, seeking one last fling before the maelstrom. Three limeys, linked arm and arm, bumped past them smelling of beer while singing "The White Cliffs of Dover."

Further down Eighth a big crowd poured out of a movie theater.

Some Jimmy Durante film, a man of no discernable talent, just a big schnozz and a rough voice, yet everybody looked happy enough. He wished Olivia was here, so he could take her to the pictures. The stuff playing in Manhattan wouldn't make it to Horton for ages, if at all. Cain picked up the pace, working the stiffness out of his gimpy thigh.

"Your limp," Danziger said. "I suppose now I know how you acquired it. A bullet in the line of duty, yes?"

"You only heard part of the story, plus a lot of bullshit."

"Granted. As I said, perhaps someday you will wish to tell me all of it."

"Perhaps someday I'll *know* all of it."

"Truly? Is it still so confusing for you? Due to trauma, perhaps?"

Cain glanced over at him for a few steps, then faced straight ahead.

"I don't know you well enough yet."

"Of course. And now I am making presumptions about you. Forgive me."

They passed two Dutch marines, chattering in a tongue that sounded almost German.

"You said you saw the report from the Schaller case," Danziger said. "Have there been arrests?"

"No. They don't even have any leads. The guys up in the one-nine weren't too happy about me nosing around in their territory, so I kept the Hansch connection quiet. Figured that would just give Mulhearn an excuse to take it away from me again. We need to lay low up there."

"Always good advice in Yorkville. For me, anyway."

Cain thought of Angela Feinman and her version of laying low—living in the back room of a shuttered theater, locked in by day and performing by night. Or maybe she was just an addict, and would be living that way anywhere.

He deferred to Danziger to choose the quickest route, and the older man steered them onto a crosstown bus to the East Side, where they climbed a covered stairway to the Third Avenue El. The train rattled uptown through the night while Cain peeped into the upstairs windows of passing tenements. He saw a man in his undershirt reading the paper, a tired woman ironing, kids in shorts running from room to room, a girl curled on a bed with a cat, a stooped butcher untying his bloody smock.

*Never take the subway.* That had been one of Clovis's lines whenever she reminisced about life in Manhattan. As a girl of privilege she'd always traveled in cabs and limousines. Cain couldn't afford the luxury. But he had grown oddly attached to the subway, despite its crowds and smells and inconveniences. The rattling old trains offered a fresh human tableau every day, a new performance on almost every ride. His wife, he decided, had never known what she was missing.

They got off at 84th and walked a block north beneath the gloomy steel latticework of the overhead tracks. It was like being in a tunnel, with the noises of the neighborhood echoing around them.

"It is just ahead," Danziger said. "You will not be welcome, not until I have spoken. So remain quiet until I say so."

Cain reached inside his overcoat, checking his holster. Danziger shook his head.

"Unwelcome, not endangered. It would probably be best for you to keep your hands out in the open. I do not even plan to mention that you are a policeman."

"Then who am I supposed to be?"

"An interested party. No name necessary. It is not your concern."

They approached a doorway wedged between the Berlin Bar, with bold gothic lettering and a noisy clientele, and a greengrocer with signs in English, German, and Hebrew, where a clerk was covering wooden trays of fruit with canvas while the proprietor cranked up the awning. The entrance was unlocked, and they climbed a narrow stairway to the third floor, where he followed Danziger to a door at the end of the corridor with no name or number. The only identifying mark was a thin block of bronze, no bigger than a pack of gum, which had been screwed into place on the right side of the door frame at a slight angle. Cain reached up to touch Hebrew lettering carved into tarnished bronze. Gouge marks in the wood made it look as if someone had recently tried to pry it out.

"What is it?" he asked.

"A mezuzah. Inside is a tiny roll of parchment, containing a verse from the Torah. When you are a part of the diaspora, it is your duty under Jewish law to post one at your door the moment you move in."

"Did you?"

Danziger shook his head.

"I stopped living by Jewish law quite some time ago, when I became a member of my own diaspora." He grimaced, as if he wished he could take the words back. Then he knocked gently on the door. "The man we are about to meet is Mordecai Lederer. He is a scholar, a very learned man, and I trust him. That is all you need know of him."

The knob rattled, and the door opened to reveal a bearded man dressed in a white shirt and worn black pants. He looked a few years younger than Danziger, and the two men clasped hands in greeting. The man noticed Cain and frowned. An exchange followed in a language which Cain guessed was Yiddish. At one point Lederer raised his voice and shook his head, but Danziger persisted. Finally Lederer sighed and impatiently waved them across the threshold.

"If you happen to see his wife, or any of the womenfolk, do not speak. Do not even look."

"He's the jealous type?"

"He is religious. And you are not of the faith."

"Why here? Why this house?"

"I was carrying the letters with me when I went to meet Schaller. When I saw what had become of him, I decided to get rid of them with the greatest possible dispatch. But I did not deem it wise to destroy them, so I brought them here, the nearest location where I knew they would remain safe."

The apartment was cramped, the air heavy with the smell of a simmering chicken. A radio blared from behind a closed door, broadcasting in a Slavic language. Lederer took them to the only other room, a square windowless chamber with wall-to-wall bookshelves and a bright threadbare rug covered with tiny angular animals, stitched in red. A small writing table and a cushioned chair were pushed into a corner. Lederer departed, shutting the door behind him without a further word. The room smelled of curling old paper, of ink and glue and leather bindings.

"His study," Danziger said, eyeing the shelf on the opposite wall. "Not even his wife is allowed in here, so consider yourself lucky."

"They only have one other room?"

"That and a shared kitchen, which tells you of the value he places on knowledge."

Some titles were in Hebrew, some in a language Cain didn't know. None seemed to be in English. Just from a glance, Cain doubted that any of the books had been printed during the past fifty years.

"Most of them are written in Yiddish or Hebrew," Danziger said.

"Those aren't the same?"

"They use the same lettering. The rest are in Czech. Lederer was born in Prague. He speaks no English, so we needn't worry about being overheard."

"What about everybody else?"

"His wife wouldn't care. His mother is quite nosy, but she is illiterate, despite all of this." He waved toward the books. "She grew up in an educated household, but not one in which learning was thought to be suitable for young ladies."

"Do you write letters for her?"

"And read them as well. Or used to. None of her letters have been answered for more than a year now. Their relations in Prague have fallen silent. It has been that way across the whole of the east of Europe for some time now. Candles flickering to darkness."

Their surroundings made his remarks seem all the more grave and ominous.

Danziger stepped over to the shelves, stood on his tiptoes, and pulled down a leather-bound red volume with gilded Hebrew lettering on the spine. He set it on the small table and opened it to the middle, revealing a sheaf of onionskin paper, neatly folded, four pages in all. Typewritten carbon copies, Cain saw. The text was in German.

"I keep these on behalf of my clients, in the event they wish to consult what they have written previously, or in case some legal question arises later, in correspondences with creditors, or public officials. I wrote three letters for Herr Hansch. Shall I read them to you in full, or just tell you what's important?"

"How 'bout the headlines for now, then a full text later."

Danziger nodded.

"This first one is from the twenty-first of January. Hansch had only just arrived from California with three friends. One, I learned later, was Schaller. From the markings we have already seen on the bodies, I think it is safe to assume that all four of them were Silver Shirts, and that they would have been readily accepted by the local contingent of Bundists. Hansch wished to write his wife in Germany. We spoke for a while about the news he wanted to convey, and how I should phrase it. I think he was uncomfortable with me, for obvious reasons, so I reassured him that I had no interest in politics, no quarrel with anything he stood for. A lie, of course, but this is part of my service, putting the client at ease. The fee is the same regardless. Still, I sensed he was less than candid in his first letter. Not much news. All he really told his wife was that he was safely in New York after a long journey, and that he was among friends and hoped to find work soon. Nothing of importance for our purposes."

"Okay."

He set aside the first page.

"This letter was from a week later, the twenty-eighth of January. Two pages. As you will see, he began to open up. I will read from the most pertinent paragraph, translating as I go:

" 'I have fresh tidings on the job front. I will soon be making a good sum of money in a new employment. It is manual labor, but I am to be paid a great amount above the standard wage, thanks to fortunate circumstances in which my skills and commitment have been noticed by people of high standing. It will be a boost for our family and for our Fatherland. With luck I may soon even have the means and wherewithal to return home.' "

"People of high standing," Cain said, repeating the phrase. "Interesting."

"I thought so as well. Then I immediately put it from my mind. It is not always a good thing to know so much about such people."

Cain thought it was a curious statement, but nodded for Danziger to continue.

"Four days later he wrote to cousins in Switzerland and sent them money, along with instructions on how to forward the amount to his wife. He was too afraid that any envelope addressed to Germany might be searched."

"How much did he send?"

"Three hundred dollars, all of it in twenty-dollar bills."

"*Wow*. That's five months' rent."

"In my neighborhood, fifteen. For Hansch, who knows? In the same letter he promised that he would soon be sending more."

"Did he say where he was living?"

"He gave no address. But from other things he said I gathered it was a flophouse, probably not so far from here."

"How would a guy like that come up with three hundred bucks? Dirty work for the Bundists? Distributing propaganda? Spying, even?"

Danziger frowned. "I suspect whatever it was came under the auspices of a more legitimate occupation. Probably a trade union position, based on his earlier reference to wage standards."

"Like in a factory, maybe. Something to do with the war effort. He could've been hired to gather information, or for sabotage."

"It could be many things, at many locations. Factories for aircraft, munitions, or almost anything on the waterfront. But, as I said, it is likely to have involved a union occupation. I base this partly as well on a connection he mentioned, the man who had assisted him in finding work."

"He mentioned the name?"

"A forename only. Lutz. From somewhere in Yorkville."

The name jogged a memory which Cain was unable to pin down, or at least not before Danziger continued.

"If it is the Lutz of Yorkville with which I am familiar—a man of considerable influence, or even 'high standing,' if you will—then we might be able to quickly narrow his employment possibilities."

"You know this Lutz character?"

"Please. We must proceed in the proper order. He wrote one more letter."

"Okay."

"It was a longer time in coming, nearly two months. By then I had concluded that I had seen the last of Herr Hansch. Then he again knocked at my door, very late on the last night in March, a Tuesday. I was in my nightshirt, and had damped the coals for the night. The house was very cold, but he demanded entry. He wanted to write to his wife, then and there, without delay. He was so angry and agitated that it took a while for him to organize his thoughts into coherent form, and even then he did not have so much to say, although his message was somewhat alarming to me."

"How so?"

"Here, I will read it."

Danziger took the final page of onionskin and held it to the light.

"'The hand of fortune has turned against me. The job I was to do was given to others, or perhaps even to fate.'"

"To fate?"

"Yes."

"Strange wording."

"I thought so as well. I asked him to elaborate. I told him that such vagueness might cause his wife to worry, but he would not be more specific. When I pressed him further, he lashed out, accusing me of working for 'one of them,' as he put it."

"Them?"

Danziger nodded.

"The letter closed with this: 'The present uneasiness of my status has put me on an undesirable footing with my employer, so I may be moving soon. Do not be frightened if you do not hear from me for a while.'"

Danziger put down the page.

"One week later I read the story in the *Daily News* with your name in it. I considered contacting you then, but was too uncertain. Maybe it was some other German laborer, with some other Sabine."

"You said earlier you knew about the tattoo."

"He had mentioned it in one of our conversations before his second letter. He made a boast of it, talking about a girl he had here that his wife would never know about. I think he thought it would raise his stature in my eyes. As if he cared at all what a Jew would think. It was my education that impressed him. A man of letters, he called me."

"What finally made you sure the body was Hansch?"

"Two days later, last Thursday, Klaus Schaller came calling. He demanded all copies of Herr Hansch's letters. I refused, of course. I told him they were the private property of Herr Hansch, and protected by United States federal law."

"Even the copies?"

"No. But he did not know this. So he offered to bribe me. Five dollars, then ten, while never once mentioning that anything had happened to Herr Hansch. I told him it was quite impossible unless he could show me some sort of authorization from Herr Hansch. He brightened somewhat at this prospect, and told me he would acquire proof of authorization the following day. Proof that would be provided by their mutual contact, this man Lutz."

Now Cain remembered where he'd heard the name. Angela Feinman. Someone named Lutz had fixed her brother's ownership papers.

"I told him to return when he had acquired this proof, but he insisted that we meet at another location. He said it would not be safe for him to come to my house a second time. He offered double the money if I would come to Yorkville. Twenty dollars. We agreed to meet at an empty apartment two blocks from here, at the address you saw in the report. A tenement much like this one. When I arrived at the appointed hour, with these letters in hand, the place was in an uproar. Children and policemen coming and going. Neighbors on their doorsteps, gossiping in a frenzy. I should have simply left, but I had to know. So I elbowed my way upstairs through the crowds and came to an open doorway. In the room I saw three policemen and some sort of doctor, who was kneeling by a body stretched on the floor, with its mouth open. From the eyes I saw that it was Herr Schaller. There was blood, quite a lot of it. It was readily apparent that he was dead. So there you are. That was last Friday night. And on the next Monday morning, promptly at six, I arrived at the station house of the fourteenth precinct, to wait for you."

"And you think both men died because of something in these letters."

"Yes."

"And now you think there will be others. Why?"

"Herr Hansch mentioned that all three of his friends had found work together. And if he and one of his friends are already dead, well . . . ?"

Cain nodded. Logical enough, he supposed.

"Did he mention their names?"

"Forenames only. Dieter and Gerhard."

"I'm guessing those names are pretty common among Germans."

"But if those forenames are logged in any trade union registry for the last several months, in close proximity with the names for Hansch and Schaller, then, well . . ."

"Good idea. Tell me more about Lutz. The girl at the theater on 96th mentioned a Lutz. Said he'd fixed her brother's ownership papers to make it look like a gentile was in charge."

Danziger nodded knowingly.

"That sounds like something he would arrange. Lutz Lorenz is his full name. A man of valuable connections."

"You know him?"

"Mostly I know *of* him. I knew his father, a man of similar skills who is now deceased. Many people know about men like Lutz. And when it is your business to gather information on your clients' behalf— knowing who to influence, for this matter or for that one—then you inevitably cross their paths."

"Have you met him?"

Danziger paused, then nodded. "Long ago. In a different time."

"Would he remember you?"

"He was a only a boy. But, well . . ."

"What?"

"I suspect that Lutz Lorenz was the person who referred Werner Hansch to me. So he certainly remembers my name."

"Which means you might not be safe, depending on how many other people know it."

"That has occurred to me. But people such as Lutz Lorenz operate with discretion. He is not likely to have kept records of any of his dealings with Hansch and Schaller."

"Which would be good for you, but maybe bad for what we need to find out. Unless we happen to catch him in a talkative mood."

"My sentiments exactly. Shall we go, then, to his place of business?"

"Lead the way."

They went back into the hallway, where Lederer was waiting impatiently, arms folded. He still seemed upset that Danziger had brought an outsider into his home, and he briskly ushered them out of the apartment without saying goodbye.

# 8

........................

THEY WALKED SOUTH TO 74TH beneath the gloom of the overhead railway as trains clattered above. The sidewalks were crowded, but they made good time.

Lutz Lorenz was proprietor of the German-American All Trades Employment Agency, which, as Danziger explained, gave him influence as a broker of well-paying jobs. It also connected him to the city's powerful unions, which in turn were tied to racketeers and crime bosses—a network that went well beyond the so-called Mafia and extended into the realms of Irish gangs, Jewish gangs, Slavic gangs, and the rival gangs of Chinatown. Interwoven through them all were the remnants of the once-mighty Tammany political machine.

"So he's got a lot of pull," Cain said. "Great. But won't his office be closed this time of night?"

"He lives upstairs, with his family."

Cain was expecting humble digs. Instead it was a five-story building, the block's newest and most prosperous-looking address. The organization's name was stenciled in gold leaf in English and German across a plate-glass storefront, but the door was padlocked. Someone had taped up a red-and-white placard that said CLOSED UNTIL FURTHER NOTICE. There was no further explanation.

"Most disturbing," Danziger said. He backed away from the building and craned his neck toward the upper floors. "The apartments are dark as well."

"He owns *all* of this?"

"He lives with his wife and children on the third and fourth floors. His mother lives on the fifth."

"How do you know this?"

"As I said, it is in the interest of my clients for me to know such things. Come. There is one other place to check. Quickly." Danziger was already on the move down 74th. "His assistant lives in the next block."

They reached another newer building, where Danziger pressed a buzzer by an unmarked glass door. A light went on two stories up. Footsteps pounded down the stairwell. A man in a silken robe, hair in disarray, appeared on the other side of the door, peering outward. When he saw Danziger he nodded in recognition and selected a key from a jangly ring of at least a dozen before throwing open the door.

"Reinhard!" Danziger said. "What has become of Herr Lorenz?"

Reinhard shook his head, and looked up and down the street.

"Not out here." He motioned them inside.

They stepped into the corridor, which was lit only by the streetlamp out front. Reinhard's words echoed up an empty stairwell.

"They came for him."

"Who did, Reinhard? When?"

"Five men, last night. He phoned me as it was beginning. I saw only the end. But there were five."

Cain got out his notebook. Reinhard noticed, and asked Danziger something in German. The two of them argued for a few seconds in lowered voices, Cain not understanding a word. Reinhard resumed in a more subdued tone.

"It was over very fast," he said.

"Over how?" Cain asked. "They killed him?"

"No, no. Took him. Took all of them."

"Everyone?"

"Lorenz and his family. There were two cars. Big Fords by the curb. They put his wife, his children, even his mother, into the first one and drove away. Then they put Lorenz in the other and headed in the other direction, toward the river."

"But why all of them, Reinhard?" Danziger asked.

"These men," Cain interrupted. "Were they armed?"

"Of course! Not the important one, the one who did the talking. But the others, yes. It was all very businesslike."

"Businesslike?"

"Very organized. Professional. No shouting, no shooting."

"Do you know who they were?"

Reinhard shook his head.

"But I think Lorenz must have. He saw me, just before they put him in the car, and all that he did was nod. He did not cry out, did not ask me to call anyone, or do anything. It was enough, I think, that I was able to witness his departure."

"Did you take any tag numbers from the cars?"

Reinhard sighed loudly and lowered his head.

"I did not. I realized later that I should have done this. But I was called from my bed. I was still half asleep. I . . . Well, I suppose that I failed. Because I have not yet heard from him, or from any lawyer, and I have not been able to enter the building. They put that lock there, the sign as well, and told me to stay out."

"Were they policemen, maybe?"

"No, no. I would have known. I also do not think they were, well . . . any of his *business associates*. From the unions or from any of those other groups." He looked at Danziger, who nodded, as if understanding exactly what Reinhard meant by "those other groups."

"If any of those people had wanted him, well, you can guess for yourself. They would have handled things . . . far differently."

Violently, he meant. Or at least that was Cain's interpretation.

"Describe him," Danziger said. "The important fellow, the one who was running the show. Did anyone speak his name?"

"No. But he was fat. Or not so much fat. More like . . ."

"Stocky?" Cain offered.

"Stocky, yes. And his eyes, they were . . ." He paused, then said something in German.

"Hooded," Danziger said to Cain. "He had hooded eyes."

"And a mustache," Reinhard said. "Kleine. A small one."

"Like Herr Hitler's?" Danziger offered.

"No, no!" Reinhard seemed offended. "Not small in that way."

"Thin?" Cain asked.

"Yes. Thin. And he was *Jude*. A Jew. I am sure of this. So, *not* like Herr Hitler."

"Stocky Jew," Cain repeated as he wrote in his notebook, "with hooded eyes and a pencil-thin mustache. And he was the guy in charge."

Danziger remained silent, as if lost in thought.

"Sound like anyone you know?" Cain asked.

Danziger shook his head.

"Okay. Then I guess for now we've got a dead end. On Lorenz, anyway."

"Yes," Danziger said darkly. "Dead end, as you say."

Reinhard ushered them outside and locked up. They caught a downtown subway. Cain slumped exhausted on the bench. He still stank of beer and sweat and sawdust. Danziger remained silent most of the way. He looked worried.

"What are you thinking?" Cain asked.

"Lutz Lorenz. If he had been shot or snatched by thugs, yes, that would be alarming. But this? It does not follow any of the usual patterns."

"And what patterns are those?"

Danziger shrugged. He looked as if he were already regretting the statement.

"You seem to know a lot about the way these kinds of abductions work."

Danziger shrugged again. "I have read about them in the papers."

"Sure. From the papers. Something's bothering you."

"Yes. Discreet or not, Lutz may have talked, especially if they threatened his family. And if he spoke freely about his recent connections, well . . . Surely you see the problem?"

"I could arrange for some protection, if you like. Or try to. No guarantees."

Danziger shook his head vigorously, seeming alarmed by the idea.

"Let *me* handle any such precautions."

"But—"

"Please! There are people in my neighborhood who will be far more helpful than your colleagues. If I involve the police, those people will want nothing further to do with me."

"But you're working with me."

"You are new. You are not yet a part of all that."

"All what?"

"Ask Yuri Zharkov. Or better still, *don't* ask him. I have said too much. I have said too little. There are stories he knows which he would never share with you anyway. Suffice it to say that most of the time police do not keep secrets well. Present company excepted, of course. You must let me take care of things on my end. Besides, it is the two associates of Hansch and Schaller who are in the most immediate danger. Dieter and Gerhard."

"Union rolls," Cain said. "I'll start checking for recent signups with some of the locals. Maybe we can track them down in time. You sure you'll be okay?"

"Save your worries for yourself. I have survived for a long time, and will continue to do so. In the meantime, I, too, will make inquiries with a few old sources. People who might be helpful."

"More guys you only vaguely know?"

The joke didn't register on Danziger, who just nodded, lost in thought. And at that moment, in the unflattering glare of the subway car, he again looked very much like the broken old man Cain had first spotted across the squad room floor.

# 9

............................

CAPTAIN MULHEARN GRUDGINGLY chalked Cain's murder case back onto the duty board. He then dropped a thick case file on Cain's desk.

"For your sins. I want it cleared by the weekend."

"Sins?"

"The boys up in the one-nine say you're poaching their goods. Said you were up there looking at one of their reports the other day."

The Schaller case, he meant. Cain said nothing. If he made a fuss and claimed it was linked to Hansch, Mulhearn might give both cases to the 19th, or to the Borough Homicide Bureau, just to spite him. He sighed and opened the file.

Before he could read a single page, Simmons was at his shoulder, seeking his monthly contribution to the squad room coffee fund. Cain dug into his pocket for what was left of his cash after the bar tab at Caruso's.

"A nickel, right?"

"Unless you're feeling generous."

Just as Simmons departed, Patrolman Dolan arrived.

"Hey, Cain, I heard about your marksmanship score. Top notch."

"You been reading my file with Maloney?"

"Huh?" Dolan looked wounded. "No, nothing like that. But word gets around, and the house has a pistol team. We shoot once a week against the other precincts, and—"

"Not interested."

"How 'bout bowling, then? You bowl?"

"No."

"What's your game, then? Gotta be something."

"Basketball. That's my game."

Dolan frowned.

"Zeke in the radio room, that's his department. I'll pass it on."

For a few seconds Cain felt pretty good about the idea of getting back into a gym—sweating, running, the echo of the bouncing ball, the burn in his lungs as he sprinted end to end, chasing down a pass for an open set shot. Then it hit him, yet again, that he couldn't run that way anymore, not since the shooting. He reached down and squeezed his knotted thigh, wondering how much of his youth was gone for good.

He returned to the file. It took only seconds to realize it was the sort of hopeless case his new colleagues would call a bag of shit. It involved a con man, Albert Kannerman, who'd been impersonating everyone from Bing Crosby's brother to the grandson of former President Taft, although lately he'd gotten into the spirit of the war effort by posing as men in uniform—a wounded air ace who fleeced adoring matrons, a naval officer selling tickets to a bogus USO show. Three detectives in other districts had already taken a crack at him. None had even tracked down a reliable address, and theories on Kannerman's whereabouts ranged from Midtown to Staten Island.

"Fuck."

He shut the file. Then, worried that Mulhearn might have yanked the Hansch case anyway, he walked over to check the duty board. Still up there, just below his name.

Posted next to the assignments, as always, was a lineup of wanted posters which never failed to intrigue him. New York criminals were cast from a different mold. Down in Horton, violent crimes were usually gut level and personal, and even the so-called professionals had tended to know the same people Cain knew. Most mug shots were of peckerwood whites or poor blacks, men who looked cornered and underfed, with forlorn expressions that said they'd just as soon shoot themselves as you. They tended to live in bleak shotgun shacks with varmints loose in the crawlspace.

Up here, every face dared you to come and get him, and in general they were a bunch of sharp-dressed fellows. Among the current offerings was a murder suspect, Emanuel Weiss, age thirty-five, in a flashy suit and a silk tie, expertly knotted. He was smirking, like he was trying not to laugh. He had three aliases—Mendy, Hoffman, and Kline—and his known associates sounded just as colorful: Louis "Lepke" Buchalter, Abe "Kid Twist" Reles, Clarence "The Jazz" Cohen, plus a murderous name that Cain vaguely recalled even from the newspapers down in Horton: Albert Anastasia, a mob killer.

Posted next to Weiss was Michael Romano, a twenty-eight-year-old robbery suspect with a winning smile and the kind of stylish haircut you saw in movie magazines. Dashing, handsome, but with a small bandage on his chin. The description said he was a "natty dresser, uses narcotics," and his aliases took up two lines: Joe Bruno, Scooter Joe, Mickey Mouse, Pickles, Pick.

The only other bunch that Cain knew of with so many nicknames was the NYPD. Colleagues were already calling him "Citizen," whether he liked it or not. Mulhearn was the Mule, Zharkov the Cossack, Maloney the Mooch. And both cops and criminals lived by their own codes, their own rules of engagement. When viewed that way, he supposed it was hardly surprising that some cops crossed to the other side, just as Valentine suspected.

"Nice look with the bandage, huh?" It was Yuri Zharkov, drinking a bottle of Orange Crush as he pointed to the Romano poster. "And you can bet he didn't get the cut from shaving."

"Sharp dresser, though."

"Mob thug. The ones with more than two aliases usually are. He's a horse player. They'll trip over him at Aqueduct before he ever turns up around here."

"So the rackets are still a problem, even after Prohibition?"

Zharkov waggled his left hand, as if to say not so much.

"Dewey, the old DA, put away most of the big ones. Waxey Gordon, Lucky Luciano—sent 'em both up the river. A lot of the others killed each other fighting over the scraps. Dutch Schultz got shot over at a chop house in Jersey. The last of the rum runners was Owen Madden, and we ran him outta town. Tried to come back for the Baer-Nathan fight, but Commissioner Valentine threw him out on his ass. They're like the last of the Comanches. Fat and drunk, and living on the reservation."

"Even him?"

Cain nodded toward the poster for Weiss, the one with ties to Albert Anastasia.

"Mendy's been back behind bars for months. Mulhearn won't take it down, though. He's still pissed off we didn't get credit for the collar. Simmons got a tip on his whereabouts, but we weren't there when they nabbed him so the papers didn't give us any ink."

"Who's left, then?"

"Well, there's Mendy's boss, Anastasia. Chief executive of Murder, Incorporated."

"I knew he was a killer, but that makes it sound more like a business."

"That's exactly what it is. Or was. Hard to say if they're even still in action. But he's over in Brooklyn, officially none of our business. Here in Manhattan?" Zharkov stroked his chin. "Socks Lanza, he's still a going concern, but he's down in the first."

"Socks?"

"Guess that wasn't on the sergeant's exam, huh? Joseph 'Socks' Lanza. Mob king of the Fulton Fish Market. He's why a fillet of flounder costs so much when you eat out, even though they get it right off the docks. Socks gets a cut from the boats, the trucks, the gutters and cutters."

"Why don't we stop him?"

"Well, he *is* under indictment. Big racketeering case by the DA. Still, you don't stop that kind of shit by nabbing just one man."

"Why not?"

Zharkov shook his head as if Cain had asked the world's stupidest question. "You sound like you been reading the shit Valentine says in the papers. It's not that easy. What's left of the mob is kind of like a fungus between your toes. The more you scratch it, the more it bothers you. Sometimes the best thing to do is leave it alone, so it don't itch so much."

Until they started knocking people off, like maybe his two dead Germans, given their connection with an operator like Lutz Lorenz.

"What about in a place like Yorkville?" Cain asked.

"What do you mean?"

"Who'd be in charge of the rackets there?"

"You'd have to ask the guys in the one-nine. Besides, in this city there are always mugs big enough to not worry about territory. Guys who operate wherever they like."

"Well, at least they'll be easy to spot."

"How you figure that?"

"Can't be too many fat Comanches with athlete's foot."

Zharkov smiled and tipped his bottle in tribute.

Cain spent the next two hours going through the tangled mess of the Albert Kannerman file. The con man was working so fast that three victims still needed to be interviewed. But the big problem would be finding him, and in a city of seven and a half million how did you track down one guy who didn't wish to be found, especially when he employed a wide variety of disguises and accents, and was an expert at fooling people?

His phone rang. Cain eyed it, wondering if it might be Harris Euston. He picked it up anyway.

"Danziger here. Where to next? I remain at your service, Mr. Cain."

"The better question is when. I've been sidetracked. A punishment detail that could take days."

"Then I shall proceed without you."

"Whoa, now. Not a good idea."

"Discreetly, of course. What is the nature of this new assignment?"

"Some con man."

"His name?"

"Probably not a good idea for me to tell you."

"Why? I could make inquiries on your behalf."

"Thanks all the same, but—"

"As you wish."

He hung up before Cain could say goodbye. Cain, miffed, stared at the receiver a few seconds before dropping it in the cradle. Maybe if he left the station house to interview Kannerman's latest victims, he could also squeeze in an hour or two on the Hansch case. Better still, pay a surprise visit to Danziger, catch him in his lair. He was eager to see where the old fellow lived and worked, maybe get a glimpse of his clientele. For all he knew, the whole business about writing and translating letters was just a cover story.

Then there was Valentine's assignment, nagging at him like a toothache. It was stalled for the moment due to his lack of access to the 95 Room. He'd either have to come up with a sneakier approach or lay low until Mulhearn was no longer watching his every move. But his hasty reconnaissance the other day hadn't been totally fruitless. Just when he'd begun to wonder how he'd ever make sense of all the files and folders, he'd spotted an index posted on the back of the doorway. Next time at least he'd know where to start looking, although he had better do it soon. Linwood Archer wasn't likely to be patient.

Kannerman's most recent victim lived only a few blocks away, which probably explained why the case had bounced into the third district. If Cain was going to clear this by Saturday, then he'd better get moving. Banking on warmer weather, he left the building with his overcoat unbuttoned, only to be greeted by gray skies and one of those blustery mid-April cold snaps that reminds you that spring is fickle.

Cain shoved his hands deeper in his pockets just as a young couple rounded the corner toward him from Sixth Avenue, chatting breezily about a Broadway play they'd seen the night before. College age, and in love. You could tell by the lilt of their voices, the spark in their eyes, their animated movements. He was reminded of Clovis, who always spoke with nostalgia of her evenings on Broadway as a girl, taking in a show and, afterward, waiting outside the stage door in hopes of glimpsing the stars on their way to Sardi's for a late bite to eat.

They'd talked about it on the night they met, in the fall of his junior year in Chapel Hill. She and three friends had come down for the weekend from Sweet Briar College, and were staying at the home of a classmate. On Saturday they'd ended up at a smoker at some frat house on Cameron Avenue, a party he'd crashed along with Rob after hearing lots of females would be in attendance. Campus women were in short supply in 1928.

Cain spotted Clovis the moment he walked through the door, standing with her friends by a bowl of punch that someone had already spiked with bathtub gin. It was hard to say what was drawing more attention—the Prohibition liquor, or the four girls from Sweet Briar. But he saw immediately that, alone among her friends, she was already a step ahead of every would-be male pursuer, looking calm and sophisticated, in no hurry to choose from among the many possibilities in the baying rabble.

He caught her eye just as she took a pack of Luckies from her purse—the only woman in the room with cigarettes. She put one to her lips, an act which so disarmed the surrounding males that Cain was easily able to beat them to the punch in offering her a light.

"Well, aren't you the Southern gentleman."

"You had us all figured out the moment you got here, didn't you?"

Already her friends were making room for them, easing away while observing closely, as if watching a performance. He felt color rising in his cheeks with the excitement of the moment, and saw to his delight that she was having the same reaction.

"Well, I *am* from New York," she said, smiling. "Used to a faster pace and all that. Or so everyone always insists whenever they meet me. Clovis Euston."

"Woodrow Cain."

She offered her hand in almost regal style, which he accepted in the exaggerated manner of a prince. He was no longer aware of anyone else in the room.

"I'm guessing you've pretty much seen it all when it comes to guys trying to make time," he said.

"And is that what you're doing, making time?"

"I'll stop right now if it's not to your liking."

"Why don't we take a walk instead, out on the lawn where those roses smelled so nice on the way in."

"Camellias, actually. Late bloomers around here."

"Well, there you go, another reason you're just the man to show me around town. I suspect you're also something of a late bloomer."

It was true. He was. She offered her arm and he took it, both of them hamming it up yet also sensing the chemistry. The crowd seemed to part for their exit. The air outside was warm, not unusual for a Chapel Hill night in early October, and, yes, there was a scent of camellias as they crossed the verandah. To Cain the air felt languidly heavy with promise.

That was the night when she first told him of her father's master plan in sending her south to Virginia, sealing her off from all those guys and gals who'd once lured her into so much trouble. Bad grades and wrecked curfews. A paternal call on an old connection had secured her a spot at Sweet Briar, an oasis of learning where her natural brightness could flourish in sobriety and calm.

"And has it?" Cain asked.

"Third in my class." She smiled, knowing he was the type who'd be impressed. "Best of all, I don't really miss any of that silly old crowd of mine in the least. And, of course, no one ever told dear old Dad about weekend trips to Charlottesville and Chapel Hill."

"Still, it's not exactly Manhattan." He tried to say it in a knowing way, so she would think he'd actually been there. "Don't you miss it?"

"Sometimes. The bustle, the crackle. I always woke up with my eyes wide open, ready to go, no matter how much I'd had to drink the night before. Here sometimes I even slumber. I luxuriate. But look around you. Is it really so terrible? Practically everyone is our age, and, well, I don't think it's a boast to say that my female competition is rather thin on the ground."

They laughed, knowing the truth of it. Then she looked deeper into his eyes.

"Besides, at times like these I feel right at home."

They wandered hand in hand to every shadowy corner of the leafy campus. Even then he could sense she was plotting to overstay her father's terms of exile. But there was more to it than rebellion.

"I think places like this are good for me," she said. "Or good for what I need. Manhattan gets me far too revved up, like one of those racing cars that overheats."

She genuinely *did* like it there, partly for the gentler pleasures of its warmer climate, its easy company, its green canopies that weren't just confined to parks.

"And how can I argue with all those camellias?" she said. "Or with your eyes."

That was the moment when they first kissed.

They stayed out until three in the morning. Cain dropped her off at the front porch of her friend's home, where the classmate's scandalized father appeared at the door in his nightshirt, tut-tutting about those ill-mannered Tar Heel boys.

From that weekend forward he borrowed Rob's car, a noisy '26 Chevy, as often as he could, bouncing and grinding his way up the rutted highways every Friday to Sweet Briar, a trip of more than a hundred and thirty miles. During the holidays, when she spurned home and hearth to stay with her classmate in Chapel Hill, they were almost inseparable.

In retrospect he realized she was already displaying small warnings which he would refuse to heed, those of a young woman who would never be quite satisfied with the slow and early nights of a small town in the South, especially once her husband started spending more of his time on the job, or with his daughter; a restlessness that would inevitably seek stimulation elsewhere. But such niggling distractions on the periphery matter little once you've set your sights so squarely on what you want most.

By March they were engaged. Harris Euston spent the better part of the spring and summer trying to subvert the arrangement until Clovis sealed the deal, so to speak, by telling him in September that she was pregnant.

A month later, the stock market crashed. A month after that, she and Cain were married.

He spent his senior year wandering in the haze of two clouds—one of marital bliss, the other of growing dismay as he watched all the job opportunities he had once counted on dissolve in a widening pool of economic panic. Olivia was born in May, only weeks before his graduation. Under other circumstances he might have felt pressured. Instead, as a scholarship student, he mostly felt blessed. By then, a fair number of classmates had already been forced to withdraw after their daddies' fortunes had fallen into ruin.

The scent of camellias—that would be a nice sensory treat about now, on this shivery spring day in New York. Honeysuckle, better still. Those were Cain's thoughts as a gust of wind blew a cloud of white petals toward him from a nearby vacant lot along 30th. The temperature made them look more like snowflakes.

His reverie came to an abrupt end with a shout by Patrolman Maloney.

"Hey, Citizen Cain, wake the fuck up!" He abruptly looked up to see a leering Maloney only six feet ahead of him on the sidewalk, hands on hips, blocking his way. "What's the matter, daydreaming about that hot and bothered daughter of yours again?"

Cain lunged forward and then snapped to a halt like a snarling dog at the end of its chain. Huge hands had latched on to him from behind. A pair of muscular arms squeezed his chest until he was short of breath. Maloney, who hadn't budged, grinned and shook his head.

"You drunken mick!" Cain gasped, barely able to squeeze out the words.

Maloney's smile disappeared. He stepped forward and, working quickly, reached under Cain's jacket to unbuckle the shoulder holster and pull it free along with the Colt revolver. Then he aggressively patted him down—arms, chest, legs, ankles—growing more frustrated by the second.

"Where is it?" Maloney snapped. "Where's your throwaway?"

"My what?"

"Your extra gun, nimrod! Ain't you got one?"

"No."

Maloney chuckled darkly and shook his head.

"Another goddamn college boy who don't know shit from Shinola. Your throwaway. The gun you use in a tight spot. Plug a skell and throw it away. Then when the lab checks your Colt, presto, clean as a whistle. No need to call in the Rat Squad while they figure out where the bullet came from. Guy with your reputation, I figured that would be the first thing you'd learn. Not that you'll be needing it today, of course."

Maloney stepped to the curb and opened the rear door of a long black Lincoln Zephyr with four doors and white sidewalls. Whoever was holding Cain pressed down the top of his head and shoved him onto the back seat. Cain tried scrambling out, but the door slammed in his face. Then a second guy inside the car grabbed him from behind and cuffed his wrists.

Maloney climbed in up front on the passenger side.

"Shut the fuck up, unless you want a lump on your head." Maloney showed his billy and thumped the seat back.

"What do you want? Maybe we should settle this on the street!"

"Believe me, Cain, I'd like nothing better. Pound those skinny lips of yours right down your throat, then stuff you in a mailbox straight back to Shit Creek. But we've got a ride to take, so shut your yap unless you want some splinters up your ass." He thumped the billy harder.

The driver started the engine. Cain saw now that it was Steele, one of the officers from the 95 Room, so there was a second name for his shit list. Out on the sidewalk, a few passersby craned their necks to see what all the fuss was about. None seemed particularly concerned. To them it must have looked like New York's finest had just collared another lowlife. Cain tried the door handle with his elbow, but it was locked tight, which only made the cop beside him laugh. A four-man job then, counting whoever had grabbed him from behind on the street. Four bad apples, minimum.

"Don't even think about taking names, asshole." This from Steele, who'd glanced in the mirror and must have noticed the calculating anger in Cain's eyes. "We're doing you a favor."

"Man's been here two months," Maloney said, "and can't even hold on to his sidearm." He held up the Colt like a taunt. "Bad training, you ask me. But don't worry, Cain, where we're going you won't need it."

"Where are you taking me?"

"Pipe down, you'll see soon enough. Get this heap moving."

Cain was still breathing deeply, although his fury was now sliding toward fear. It would be easy enough to dispose of him, and for all he knew Mulhearn was also in on it. The captain must have known that the Kannerman assignment would get Cain out of the building by lunchtime, and the latest victim's address had told him which direction

Cain would head. All of them would be on Valentine's shit list soon enough, provided he was still in one piece to put them there.

"What's this about?" he asked, trying to steady himself.

"I said shut it." Maloney whipped the billy across the seat back toward his forehead. Cain reeled out of the way just in time.

"It would be bad form if you was to arrive scuffed up, so keep it quiet."

Did that mean they intended to keep him alive? If so, maybe somebody else was waiting to do all the dirty work. Cain had visions of a long, grim ride to the furthest reaches of the city, up through a tunnel beneath the Hudson, or maybe across a bridge to Queens, out to the remote wasteland near the new airport. Or over to the lonely sawgrass marshes of Jersey, where it was so quiet you could hear the wind blow. He might never get a chance to make a move, not with these cuffs on.

Steele surprised him by heading deeper into Midtown and turning north on Park Avenue, where the sidewalk was filled with serious looking men in suits, glamorous women out shopping. Bankers and secretaries, prosperous housewives walking pampered dogs on jeweled leashes. Grand Central Station loomed far ahead. Maloney rested an arm across the seat back and turned to face him.

"Heard you were seen coming out of headquarters the other day. What was the occasion?"

Had Linwood Archer ratted on him? Cain offered the first explanation that popped into his head.

"Paperwork."

"What the hell's that mean?"

"Forms to sign. Payroll, you name it. They're running people through the Academy so fast that the pencil pushers can't keep up, and I'd kind of like to get paid."

"Forty-day wonders." Maloney said, shaking his head. "No wonder you can't do shit."

Maybe he bought it. Maybe they didn't know a thing. Or maybe none of that mattered because they were about to kill him simply because he'd been snooping around the other day, or just on general principle. Cain was surprised at how little emotion he felt at the prospect. A pang of loss on Olivia's behalf, but not a whole lot more. Fear at some level, but less than he would've expected. Was this the toll of the last six months? Numb at the core? Or maybe not. His anger was stirring again. If it came to it, he'd go down fighting, graceless or not. Butting his head and running like a coward. He clenched his fists behind his back, the cuffs biting into his wrists while he stared out the window at all of the lives in progress, all of the people who still had a future.

No one said anything more until the car turned left onto 37th, where it pulled up in front of a red brick building with a marble foyer and a green awning. A doorman stood guard in a uniform worthy of a pasha.

"This is your stop," Maloney said. "Take off the cuffs, Mabry."

Mabry. Another name for the list.

"Now get out."

Whatever had been squeezing Cain's heart eased its grip. He surveyed the landscape. A flag over the door identified the place as the Union League Club. Cain had never heard of it.

"Here?" He was beginning to think he might survive the afternoon.

"I said *get out!* Go straight upstairs, second floor. You'll see a guy with a big book. You're expected. Oh, and before you go." He tossed a necktie across the seat. "Put this on, you fucking slob. That one you're wearing looks like you been washing cars with it."

# 10

........................

SUDDENLY IT FELT LIKE SPRING AGAIN. A reprieve. Rebirth.
Cain stood on the sidewalk, breathing deeply in the harmless cold
breeze as the Zephyr pulled away. He knotted the new tie while whistling an ad jingle he'd heard that morning on the radio. The doorman
smiled as if he approved, and nodded as Cain entered the foyer of the
Union League Club, where he was greeted by varnished wooden columns supporting a grand marble double staircase that curved upward
from both sides of a central landing.

With its classic design and wrought-iron banisters, it looked like
a set from a Busby Berkeley musical. All that was missing was the
lineup of high-stepping showgirls, doffing top hats as they tap-danced
down the stairs toward him from either side. It made him feel like he'd
arrived, which he supposed was the whole point.

For a fleeting moment he considered leaving—why should he do as
Maloney asked, especially now that the car was gone? But curiosity got
the better of him, and he climbed to the second floor, where a man in
a dinner jacket was indeed posted with a big reservation book outside
a dining room.

"Your name, sir?"

"Woodrow Cain."

The man frowned and ran his finger down the page.

"Yes," he said, as if he could hardly believe it. "You're expected. Mr. Euston is waiting."

His father-in-law. Cain should've guessed.

A maître d' materialized and escorted Cain across the carpet to a corner table where Harris Euston sat, reading *The Wall Street Journal*. It was a venerable old room with dark paneling and a molded plaster ceiling. Gilt-framed portraits of dour old men stared from every wall. There were starched tablecloths, and each place had a full setting of silver, most of which would never be needed. A bit stuffy, in other words, which is probably why Euston looked right at home as he folded his paper and rose in greeting.

Up to now, Cain had only met his father-in-law while in the company of his wife, and even those occasions had been few and far between. A widower, Euston had always struck him as a bit of a prig, smoking thin cigars and wearing clothes from another era. Starched shirts with detachable collars. Black suits with an outdated cut. He sometimes wore a cravat instead of a tie. He was trim, except for the paunch of his belly, which poked out as if it were a strap-on fashion accessory, a symbol of prosperity ordered from some high-end haberdasher.

Cain's knowledge of Euston's habits as a New Yorker were sketchy at best. The man had a roomy apartment further up Park, where he lived alone. His wife had been dead for fifteen years, yet he still regularly attended the church she had chosen for them, St. Thomas Episcopal, on Fifth Avenue in Midtown, where he always sat in the same pew up front on the right. Over the years he'd contributed enough to merit a brass plate under a stained glass window. Cain had never warmed to his company, and, odder still, he had always sensed that Clovis hadn't, either. Yet, she had often turned quickly to her father whenever they were in need, and without fail Euston had responded promptly, and usually generously.

Euston had never showed much regard for Cain's profession. In his circles, being a cop was something that Irishmen and Italians did, and Cain's status as a university man only seemed to make his employment more ludicrous. He was also a bit of a snob about the South. On his one visit to Horton—arriving in a glossy green Packard with white sidewalls—Euston had always frowned and kept his mouth shut whenever they'd encountered some quaint regional custom or local personality.

He was a partner at Willett & Reed, whose clients were mostly bankers, investment houses, and large corporations. Cain had the impression it was the kind of outfit capable of accomplishing more with a few well-placed phone calls than most law firms could manage with a pile of legal motions. The firm's name stood for money and influence with a patrician gloss, but it now occurred to Cain that in at least one way it bore a striking resemblance to the one-man information shop of Max Danziger: It valued discretion above all, especially for clients who were quietly up to no good.

Euston checked a pocket watch and shook his hand in greeting, probably more out of deference to club decorum than to Cain.

"Woodrow. Right on time. Cocktail?" A waiter stood at the ready.

"I'm working."

"Bring him a double Scotch. No, make it a bourbon. Neat. And bring me another of these." He held up a beaded crystal glass, nothing left but ice. The waiter glided away. They sat.

"I've been wondering what a man has to do to get his phone calls returned by his cop son-in-law."

"And you settled on kidnapping. I take it you're a friend of that blunt instrument, Maloney. Mulhearn, too."

"I'm a friend of a lot of people in the third district, and the fourteenth precinct in particular. Friendships that don't always come cheaply, I have to say." He smirked. "How do you think you got this job, from your test scores?"

Cain bit his tongue. He wished Valentine could be here. It would be enjoyable watching the two self-important blowhards clash in such polite surroundings, their egos as overinflated as those big balloons in the Macy's parade—Felix the Cat versus Mickey Mouse, bumping their way through the crystal and china while Cain sipped his bourbon. It was almost a relief to have the hostility out in the open. He wondered how long Euston had been holding it back. Probably since his daughter's wedding day. And it wasn't as if the man's daughter had been blameless in what had happened in Horton last fall. Far from it. A few months ago Euston had even appeared to be shamed by events, but obviously not anymore.

His drink arrived along with the menus. Cain thought about pushing it aside, then reconsidered and downed half the bourbon in one go, shuddering at the amber pleasure of it. He needed it. His nerves were still shaky from the car ride.

"I thought I might at least warrant a courtesy visit, but as I suspected you're not well schooled in courtesy."

"You know how it is with Southern provincials. It's all we can do to keep our shoes tied and our napkins in our laps. What's the agenda here, sir? Other than showing me which cops are in your pocket."

"Mostly I wanted an update on your situation. I do feel *some* sense of responsibility now that you're living in my town. Although I'll confess that my primary concern is for Olivia's welfare. She'll be arriving fairly soon, and I wanted to inquire as to what your plans are for extra help once she's present. Who will take care of her while you're at work?"

"I'll manage something."

Euston shook his head.

"Just the sort of half-baked answer I expected, which is why I've taken the liberty of arranging for a housekeeper. Someone with hours as flexible as yours, and she'll be ready to go at a moment's notice. An Irishwoman. They're especially good at that sort of thing. You certainly wouldn't want a Negro, not in Chelsea. I'll pay her wages, of course, so don't bother to protest. You might even say thank you if the thought ever crosses your mind."

"I'm still trying to figure out how to say thanks for that deluxe ride that brought me here. Top of the line, sir."

"Her name's Eileen. A bit partial to popery, but I suppose that comes with her kind. She doesn't drink, so you needn't worry about locking away the whiskey. She's a firm hand, and I think Olivia will need that. She'll be, what, thirteen in a few months?"

Cain nodded, sobered by the thought.

"I've seen perfectly well-behaved children arrive here and run completely wild."

*Like your daughter?* Cain thought it, but didn't say it. Besides, he shared Euston's concerns, and knew he couldn't afford anything comparable.

"What do you hear from her?" Euston asked.

"She's doing about as well as expected. I'll let you know if she ever asks about you."

"I do worry a bit about that location where I've put you, down there in the garment district. For her sake."

"The building's fine."

"Not the building. The neighbors." He glanced around and lowered his voice. "A trifle too Hebrew for my granddaughter, I should think."

"Or maybe just for you."

"Me?" He laughed dismissively. "I wouldn't last very long in my profession, or even in this club, if that was my attitude. Although there *are* parts of town where it's beyond belief. Go down to Hester Street one morning and we'll see how long it takes before your broad-minded superiority begins to crumble. The men with their side curls, the women covered head to toe, every sign a nightmare of Semitic squiggles. You do know, don't you, that pretty much every Leninist and Trotskyite in this town is a Jew? Just read the names on the hand-bills. Goldman, Steinberg, Cohen."

"Greenberg."

"Of course."

"I meant Hank. Fifty-eight homers for the Tigers last year."

"No one's saying they're *all* up to no good. It's a matter of propor-tion. In New York they've engineered a striking degree of control over the newspapers, the investment houses, you name it. Although soon that will matter less. The city's boom has peaked. There was a piece on it in *The New Republic*. Not my kind of magazine, but this time they got it right. New York's heyday is over. Were you aware that one fifth of this country's unemployed live right here in the city?"

"I wasn't. I doubt our reading habits have a lot in common."

"We'll get a boost from the shipyards, of course. In wartime every-one booms, it's the only thing that makes them worth fighting. But all the new production is going to places like Bridgeport, Hartford,

Detroit. Now there's your city of the future, Woodrow. Detroit." He leaned closer and again lowered his voice. "So, while the reign of the Jews may continue here, the realm itself will inevitably fade in power and influence. And no one will ever again buy stocks the way they used to, not after what happened in '29."

"Then maybe you should move to Detroit."

"Maybe I will. You'd like that, wouldn't you?"

The waiter returned. Euston ordered for them. Sweetbreads, roast duck, spring vegetables and red potatoes, thick slices from a juicy rib roast. All arrived promptly, and with an impressive clatter of china and silver plate. It was easily the best meal Cain had eaten since he'd come to New York, and it cooled the simmer of his anger. He decided to be civil for a while, if only for Olivia's sake. He imagined Clovis at the seat to his right, squeezing his hand beneath the table to keep him from picking a fight.

"How is the war affecting the legal business?" he asked. "Hard to imagine it would be much of a help."

"You'd be surprised. Chase Bank is worried about the legal exposure of its interests abroad, so there's that." Chase Bank. Quite a client. Cain was impressed, but that was probably why Euston had brought it up. "Then there's General Motors, a few of the other industrials. You can't imagine the litigation they're facing."

"Even now?"

"Especially now, given who their enemies are. Do you think the unions have called a truce just because everybody's supposed to be pulling together? No more than the criminal element has, I'm guessing. Speaking of which, I seem to have read in the papers that you've already gotten involved in a murder investigation."

"I've never thought of you as a *Daily News* man."

"When your son-in-law turns up in the coverage, word tends to get around."

"I didn't plan on that, believe me."

"Interesting case, though."

"Not really."

"Sounds like you haven't made any headway."

"I haven't closed it, if that's what you're asking."

"But definitely some sort of German connection, I gather."

"I probably shouldn't discuss it, in case it ever goes to trial. As a lawyer I'm sure you understand."

"Certainly. Of course, there's also the concept—in both our professions—that by sharing information you can sometimes acquire some. Quid pro quo. My firm and, more to the point, our clients have contacts all over this city. They often know things that a brand-new detective, or even his more experienced colleagues, might not."

"Even in a low-rent place like Yorkville?"

"There's more prosperity up there than you'd think. Plenty of Americans with Germanic backgrounds have done quite well for themselves, and those are the very people who tend to keep their ears to the ground."

"Seemed like a bit of a Nazi enclave, far as I could tell."

"See? Only an unsophisticated newcomer would paint it with such a broad brush."

"Like with life down on Hester Street?"

"I've heard you finally came up with a name for the victim. Hansch, is it?"

"Mulhearn tell you that?"

"As I said, lots of friends in the one-four."

"Well compensated, you said that, too. Which of your clients pays their tab? Chase? GM?"

"Same fellow who's paying yours. Think of me as a patron, Woodrow. Like one of those philanthropists who gets the best seats at the Philharmonic."

"I doubt I'll forget your role in my life anytime soon. But as a long as you're offering contacts, maybe I'll bounce a name off you. Lutz Lorenz, sort of a jack-of-all-trades. Runs a little labor agency up that way. Ring any bells?"

Euston frowned, then shook his head. "Can't say that it does. How's he mixed up in all this?"

"Sorry. Like you said, quid pro quo. You want more, you'll have to help me first. Don't say I never asked."

The waiter materialized to Euston's left.

"A telephone call for you, sir. He insists that it's urgent. Shall I bring the phone to table?"

"I'll take it in the reading room." Euston frowned, put down his napkin, and rose from the table. Then, turning to Cain: "This should only be a minute."

Cain sat in silence while watching Euston cross the room. One of his bigshot clients, perhaps. Or Mulhearn, checking to see if Maloney had delivered the parcel as promised.

The irony of this meeting was that, under other circumstances, Cain might easily have been dining with Euston as a colleague of sorts. After two years on the job in Horton, when Olivia was a toddler and he and Clovis were still scraping together a down payment on a small house, Euston had cruised into town on his one visit south to offer him a job at Willett & Reed. Not a lawyer's position, of course, although Euston made vague intimations that the firm would help pay Cain's way through law school on the side.

He had refused the offer outright during a long and testy evening. It was the one time Clovis took her father's side in an argument, but Cain refused to budge. Too prideful, or maybe he just hadn't liked the idea of making New York his home. To Clovis's credit, she had never again raised the subject.

Cain had never second-guessed the decision, but looking around him now he wondered. He might yet be married, not to mention more handsomely employed, their daughter in a stable home, safe from all that had happened. Or maybe things still would have ended in disaster, but in a different way—Clovis's passions burning even more danger-ously brighter in this city of motion, Cain driven to drink or depres-sion by homesickness and dissatisfaction. Although one thing was inescapable: Rob Vance would be alive. Cain had to wash down that thought with another swallow of bourbon.

Whatever the case, here he was in Manhattan all the same, with Euston still trying to run his life. He felt the roast going cold in his belly, and then saw Euston returning to the table, looking a bit disconcerted.

"Bad news?"

"Nothing that you need to know."

"Words to live by."

Euston ignored the barb and began picking at the margins of his lunch.

"So how are things going for you otherwise, Woodrow? Personally, I mean. Are all of your needs being addressed?"

His needs? The question made him flash unbidden on an image of Clovis, a moment from their honeymoon in Florida. She stood naked in bands of slatted sunlight through a jalousie window, both of them sunburned. They touched each other, lightly at first, and then with passion, no longer caring if it stung as they climbed into bed.

Euston was staring at him, as if reading his mind. Cain impaled a green bean on his fork and replied: "Sure. Mostly. I did have a question for you. Partly because I'm guessing Olivia will want to know."

"Then by all means."

"Where's Clovis?"

Euston frowned. He dabbed his mouth with a napkin as if someone had struck him across the jaw. "That's not your concern."

"As I said, Olivia will want to know. Believe me, she'll ask."

Euston looked him in the eye. "She's someplace where she's being well cared for."

"A place for drying out?"

"You never did understand her properly, you know, or maybe she wouldn't have developed such a thirst."

"Her thirst predated me, as you might recall. You might also remember that toward the end of things she developed a certain hunger."

"Which you could have deterred by paying her the proper sort of attention, instead of leaving it to others. But I'm not here to judge you, or to make her out to be a saint. It's why I've agreed to help provide for your needs. Olivia's, too, of course. That's my main concern. It's Clovis's concern as well."

"She knows I'm here?"

"I keep her apprised of *some* things about you. Not all of them, of course. Not until she's ready for it."

"And when will that be?"

"That will be my decision. And hers."

"I'm a little surprised she cares at all."

"Proving once again how poorly you know my daughter." He leaned forward, eyes narrowing and his skin turning red. All that other business—the big shot clients, his ready supply of cops—was behind him for the moment. Now it was deeply personal, and his voice took on an edge. "Tell me, Woodrow. Once you put my daughter down there in that quiet old backwater, this beautiful cosmopolitan girl who used to be so vibrant and alive, did you really believe that your bashful Southern charm alone would be enough to keep her satisfied and entertained? And on a cop's salary, no less?"

Cain opened his mouth, but no words emerged, and Euston jumped right back into the breach.

"Yes, I thought so. And now that everything's gone, here you are, still eating on her daddy's tab."

Neither of them had much to say after that. When the waiter asked about dessert or coffee, Cain declined and Euston signed for the bill. Paid by Willett & Reed, or even Chase National Bank, for all he knew.

Cain dropped his napkin on the table and stood to leave. Euston kept his seat. His face was no longer red, and his voice was calm.

"Remember, Woodrow. Keep me abreast of things. In my business it's always useful to have information from a wide range of sources. And while I do have friends in the station house, family is always a more reliable conduit."

"I don't recall making any promises to that effect."

"Who said anything about promises? It's an implicit part of our arrangement, presuming you wish to stay housed and employed. The fine print, if you will, and you know how lawyers are about fine print."

"Then I guess you should have gotten it in writing."

Euston smiled. "If I didn't know better, Woodrow, I'd say you didn't learn a thing from today's chauffeured ride. I can always arrange for other destinations, you know. Bear that in mind next time you're debating whether to return one of my phone calls."

Cain felt the blood rise in his cheeks. He squeezed the back of the chair, then turned to leave before he said something foolish.

He walked the entire way despite the throbbing in his leg, and he needed all eleven blocks to cool down. Not that it did him much good once he reached his desk, where he saw that Maloney had placed his gun and holster right on top of his paperwork, perched where everyone could see them, for maximum embarrassment. There was a note on top, scribbled on a page from a memo book. Maloney had signed it with a flourish, so that everyone who looked would know who was pulling Cain's chain.

"Better brush up on your gun security, Citizen Cain. Never know when you'll need one of these."

He angrily crumpled the note and was about to toss it in the trash when his more practical side prevailed. He smoothed it out, put it in the top drawer of his desk, and locked it away. Maloney, Steele, and Mabry. Names worth remembering. He vowed to make it into the 95 Room as soon as possible, even if Mulhearn again caught him in the act.

No one in the squad room said a word as he strapped his Colt back on. He looked from desk to desk, wondering how many more of them were on his father-in-law's payroll.

# 11

........................

CAIN CAME UP FROM the subway onto Delancey, entering Danziger's world for the first time. He couldn't help but smile. It was the very sort of place Euston had been railing about the day before in the sterile sanctity of the Union League Club. The "Semitic squiggles" of Hebrew were on plenty of signs, and many women were indeed covered head to toe. But here, too, the wider world had infiltrated deeply. There was even another Thom McAn.

The sidewalks were bustling on a sunny market day as vendors called out their wares and prices. The air smelled of freshly butchered meat and of washed fruit and vegetables. Plucked chickens hung by their necks all in a row in a shop window. Cain supposed he might just as easily be in some urban corner of Europe as Manhattan, and he found himself liking it, buoyed by the vibrancy, the intensity, the enveloping noise.

A newsboy in shorts and a flat hat bumped past on his right, carrying a sack of fresh copies of the afternoon edition, which smelled of ink. The boy held aloft a copy and began shouting the day's headlines even as the heavy bag banged against his knobby knees. A fishmonger, white apron smeared with blood, poured a bucket of ice onto a gleaming row of the day's catch.

"Haddock fresh from the docks, sir. You won't find a better price."

Cain nodded in passing but didn't dare open his mouth, knowing his accent would immediately mark him as an outsider. He was having too much fun pretending he belonged, a feeling that carried him all the way to the narrow tenement house at 174 Rivington Street, where there were two front doors. The one on the right opened onto a narrow hallway with a stairwell. The door on the left was painted black, with one of Danziger's business cards tacked above a mail slot. Cain knocked loudly until Danziger opened. The man's look of surprise quickly gave way to an irritated frown.

"You should have given me warning."

"Warning? I'm a policeman."

"I am with a client."

Another voice, a man's, shouted from somewhere behind him:

"A client? Is that how you refer to me behind my back, Sascha? A *client*?"

"Sascha?" Cain asked.

"A term of endearment. He is an old friend."

The man shouted again: "Ha! Friend! Now that's more like it!"

"We are discussing deeply private matters for his correspondence. So if you could please return later. Half an hour, perhaps."

"Nonsense!" the man shouted. "I have no secrets from anyone. You know this, Sascha. Besides, I doubt that any man sounding as he does will understand a word of Russian. Invite him in at once!"

Danziger sighed and stepped back from the doorway. "Wait here at the front while I conclude with his letter. I will be with you in a moment."

"Greetings, sir!" An older man stood from a chair in the back of the room and nodded toward Cain, smiling broadly. He wore a black waistcoat and pants, and a starched white shirt. His silver hair was long and uncombed. He looked at least sixty, possibly older, but the shimmer of his watery brown eyes was visible even through the dusky gloom of the long, ill-lighted room.

Cain looked around him with a growing sense of wonder. Danziger's office appeared to take up the entire floor. There was no bed or lavatory, so presumably he slept and bathed elsewhere. Up front where Cain stood the room was furnished as a sort of narrow parlor, with a ratty brown love seat and an emerald wing chair with stuffing poking from its cushions. The walls were covered floor to ceiling with bookshelves. The titles were in many languages, and included thick volumes that appeared to be dictionaries and reference works. It smelled like a library, a mustier and more raffish version of the study they'd visited the other night in Yorkville.

In the rear, where the old man stood next to a ladder-back chair, the space was anchored by a massive rolltop desk of varnished walnut, cluttered with books and papers. But the real wonder was on the wall above it—row upon row of cubbyhole mail slots—at least a hundred, maybe even two hundred, and every last slot had something in it, including some that bulged with a dozen or more envelopes. Cain marveled at the magnitude. All those lives, past and present, and this was their nerve center, possibly their only connection to the wider world beyond these crowded blocks.

Beside the rolltop desk was a broad writing table with a row of four aging typewriters, side by side, presumably one for each of the different alphabets Danziger employed—Cyrillic for Russian, Hebrew for Yiddish, a German model to handle the umlauts of that language, and then the last one for English. The writing desk sat beneath a high frosted window that loomed above the cubbyholes. It was louvered open at the top to let in fresh air, along with a slanting shaft of sunlight which illuminated tumbling motes of dust.

Over to the right was a large woodstove. The floor, which creaked and moaned with every step, was covered by an overlapping series of Oriental runners and rugs of varying shapes, designs, colors, and thicknesses. This patchwork nature gave the room a palpable sense of topography, as if you might have to negotiate your way to the rear via a series of footpaths and valleys. All in all, the room was a bit of a firetrap, a bit of a museum, a bit of a riddle. But above all it felt like an embodiment of Danziger, a man with so many of his own nooks and crannies.

Danziger briskly made his way across the undulating floor to the back, where he settled into the office chair with a deep groan of its universal joint. The old man sat down as well, in the chair facing Danziger.

"Now," Danziger said, continuing as if Cain weren't there. "Where were we?"

"Come now," the man said. "First you must introduce me to your guest."

Danziger stood slowly, looking somewhat put out. The other man stood again, so Cain followed suit, feeling a bit mannered, as if they were gathered in a sitting room in Bohemia.

"Mr. Cain, this is Fyodor Alexandroff, an old and trusted friend who has been using my services for years. Fedya, this is Woodrow Cain, a detective sergeant in good standing with the New York Police Department. We are assisting one another on a private matter of some import."

"Are you now? Well, then, greetings to you, sir."

"Pleasure to meet you, sir," Cain said.

"My niece may be arriving shortly to join you. She always enters without knocking, and is often nosy to the point of rudeness. Please feel at complete liberty to ignore her."

"I shall."

Shall? Cain never talked like this. He felt as if he'd walked into a different century, and was adapting on the fly. He pictured Alexandroff's niece as a weathered old crone, smelling of cabbage and dressed in a black wool skirt that would brush against the floor with every step.

"He is exaggerating, of course," Danziger said. "She is quite harmless. A do-gooder of the first order. So, once again, Fedya. Where were we?"

The two men sat back down. Cain did as well.

Alexandroff answered in Russian, and the two men were soon deep in conversation, leaning closer until their foreheads were only inches apart, while Danziger took notes in a thick ledger, nodding occasionally. They continued in this way for another ten minutes while Cain watched, fascinated by their body language. At times they seemed to slip into a trance as they stared into each other's eyes, exchanging words in Russian.

The door opened. The two men looked up, the spell broken. Cain turned and squinted into the sudden glare. He beheld the silhouette of a young woman in a thin coat. Her face slowly came into focus as his eyes adjusted to the light.

He swallowed hard, momentarily speechless. It wasn't beauty that struck him with such force. If anything she was a bit plain, and quite unadorned. It was more a case of her presence, or perhaps of her movements—a sense of sureness and energy that radiated from her like a force field, as if it were part of the nimbus of sunlight, although the effect didn't diminish in the least even after the door shut and she was enveloped by the gloom. Her eyes, that was part of it. Brown and welcoming, carrying their own light. Full of empathy, wit and—to Cain's eyes—allure.

"Who are you?" she asked, not rudely, but with little warmth.

"Woodrow Cain. I'm waiting on Danziger."

"Not as a customer, surely?"

"No. I'm ... we're ..." He could hardly get the words out. He felt like an imbecile, and a thirteen-year-old imbecile at that. "We're working together."

Fyodor Alexandroff shouted to her from across the room.

"He is a police detective, Beryl dear, so you must be on your best behavior!"

Alexandroff said it as a joke, but Beryl—at least he knew her name now—didn't seem amused or impressed.

"So, Sascha is collaborating with the authorities now?" Then, to both of the older men. "Don't rush on my behalf. I brought a book."

She settled into the ratty wing chair, pulled a book from her shoulder bag, and immediately began to read. The signal couldn't have been clearer: Leave me in peace. Cain chose to ignore it.

"*China Sky*," he said, reading the cover. "How does it compare to *The Good Earth*?"

"Policemen are reading Pearl S. Buck now?" She spoke without looking up.

"I was an English major."

"Where?" This time she at least peeped above the pages.

"Chapel Hill."

"Ah. Where Thomas Wolfe learned to overwrite. I met him once, at a party in the Village. He was being swarmed by girls who didn't know better. He was quite vulnerable and charming, exactly the way you'd expect for a rough-hewn mountain boy. He was huge."

"Does he still live up here?"

"He's dead."

"Oh, right. I knew that. Only a few years ago, wasn't it?"

"Yes. Tuberculosis."

She looked back down at her book. Cain knew he'd blown it, but he couldn't stop now. He wondered if he could find some way to finagle an address, or a phone number. It occurred to him that it was no sure thing that her last name was Alexandroff, or even that she was single, although he had already checked her hand and seen there was no wedding ring. If he had to guess, he would've said she was twenty-nine or thirty. Nearly his age, or close enough. He groped for something to say that wouldn't sound ridiculous.

"He does interesting work."

"Wolfe?"

"Danziger."

"Oh. Yes. I suppose he does." She put her book facedown in her lap and glanced toward the two older men, who had resumed their trance and were muttering in Russian.

"My uncle has been coming here for years. He's not illiterate like most of the customers. But one of his cousins from Minsk reads only in Yiddish. My uncle lost that years ago, as an act of rebellion against his parents, I suspect. So Sascha translates for him, into Russian. Reads the incoming letters and types up the outgoing ones, from his notes of their conversations. Although that's never the reason they're talking for this long. Uncle Fedya comes as much for the fellowship and the neighborhood gossip. They go way back. And they met while speaking Russian, so that's how they often prefer to converse. The letters themselves, well, they're nothing to write home about."

"Good one."

She smiled for the first time. For a moment the room was a hundred watts brighter.

"I've watched him working with women, though. Sascha, I mean, and that's where he really earns his keep. With the men like my uncle it's usually just 'I am fine, I hope you are well,' plus one or two events of the day. Boring. Skeletal. Nothing of real substance or energy. But these women, you should see them, you should *hear* them! Old World to the core, and Sascha is their town crier, their daily newspaper. He draws it all out of them—he is quite gentle, when he wishes to be, very courtly and respectful—and once they get going, goodness, they spill everything. Truly everything, until they have drained the deepest well of their souls. I've seen some leave in tears. Catharsis, I suppose. And from what I'm told, Sascha really makes their words sing."

"But how would they know, if they're illiterate?"

"Good one," she said, smiling again. "I asked that very question. It seems that oftentimes the replies, often as not written by *other* paid letter writers, include effusive compliments for the style of his prose."

"Or maybe he just says that."

"Now you're thinking like a policeman."

This time Cain smiled.

"You and your uncle call him Sascha."

"Yes. The diminutive for Alexander." She reopened her book.

"But his name is Maximilian."

"The name on his business card, you mean."

"Yes. Well, no. That just says Danziger."

"Obviously you don't know him very well."

"Not for very long, anyway."

"I see."

She went back to her reading, but now Cain was too curious—about Danziger, and about her—to stop. And he still didn't have an address, or even her last name.

"He told me the other day that he tries to forget everything people tell him, all of their secrets."

She looked back up, a little wearily this time. "You sound skeptical."

"Well, for a man whose business is supposedly information, it didn't sound very likely."

"I think it's quite plausible, especially considering what his customers are often hearing from their friends and family lately, from all over Europe. Who'd want those dark stories shunting around in your head all night, like boxcars in a switching yard? I know they'd keep me awake. Besides, to hear my uncle Fedya tell it, Sascha has had quite a lot of practice at forgetting."

"Meaning what?"

"Ask Sascha. Or Max. Whichever name you prefer."

She went back to her book. This time Cain did not interrupt. He was too busy thinking about all she'd said. A few minutes later, Danziger and Alexandroff concluded their business. Alexandroff shook Cain's hand in parting. Cain was hoping to speak more to Beryl, but she ducked out the door to wait on the stoop for her uncle. Then the door shut behind Fedya, and she was gone. Cain sighed and decided he might as well get down to business. But that aspect of his visit was also destined to end poorly.

"You should have let me know you were coming," Danziger said, a little irritably. "When you told me yesterday of your nuisance assignment, I went ahead and booked myself fully for the rest of this week, and these are not appointments that can be cancelled upon a whim."

"Sorry."

"Perhaps we can meet on Monday."

"Okay."

"At your office?"

Cain was about to assent, until it occurred to him that if he returned here he might at least have a remote chance of bumping into Beryl.

"I'll come here instead," he said. "Ten a.m.?"

Danziger frowned, then nodded. "As you wish. Oh, and before I forget. I made a few inquiries in the matter of Mr. Albert Kannerman."

"Who?"

"Your con man at large. Your punishment detail."

"Who told you his name?"

"Here. Try this."

He handed Cain a folded scrap of paper which contained an address on Grand Street. Nothing more.

"My understanding is that your best chance of finding him at home is between the hours of two and three a.m. I am also told he is a heavy sleeper."

Cain was about to ask how Danziger had learned this when the door opened. For a moment his spirits leaped, but it was an older woman with a baby in her arms and two toddlers in tow, their faces smeared with bread crumbs.

"Ah, Mrs. Stern," Danziger said, his voice rising an octave. "What a pleasure to see you. My visitor here was just departing. Come right in and I will retrieve your latest correspondence. One from each of your sisters!"

Cain slipped out the door as they entered. He headed back toward the maelstrom of Delancey Street, where he forded the crowds until reaching the stairway down to the subway. When he reached the platform he dug into his pocket for the address Danziger had given him for Kannerman. He chuckled to himself, wondering once again at the old man's resources. Maybe the info was worthless, although he doubted it. Another act of sorcery by Max Danziger. Or was it Sascha instead?

Information, indeed.

The Kannerman address wasn't far from here. Perhaps he should try it now, or at least scout out the best ways of entry and exit. He was on the verge of heading back up the stairs when he spotted Beryl, leaning against a support pylon maybe thirty yards down the platform, again reading her book.

Cain carefully worked his way toward her, weaving through the crowd while hoping she didn't look up and spot him. He stopped about ten yards short, wondering awkwardly what he could say to break the ice, when the train pulled in. He watched her board before he entered the same car at the opposite end. Peering between the heads and bodies he saw her take a seat just beneath an ad for Old Gold cigarettes, printed with the words of the jingle he'd heard that morning on his neighbor's radio—*Not a cough in a carload!*—which somehow made the moment feel fated. Then he picked his way forward through the standers and strap-hangers until he stood just in front of her bench.

She looked up, noticing him right away. He feigned surprise.

"Oh, hi! What an unexpected pleasure."

She looked annoyed, as if she'd instantly figured out his entire maneuver. Not a frown, but something close. "Hello," she said curtly.

She looked back down at her book. Cain was beginning to feel quite resentful of Pearl S. Buck.

The train lurched into motion, lights flickering. At the first stop it took some effort to hold his position as more people boarded. He wondered if he should try to speak to her. Twice she glanced up at him. The first time he looked away, embarrassed. The second time she frowned and spoke up.

*"Do you mind?"*

She said it sharply enough that half the car must have heard. Heat rose in his cheeks, and when Cain glanced left an older woman was scowling at him. Public enemy number one, at least on this car. Suitably shamed, he worked his way back toward the other end of the car, where he spent the next few minutes staring at an advertising placard for the March of Dimes China Relief Fund, which only reminded him of Pearl S. Buck.

So, then. Was this what the city inevitably did to the lonely? Turned them into furtive stalkers in futile pursuit of companionship? In the course of a day he saw so many passing faces that he supposed he was bound to run across one now and then that would light something inside of him, a face that would inexplicably hit him just the right way—or just the *wrong* way, considering how idiotic he now felt. He was behaving like a lecherous old man on a park bench with a runny nose and a bottle of hooch in a paper bag.

Between the next two stops the lights again went out for several seconds at a time. When they came back on Cain saw that an older Japanese man—mid-fifties, dressed head to toe in British tweeds—had taken a seat on the opposite side. The seats to either side of him were empty, even though at least a dozen people were standing. People near him were frowning with even more hostility than they'd exhibited toward Cain. Germans and Italians could blend in, Cain supposed, but not Japs, and the assumption of course was that none could be trusted, not since Pearl Harbor. He had been mildly surprised to see this theme turn up even in a recent *Times* review of Gilbert and Sullivan's *Mikado*, in which the critic praised the libretto for "depicting the Japanese in the light that history now records—sly, witty and deceitful, unconsciously corrupt, and treacherous." But did that also go for this poor fellow? He looked like nothing more than a weary businessman, briefcase in his lap.

The man stood to get off at the next station, which was also Cain's stop. Cain paused to let him exit first, only to have a glowering young tough shoulder past him along with a friend and then several other people.

The moment Cain stepped onto the platform he knew something

was wrong. From just ahead he heard the sound of grunting, a loud gasp, a tumble of bodies. When the crowd cleared Cain saw the Japanese man on his knees at the edge of the platform next to his open briefcase, which was spilling papers into the breeze created by the departing train. Passersby moved briskly on their way, ignoring him, although one or two bumped his shoulder as if determined to add to his misery. One such bump caused him to teeter alarmingly at the edge of the platform before he steadied himself.

"Fucking spy," someone muttered.

"Why isn't he locked up?" said another.

Cain stepped forward and began picking up loose papers. Then he knelt by the man, who, recoiling instinctively, held up a hand to protect himself.

"It's okay," Cain said. "I'm here to help. Speak English?"

"Of course!" the man hissed, no trace of an accent. "I'm an American. I've lived in this country for thirty-nine years!"

"Hey, pal!" It was the young thug from the subway car, with his buddy. "Let the rest of us take care of this."

Cain turned to see both boys grinning, hands in pockets. The first one cocked a leg, as if preparing to kick a football. Cain sprang from his crouch, grabbed the foot as it came forward, and then twisted the leg to tumble the boy onto his back.

"Whose side are you on, asshole!" the second one shouted, already in motion.

Cain released the boy's foot and pulled out his shield, flashing it in their faces.

"I'm a cop," he said. "Get a move on." Then, to the gathering crowd. "Everybody move it. This man's an American citizen on his way to work. Nothing more to see here."

The last part was a New York cop's line if Cain had ever heard one. All that was missing was the local accent. As it was, the two young thugs seemed as shocked by Cain's drawl as by his actions. But the badge did the trick, and they eased slowly toward the exit.

When Cain turned back around a young woman was helping the Japanese man to his feet. It was Beryl. This time she didn't frown or look away.

"Thanks for doing something," she said. "I've seen far too much of this kind of thing. No one ever raises a finger to stop it."

The man clasped the briefcase to his chest. It was scuffed but intact, and so was he.

"Thank you," he said to Cain.

"Don't mention it. Take care of yourself."

Bystanders, already back on the move toward their destinations, frowned in disapproval, but none seemed perturbed enough to intervene. The man brushed himself off and was on his way, which left Cain and Beryl standing side by side. He glanced at her, and caught her glancing back. He still didn't even know her last name.

"Sorry about being, well, so rude," he said. "It's just that . . ." He ran out of words. He was going to blow it again.

"Well." She brushed a lock of hair from her face. "I should get to work."

"Me, too."

She turned and strolled away, the opportunity gone. He was an idiot, a fool.

Then she abruptly wheeled around, and almost before he knew what was happening she blurted out the most vital information he'd heard in days.

"Beryl Blum," she said. "No *e* on the end. Cadman six, two-four-three-seven. The phone's shared by the whole building, so ask for Beryl in 2C."

Before he could answer she turned toward the stairs and was swallowed by the crowd.

For several blocks Cain repeated the phone number over and over to himself so he wouldn't forget. Finally he stopped just outside the station house and took out his notebook to scribble it onto a blank page, along with her name.

Seeing it in black and white reassured him. Yes, he would see her again, and possibly soon.

He breezed into the building and climbed the stairs two at a time.

# 12

.......................

DANZIGER

EARLY ON THE THIRD SATURDAY of every month, unbeknownst
to neighbors and friends, I treat myself to a personal metamorphosis,
briefly shedding the drab trappings of my current existence in order
to spread the bright butterfly wings of my distant past. It is a sort of
therapy, I suppose, a means of reminding myself of a time when life
was not quite so fraught with need.

I begin this transformation shortly after rising, by packing a small
leather suitcase. Then, at around eight a.m., bag in hand, I set out
from my doorstep dressed in my usual shabby clothes. I nod politely to
passersby. Many of them are already walking to synagogue, to devote
themselves to higher pursuits on this morning of the Sabbath, and I
am happy to let them believe that I am doing the same.

Instead, I proceed west on Delancey until I reach the Bowery, with
its rogues' gallery of gin mills and flophouses, deathly quiet at this
early hour. I then head uptown, walking all the way to Astor Place. I
prefer to be well north of my usual environs before boarding a subway,
lest some believer catch me in the act.

Deceiving neighbors and clients is not my only motive. My precautions also protect them from knowledge which might only bring them
harm. Their lives have become important to me, and to visit calam-

ity upon their houses through some careless disclosure or unwanted entanglement from my own fading history would be unforgivable.

Upon arrival at Grand Central Terminal, I visit two fine establishments owned by the recently retired James P. Carey, a master entrepreneur of an earlier era. The first of these, located in the men's waiting room, is a once grand barber shop with an adjoining public bath. There, for the rather steep sum of fifty cents, I luxuriate in the heat and fog of a Russian steam bath, letting the cares and labors of the previous month rise like a vapor from my sweating pores.

Suitably refreshed, I unpack my suitcase and change into the laundered clothes folded neatly within—charcoal gray suit, with wide lapels and pleated pants, smelling faintly of mothballs; a starched white shirt; striped silk tie; black wool socks; and a polished pair of lace-up wingtips in black and white Italian leather, even though in recent years they have begun to pinch my toes.

I adjourn to the spacious barber shop with its sixteen chairs, tile walls, and marble basins, where my regular barber, Sandro, trims my graying locks with scissors, and then shaves a week's worth of stubble with a straight razor. He finishes by applying a layer of steaming towels. I remain silent throughout, content to eavesdrop on the political gossip of neighboring patrons. Before continuing on my way, I visit Mr. Carey's baggage check service, where I drop off the suitcase with my old clothes packed inside.

From there I catch an uptown subway, emerging into the part of Midtown which always reminds me of the music of Gershwin— bouncy, optimistic, and brashly American, with a human pulse beating deep within its many layers of noise. After the crowded lanes around Rivington Street these boulevards feel as spacious as the canyons of the American West, and I exult in the vista of skyscrapers with their clean and rigid lines stretching all the way to an open sky, with nary a clothesline in sight. If any of my current contemporaries were to pass me on the sidewalk during this final leg, I doubt they would recognize me. Even my posture is different. Shoulders back, chest forward, a longer and more confident stride.

My footsteps carry me deeper into Midtown, to the Longchamps restaurant on 57th, between Fifth and Sixth Avenues, where I take a seat, order breakfast, and, with a flourish worthy of a banker, shake open my broadsheet newspaper.

I confess that Longchamps is a fallback destination. My first choice would be Lindy's, on Seventh, where my old employer used to hold court almost every night at his regular table, with his usual entourage. But even after all these years, an appearance there would feel too risky, too foolish, for someone who has become as careful as I. And it is not as if I set out on this monthly excursion in order to re-create history. I am engaging in harmless nostalgia, if only to remind myself of a time in which I believed in a future without war and without want, a more enlightened age in which the concerns of the Old World would no longer matter in this brash new country of ours. Such is the foolish optimism of youth and easy power—a foolishness that seems especially acute when I also recall the manner of people I worked and played with at the time.

So, I settle instead for my secondary location, the 57th Street Longchamps, with its art deco air of elegance, from its murals to its menus. It, too, was once popular with my old crowd, particularly with one fair friend who has long since passed from my life, her face a mere memory. From time to time the place still attracts a few holdovers from those days, so I suppose that even my fallback choice comes with an element of calculated risk. That may even be part of its charm.

The current waitresses, however, know me only as a quiet, uncelebrated man who wishes to be left in peace as he reads his paper and enjoys his poached eggs on toast, with plenty of refills of coffee.

Usually I take a table in the back. Today it was occupied. Business has been picking up. During the first months of the war the place was practically empty. Now people are spending money again—those who have it, anyway. Or maybe Longchamps is succeeding with its new ad campaign, which I recently spotted in the *Times,* a crass appeal to patriotism that proclaims sit-down dining to be a key element of overseas military success: "Don't be a 'sandwich grabber.' Make every meal a VICTORY meal at Longchamps." Ludicrous puffery, of course, but what could possibly be more American?

I was just tucking into my eggs when three customers walked in whose presence made me pause with the fork halfway to my mouth.

One I recognized from the newspapers as a prosecutor from the district attorney's office. His face jarred loose a recollection from the recent past, but I was unable to identify its nature before the second gentleman commanded all of my attention. I had last seen him when I was much younger, and the sight of his face prompted me to drop my fork to the plate and duck behind the pages of my newspaper. One reason is that he is the sort of fellow who never forgets a face, no matter how much that face may have been altered by the passage of time. The other is that he is one of those people "who you see, but you do not watch," as a wise man once said of my former employer. I knew him best by an old nickname, the Little Man, and the sight of him immediately reminded me of why I have always taken such scrupulous precautions in these monthly transits between one era and another.

For a few perilous moments I dared not even move the protective curtain of my newspaper. Only when I finally mustered the nerve to take another glance did I clearly see the third member of the party. His face was not familiar to me, and when the others spoke his name I did not recognize it, although I soon gathered from the way he was dressed and the words he favored that he was a lawyer for a client of dubious reputation.

They took seats at a nearby table, and although they endeavored to keep their voices low I was able to make out a fair amount of their conversation. Had I not done so, I would not even be relating this incident to you.

After a few minutes of small talk, in which they discussed General MacArthur, Herr Hitler, and the pitching staff of the New York Yankees, I began to lose interest. One of them then mentioned the name of someone in the same line of work as the Little Man, a name which would have been recognized by almost anyone in the restaurant. I snapped to attention and raised my newspaper into a position of even greater privacy.

Even then, it was not until several minutes later that I became convinced of the meeting's importance with regard to my own circumstances. Because that is when I heard them discuss, albeit briefly, the current status of Lutz Lorenz. Astonished, I strained my ears for more. When the waitress approached with the coffee pot, I waved her away with uncharacteristic rudeness. It then occurred to me why the fellow from the DA's office seemed so familiar, even beyond the fact of having seen him in the papers. The realization left me feeling quite troubled.

At that point I knew that this day would not proceed like any other third Saturday of the month. Usually I conclude these meals with a full stomach and warm memories. On this Saturday I was already thinking ahead to Monday, when I would be obligated to report my findings to Detective Cain, and in doing so would risk revealing a side of myself that I had hoped to conceal from him—from practically everyone— for the remainder of my days. Mr. Cain is a man of abiding curiosity, and I was certain he would ask many unwelcome questions. I would have to tiptoe through my answers, while avoiding any stumbles. My immediate concern, however, was to gather as much intelligence as possible.

I watched and listened closely, hoping for more. More is what I soon got, although not without some extra effort requiring the use of skills I have not employed in ages. And so, for the second time in as many weeks, I contemplated the inexplicable ways of old and sub-merged secrets, while wondering how many more of them would soon be rising from the deep.

The war was here. It had come right to my table. And on Monday I would be carrying a fresh dispatch from the front to Woodrow Cain. Further casualties now seemed inevitable.

# 13

....................

CAIN WALKED INTO THE STATION HOUSE to see a crowd forming by the notice board, where Desk Sergeant Romo had just put up a memo from the commissioner. Simmons, a colleague from the detectives' squad room, complained loudly.

"Fifty-five cents? And we gotta pay it ourselves? That's eleven months of house coffee!"

"But you get your very own halo, Simmons," Romo said. "Pretty cheap for getting to look like an angel."

The uniformed patrolmen who were reading the notice didn't seem at all upset, and Cain realized why when he saw that it was headlined "To All Detectives."

"You seen this?" Simmons asked. "Downtown says we gotta buy some blue cap with a ring around it that glows in the dark, to wear during blackouts."

"It's so we can spot you in the dark," a patrolman said. "So we'll know you're not up to no good."

Cain read the fine print. The caps would be available next Monday at the equipment room down at headquarters. Every detective had to buy one by the end of the week. Yet another waste of his time, yet another irritating expense.

"Hey, Sergeant Romo," a patrolman said, "speaking of equipment, I need the key for the stationery closet. My memo book's full."

"What, you think I'm turning you loose with the keys to every room in the house? Not on your life. Give me a minute and I'll walk you down there."

Romo reached beneath his high desk, emerged with a large jangling key ring, and stepped down from his perch. It gave Cain an idea. He'd checked the 95 Room several times the day before. On two occasions, Steele and another officer were on duty, so he kept going. The third time, the door was shut and locked up tight. Presumably, Romo had one of the keys.

Cain looked up to see the desk sergeant eyeing him closely. Expecting a rebuke, he turned quickly toward the stairs, but Romo called out before he could duck out of sight.

"Citizen Cain, just the man I wanted to see. Your crazy old coot is back!"

"Who?" Cain turned around.

"The weird old guy in the big coat. The one who smells like soup." Danziger, he meant. Had to be. "Showed up at seven again, badgering the overnight squad. Told him you wouldn't be in till nine and he just about blew a gasket. Then he left, said he'd wait for you at the Royal."

Romo twirled a forefinger by his head. *Crazy.*

"Thanks, Sarge. I'll keep him out of your hair."

The Royal was a greasy spoon just up the street, wedged between a shoe repair and Schonfeld's Men's Shop. Big signs on the front window touted triple-decker sandwiches for a dime, a nice deal as long as you could put up with the rude counter man, Freddie.

Cain walked in to see Freddie in a white smock, snapping a small towel like a bullwhip at a lumbering horsefly. The place was empty except for a table in the back, where Danziger was hiding behind a *Daily News.* Cain slapped a quarter on the chrome countertop.

"That's for a cup of coffee, and so you'll leave us alone. I'm doing business here."

"Yes, your honor." Freddie bowed theatrically, but didn't argue the point.

Cain took the steaming cup to the table, where Danziger sat before his own half-empty cup. His eyes were bloodshot, his face haggard.

"Thought we were meeting at your place," Cain said. "Ten o'clock, wasn't it?"

Danziger leaned forward and whispered urgently. "This couldn't wait. This entire matter has become more complicated than we thought."

"Complicated comes with the job."

"All right, then, if a euphemism will not suffice. *Bigger* than we thought. More *dangerous*. There are people involved who are . . ." He searched for the words. ". . . beyond our capabilities."

"Whoa now. Let me be the judge of that." Cain glanced around to make sure Freddie wasn't listening. He was at the griddle now, scraping it down with a metal spatula. "You look terrible, by the way."

"I have been working nonstop throughout the weekend, calling upon contacts I have not utilized in years. I have scarcely slept, not since what I witnessed Saturday morning, during my breakfast at Longchamps."

"Longchamps?" Cain raised an eyebrow. "That's a few cuts above the Royal. You'd have to write a lot of letters to swing that."

"Breakfast is their least expensive meal. It is a monthly ritual." He sounded defensive, like he'd just admitted to visiting a prostitute. And, frankly, he was a wreck, looking like he hadn't slept for days, although for a change his hair was neatly trimmed, and it looked like he'd even shaved.

"Sorry. Didn't mean to make a big deal of it. So you were at Longchamps. Tell me what you saw that's got you so keyed up."

"Three men came in. Men whose names you read in the papers. They took a table near my own, close enough for me to listen. It was a business meeting, and one of their topics for discussion was the whereabouts of Lutz Lorenz."

"Okay. I guess that's pretty unusual, depending on who we're talking about here. But all it really tells us is that word must be getting around about his disappearance. You said yourself he was well connected. So who were these guys?"

"No. You don't understand. They *knew* his whereabouts. One of them assured the others that Lorenz was 'in safekeeping.' Although, regrettably, he did not otherwise share details of the location."

"Whoa now. Back up. I need names. You said you knew them from the papers?"

"Murray Gurfein. He was the first one."

"From the DA's office?"

"Yes."

"He's the head of their rackets bureau."

"And on Saturday morning he was breaking bread with a hoodlum, and a hoodlum's lawyer."

"A rackets investigator can't very well do his job without rubbing elbows with a lot of dirty customers."

"This is what I told myself as well. But you will see. The second man was the hoodlum's lawyer. I believe the proper slang is 'a mouth-piece.' Moses Polakoff."

"Never heard of him. And the other guy was his client?"

"No. Mr. Polakoff's client currently resides in upstate New York."

"Albany? Buffalo?"

"Clinton State Prison, in Dannemora. He is an inmate, Charles Luciano, the man the papers refer to as 'Lucky.'"

"*He's* tied in to Lorenz?"

"Along with the third man at breakfast, Meyer Lansky."

"That sounds vaguely familiar."

"Vaguely is how he prefers it. He is very successful at avoiding pub-licity. He lives well, steers clear of the police, and tells everyone who will listen that his business interests are legitimate, that he is a gam-bling concessionaire and nothing more."

"Sounds like you know all about him."

"I told you, I have been working."

"If he keeps his face out of the papers, how'd you recognize him?"

"Do you wish to interrogate me, or shall I tell you what transpired?"

"Go ahead."

"I could not hear everything, but from the snatches of conversation that I *was* able to understand it became clear that the affairs of Mr. Luciano and of Lutz Lorenz have somehow become intertwined, and as a result the whereabouts for both of them are currently subject to change."

"Luciano's getting out?"

"No, but they discussed moving him. The Dannemora prison apparently has a nickname. It is known as 'Siberia' because it is far from everything. There is snow still on the ground. And apparently all parties to this meeting wished for him to be closer, so they agreed that efforts will be made to move him to another venue. Sing Sing, perhaps."

"Why closer?"

"For the greater convenience of regular visits."

"By who?"

"By all of them."

"For what purpose? Because of *Lorenz*?"

"I do not know, but they mentioned Lorenz's name directly afterward. It was the next item they discussed, so I could only presume the subjects were related. Mr. Lansky was the first to mention Lorenz by name. He inquired after his well-being of Mr. Gurfein, and Mr. Gurfein is the one who said, 'It has been taken care of. He is in safekeeping.'"

"Gurfein? An assistant district attorney said that?"

"His exact words. At this point, perhaps it would help if I described to you what Mr. Gurfein looks like. Stocky, to use your own word from the other night. Stocky, with hooded eyes and a pencil-thin mustache. Familiar?"

"The guy who led the raid. Has to be."

"Precisely."

"Then maybe Lorenz is some kind of witness in a big case we don't even know about. You said yourself he has shady contacts, a lot of varied interests. This might have nothing at all to do with Hansch and Schaller."

"Then please explain the timing. Hansch dies and is fished from the Hudson. Four nights later, Schaller is killed. Not long after that Lorenz is rounded up by the DA's rackets investigator, who happens to be in league with two of the city's biggest mobsters, one of whom is incarcerated."

"Well, when you put it like that . . . But who says Gurfein's 'in league' with these creeps, just because they had breakfast? He might be cutting a plea deal. A better prison for Luciano and some dropped charges for Lansky, maybe, in exchange for their help in putting away Lorenz."

"A deal with two kings to bring down a pawn?" Danziger shook his head. "Where is the utility of that? And on what charges?"

"It could be for anything, up to and possibly including the deaths of Hansch and Schaller."

"Gurfein and his boss, Frank Hogan—would they make such an arrangement without telling the police? In your experience as a policeman, is that the way business is done?"

"Well, no. Not in most places. But I don't know how things work up here, especially in the DA's office. Did any of them mention Hansch or Schaller by name? Or any of those Bundist groups like the Silver Shirts?"

Danziger shook his head.

"Lorenz was the only name I heard besides Luciano's. Soon afterward they paid their bill and adjourned to a more private location, presumably to resume their discussions in greater detail."

"And how do you know that?"

"I followed them."

"Are you crazy? You don't exactly blend in with the crowd."

"I was dressed very differently on Saturday. I do not believe that they noticed me. Besides, there are ways of doing these things to prevent your intentions from becoming readily apparent."

It was a loaded answer, and Cain already had so many questions about Danziger that he couldn't help but smile. He was excited and curious, but still a bit wary. He well knew the way a few snatches of overheard conversation could seem to add up to something far more nefarious, although he was deeply intrigued by the possible involvement of such a strange collection of well-known characters. He was also more than a little interested in this side of Danziger that the old man was finally revealing.

"So tell me what you saw, then."

"They went out onto the street. I watched through the window while I paid my bill. I expected them to go their separate ways, but when a taxi pulled up all three of them climbed in. So I hailed a taxi as well. Traffic was heavy and it was easy to keep pace. I saw them turn onto Sixth Avenue. Then they traveled downtown, sixteen blocks, and got out near Times Square, at the Hotel Astor, where they went inside."

"All three of them?"

"All three. So I stepped into the lobby, trying to act like I belonged in such a swank place as the Astor. I spotted them by the elevators, on the other side of the lobby. Fortunately it was a busy lobby. Bell-hops, people of leisure. They boarded an elevator. I waited for the doors to close, and then I walked over and pushed the button for the same elevator. I looked above the doors to watch the progress of the arrow, which stopped right away on M, for mezzanine. The elevator then returned and the doors opened. Empty, thank God, except for the operator, who asked me what floor I wanted. I acted as if I had forgotten something and begged his pardon.

"An hour later I returned, and even then I was at first too nervous to venture to the mezzanine. I took a walk around the lobby, waited another twenty minutes, and finally went upstairs. There were no guest rooms on that level. I checked every doorway. There was an empty meeting room. There was a banquet room, lushly appointed, where a bride-to-be and her bridesmaids were preparing for a lun-cheon. There was a hotel catering office. There was a meeting in progress of rather sleepy-looking old bankers from the Midwest. And there were two more offices, unmarked, with locked doors. And finally, in the middle of the corridor, there was a suite of three offices, rooms number one ninety-six, one ninety-eight, and two hundred, with a nameplate for the suite on the doorway of two hundred, stating that these were the premises for the Executives Association of Greater New York. It was the only office other than the hotel caterer's that was open for business."

"The only one?"

"Yes."

"But this was more than an hour later. Maybe they used one of the other offices and locked up before you came back."

"I thought of that as well. Still, this association is a possibility. And the name does make it sound like the sort of organization that might, well . . ."

"Be a front?"

"Yes."

"Certainly worth checking."

"Or . . ."

"Or?"

"It could be legitimate," Danziger said, "representing the very heart of wealthy, establishment New York. Which, in its own way, would be equally disturbing."

Cain let that sink in. He eyed Danziger carefully. "You seem to know a lot about mobsters and mouthpieces, about front groups and how to follow shady characters. I also find your choice of restaurants interesting."

"As I told you, it is a monthly extravagance."

"Right. But Longchamps must have, what, a dozen locations? And you just happened to pick the one where these three guys showed up to conduct a little business?"

"If you must know, I am told that it is a location where such people are commonly known to gather. Their presence, in and of itself, should not come as a surprise."

"Exactly my point. And how'd you happen to come by this knowledge?"

"In the course of serving my clients, of course, as I told you the other night."

Cain smiled and leaned across the table so that Danziger had to look him in the eye. "You know, at some point you're going to have to level with me about your past if you expect to maintain my trust and confidence."

"I could make the same demand of you."

"And if we're ever working a case in Horton, you'll have every right. But we're in your old haunts, chasing your old ghosts. Or avoiding them, I'm not sure which, and that uncertainty is a little troubling."

Danziger looked down at his coffee cup. Cain waited through several seconds of silence before Danziger spoke. "When I was young,

I moved in different circles from the ones I move in now. Somewhat recklessly so, as the young are inclined to do. A fast crowd. That is how my mother would have described it, had she lived to see it."

"Was this back when you used to ride to big-shot funerals in taxis? In '28 you wouldn't have exactly been a callow young buck."

"I have had experiences of which I am not proud, but I have most assuredly put them behind me. I serve a different calling now, as you have seen for yourself at my place of business. A different clientele, one that depends upon my good offices for vital information. And, as I said, that other life . . ."

"It's behind you now?"

"Yes." His eyes flashed. "Besides, you are hardly one to be talking about withholding information. It is said that you are already pursuing an interest in my friend Fedya's niece, Miss Beryl Blum."

Cain, caught off guard, couldn't help but laugh, if only because Beryl's name immediately put him in a cheerful frame of mind. He was impressed that Danziger already knew that he had telephoned her, having finally gotten up his nerve late Sunday afternoon. In his experience, most women would've expected him to follow convention by asking her out for the following weekend. Beryl had instead insisted that they meet on Monday, today, after work.

"Why wait all week?" she'd said, her frankness as thrilling as it was jarring. "We're both interested in each other, and we're no longer seventeen. How about tomorrow?"

Maybe that was the way of all New York women, although Cain doubted it. She seemed to broadcast an air of independence, as if daring others to object. If he were still living in Horton it might have put him off. But after everything he'd endured over the past several months it felt bracing, refreshing. So they'd arranged to meet, and this morning he'd dressed in his newest shirt and cleanest suit, and he'd walked to work in a fine mood indeed.

"You don't sound too happy about it," he told Danziger.

"Fedya has already come calling to berate me for unleashing the ravening goy on his favorite niece. And a policeman, no less. He is an inveterate snob in these matters. He would prefer a surgeon, or a university dean. Some nice boy whose mother was still close at hand."

By now Danziger was smiling. Cain figured it was partly out of mischief, partly because he'd managed to so deftly change the subject. Feeling magnanimous, Cain decided he didn't mind. "Tell your friend I'll be on my best behavior."

"Yes, but will she? That is his real worry. She is a young woman of modern ideas and immodest habits. But that is your life, your concern. Not mine, yes? So perhaps we should refrain from discussing these kinds of private affairs, especially when there is still so much work to be done."

Cain got the message well enough: Stay out of my private affairs and I'll stay out of yours. He decided to play along for now. Their working arrangement was beginning to feel dangerous enough without adding further complications.

They left the Royal just as Freddie snapped his towel at another horsefly. To Cain it sounded for all the world like a gunshot.

# 14

SHE WANTED TO KNOW everything there was to know about him, and for the first time in ages Cain was inclined to tell it. A year's worth of sexual deprivation certainly explained part of his eagerness. But something more was at work, too—a deeper need to start unpinning the tight wrapping he had pulled up around himself beginning with the sad events of the previous fall.

Spring had started the process, and now Beryl Blum was accelerating it with each and every question. He felt himself opening like the petals of a flower, breathing in light and energy in rejuvenating gulps with each revelation. And so, fairly early in their dinner conversation, Cain found himself uttering these words, even though he was elbow to elbow with other diners at Guffanti's, an Italian place on Seventh:

"I have a daughter. You should know that about me. She's coming up to join me at the end of the school year."

"So you're . . . ?"

"Still married, with a divorce in the works. It's not a question of if, but when. My wife's institutionalized somewhere, getting treatment for her drinking. For other things, too, I think, although my father-in-law won't say. Plenty of it was my fault, some of it wasn't. There's a long story behind it. I can tell it to you whenever you'd like to hear it."

She leaned forward and didn't frown, didn't look away. Already he believed she was extraordinary, and this seemed like further proof.

"I'll take you up on that offer when we're in more private surroundings. Thank you for leveling with me. I gather it's a painful story."

"Embarrassing, too, most of it." He took a sip of his drink, relieved to have that off his chest. Before the evening, he had worried that he would feel Clovis's presence hovering nearby. Instead, the opposite seemed to be happening, which was one reason he felt able to talk about her with Beryl, and about everything else that had happened.

"What about your life?" he said. "I haven't shut up since we sat down. I've hardly asked you a thing."

"My fault. I've been asking all the questions."

"Is that because I'm a cop? Trying to find out if I pass muster?"

She smiled. "I wish I could answer with an absolute no, but it wouldn't be honest."

"It's a common enough phenomenon among certain types of women."

"Oh?" She raised an eyebrow. "And what type would that be? Snobby?"

"That's part of it. Usually involving either a certain caliber of family name or a certain caliber of university."

"Well, you definitely won't find me in the Blue Book, but would Columbia qualify for the latter?"

"Absolutely."

"Chapel Hill is no slouch."

For a state school in the South, she thought, but was too polite to say. She lowered her head and laughed softly, an appealing gesture. Then she reached across the table and touched his hand.

"I hear you also thought about graduate school."

"Someone's been talking about me."

"My uncle Fedya was determined to vet you on my behalf. He blames himself for this entire evening, so he demanded an immediate audience with Danziger."

"So I heard."

"But Danziger didn't breathe a word about a wife and a child."

"Maybe he was protecting me," Cain said, warmed by the thought.

"I think he was. My uncle said Danziger seems quite attached to you."

"I like him, too. But, speaking of someone who needs vetting, well . . ."

"I take it he hasn't exactly clued you in on his wayward youth."

"He's told you?"

"No. But my uncle has a few stories."

"And?"

She lowered her head again, hiding her smile. Cain knew he was becoming far too enchanted, but saw no reason to fight it.

"I'd be talking out of school if I were to reveal them."

"You're probably right. And don't think I didn't notice that you've stopped calling him Sascha. You're looking out for him, aren't you?"

"You really don't know the first thing about his life, do you?"

"That's certainly what I'm beginning to suspect."

"'Beginning to suspect.' He even has you talking like him. He has that effect on everyone. Tell me, when you're with Danziger do you ever start feeling like you're reading lines straight out of a nineteenth-century English novel?"

"At least half the time I'm with him."

They laughed. Then she turned serious.

"Not to overdo it, but if the two of you are truly pursuing anyone with, as Danziger might say, a dubious enough background that they might actually do you harm, then wouldn't it behoove you to learn a little more about him?"

Another touch of his hand, with a thrill reaching to his toes. A grown man of thirty-four, and Cain was reacting like a teen in a soda shop, enthralled by the idea of so much as a good-night kiss.

"What are you trying to tell me?"

She shrugged.

"I'm not sure. I probably don't know the half of it. Only a few legends, from Uncle Fedya. But there are bound to be records, aren't there? As long as you know his real name."

"Sascha?"

"For Alexander. Maximilian is actually his middle name."

"Is he really a Danziger?"

"He is now."

"He changed it?"

"So I'm told."

"Legally?"

"That seems to be a matter for debate. He chose Danziger because one side of his family was from Danzig, in West Prussia."

"His father's side."

"So he did tell you that much."

"Yes. But I don't know his old name. Do you?"

She smiled uncomfortably, saying nothing. He decided not to press the point, and was about to move on when she spoke again.

"There was a woman, once. I do know that."

"Was? How did he lose her?"

"I don't know. But I gather it's not something that he talks about anymore, even with Fedya."

"Maybe that explains why he's a bachelor. What else do you know?"

"Not all that much. Or nothing that I'd feel comfortable telling you, even though I'd like to help, because, well, I'd hate to think the two of you might be ambushed."

"Ambushed? By what? Or who?"

"I'm not sure. It's all sort of hazy, even from what little I know, and I'm probably making it sound far worse than it was. But, well, I'd feel terrible if I were to hurt him by saying something I shouldn't. And not just for his sake. Maybe you don't realize how important he's become in so many lives. People who are vulnerable and old, people whose way of life has almost vanished."

"Oh, I think I have an idea of that."

"Do you? For them he's the last link to everything they left behind. Their families, their pasts. If he disappears, so will all of that. Dust to dust. And if by telling you too much I somehow destroyed his work . . ." She shook her head.

"Who said anything about destroying him? Or even hurting him. I wouldn't dream of it. I happen to like him. A lot."

"I know. I can see that, and I believe it's genuine. But sometimes when you start poking around in someone else's shadows . . . Well, you're a policeman, you know how that can go. Things come out of hiding. Things that can't be put away twice. And then the whole edifice crumbles."

"Edifice. Exactly how Danziger would have put it."

She smiled, but still looked troubled. "Then I think of the two of you, walking into some situation for which you have no warning, partly because you know so little about him, and that worries me as well."

"How bad can it be? All he's told me was that he ran with a fast crowd."

She shook her head and rubbed her arms, as if she had taken a chill.

"Let me think about it some more," she said.

"Sure."

Their dinner arrived—two plates of spaghetti along with a chilled bottle of Orvieto. Cain broke off the end of a long breadstick. He twirled his fork through the noodles and the thick red sauce, the likes of which he'd never seen down south—rich with chopped onions, peppers, and chicken livers. He overheard the man at the next table ordering a cocktail called a Clover Club, and he marveled that he was here at all—in a Manhattan restaurant with an interesting woman, seated elbow to elbow with what felt like half the noisy city.

The waiter poured more wine, and their conversation drifted comfortably toward other topics—their childhoods, their neighborhoods, their jobs.

Beryl worked for the Red Cross, in programs aiding newly arrived immigrants, often from war zones. Sometimes her wards were from enemy nations, and many had already been tagged for deportation. She spoke German, Russian, and a smattering of Polish, which meant she often dealt with people who'd suffered quite a lot, and, in the case of the deportees, whose suffering was likely to continue.

"That Japanese man on the subway," she said. "What made you want to help him?"

"It's part of my job."

"I doubt many of your colleagues would see it that way."

He considered arguing the point. Then he thought of Maloney, and the other night at the bar.

"You didn't exactly back down, either."

"It's my job, too, working with people like him. People who are in a fix, even the ones from places that aren't very popular right now. My boss seems to think they're the ones I'm best suited to help."

"And you don't?"

"What I really want to do is go overseas. Europe, anywhere near the front. But I'm not a nurse, and they've got plenty of volunteers for the glamor jobs. My boss says I'm needed more here."

"Remind me to send him a thank-you note for keeping you ashore."

When the check arrived she again surprised him by insisting on paying her share. Although he was secretly relieved—the meal had set him back more than he expected—he was embarrassed, too.

"We should all do our part," she said. "It's the wartime spirit."

"Yeah, but . . ."

"You'll just have to get used to the way I do things."

He supposed that would be easy enough.

They went for a walk afterwards. It was a beautiful night, soft air blown free of grit by a spring breeze off the Hudson. The pale glow of twilight still lit the western sky as darkness fell on the dimmed skyline. The usual crowds were out, jostling and weaving. But with Beryl at his side Cain no longer felt hemmed in. Each passing face seemed filled with potential. Every stray voice told a story worth hearing.

"This place never stops amazing me," he said, invigorated by the energy around them. "You've got the whole world on one island. People from everywhere."

"Even from Horton."

"Yep." He smiled. "Even from there."

She took his right arm and returned his smile. He hadn't felt this content for longer than he cared to remember. She could've said good night at that very moment and there still would have been enough residual goodwill to coast him straight on through to dawn. Rounding a corner his leg stiffened, and he reflexively reached for his thigh, as if to stroke the long wrinkly scar where his muscles were knotted beneath the skin.

"Your limp," she said, the words making him flinch. "Is that part of what brought you here?"

"Yes."

"Don't be ashamed. It makes you a better cop."

"I doubt the department sees it that way."

"Well, the department's wrong. Pain, humility. They change you.

I see so many cops—sorry, police officers—who've never experienced much of either, and it shows in their work, their attitude."

He shrugged. "I was never exactly a bust-'em-up kind of policeman, even beforehand."

"You weren't exactly living in a bust-'em-up town."

"You'd be surprised. Especially on a Saturday night, in some road-house or shotgun shack where a guy was beating his wife half to death. A drunk with a sawed-off and a belly full of corn liquor. Throw in a few rowdy friends and neighbors and that's as bust-'em-up as it gets. Makes the Bowery look tame."

"Maybe so."

"Definitely so. Where would you like to go?"

"Anywhere with a little peace and quiet."

He wanted to suggest his apartment, but felt like that would be mov-ing too fast, although with Beryl maybe the usual rules didn't apply.

"There's a quiet little bar around the corner. In the old days I'm told it was a speakeasy."

"How about your apartment?"

He blushed in spite of himself. The sheltered boy, out on the town with the bold woman.

"Sure. Fair warning, though. All I have to drink is beer."

"My mother's side of the family is from Bavaria. They'd say you're well stocked."

Pete, the night doorman, greeted them with a smile and uncharac-teristic courtesy. He seemed to approve of Cain's choice in women. Or maybe he was just relieved to finally witness a spark of happiness in the life of his loneliest tenant. No one wanted one of those depressed lodgers who ended up hanging himself from a ceiling pipe.

Cain fetched beer from the fridge and threw open a window. Kids squealed in the street below, playing kickball. From a radio came the voice of Red Barber, informing Dodger fans that pitcher Kirby Higbe was sitting in the catbird seat. That's how Cain felt as he settled onto the couch next to Beryl. He handed her a beaded bottle of Schlitz.

"Are you always so polite? Holding open doors, staying to my left on the sidewalk. Almost courtly."

"Way I was raised."

"A Southern gentleman." Clovis's old line, but the image didn't linger. "The shyness, though. I didn't expect that."

He looked down at his feet. "It's been a while. Dating, I mean."

"I suppose it has."

She touched his cheek. He set his beer on the floor. They searched each other's eyes for a moment, and then kissed, gently, lips barely brushing. Then again, easing closer on the couch as the springs groaned.

She wore no makeup. Not a drop of cologne, nor the slightest hint of powder, cream, or rouge. No eyeliner or mascara. He should have known this already just from looking at her, *staring* at her the way he'd been doing all evening. But the moment of revelation came instead with these first kisses, his cheek against hers, and from her scent—soap and skin, nothing more. At that instant he realized that with Clovis and all other women he'd known back to high school this moment had always been accompanied by a smell of cologne or cosmetics, the very scent of arousal, and it was missing here, as if Beryl and he had skipped some step in an instruction manual. For the briefest of moments the absence almost threw him. Then she again stroked her fingertips across his cheek, and he pulled her closer, and just like that they were off and running. Soap and skin were plenty.

Afterward, in his bed, she was the first to break the silence, unless you counted Red Barber, who had provided play-by-play throughout. *Smash to third. Slow roller up the middle.*

"He missed the big play at the plate," Beryl said, laughing.

"What was the call?"

"Safe by a mile. Game winner."

"I didn't expect this."

"If you had, it never would have happened. My uncle Fedya calls me a shameless libertine. Maybe that explains it. I do subscribe to the notion that consenting adults need not wait to satisfy their desires. Especially at our age."

"I haven't even asked how old you are."

"Like I said, a gentleman. Thirty-one."

"Thirty-four."

"I know. Danziger *did* offer that."

They moved closer. A kiss, a caress. She reached down, fingertips stroking his thigh like a breeze through the window, while Red Barber chimed in.

*Well, now we've got a real rhubarb going down at third.*

They smiled. Then someone switched off the radio and it was just them on the bed, serenaded by the distant tooting of car horns. She touched the scar on his leg and he didn't flinch, so she left her hand in place, warm, an assurance.

"Tell me what happened," she said.

Cain answered without hesitation, the words coming easier than he would have expected.

"My partner Rob and I, we went looking for a suspect, late afternoon. We'd heard he was holed up in some old bootlegger's shack, the edge of a tobacco field, broken-down place with vines all over the windows, a hole in the roof. We knew the guy. Mean old cuss, but not much of a threat. Tom Strayhorn. Loved to hunt squirrels, drink all weekend in his fishing skiff out on the Neuse. He'd never been much trouble up to then, but he'd roughed up his wife a few days before, and that Saturday he'd knocked over a general store, so it was time to haul him in.

"His car was there, stuck in the mud up against a line of trees. He'd put some branches over it, like a duck blind, but he must have been drunk because even that looked half-assed. We knocked first, announced our names. He knew us, so we didn't expect the worst. He said come on in. We drew our guns because it's procedure, the way you're trained. Then I opened the door, went in first."

Cain paused, remembering the way the room had looked in the November gloom. Water dripping from warped crossbeams. Weeds sprouting through gray floorboards. Cold air, smelling of corn liquor and spoiled meat, with Strayhorn grinning at them from a crouch in the corner, a big pistol curled in his hand like a mutation.

"And then?"

"Our training was to show restraint. Be ready to shoot but give him a chance to put his weapon down. Then he shot Rob. Just pointed and *bang*. Smiled and pulled the trigger. I let it happen. The shot killed him, just like that, straight through the heart. Then I shot back, and he shot back at me, hit my leg. Hard to say which happened first, or if it was all at the same time. It was so damn loud in that small room, and Rob broke the floorboards when he fell, his blood all over me, all over everything."

"Good God."

"Rob was more than just my partner. My oldest friend from the first week of college, and ever since. Best man at my wedding. One of those guys who always knew what I was thinking, and I was the same with him. Or that's what I'd always figured. That morning I'd just found out he'd slept with my wife. Clovis told me at breakfast. Said she was moving out."

"Oh my. I'm sorry."

"Yeah. Me too." Cain paused, took a deep breath. This part was still the hardest.

"Did he know you knew?"

Cain shook his head.

"I'd avoided him all day, then we got called out to get Strayhorn, and it wasn't the right time. I couldn't even look at him, we hardly spoke the whole way out there. Maybe that's why I waited. You know, waited to shoot. That's what the DA's people wondered, anyway, once they heard everything else."

"They questioned you?"

"My shot killed Strayhorn, so yeah. With me as the only surviving witness they pretty much had to. They broke it down, step by step, over and over. My boss invited them in on it. Didn't want the whole town thinking he was covering for me, not once he heard about Clovis and Rob, which, it turned out, everybody but me had already known about. Small towns, that's how it happens sometimes. You're always the last to know. So when the other two got killed and I didn't, well, you can imagine the kinds of things people would say. Three damn shots, maybe two seconds in all, and that's how long it took to lose my best friend, my wife, my career, my reputation. Every bit of it dripping away between those floorboards, with the blood of all three of us mixed in with it."

"But you said yourself, you played it by the book."

"I did. But now I wonder if I knew all along that the book wasn't the right way to play it. Not once I saw Strayhorn's face, the way he was grinning. And I was the first one through the door. I think part of me knew right away what he was going to do."

"Meaning he could have just as easily shot you."

"Maybe I wanted that, too. I'm not sure which is worse, a death wish for Rob or for me. I might have been figuring he would just take care of both of us."

"If that was true you wouldn't have fired back."

"By then I was operating on instinct."

"What about Rob? He didn't fire first, either."

"I think that's what saved me in the end, with the DA anyway. That and Strayhorn being a good-for-nothing sack of shit who deserved whatever he got. It's the one thing I keep going back to, to tell myself I couldn't have handled it any better."

"And?"

"The jury's still out. It always will be. But I know how Clovis would vote."

"She blamed you?"

"Blame doesn't describe it. She pretty much went round the bend. She'd always been a drinker. It was already a problem, but we managed. After that? She was a mess, dawn to dusk. Screaming one minute, sobbing the next. Or just staring off into space. Couldn't finish half her sentences. And poor Olivia. It was like she didn't exist anymore, not for her mother. It went on like that for days. Clovis's dad sent someone down, who drove her away, back up north. To someplace upstate, I think, but he's never told me where. Then he got me this apartment, this job. To help Olivia, he said. I think mostly he wanted to keep an eye on me. And on Olivia, too, once she gets here."

"You couldn't stay in Horton?"

He shook his head.

"Raleigh, maybe, that's where my family's from. But I'm not sure what I could've done for a living. And even there, well . . . Rob's family lives on the other side of town. I'd spent all kinds of time with them until this happened. Every summer during college it was practically a second home. But there was no going back now."

"They blamed you?"

"His younger brother, James, decided pretty early on that it was all my fault. He'd always idolized Rob, and he made a crusade out of it. Wrote eleven letters—*eleven*—to the DA, trying to get me indicted. And when that didn't work he wrote the U.S. Attorney. Offering to testify against me, tell them all kinds of wild conspiracy shit that wasn't even close to true."

Cain had bunched a corner of the bedsheet in his right fist, which was shaking. Beryl pulled the fist to her face and kissed it. He let go and slowly flexed his fingers, the knuckles stiff.

"How did you hear about all that?"

"The guys in the DA's office told me."

She raised her eyebrows.

"I know. Not exactly by the book, but even they thought he'd gone off the rails. Another good reason to leave the state. I half expected him to be at the train station when I left, with a gun to finish me off. I don't think he'd ever do harm to Olivia, but, well, I'll feel better when she's up here, as tough as it's going to be for her."

"What's she like?"

Cain smiled, exhaled. It felt good to have everything out, but now he needed to push it away, back into the corner, and thinking of Olivia helped do that. He'd been lying on his side, facing Beryl, but now he rolled onto his back and breathed deeply.

"She's wonderful. Sweet and curious, smart as a whip. I miss her, and I think she misses me. We write pretty much every day."

"Does she know about . . . well, all of what happened?"

"We never told her about Rob and Clovis, but kids are smart. They hear things anyway, especially in a small town. They see the papers. And why else would her mother have gone crazy like that, when all I ended up with was a bad leg? She probably knows all about it. But I don't think she blames me. If she does, she's good at hiding it, 'cause if there's one thing kids her age don't hide well, it's resentment, mistrust."

"Probably because she knows you love her."

"I hope so. I say it every time I write. We'll find out, I guess."

Beryl put an arm across his waist. They lay in silence, savoring the peace and quiet, the remnants of the breeze. Then she propped herself up on an elbow and spoke again, whispering her words like a lover's secret.

"Dalitz. That was Danziger's name. Alexander Maximilian Dalitz. Only because I trust you to do no harm. And that's the last story you'll get out of me tonight about Sascha."

He nodded, grateful and solemn. Then he kissed her, quickly the first time, slowly the second, and the last thing Cain did before drifting off to sleep was to pull her closer, either for ballast as he fell, or so he knew she'd be there when he awakened.

# 15

.....................

A KNOCK AT THE DOOR woke them—faint at first, then loud and insistent. Cain sat up in bed, fumbling for his watch.

"Are we breaking one of the landlord's rules?" Beryl asked sleepily.

"Doubtful."

It was a few minutes after midnight. He threw on a robe and crossed the hall barefoot while the banging continued.

"Hold your horses! I'm coming!"

He opened the door to see his sister, Sue, looking tired and put out, a suitcase in her left hand. On her right, clinging to Sue's bedraggled white cotton dress, was an exhausted Olivia, whose eyes suddenly came to life at the sight of her father.

"Olivia! Sweetie!"

He knelt to welcome her. Had she grown an inch? Had her face really changed in the space of a few months, or was she just tired? She said nothing, but launched herself through the doorway and clung to him like she'd been waiting all her life to do it.

"We looked for you at the station," his sister said crossly. "Didn't you get my letter?"

"No." His voice was choked with emotion. "Train must've beat it here. I had no idea."

He wanted to sob, feeling Olivia's thin body pressed against his rib cage, against the robe that, he now realized with embarrassment, smelled very much like Beryl, like sex, the essence of their intimacy seeming to fill the air. Sue stepped past him, heels hammering the wood floor. Out of the corner of his eye Cain saw her appraise the room, face tilted upward, nostrils flared, as if already receiving every important signal.

"You should've telephoned," he said softly, not wanting to argue while Olivia was holding on. "Or sent a telegram. I could've had everything ready for you."

"Money doesn't grow on trees, Woodrow. We don't lead a profligate life the way you do."

Talking like a Baptist.

"Yeah, I'm just high on the hog up here, as you can see from all the furniture."

He wondered what Beryl could hear, and how he was going to handle this.

"Well, if Uncle Sam's postmen can't beat Southern Railway to New York City, then I don't see how he expects his soldiers to beat Hitler and Tojo."

Cain unclasped his arms and looked Olivia in the eye. She was already half asleep.

"Sweetie, I'm thrilled you're here, but what about school? You couldn't have finished the year, have you?"

Olivia yawned and buried her face in his chest while Sue supplied the answer.

"Her teacher said it was becoming too much for her, being without her daddy. Said she'd be better off finishing the year up here. I've got her permanent record in the suitcase. You ask me, the real reason was that this girl was becoming such a handful. Nobody could half control her anymore. Me, Don, her teacher. You know how stubborn she can be, once she's made up her mind. And she keeps secrets, this girl, all kinds of them."

All of this with Olivia standing right there, although by now she seemed too tired to care. Or maybe she'd heard it all before. Cain stood and took his daughter by the hand.

"Let's get you to bed, sweetheart."

But where? He had planned to give her his own room once she arrived, and then find a foldout bed for himself that he would store in the living room. But for the moment his bed was occupied, and he felt color rising in his cheeks. He glanced toward the hallway, but Beryl was staying out of sight. He believed now that he could smell all sorts of giveaways and guilty secrets, swirling in the night air. Then he turned toward Sue and saw that she knew.

His sister stepped into the corridor to retrieve a second suitcase and then shut the door.

"I'll put away your things for you, dear," she said, heels striking like a gavel as she headed straight for the bedroom with Cain in pursuit.

"Let me do that, Sue."

"I'm fine," she snapped, gaining velocity, a locomotive determined to smash through the crossing. "I'm a big girl. I'll handle whatever there is to handle."

Yes, she knew all right.

He gave up the chase and was still holding Olivia's hand as Sue rounded the corner. He braced for an outburst, a collision. Instead he heard a brief, muffled exchange of female voices, and then Beryl emerged from around the corner. She was fully dressed and, all things considered, remarkably poised.

"I told her I was just leaving, so I guess this is good night." She spoke in a half whisper. She was not angry, not flustered, and Cain realized he wasn't all that surprised. She was remarkable.

He smiled warmly, reaching toward her with his free hand and then letting it fall away as Sue appeared in Beryl's wake, her face a thunderhead of triumphant disapproval. Beryl touched his arm in passing, and then paused in the open doorway.

"I'm sure I'll be seeing both of you soon enough," she said, pointedly directing her words at Cain and Olivia.

"I'm sure you will," Cain said. "This is Beryl, sweetie. She's a friend of mine."

"Friend!" Sue chimed in from behind, punctuating it with a snort.

Olivia, unfazed, nodded and yawned. Her calmness probably had more to do with exhaustion than with any sense of solidarity, but it was nice to pretend they were showing a united front.

After the door shut he turned to see Sue pulling a fresh set of bed-sheets from Olivia's suitcase. She began tucking them onto the couch.

"Daddy, can I go to bed now?"

"I don't think your daddy has a bed for you yet, dear, so I'm making you a place to sleep right here." Sue's strained cheeriness had forced her voice into falsetto.

Cain shouldered past her and pulled the sheet off the cushions.

"I'll do this. Olivia will stay in the bed. I'll just put her sheets on it. Sue, you can stay out here, and I'll take the floor."

Sue's mouth flew open in surprise. She shot him a glare of deep disgust, the implication clear. *You'd put your daughter to bed right where you were just lying with that woman?*

"C'mon, sweetie." He took Olivia by the hand.

Sue folded her arms as they left the room together.

He stripped off the sheets and tossed them into the corner while Olivia watched, wide-eyed. She stepped forward to help him put on the fresh one, and then looked up as he puffed the pillow.

"This is a big place, ain't it, Daddy. New York City, I mean."

"Sure is, sweetie. But you'll get used to it. This is your new home."

She nodded, kicked off her shoes, and slipped her plain wool dress over her head. Then he tucked her into bed. She was asleep almost the minute she laid her head down. He kissed her on the forehead. Yes, she definitely looked older, and she had grown an inch. Almost thirteen. Like a child for the moment, because she was worn out, but later? He switched off the light and returned to the living room to find Sue in the same pose as when he'd left—standing with arms crossed, lips in a tight seam.

"I see why you like it here so much. Some harlot in your bed whenever you want, without any family for miles."

"I don't recall saying I liked it, but it'll do for now."

"Why'd you even want to come to this horrible place? You know you would've always had a home with Don and me."

"Would've? Sounds like the offer has expired."

"You know what I mean. And listen to you, talking like a Yankee. You should be with your own people."

He was too tired to argue.

"Thank you for bringing her all the way up here," he said, trying to take things down a notch. "You look worn out. Are you hungry?"

"What do you have?" she said, making a beeline for the icebox.

He would've offered to fix her something, but knew better than to get in Sue's way once she'd decided to commandeer a kitchen. Within seconds she'd rounded up the essentials, and soon afterward she had eggs and bacon popping side by side in a cast-iron skillet. Slices of bread were toasting, and a fresh pot of coffee was bubbling up brown in the glass knob of the stove-top percolator.

Cain watched her eat while they exchanged small talk about people they both knew, keeping the field of play neutral to avoid further confrontations. After a few minutes, he decided to tempt fate.

"Have you been to Horton?" he asked.

She paused with her fork halfway to her mouth. A glistening shred of egg white dangled like bait from a fisherman's hook.

"Once. To pick up some of Olivia's old things."

"Are they still talking about it?"

"Worse. No one would even say your name. I think they were afraid to even bring it up. When Olivia showed her face they had no idea what to do. Old Miss Lawing's mouth flew right open, and her hands were all aflutter. When I told her you'd gone to New York you'd have thought I'd just told her you'd enlisted in the Jap army. What time is it?"

He checked his watch.

"Almost two. When's your train?"

"Six. I didn't come here to linger, and there's work to be done back home. I'll freshen up, wash my face. But when that's done I'd just as soon wait at the station." She looked around the room with an air of renewed distaste. Keep talking much longer and they'd be right back on disputed ground, tooth and nail, so Cain let it go.

"Let me call you a cab, at least, when you're ready. I'll get the fare."

She nodded, then stood to clear away the dishes.

Later, after she'd gone, Cain was falling asleep on the couch when a voice called faintly from the bedroom.

"Daddy?"

He got up, made his way to the bed, and sat down beside her. Olivia's eyes were wide open.

"What's wrong, sweetie?"

"I forgot to say my prayers. Do you think it would be okay to say 'em now?"

"Sure. Go ahead."

She sat up straight, pushing her pillow back against the headboard. Then she placed her hands together and bowed her head, just like her mom taught her.

"Now I lay me down to sleep, pray the Lord my soul to keep. If I should die before I wake, I pray the Lord my soul to take. Bless Daddy, my school, my teacher, Aunt Sue, Uncle Don, Grandma and Grandpa Cain, Grandpa Euston . . ."

She paused and looked up.

"Is it still okay to bless Mama?"

"Absolutely, honey. She'd like that."

"Aunt Sue never let me. She said it wouldn't be right to bless a wicked woman."

"Don't ever let anyone tell you who you can and can't bless, okay?"

"Okay."

"And your mama's not wicked."

"I know."

She bowed her head again.

"And bless Mama, too. Amen."

Olivia, eyes shut, nodded firmly as if to settle the issue once and for all. Then she opened her eyes, unclasped her hands, and eased back onto the pillow. Cain pulled up the covers.

"Do you think I'll ever see her again?"

"Your mama?"

She nodded solemnly.

"Probably, but maybe not for a while. I'll have to talk about that with Grandpa Euston."

"Will he come and see us?"

"I don't know if he'll come here, but I know he'll want to see you, one way or another."

Olivia nodded again, then closed her eyes. He stayed awhile, listening to her breathing. Then he thought of a question, but by then she was asleep, and that was okay, too. Her face looked free of worry, an innocence and simplicity he envied. He was relieved she could still ask him about her mom. But who knew how long that would last, once she started learning more of the story. He wondered what version Sue had told her, and what else had been said.

Keeping secrets, Sue had said. Well, that was natural at this age; within another year it would probably be second nature. A lot of big changes were right around the corner for Olivia. She'd get her period, start turning into a young woman, seeking boys and independence. Girls needed their moms for all that, as guides and as sparring partners. He would need advice to help sort it out. A big job, and he wasn't sure he'd be good at it.

He wondered about all the rough kids he'd seen in the neighborhood, holding court on street corners and running the stickball games. Then he remembered gentle Olivia and the way she'd always favored the underdog, sticking up for the boy with polio who walked in braces, releasing fireflies from her friend's mason jar when the friend wasn't looking. How could she possibly fit in here? What would this place do to her?

Cain sighed and stood. He walked back to the couch, but was too restless to sleep.

# 16

....................

CAIN AWOKE TUESDAY MORNING to the realities of a rearranged life. He was a dad again. A dad with a lover, no less, unless Olivia's arrival had scared Beryl away for good. He hoped not, but for the moment he was still a bit bewildered by the events of the night before.

Everything with Beryl had moved so fast, almost headlong compared to what he was accustomed to in his dealings with women. He had enjoyed the seeming recklessness of it—how fine to again experience abandon, and with no one looking over his shoulder in disapproval. Now, with the light coming through the blinds and his daughter asleep, it all felt like a mirage, or maybe a deception. Yes, he was still a father, and happy to be one. But in coming to the city Olivia seemed to have brought Clovis right into the apartment with her.

He thought of Beryl, back in her own bed, the one person with whom he might be able to talk about some of these feelings. But would she really want to hear them? Only one way to find out.

He went to the phone, lifted the receiver, dialed her number. Some other tenant answered, her voice echoing in the apartment house hallway. He asked for Beryl. The receiver went down with a thud and he heard footsteps, followed by a shout. Then Olivia appeared in the doorway, barefoot and yawning. She had her mother's eyes, wide and watchful.

"I'm hungry, Daddy."

He put the phone back in its cradle just as someone was answering.

"Then let's fix breakfast. We've got a lot to do today."

"Can I have scrambled eggs?"

"Sure can. Bacon and toast?"

She nodded.

"Is that the newspaper?"

"Yep. Not much good news today."

She scanned the headlines. Before she only used to read the comics.

"Where's Corregidor?" she asked, pronouncing it slowly but getting it right.

"It's part of the Philippines, in the Pacific. Our army's having a rough time there."

"What about Leningrad?"

"Russia. It's where the Germans are. Hand me that."

No sense filling her head with thoughts of the war on her first morning, especially when almost all of the news was bad. Cain glanced at the front page. The new premier of occupied France had thrown in his lot with the Nazis. Hitler had celebrated his fifty-third birthday on the eastern front, while in New Jersey FBI agents raided sixty-two locations to see if any of the local celebrants were up to no good. The Navy's inquiry into the burning of the *Normandie* had concluded that the fire was the result of "gross carelessness and utter violation of rules and common sense." Citing slow production, the Navy had also seized control of four aircraft factories, while also noting that in some parts of the plant every employee was an enemy alien. Cain wondered how Harris Euston would view that development: A blow against unionism, or undue government interference? Hidden little battlefronts, wherever you looked.

Hoping to find something cheerier for Olivia, he turned to the sports pages, where the results were mixed. Dodgers win. Giants lose. Yanks idle.

Cain had already called the station house to say he'd be late due to a family emergency, and after breakfast he and Olivia ventured into the streets on a few errands. Now he was the seasoned New Yorker with a novice to instruct, and he found himself hastily imparting lessons that suddenly felt like matters of life or death. Stay on the sidewalk. Don't talk to strangers. Memorize our address. Get to know the doormen. Pee before you leave the house. Don't stare on the subway. And so on, all the way to a secondhand furniture store on 14th Street, where he bought a fold-up bed and a thin mattress.

Olivia seemed overwhelmed, and who could blame her? Block after block, she kept her head down and held his hand tightly. Maybe he shouldn't have been so emphatic in his warnings about strangers. Just north of 20th she let go of his hand, and Cain took another two steps before he realized she wasn't keeping pace. He turned in a panic and saw her standing on the grating of an air shaft to the subway, looking straight down while crowds parted to either side of her.

"Sweetie, what is it?"

He saw that she was gazing at hundreds of discarded cigarette butts which had accumulated on a grimy ledge a few feet below.

"Look at that," she said. "You think anybody will ever pick them up?"

"I doubt anybody can reach them, sweetie."

"Then why does everybody keep throwing 'em down there?"

"I don't know."

She looked up. "This place is a mess."

"Big cities aren't easy to keep clean."

"Then this one must be *really* big."

Cain was on the verge of a smile when he felt a cold spot in the middle of his back. He was immediately on his guard, sensing someone's eyes were on him. He wheeled around, and rapidly scanned one face after another, half expecting to see Maloney, or Linwood Archer from the commissioner's office. No one was familiar. Everyone seemed intent on his own business. Only a grocer stared from a doorway, probably drawn by Cain's pose of alertness. Yet the spot on his back still tingled, like a button that had been pressed to sound the alarm.

"What's wrong, Daddy?"

"Nothing, sweetie. Hold my hand."

It hit him anew that his girl was here in New York for the long haul—meaning double the responsibility, triple the stakes. Maybe that's what gave him the sudden case of the heebie-jeebies, but to make sure he took a last glance over his shoulder, and couldn't help but shudder slightly even though he saw nothing out of the ordinary.

"What are you looking for?"

"Just people."

"Well, there's plenty of them."

He smiled. "That's for sure. Let's go home."

When they arrived back on 25th Street, a frumpy woman in her forties was waiting just inside the entrance, seated on a folding chair provided by Tom, the day doorman. She rose uncertainly while Tom provided the explanation.

"Mr. Cain, this is Eileen. She was sent by Mr. Euston to work for you."

He handed over a folded piece of paper, a typewritten message from Euston on Willett & Reed stationery. Cain read it while Eileen nodded and blinked nervously:

Woodrow,

This is to introduce Eileen O'Casey, at your service. She comes highly recommended and ready for flexible hours, so I trust she is suitable. I would appreciate a visit from Olivia at your earliest convenience, although perhaps it would be better to have Eileen arrange it.

Let it never be said that I am not a man of my word, or that I am a shirker of obligations. I hope the same will be true of you.

Harris

Cain folded the letter and put it in his pocket. He cleared his throat, trying to bury his anger beneath his gratitude before addressing the woman who, from now on, would probably be spending more time with Olivia than he would. He wondered how Euston had even known Olivia had arrived. Tom, maybe, or the night doorman. A hazard of letting your father-in-law decide your living arrangements.

"I'm Woodrow Cain, Miss O'Casey. Pleasure to meet you. And this is my daughter, Olivia."

Eileen nodded, her lips sealed primly, although they broke into a smile as she turned her gaze to Olivia, who didn't shrink from it but didn't step forward, either. And why should she? She'd now been passed from Aunt Sue to Dad to Eileen in the space of a dozen hours.

"Mr. Euston said he'd be handling my salary, so you're not to worry yourself on my account," Eileen said.

So, then. Another spy in his midst, although he had to admit she was a godsend.

"Welcome," he said. Then, turning again to his daughter, "Olivia, you're to treat Miss Eileen with the same politeness and respect that you'd show to me." He hoped he was handling this correctly. He'd crossed onto foreign soil, and was desperately in need of a map, a translator. "Okay, sweetie?"

Olivia nodded solemnly. You could see in her eyes that, for her, the day had just taken a turn for the worse, and it stabbed him deeply. Fresh in town, and already left to the mercy of strangers. He knew the feeling.

"So, does that mean Aunt Sue ain't coming back?"

"Isn't, sweetie. Not ain't. And, no. I'm sure she's on the train to Raleigh by now."

Cain escorted them upstairs, no one saying a word as they climbed the steps single file. Once they were safely behind the closed door, he knotted his tie, grabbed his notebook, and prepared to depart for the precinct house. Then the telephone rang. Beryl, perhaps? Had she heard his voice on the earlier call?

It was Captain Mulhearn.

"I hear you're arranging your own shift changes now, Citizen Cain, completely on your say-so. If true, that's some brass balls, but it don't mean I still can't bust 'em."

"My daughter arrived late last night, sir. I've been making arrangements for her, but I was just leaving. Be there in half an hour, and I can double up tomorrow."

"Not so fast. I've got a detail for you to take care of on the way in, especially since you can't seem to get enough of punishment duty. Good thing you never enlisted or you'd be spending the whole time peeling potatoes and digging latrines. Now, you got that bogus notebook of yours handy?"

"Yes, sir."

"Got five names for you. I want you to run them down at the Bureau of Criminal Identification, right up the block from headquarters. We'll need their prints and their criminal index files. Those people down there can be a royal pain in the ass, so I figure you're just the man to deal with them. Ready?"

"Ready."

Mulhearn spelled out the five names while Cain wrote them down. This would kill the bulk of the afternoon, when what he'd hoped to do was to link up again with Danziger, preferably on the old man's turf, well beyond Mulhearn's reach. Although he brightened a bit when the fifth name turned out to be that of con man Albert Kannerman, who, true to Danziger's tip, had been rounded up by the overnight shift at the very address Cain had provided, which meant he'd at least get some credit for the collar.

"Got all that?" Mulhearn asked.

"Got it, sir."

He was about to hang up when Mulhearn said, "Oh, and speaking of headquarters, some pencil pusher named Archer was calling here looking for you. Said he had some payroll questions, but that you had his number. No rush, unless you actually expect to get paid for your brand of slack-ass policing." Mulhearn slammed the receiver in mid-laugh.

So Linwood Archer was after him. Did Mulhearn really believe Archer was from payroll, or would he now know that Cain was up to some sort of dirty work for the commissioner? Either way, it was unwelcome news. Probably Archer's way of expressing his disapproval of Cain's lack of progress. It made him think back to the moment on the street when he'd been so certain he was being watched. Archer, maybe? Or one of his goons? He had better find a way into the 95 Room as soon as possible.

"Daddy?"

"Yes, sweetie."

"Do you think it would be all right if Miss Eileen took me to a park?"

He looked at her face, needful and glum, and for a moment the thought of her being out in the open on a swing set, or climbing some jungle gym, scared him out of his wits. Then he searched her eyes and saw restlessness and boredom. A energetic young girl on a fine April day, about to be cooped up with a matronly stranger who smelled vaguely of rosewater and lye soap.

"Sure. Just be careful." He bent down, gave her a hug and kissed her forehead. Then he headed off to do his job.

# 17

........................

THE BUREAU OF CRIMINAL IDENTIFICATION was a shrine to archival zeal; a multi-story vault of arrest records, rap sheets, summons reports, fingerprint files, ballistics reports, modus operandi files, and photographs. With its musty smell and hallowed silence it felt like a library, cataloging crimes and criminals going back for decades.

In Horton, tracking down old information on lowlifes could take days, even weeks, and there was little or no cross-referencing between jurisdictions. Up here they'd amassed almost everything you'd want to know in one place, and each year the department spit out voluminous statistical reports with a seemingly endless array of totals on the city's criminal misbehavior. How many people between the ages of thirty-one and thirty-five had been arrested the year before for felonious assault with a knife? Two hundred eighty-two. How about people between the ages of sixteen and twenty, and arrests for larceny from intoxicated or sleeping persons? Six.

Best of all, like an all-night diner the Bureau of Criminal Identification never closed.

Impressive.

Yet, as with his trip to the Automat, Cain found himself mildly disquieted by such efficiency. Keep it up and eventually you'd be able to find out almost anything about anybody, and by barely lifting a finger.

"Whatcha need?" the counter clerk asked.

Cain showed his shield and presented the list of names.

"Fill out a form." He handed one over. "Detective, huh, and from the third district?" He chuckled. "Mulhearn usually sends some rookie from radio patrol. You must really be in his doghouse."

"Woof, woof," Cain said glumly, drawing a smile.

"So, these five names and that's it?"

Cain was about to nod when an idea struck.

"One more," he said. "Almost forgot."

He added a sixth name. The clerk nodded and read it aloud. "Alexander Maximilian Dalitz. Got it. Should have everything within an hour or two. You gonna wait here or come back? Most guys like to step out for a bite to eat." He leaned across the counter and lowered his voice. "Joint around the corner called Clancy's has an all-day happy hour for any member of New York's finest."

"I'll wait here."

"Suit yourself."

An hour later, bored out of his mind, he headed out after all, opting for coffee instead of a drink. One nickel and one scalded palate later he was back, greeted by a stack of files on the counter with his request form sitting on top. The clerk was somewhere in the back.

He made a quick count. There were only five—one for each of the names Mulhearn wanted, and nothing for Dalitz. He sighed in relief, surprised at how good it made him feel. So maybe it was all a bunch of talk and legend, a couple of old guys spinning tales about their youth. Or maybe Danziger had been so good at his chosen line of misbehavior, whatever it might have been, that he'd never been caught. Whatever the case, Cain felt several pounds lighter than when he'd walked in. He began whistling as he signed the form to show he'd gotten what he asked for, and his tune brought the clerk through the door from the back.

"Thought that might be you," he said. "Just so you didn't think I was shorting you, wanted to let you know it'll be a few days on that Dalitz file."

Cain's smile faded. "There's a Dalitz file?"

"It's what you wanted, right?"

"Sure."

"It's just, well, it's been in cold storage quite a while now, given his circumstances."

"Circumstances?"

"He's deceased. Has been since twenty-eight. You knew that, right?"

"Sure."

The remnants of all those good feelings bottomed out in his stomach, stewing with the burned coffee.

"They keep those closed files down in some rat hole over at the Hall of Records, and getting those slugs to jump when you want something, well, you know how that can go. How 'bout I give you a ring when the corpse surfaces, so to speak?"

"Yeah, you do that."

Cain walked back into the sunlight. Dead since '28, the same year in which Danziger had last used a taxi, at least until this past weekend. To go to a funeral, he'd said. His own? The man *was* a bit of a sorcerer, and that would certainly be the ultimate trick. Or maybe the whole thing was the result of some clerical blunder, a bit of misplaced paperwork in a city that at times seemed built on the stuff, offering another form to sign everywhere you turned. Besides, it was one thing to fake your own death. It was quite another to then return to the same neighborhood without anyone noticing. Fourteen years of living a new life right around the corner from where the old one had supposedly ended? Even Danziger wasn't that good.

But now that Cain had the name—Dalitz—and the fact of the death, he intended to confront Danziger about both items. And he vowed to do it before the day was out, even if that meant asking Miss Eileen to work overtime on Olivia's first full day in New York. His daughter was right. This place was a mess.

Cain sighed, snugged up the files in his arms, and pushed back into the crowds.

# 18

................

## DANZIGER

HE IS OUT THERE, LOOKING FOR ME. Or, rather, looking for the *old* me. I know this intuitively, in the same way I was once able to detect menace approaching from around the corner before it even showed its face. It is an awareness which never leaves you once you've experienced the bruising consequences of lowering your guard, although this time I can take comfort that my pursuer is relatively benign. Mr. Cain, I am quite confident, does not intend to do me harm. He will be dogged, yes, annoyingly so, but he will pursue his course of inquiry out of curiosity and a misplaced sense of duty, not out of malice. It is his inexperience that worries me more; the prospect that, in his blithe efforts to learn all, he will unintentionally reveal far too much to the hungry eyes beyond my walls.

I suppose that Beryl Blum is to blame. Fedya told me as much earlier this afternoon, after the poor girl confessed to him that she had revealed my former name in a moment of weakness—carnal, probably. Proving once again that, with secrets, even the involvement of a single additional person is one too many. But I will make no recriminations. Beryl is a good girl. *Girl*, I say, when she is thirty-one, well beyond a marriageable age, a status which probably makes her and Cain perfect companions. Lust and longing, truth serum of the lonely. No secret will be safe between them until the first flames of infatuation have been extinguished.

I cannot deny that this will require extra precautions of me. The next time I see Mr. Cain, he will doubtless be full of additional information, and thus, additional questions. For the moment, I will have no choice but to deflect, to parry, to misdirect; for his own good as much as for mine. Because the time has come for me to be his guide into the fringes of my former world.

You may justifiably ask why I would take such a risk for the sake of two dead Germans with Nazi inclinations. One motive is self-preservation. A shadowy cabal would appear to be at the center of these recent events, and if its fears and suspicions led its participants to silence Hansch and Schaller, then surely at some point will they not also reach out for me? Surely Lorenz, silenced in a different manner, must have revealed my name by now, since he was the one who directed those two Germans to my door.

But only with my help and guidance will Mr. Cain be able to reach the heart of these matters. I know the codes of these people. I speak their language, literally and figuratively. Without me, he would surely misread vital cues and messages, perhaps with disastrous consequences.

So, for his benefit and for mine, I must resume more of my previous ways of behaving. I must once again seek out dangerous company and, in doing so, beg the forgiveness of whatever deity has spared my life to this point. Because I confess that I again find myself beguiled by the prospect of tasting the voyeuristic pleasures and excitements which once guided my life, and once nearly ended it as well.

# 19

......................

THAT AFTERNOON CAPTAIN MULHEARN made damn sure Cain had no time to even think about Danziger, much less sneak off to see him. He began by once again dropping a thick file folder on Cain's desk.

"Here you go, Citizen. You're on Civil Defense duty."

CD Duty, as the cops called it, was a wartime job that mostly involved dealing with civilians who'd volunteered as air raid wardens or as foot soldiers in civil defense patrols, which functioned as auxiliary policemen at a time when extra manpower was needed, like during parades, riots, or big demonstrations.

Cain's first order of business was to check out a rumor that a couple of ne'er-do-wells living on 37th Street had applied to become air raid wardens to make it easier for them to rob stores during blackouts. Five phone calls and a quick trip to the nearest Army recruiting station soon established that both men had left for boot camp weeks ago, and had never even applied to be air wardens. He nonetheless had to type up a detailed report, because the tip had come in a handwritten letter from some nosy New Yorker to FBI director J. Edgar Hoover, who had forwarded it to Mayor La Guardia, who had passed it down to Commissioner Valentine.

"Handle *carefully* and *thoroughly*!" Valentine had scribbled on an attached note. So much for being immune to political influence, Cain thought ruefully. And nice irony that it had ended up on Cain's desk. He resisted the urge to scribble an aside to Linwood Archer.

His other CD duty for the day was far more pleasant: registering six new female air raid wardens, a task that became the object of station house levity when he marched them downstairs for fingerprinting in full view of officers coming in off the street from patrol duty.

*"Need some help rolling those fingers, Citizen Cain?"*

*"You're turning a little red there, Sergeant. They making your temperature rise?"*

*"Or is that something else rising?"*

Several of the young ladies blushed. Cain took it in stride. This was one reaction that would have been no different in Horton. Usually the only women you ever saw in the station house were either the rare female plainclothes officer, working upstairs, the hard cases from the Tenderloin who'd just been arrested, or the distraught victims of crime. Even most of the clerical work here got done by men, and the sight of six well-meaning young women in smart CD uniforms was therefore bound to be a distraction.

Twice Cain had to shoo away overly curious patrolmen, but all the extra attention eventually gave him an idea which he decided to put into action as soon as the fingerprinting was done. He marched the women up to Romo's high desk and whispered conspiratorially, "Got a second, Sarge?"

"Considering your present company, I got all day."

"These gals could use an escort upstairs while I go use the can. To keep 'em out of harm's way until I'm back, if you know what I mean."

"Absolutely, young man!"

Romo sprang to his feet with a bounce in his step and led the women toward the stairwell. Everyone watched their progress except Cain, who reached beneath the desk for the ring of keys. The one for the 95 Room was clearly marked. Cain worked it loose, dropped it in his pocket and returned the ring to its hook just as the last of the women disappeared up the stairs in a chorus of wolf whistles. He'd be fine as long as no one missed it between now and the shift change. That gave him an hour to get a copy made. He'd worry later about how to put the key back.

After completing the paperwork for the women he followed them out of the building and veered off toward the nearest hardware store. The clerk, not accustomed to cops asking for copies of official-looking keys, frowned doubtfully until Cain slipped him a dollar and said, "I screwed up. Lost the duplicate, and the less my lieutenant knows about it, the better."

"Got it."

By then Cain had come up with a plan for how to return the original. After leaving the hardware store he headed straight for Logan's, a tavern that was a mandatory after-hours stop for some of his colleagues. The bartender was accustomed to special requests from his law enforcement clients, and Cain had heard talk of some of the tactics. He eased up to the bar. Ten minutes from now, every stool would be filled by officers from the day squad. But for now the place was practically empty.

"Special order for the lou on the night squad," Cain said, using house slang for the squad lieutenant. "A flute would make his day."

"Coming right up."

The bartender pulled out an empty brown pop bottle from below—Orange Crush, which made Cain wonder what Zharkov had really been drinking in the station house the day before—and filled it with a few shots of Old Bushmill's.

Cain reached for his wallet, but the bartender waved him off.

"With my compliments to the lou."

Back at the station house, Cain followed established procedure. He approached the desk just as the night squad's desk sergeant, an agreeable rail-thin fellow named Walker, was settling in.

"Got a flute here to wet the lou's whistle," he said, keeping his voice down.

Walker's eyes lit up.

"You're a gentleman and a scholar. Sergeant Cain, is it not? The new detective?"

"Yes, sir."

He took the bottle in hand.

"Well, then. I'm sure the lou will remember you in his prayers. As will I."

He winked and poured a toot into his coffee mug.

"Carrying charge," he said, before heading off to complete the delivery. Cain checked his flanks, saw his chance, and grabbed the key ring. He slipped the key back on and headed upstairs to complete the last of the day's paperwork. Shortly afterward he left the station house with two errands to run. An hour after that he arrived at Danziger's doorstep on Rivington Street.

This time Cain entered without knocking. Danziger looked up in annoyance.

"I am with a client, my final one of the day," he said testily, before turning back toward a heavyset woman in black, seated in a chair facing his. "My apologies, Mrs. Hartstein. You may resume in full confidence of privacy, as I can assure you that the gentleman who does not act as a gentleman neither speaks nor understands German. Nonetheless, I will ask him to wait outside if that is your wish."

She eyed Cain, who smiled sheepishly, the way he used to whenever his grandmother caught him stealing icing from a freshly baked caramel cake.

"It is quite all right," she said in English. "I am nearly finished."

"Very well." Then, in a sterner tone to Cain. "Please wait quietly."

She may have been nearly finished, but, as Cain soon discovered, she still had important things to say. Danziger scribbled quickly while she spoke German in a low, urgent tone, gesturing with both hands. When she paused, he nodded solemnly and retrieved a folded page of onionskin paper from an open envelope. He then began reading from it in German while she listened closely, head bowed. At one point she stopped him with a hand on his arm. She reached into a large black handbag and dabbed at her eyes with a lacy handkerchief. Danziger continued reading in a lowered voice, and the silence afterward felt like a pronouncement of death. He gently refolded the paper, slipped it back into the envelope, stood, and slid it into one of the cubbyholes on the back wall, near the end of the top row. She rose with a mournful sigh, and he accompanied her to the door, neither of them glancing at Cain as they passed. Her eyes were off in some bleak world across the seas.

The door opened to the noise and dust of the neighborhood. Danziger guided her across the threshold. "I am walking her home," he said to Cain. "It is a few blocks only, the least I can do for her in such a difficult time. You will wait."

"Sure."

The door shut behind them.

It took only thirty seconds for Cain's curiosity to get the best of his sense of propriety. He rose stealthily from the wing chair, already feeling like he was up to no good. First he tried the drawers of Danziger's desk. The biggest one was locked. The smaller ones were stuffed with bills, invoices, torn scraps of paper with scribbled names and numbers, none of them familiar. On top of the desk was a well-thumbed old book, open to the middle. Cain checked the spine: *Harkavy's American Letter Writer and Speller, English and Yiddish*, a reference work by some fellow named Alexander Harkavy, and printed forty years earlier by the Hebrew Publishing Co., New York.

He saw now there was also a small framed photograph, an oval barely bigger than a silver dollar that was walled off from the rest of the room by a pile of recent correspondence. It was a yellowed portrait of a young woman, beautiful but unsmiling, with black hair and a prim collar, buttoned to the neck. He turned it over but there was no date, only the name of a photographer's studio in New York. He was careful to place it in the exact spot as before.

Cain looked up at the two hundred or so cubbyholes. As before, every single one had something in it. Impressive, yes, but looking closer he now saw that for an alarming number the envelopes and papers were yellowed, or even curling at the edges. The ink was faded.

He gingerly pulled out a letter and unfolded it. It was dated October 1932. Ten years old. The onionskin stationery was brittle, almost to the point of crumbling. The other three envelopes in the slot were all postmarked before 1931.

Who were these people? What were their stories? And were some of them dead? If so, why had Danziger held on to their letters, especially since he seemed so keen on erasing their stories from his memory? Or so he'd said.

Cain slid everything back into place, taking care to do no harm. He felt like he had come across an ancient archive. The door creaked open behind him. He flushed in embarrassment, and took a moment to compose his expression before turning to face Danziger, who stood at the entrance with arms folded, staring. As the door slowly closed behind him, a band of sunlight lit his white hair and pale skin, making him look like an avenging angel. Yet he did not seem angry, or the least bit surprised.

"You will not find it there," he said, "or anywhere on these premises."

"Find what?"

"Any sign of my previous life."

Cain was tempted to ask about the photo of the woman, but something in Danziger's expression warned him off.

"That sounds like you're admitting to one."

"One? By my count there are at least three. We all have past lives, wouldn't you agree? There was my childhood, happy but impoverished, in a city now lost to memory. Lost to everything, if newsreels are to be believed. Then my passage to New York, which landed me far too soon upon the shores of orphanhood. Followed by a life on my own in an era of self-education and rising status. That is the one you seek evidence of, is it not? But, as I said, no trace of that life resides here."

"No trace of it seems to reside in the police records bureau, either." He decided not to mention the files he'd requested from the Hall of Records. "They say you're dead. Or that Alexander Maximilian Dalitz is dead, anyway. Has been since 1928."

Danziger flinched, and Cain could tell he hadn't wanted to.

"He died for a good reason. Several good reasons. But let us not speak ill of the dead. Instead, look up again at those letters where you were just poking around. Go ahead."

Cain obliged him.

"Now, tell me what you see."

"Mail, some of it pretty old."

"No, no. What you see are lives. Lives which depend upon me. And, yes, I have cultivated their dependence, perhaps out of a need to feel worthy and wanted. But it has occurred all the same. And now you would propose, with a little further meddling, to render me null, or perhaps damaged, and at the very least compromised in my standing here. So do it, then, if the only way you know how to behave is as a policeman, operating by his manual of procedure. But be prepared to live with the consequences for all of them." He spread his arms wide. "Mrs. Hartstein, who you just saw leaving, would you care to hear the news of hers which has just been revealed to me?"

"News revealed in confidence?"

"Don't be impudent. Just listen, for a change. Four months ago she received a letter from her sister in Hamburg. Their entire family was in hiding, but the police were going door to door, searching for Jews. There were reports that entire crowds of them were being escorted to the *Bahnhof* and loaded onto rail cars. Cattle cars, Mr. Cain, not passenger compartments. These trains were seen leaving town, traveling east.

"During the next four months she heard nothing. Not a word. She feared the worst, but hoped that perhaps they were in a new location, someplace where even sending a letter through trusted intermediaries was too risky. Until today, when she came to me with a letter that had just arrived from an old neighbor, a sympathetic member of the *goyim* who only the week before had come across all of her family's belongings in a secondhand shop. Their furniture, their jewelry and silver, their candelabras. Even their *clothing*, Mr. Cain, right down to their laundered undergarments. Folded neatly on shelves and hanging from racks in this terrible little shop, every piece of their lives. As I sadly explained to her, this is not at all uncommon news, Mr. Cain, and its meaning can only be ominous."

"Maybe they sold everything, lock stock and barrel, to buy their way out of town?"

"To go where? Berlin? Where these cattle trains are said to be running with even greater frequency? It is very likely, Mr. Cain, that everyone in Mrs. Hartstein's family has disappeared forever. Meaning that all that remains of her past, the only traces, are those which you see in her mail slot, third from the end on the top row. The top row, because she is one of my oldest customers. And without me to curate and translate those relics, where would she be?

"Whereas you, Mr. Cain, need me only as a cop needs a source, a guide, a clue. I will be expendable the moment you have obtained what you want. Yes, I know that I speak too highly of myself, and perhaps also too lightly of your work. But if my vanity engenders doubt, then ask someone you trust. Ask Beryl Blum."

"Oh, I trust you. This version of you, anyway."

"Seeing as how that is the only one which currently exists, shouldn't that be enough?"

"Except that your connections from those earlier times—you said it yourself—they're still dangerous. For both of us. And you've already trespassed back into that part of your life, whether you intended to or not. You crossed back the moment you took on Werner Hansch as a client. Or that's what I'm guessing."

Danziger looked at him closely, as if reassessing.

"You guess well, Mr. Cain. Although even I was not aware of how seriously I had trespassed until I witnessed that formidable lineup of personalities at the breakfast table at Longchamps."

"Where does that leave us?"

"You're the detective. You tell me. What more have you learned?"

"For one thing, I stopped by the Hotel Astor on the way over."

"Was that wise?"

"It seemed like an obvious starting point."

"But if certain people hear that they have captured the interest of the police, well . . ."

"I was discreet. I also shelled out a little cash, to keep my source quiet."

"So, then. Even Mr. By-the-Book is not above the employment of certain unsavory methods. I am encouraged."

"She had a low price tag. It was the switchboard operator at the hotel."

"A wise choice. She handles virtually every call in and out of the building, does she not?"

"Except that the office for the Executives Association of Greater New York has its own direct line. It was installed back in December. She remembered because it was the week after Pearl Harbor."

"Then I suppose she knows little or nothing of their operations."

"Almost nothing. She knows the guy who runs the place, a fellow called Haffenden."

"Haffenden? Spell it, please."

Cain obliged him, then told him the rest. "Charles Haffenden, but everyone calls him Red."

"I daresay that anyone calling himself Red instead of Charles is likely to run in the same circles as Mr. Lansky and Mr. Polakoff."

"Not exactly."

"You know more?"

"Agnes, the gal on the switchboard, says he's a real peach. A gentleman, even."

"Gentlemanly behavior and the rackets are not mutually exclusive."

"She says he's a man in uniform."

"Military?"

"The U.S. Navy. An officer, to boot. Lieutenant commander. So I made a few calls. Discreetly, once again. And this is where it gets kind of interesting. Before the war he was in the reserves, just a businessman. Some big-shot glad-hander in advertising and marketing, which probably explains why he's running the Executives Association. When the Navy recalled him for active duty they made him chief officer of the district for Naval Intelligence."

"Intelligence? As in spies and secrets?"

"And his real office, or at least the one he runs for the Navy, is down near Wall Street, in the federal building on Church Street. As for why he hired his own private line at the Astor, that's anybody's guess. But Agnes says lately he's there two, three times a week, holed up for hours at a time."

"Where he meets with the likes of Meyer Lansky, Murray Gurfein, and the mouthpiece for Mr. Luciano."

"Yep. And she knew one other item. She says just the other day Haffenden rang her up and asked for a phone number for some place not too far from here, down on the East River." Cain took out his notebook and flipped to the page. "Meyer's Hotel, at one seventeen South Street. Not much, I guess, but . . ." Danziger was smiling broadly. "You've heard of it?"

"A foul and seedy establishment. Little better than a flophouse for seafarers and wharf rats. But it is also a place of business for a celebrated figure of whom you may have heard. Joseph Lanza."

"As in 'Socks' Lanza?"

"Of the Fulton Fish Market, which is right next door."

"Why would Lanza be mixed up in this?"

"Jobs, perhaps. The ones Lorenz brokered for Werner Hansch and his Bundist friends. Lanza could have provided them through the Seafood Workers Union, which he practically runs. No one gets aboard a trawler, or onto the weighing lines at the market, without his say-so."

"Makes sense."

"Perhaps. Perhaps not."

"Because he's under indictment, you mean?"

"Yes. Conspiracy and extortion, multiple counts, if the newspapers are to be believed. Which makes his involvement with these people all the more puzzling. When you're in his shoes, the last thing you want to do is start acting as if you're cooperating with anyone in authority. People who do can suddenly find it very hard to conduct business. Or to even live a life."

"Unless the authorities he's working with are crooked."

"There is also that possibility. Mr. Lanza was indicted by the previous DA, Mr. Dewey. Perhaps the new DA, Mr. Hogan, and his man Gurfein do not think so highly of the case against him. Either way, Mr. Lanza is keeping curious company. We will ask him why, provided he chooses to speak with us."

"*Us?*"

"My trespass that you spoke of, the one which led into my past. You are correct, of course. I have crossed a line. But there are other lines still ahead which I had hoped to avoid crossing. Yet now I believe I must do so if I am to be of any further value to you."

"You're sure?"

"Only if you are prepared to stop asking so many questions of me. You must also be willing to operate beyond your usual codes and strictures, if only out of loyalty to all of those people you see in this room." He gestured toward the cubbyholes. "So, do we have an agreement?"

Cain had no choice but to say yes, even as he wondered what sort of compromises lay ahead—and with Linwood Archer waiting right around the next corner, for all he knew.

"Okay," he said. "Count me in."

"Very well. Let us begin your education, and my next trespass."

"Where?"

"Meyer's Hotel, at the Fulton Fish Market. We shall go straight to the heart of things."

Cain sensed the momentous nature of this move, and for a second he wondered if it was worth the cost.

"You sure you're ready for this?"

Danziger nodded.

"But let us wait until morning. Far too soon it will be dark. Not the right time to breach their defenses."

"You make it sound like an armed assault."

"Reconnaissance only. But we should go as early as possible. Sunrise, no later."

"To catch them unawares?"

Danziger frowned.

"It is clear you have never been to the fish market. Sunrise is when the place is at its busiest. We will have safety in numbers. Perhaps their lookouts will even be too preoccupied to notice our approach. But if you wish to question my tactics, then, please, offer an alternative."

"You know an awful lot about this stuff."

"For which you should be grateful, not questioning."

Cain watched him closely, but Danziger remained poker-faced.

"Okay, then. I'll come by for you, bright and early."

Danziger nodded. Then he looked around the room, with the air of a man accounting for all his worldly possessions just before embarking on a lengthy and perhaps perilous journey. Without a further word, he escorted Cain to the door.

# 20

...................

CAIN INHALED A GUST OF BRINE as he slipped on cobbles slimed with blood and fish guts. His aching leg was just beginning to loosen up. Beneath a tattered awning to his left, a shower of fish scales glittered like silver confetti in a band of low sunlight. In the next doorway down, a large man in heavy gloves slid a pink bundle of entrails from the belly of a huge swordfish.

They were enveloped by noise—the banging of cleavers on cutting boards, the splash and sluice of hosed water, the hungry cries of seagulls and, loudest of all, the call and echo of rough male voices shouting prices and poundage at the weighing stations of every storefront, where teetering metal baskets sagged and creaked. Tails of red snapper overlapped the edges of one like waving hands, stilled in a cold farewell.

Down here on Fulton Street, at ten minutes past dawn, not a single woman was in sight, although here and there Cain saw scrawny boys in shorts and smocks, darting between shadow and sun.

"Watch yourself, Oscar!" someone called loudly from behind, Oscar apparently being the preferred name for anyone who didn't belong. Cain stepped aside just in time for a handcart to rumble past toward the East River. From the opposite direction someone approached with wooden boxes of ice hefted on both shoulders.

For all the activity, Cain sensed an edge of weariness taking hold, which told him that everyone had been at their jobs for hours, having risen long before him.

"Is it like this every day?"

"A little slower on Sundays," Danziger said. "Slower still during storms, when the boats stay in harbor."

Cain took stock of his companion and noticed a change. A few blocks ago Danziger had led them into the mouth of Fulton Street almost warily, with careful steps that seemed to betray the frailty of advancing age. Now his stride was longer, bolder, as if with each step he was easing deeper into familiar territory. Cain settled in just off Danziger's right shoulder.

On their left they continued passing what seemed to be endless storefronts. All were open to the elements on the ground floor, and the name of each establishment was painted overhead in big black letters between the windows of the floors of these three-story brick buildings. Most of the brickwork was painted white, perhaps for better visibility during the pre-dawn hours when the market first stirred to life. Cain scanned the names: MARKET SHELL FOOD CO.—OYSTERS, FILLETS, CLAMS; JOHN DAIS CO. WHOLESALE FISH; FLAG FISH CO.; BEYER FISH CO., one after another, all the way to South Street and the water's edge, where the masts and pilot houses of trawlers cast long shadows across the wharves.

On the opposite side of Fulton, trucks were parked side by side in a long row, rear doors open to accept whatever the restaurateurs and grocers bought. Other trucks had arrived full, to unload the day's catch from elsewhere—crabs and oysters from the Chesapeake, cod and lobster from points north. No sooner did one truck leave than another took its place.

Elsewhere in the city, meat and fresh vegetables were in short supply. Sugar was already rationed, and meat and coffee were said to be next in line. But down here the sea was still issuing its bounty without limit. No wonder the mob loved the place and jealously clung to its power. It was a nonstop profit center, unhindered even by war, with every part of the supply chain gathered conveniently in one spot—trawler, trucker, gutter, seller, shipper, grocer, and chef—which no doubt made for easy, multi-level skimming. And, indicted or not, Socks Lanza was still lord over all.

Cain saw now that the last and biggest building on the block, rising five stories in red brick, was Meyer's Hotel. It announced itself with white letters mounted on its two fire escapes. Just below was a sign of equal importance for any thirsty fisherman: BAR.

"That's our destination?"

"Yes." Danziger stopped, and held out an arm to stay his progress. "Observe it for a moment. Tell me what you see."

Cain saw fishermen in overalls and rolled sleeves heading into the bar for breakfast, or perhaps for a morning pick-me-up. A newsboy laden heavily with a fresh edition slumped by an open window, smoking a cigarette although he was no older than twelve. Further to the left, two fellows flanked a narrow, unmarked doorway. Compared to the fishermen and merchants they were almost dandyish, dressed in wide-lapel suits and cocked fedoras, the brims shading their eyes from view. One chewed a toothpick, his jaw rolling slowly. The other smoked a cigar.

"Those two fine young specimens kind of stand out, don't they?"

"They are there to be noticed," Danziger said. "Move closer and you'll also observe the bulge beneath their jackets. Also intentional. Mr. Lanza posts them as a sign to be heeded by one and all."

"He's telling people to steer clear?"

"Heavens, no. He is telling the world that he is present and accounted for, and currently receiving petitioners. Not that you'd ever see *him* in a suit. Mr. Lanza favors the uniform of his fellow tradesmen. Even when seated behind a desk he wears overalls begrimed by oil and offal. But his visiting hours will remain open for as long as those two well-dressed goons remain at their stations. Although not open to everyone, of course. That is our challenge."

"How do we get past them?"

"Your shield would no doubt suffice, but under their rules that would constitute an entry by force, and we would receive such a chilly reception as to make our visit worthless. Your presence would also be remarked upon, no doubt, to someone of high standing at the fourteenth precinct, whereupon your Captain Mulhearn would be duly notified."

"The last thing I need."

"Then I suggest you leave matters in my hands. I will speak for us both."

"They won't make me as a cop?"

Danziger shook his head, as if Cain still didn't get it.

"If they make you as anything, it will be as a bumpkin. Although they *will* detect your sidearm, so please keep your hands at your sides."

Cain, who'd figured that by now he blended in like any other New Yorker, felt mildly affronted, but this was no time for hurt feelings.

"Lead the way."

They approached. Danziger walked briskly, with head held high. Cain followed his lead, trying to disguise his slight limp. Moving closer, he saw that both men were freshly shaven, unlike the fishermen and merchants, who were already sporting five o'clock shadows. He detected a whiff of aftershave. When they were almost upon them, the man chewing the toothpick spit it out to a point five feet in front of him, as if to signal they were to come no closer. Danziger spoke to that one.

"We have business with Mr. Lanza. I am Mr. Danziger." Cain was a little surprised he'd given his real name, but why offer yet another alias when he was already living under one? "My companion is Mr. Pierce. We're here on a delicate matter of some urgency. Union business."

"We wasn't told to expect anyone of your names, but Lester here will go see if he might squeeze you in."

Lester disappeared into the doorway and up a flight of stairs. The first guy produced a new toothpick from a lapel pocket and resumed chewing, eyeing them carefully all the while. A few minutes later Lester returned with another man in tow. Cain had checked a few photos the night before, so he knew this wasn't Lanza. But the fellow looked several cuts above the sentries, and he, too, wore office attire, although he had shed his jacket.

The man said nothing as he inspected them, slowly and carefully, as if assessing strengths and weaknesses. Then he nodded and turned back around.

"Okay," the first guard said. He turned to Cain. "But first you'll have to check your hat here at the door."

Cain, bare-headed, frowned in puzzlement until Danziger said, with a hint of impatience, "Your sidearm, he means."

Cain reluctantly handed it over. The guy reacted as if he'd been handed a dead skunk.

"So how come you're carrying a Colt .32, like one of Valentine's flatfoots? We got enough Lizzie Louses cruising through our waters as it is."

Danziger answered. "His choice of arms is a personal decision. I am the brains, he is the muscle. But I can assure you that he is quite harmless."

"And mute, too, huh?"

The guy smirked. Cain held his tongue and clenched his fists at his sides, while wondering what the hell a Lizzie Louse was.

"Upstairs, then. Go on up."

The man who'd come down to inspect them was waiting on the second floor landing, where he led them to a small office dominated by a battleship-gray desk with at least a half-dozen dents. A faded wall calendar advertised a local ship's chandler, but there was little else in the way of décor. The window was open, and the room smelled like fish and boat fuel. Venetian blinds banged and rattled in the breeze. The man settled in behind the desk, lit a cigarette, and then put away his pack without offering one.

"Which of you is Danziger?"

Danziger nodded.

"And you're Pierce?"

"Yes," Cain said. "And your name is . . . ?"

The man ignored the question and turned back toward Danziger.

"So you're the guy in charge?"

"I am the one who has been appointed to speak for the interests of my clients."

"You a mouthpiece, then?"

"A personal representative."

"On a union matter?"

"Yes. Two members of your union, it seems, have come to rather unfortunate ends. We're here on their behalf, seeking to collect any pension or compensation due to their families."

The guy showed no visible reaction. He studied their faces for a few seconds longer.

"Names?" he asked, picking up a pencil.

"Werner Hansch and Klaus Schaller."

He wrote them on a pad without batting an eye.

"Never heard of 'em."

"They were German citizens, hired in the past month or two. They were referred by the German-American All Trades Employment Agency, operated by a Mr. Lutz Lorenz."

The man raised his eyebrows. Then he tilted his head and took a long, slow drag from his cigarette before rolling his chair backward without once taking his eyes off them. He stood.

"Back in a minute."

They heard him climbing the stairs to the next floor.

"Think he's gone to see Lanza?" Cain asked.

"Probably. He is the second in command. Or so it is said."

"You know who he is?"

"Benjamin Espy."

Danziger didn't volunteer how he knew, and there was no sense in asking. Espy returned within a minute or two and quickly settled in behind the desk.

"My boss ain't never heard of these people. So there you go."

"It is certainly plausible that the names would not be familiar to him," Danziger said. "But perhaps if we could peruse your membership records for any recently issued cards for your local? Number three fifty-nine of the Seafood Workers Union, is it not?"

Espy eyed them for a beat or two. He had just started to shake his head when Cain lost his patience. The opportunity to obtain any possible information was about to slip through their fingers, and Danziger seemed ready to acquiesce. Not him.

"Maybe your boss could also tell us what he knows about a fellow named Red Haffenden. And before both of you claim you've never heard of him, we know for a fact that Haffenden has been making calls to Mr. Lanza at this very office."

Cain looked over at Danziger, expecting a nod of gratitude. Instead, the older man sighed and lowered his head in an elaborate show of embarrassment, as if Cain had just used the wrong fork at a dinner party. Espy, meanwhile, had gone red in the face and had risen halfway out of his chair. He shouted in reply as he leaned across the desk.

"What is it with this one?" he said to Danziger. "He comes in here talking like a hayseed from the sticks and waving some cop's gun under our noses. Then he starts claiming to know our business better than we do?"

"My colleague is impulsive and inexperienced," Danziger said. "And, as you have surmised, he comes from elsewhere. Despite his regrettable display of impertinence, I personally assure you that he is a one-way guy."

The words seemed to momentarily appease Espy, while Cain was left to wonder whether he should be offended by the description. Danziger held out his hands in a gesture of forbearance and spoke again.

"Let us speak candidly for a moment, sir. As you and I are both aware, what your boss says is word, from the Brooklyn Bridge to the Battery, and in certain points beyond. If he gives the go-ahead, a man may join a waterfront union, whether it happens to be Mr. Lanza's local or one of the Longshoremen's."

"Hey," Espy shouted. "You want to speak candidly, and after that crack by your friend? Then try this on for size. What my boss is, first and foremost, is a patriot. So we ain't running nothing with no Germans, and if you've got some kind of idea that we are, then you're dead wrong. And he's a patriot for no pay, I might add. He's not getting one penny outta this deal. He's a seventy-five-a-week union man living in a three-room apartment, because that's all he and his old lady can afford. And now you're gonna question his patriotism?"

"We are doing nothing of the sort," Danziger said gently, although he looked thrown by the turn the conversation had taken. So was Cain. What sort of "deal" was Espy talking about? And why was he suddenly making such an issue out of Lanza's patriotism?

"Then you need to stop throwing around certain names and places like my boss has got something to do with it."

"Of course. We wish only to peruse the local's records. Which we can accomplish with minimal disruption, I assure you."

Espy eyed them both for a few beats more, then nodded.

"Then you do that. Two doors down. Ask Hal, he'll show you. There's nothing to see about any damn Germans. When you're done I want the both of you out of here. Don't be coming back, and don't be asking any more questions about Mr. Lanza. To nobody. Understand?"

"Of course."

"And that goes double for him." Espy jerked a thumb toward Cain without turning his head. Cain wasn't sure what was worse—feeling completely disrespected, or feeling so far out of his depth.

Espy escorted them to the room in question. The search, through a single file folder that held the membership rolls for Local 359 of the Seafood Workers Union, took all of ten minutes, and was fruitless. There was no record for a Hansch or a Schaller, either for the past month or for any month dating back as far as 1936. The man named Hal escorted them downstairs, where both sentries smirked as they handed back Cain's police-issue weapon.

"Nice pop gun, kid."

"What would you know about it?"

He was about to say more, but a glare from Danziger warned him off. They walked away, Cain barely containing his anger. The fish market was still in full swing, and now that the sun was higher the smells were more intense. Neither man spoke until they'd gone three blocks and turned onto Pearl, where Danziger stopped and tapped a bony forefinger against Cain's chest, as if to drive home every word.

"You are never to do that again."

"*Me?* What about you? And what the hell's a one-way guy? Some kind of crooked cop?"

"A straight shooter. An honest man. It was a compliment."

"Only if you believe in honor among thieves. And Lizzie Louses?"

"Police patrols. It is usually the best policy to address those sorts of people in their own tongue. And your sin, if I might continue with my previous point, was in revealing the information about Haffenden. It was not something we should have shared."

"Well, sometimes you've got to light a fire under people, and—"

"And sometimes when you light a fire the whole building goes up! With you inside of it!" Danziger's voice was raised, his eyes flaring. Cain had never seen him so angry. "You must let *me* decide what is best in our dealings with these sorts of people, Mr. Cain. If only to help you live a longer life. Yes?"

"Okay." Cain waited a few seconds, letting him calm down. "But weren't you surprised by the way it set him off? I was."

"It was beyond strange."

"All that mumbo-jumbo about his patriotism, about some deal that he's not getting paid for."

"Useful material, perhaps. But only if we learn more. Mr. Haffenden would seem to be the key. Perhaps it is a Navy secret."

"If Haffenden was on official Navy business, I doubt he'd be doing it from that private office at the Astor."

"I agree. This arrangement, whatever it is, does not smell any better than those wharves we just inhabited."

"Where do we go next, then?"

"I need time to think. And perhaps a day or two for checking with a few contacts. In the meantime, you are to do nothing that might stir up these people further. Stay on the Erie, as Mr. Espy would say."

"Lay low?"

"Good. I may yet succeed in making you bilingual."

"Fluent in mugs, mopes, and mobs. That'll open doors."

"We should part ways here, in case someone is following. Two are harder to keep up with than one."

Cain, jarred by the idea, spun around to check behind them, realizing as he did so that he had no idea who or what he was looking for. What kind of tail would Espy employ? A mug in a suit? A fisherman on the take? A newsboy, even, earning an extra nickel? It might be anyone.

He turned back around to ask Danziger's advice, only to find an empty space and a view of a vast, milling crowd, placidly going about its business on a fine spring morning on Pearl Street.

# 21

...................

## DANZIGER

I MADE HASTE TO DISENGAGE without Mr. Cain noticing, in no small part because I did not wish to field any further inquiries, lest he pry loose the truth of the matter, which was this: Mentioning Haffenden's name had been a stroke of blind genius. Without it, we might have departed Meyer's Hotel empty-handed. Instead, the intemperate Mr. Espy had clumsily let his anger master his words, and in doing so momentarily opened a doorway onto a deeper chamber of his thoughts.

The problem is that our knowledge is not yet sufficient to illuminate the room beyond that doorway. And I would certainly not encourage further such impulsive behavior on the part of Mr. Cain, or not until he has progressed in his education regarding the rough ways of these grubbier environs. I say this not out of vanity for my own expertise, but because I am certain he never realized how close he came to losing his life only moments ago.

He did notice, as I did, that as soon as Mr. Haffenden's name was mentioned, Mr. Espy's right hand reached stealthily toward an open drawer of his desk, just to the right of his knees. This grope into "the dynamite hole," as Lanza's minions supposedly call it, was for the purpose of procuring a fully loaded pistol, with which Mr. Espy has been known to dispatch without hesitation any particularly troublesome petitioners of his lord and master. Only my immediate verbal efforts at appeasement stayed his hand. An easily angered man, our Mr. Espy, even though his police record shows only small-time convictions for such crimes as robbery, rum running, and the thieving of automobiles.

What puzzles me most about his inadvertent revelation—the news that some sort of "deal" may have been struck between Messrs. Lanza and Haffenden—is that, for the moment, there are no financial considerations in play. Working for free, Mr. Espy said of his boss, even though the time-honored tradition of deals between men on the public payroll and mugs such as Mr. Lanza is one of lucrative payoffs, for one party or another, and often for both.

There is, however, another currency which sometimes enters into these agreements: human lives. The erasure of certain inconvenient individuals, for example. Is that what Mr. Lanza has bargained for? If so, it leaves me cold and worried. Werner Hansch and Klaus Schaller may have been unworthy individuals, but if I was to learn that our own Navy, in concert with the district attorney, had guaranteed their disposal—and perhaps Lutz Lorenz's as well—in exchange for considerations from the likes of Mr. Lanza (and, by logical extension, Messrs. Lansky and Luciano), then I would find it objectionable, even alarming, wartime or not.

But, as I said, the room beyond this newly open doorway remains dark. My guesses and postulations are exactly that. Meaning that Mr. Cain and I still have much work to do.

I should also use this moment to correct a wrongful impression you may have formed during an earlier conversation at my house between Mr. Cain and me, lest you accuse me later of having aggrandized my importance to my neighborhood.

When I look up to those mail slots above my desk, I do indeed see lives. But that is not all. I see tombstones as well, more of them every month. Because mine is an aging clientele, and my occupation itself is on its deathbed, despite my protestations to the contrary on the occasion of our first acquaintance. Language schools and public education are seeing to its demise, and within a generation there will no longer be enough need for my services to support a livelihood.

I should have foreseen this, perhaps. But I took up this profession at a moment in my life when I needed to feel useful, valid, helpful. And, considering recent events, it is probably a good thing that my declining business has freed me to attend to the task at hand.

I am now convinced that I must redouble my efforts, and become even more vigilant in my efforts to protect those who may come to harm. For the second time in my life, I must become a watchful presence in the lives of others, except this time in a role of benevolence. Or so I hope.

That is why I scurried away the moment I saw the opportunity, evading Mr. Cain's notice to proceed back to Rivington Street, where I shall lay the best possible plans for our progress, and for our survival.

# 22

........................

AN EXHAUSTED CAIN made it back from the fish market to the station house in time for the beginning of the day shift. He needed three cups of java to steel himself for his next leap into the unknown. That was due to occur at eleven a.m., when, based on what he'd heard from gossipy colleagues, Officers Steele and Rose of the 95 Room would head out for their daily coffee break at the Royal.

Cain went downstairs at eleven. Sure enough, the room was locked. He looked both ways in the corridor and used his duplicate key to let himself into the darkened office. He quickly relocked the door behind him, switched on the light, and checked his watch: 11:02. The earliest Steele and Rose ever returned was 11:30, or so everyone said. He had less than half an hour to get down to business.

It was a bit disconcerting, seeing the many shelves and file drawers arrayed before him, all of them stuffed to their limits. So much documentation. In Horton, police paperwork was fairly rudimentary, and the filing was uneven at best. The NYPD, however, was in many ways an edifice built upon a bewildering array of paper. Cops had to deal with roughly two hundred and fifty different forms in their daily work, which varied from the basics, like the UF-7F, a fatal accident report, to the relative obscurity of the UF-17A, a report of a burned-out street lamp.

Fortunately, from his earlier reconnaissance he knew that the index to all the files was posted on the back of the door. In addition, the trail of police paperwork following an arrest was fairly straightforward. Every arrest was reported on a UF-9 form, each of which was noted in the precinct's arrest record, which listed cases in chronological order and by serial number. The UF-9 forms were then bound in monthly volumes. Summons reports, disposition records, and other papers were also stored in the 95 Room, but Cain figured that the arrest record was the best starting point.

Scanning the index, he quickly found the shelf and binder number for the precinct's arrest record ledger. He went to the shelf, took down the big ledger, and opened it atop a worktable next to the framed fishing photos that Steele and Rose had gushed about his last time here.

Cain flipped through the pages to January, which Valentine had cited as the month when things began to go awry. He scanned the dates and names, not sure what he was looking for until he saw "Ericson, Stanley," who'd been charged January 17 with illegal bookmaking. Recalling that Valentine had singled out "a bookie named Ericson" as someone who inexplicably remained at large, he looked closer. Curiously, the faint remnant of an erased check mark was in the left margin next to Ericson's name. Cain noted the serial number for the case, and then consulted the index on the door for the location of the January binder of arrest reports. He grabbed it off the shelf and flipped through the pages of reports, filed by serial number, until he reached the space where Ericson's arrest report should have been filed. There was nothing.

Cain logged the serial number of the missing report in his notebook and went back to the arrest record's pages for January, this time paying special attention to the left margin. He found eleven more cases with the ghostly remnants of erased check marks out in the margin. He wrote down the name and serial number for each one, and went back to the January binder of arrest reports. The report for the first of the eleven numbers was missing. So was the second. With time limited, he decided to assume that the same would be true for the other nine. He then went back to the arrest record to search for more erased check marks in subsequent months.

He glanced at his watch: 11:18. Twelve more minutes before he had to scram. A droplet of sweat fell onto the ledger, smudging a name. He flipped through the pages for February and found at least seven erased check marks, although he was moving so fast that he might have missed a few. He saw six more for March until a notation for an arrest on March 19 stopped him. The check mark was still there, not erased. There were two more on the next page. Did that mean those arrest reports would still be in the binder for March?

He took down the March binder, rifling through it so fast that he tore a page. The checkmarked arrest report for March 19 was present and accounted for. The subject was Clarence Cohen, charged with running an illegal crap game on 41st Street. Someone had paper-clipped a short note to the report, but just as Cain began trying to decipher the handwriting he was startled by the sound of voices from the hallway.

Shutting the binder, he froze, as good as dead if anyone entered. He watched the door knob for movement as the voices passed and then faded. Cain exhaled and checked his watch: 11:27. Time to finish and get the hell out of here. He slid the arrest report binders for March and January back onto the shelves, and then the arrest record.

He put his ear to the door. All quiet. He turned the lock, shut off the light, and then flipped it back on, remembering in the nick of time that he'd left his notebook on the worktable.

"Shit!"

He grabbed it, again shut off the light, and stepped into the hallway, where he quickly locked the door and headed toward the stairs. No sooner was he under way than he heard voices approaching from the end of the hall. He didn't wait to see if it was Steele and Rose.

There was still plenty of work to do, but at least now Cain knew he was on the right track. The system seemed simple enough. Someone was checkmarking cases for special handling, presumably in exchange for bribes. Once the arrest report was disposed of, the check mark was erased.

But why not just dispose of the reports right away, rather than risk leaving a trail with the check marks and erasures? Easy, he thought. You didn't make a report disappear until the client paid for special handling. It was a ham-fisted way of doing things, and easily spotted by anyone with half a brain who could get access to the 95 Room. Then again, no one got a job in the 95 Room by being the brightest bulb in the precinct. And it was pretty easy to see why Mulhearn, and perhaps other ranking officers in the precinct, would gladly look the other way in such a scheme. Even if they weren't sharing in the payoffs, they'd be enjoying the benefits of a lowered crime rate in the precinct every time yet another arrest report disappeared. Crude, but effective, and probably foolproof as long as the precinct followed its own rules of keeping all its records under lock and key. Copies of the arrest reports weren't sent to headquarters until the end of the month, and by then all the ones getting special handling in the 14th would have disappeared.

As Cain entered the squad room, the name from the March 19 arrest report snagged in his memory. Clarence Cohen. He opened his notebook and walked over to the lineup of wanted posters. There he was, Clarence Cohen, listed among the "known associates" of Mendy Weiss, the suspect from Murder, Inc. Whoever had engineered this scheme was helping an associate of one of the city's most notorious criminal enterprises.

That gave rise to another thought. Anyone willing to help murderers might also have a murderer's services at his disposal. Money wasn't the only means of bribery. Cain swallowed hard. He reached into his pocket and fingered the duplicate key as if it were a rabbit's foot, hoping its charm didn't wear off anytime soon. On his next trip to the 95 Room, he'd better not cut it so close.

Cain was so shaken by his findings that he could only eat one of the piroshki that Zharkov brought him an hour later in a greasy paper bag. Maybe this kind of scam was inevitable, he thought, especially once a department started putting so much reliance on record-keeping. Fortunately for him, these early practitioners seemed to be working at it with Stone Age tools. But that would change. Send the cavemen like Maloney off to jail and the next bunch would come at it with sharper tools that left fewer traces.

He spent the rest of his afternoon muddling through his own paperwork in an exhausted daze. Captain Mulhearn then rounded out his day by dispatching him to the furthest corner of the third district, way up on West 83rd Street, in search of a witness in one of Simmons's cases, a fellow who turned out to be out of town.

By then he was wrung out and hungry, and almost desperately in need of the humble comforts of home. He also felt like a lousy dad. Miss Eileen had been on the job for only a few days, and already he was asking her to care for Olivia for loads of extra hours. That morning she'd had to catch a bus well before dawn, and, as if that wasn't bad enough, Cain hadn't been around to see Olivia off for her first day at her new school. His daughter hadn't been at all thrilled about the idea of heading off to a strange classroom full of unfamiliar faces.

He made his way wearily through the crowds on the subway platform for the ride downtown. Finally reaching his stop, he rushed up from the tunnel only to end up with his face practically pressed against the backs of two women just in front, close enough to smell the damp wool of their skirts, the laundered cotton of their blouses. Behind him, two brisk men in suits pressed closer as the people in front of him made way for an onrush of people coming down the steps. For a moment everyone came to a halt. Cain, breathless and confined, flashed on Danziger's account from the day before, with its haunting tales of crowded boxcars, human cattle struggling to survive.

Finally the crowd surged upward again, and he spilled into the open air with a palpable sense of release before colliding with a newsboy who shouted in his face.

"Watch where you're going, mister!"

Other faces came at him too fast to process—an older woman with an elegant strand of pearls, a down-and-outer smelling of urine, a grocer in his smock, brow gleaming with perspiration as he swept the sidewalk in front of his store. Then, from out of the blue, he sensed eyes upon him, just as he'd done the day before while walking with Olivia. The eerie sensation triggered a rush of blood to the brain, a heightened awareness. Once again he felt a cold spot like a target in the middle of his back.

He stopped abruptly, causing two people to bump him from behind.

He wheeled around almost drunkenly, looking in several directions at once, but saw nothing suspicious. No Archer. No Maloney or Steele or Rose. No thugs belonging to Espy and Lanza. The list of would-be stalkers was growing longer by the day. Maybe that in itself was enough to trigger these episodes.

Cain maintained his watchful pose a moment longer. A gust of steam from a hot dog wagon blew through him like a spirit, but no one seemed to be paying the slightest bit of attention to him, aside from the frowning pedestrians forced to weave around him on the sidewalk.

Nerves, then. Or exhaustion. Had to be. Yet, he still felt a deep sense of relief as he reached his building, where the big door swung open courtesy of Pete, the night doorman.

"Evening, Mr. Cain. I've been asked to inform you that your daughter and Miss Eileen are at the park, and will soon return."

"Thanks, Pete."

He took the steps two at a time, trying to outrun something he still couldn't identify. Closing the door behind him, he finally experienced the relief of solitude. Deep breath, with sweat cooling on his back. He went to the refrigerator, opened a bottle of beer, and swallowed greedily as he stood in the kitchen. Noises filtered in through the window—a police whistle, a car horn, the mumbling hubbub of the crowd. Not peace, really, but the best he could do under the circumstances. He would've gladly paid a few dollars to hear the lullaby of crickets, the fluted call of a wood thrush, with a whiff of honeysuckle for good measure.

Or maybe what he needed instead was a sympathetic ear, a warm body. He picked up the phone, dialed the number. A woman with a heavy accent answered, and it took a few tries to get her to understand who he was asking for on the communal phone. Moments later, Beryl answered.

"I've been meaning to get back in touch," he said. "I've been hoping you don't think my house is too crowded for a return visit."

"As long as Olivia doesn't mind."

"Oh, I think she'll like you. Although, well . . ."

"You're not so sure about the sleeping arrangements?"

He was glad she couldn't see him blush. He hadn't intended to cross into that territory, or not now, but he should have known Beryl would get right to the point.

"You can always visit me here, you know. I wouldn't be upset if you didn't stay for the night."

"Mostly I just wanted to talk about my day."

"The way you sound, it must have been pretty terrible."

"Pretty strange, that's for sure. And way too long."

"Would you like to meet for a drink?"

Behind him, the doorknob rattled. Olivia's footsteps clattered across the floor. He turned with an awkward smile, then melted when he saw her eager face. What was he doing, acting like a sneak on the phone? His daughter was home from her first day of school, no doubt with her own tales to tell. Olivia launched herself toward him, and he had to set the receiver on the kitchen table in order to catch her in his arms. She smelled like grass stains and playground sand, more of a little girl than an adolescent, at least for the moment.

*"Hello? Are you there?"*

Beryl's voice called faintly from the receiver. Olivia turned alertly toward the phone.

"Is that Mommy?"

"No, sweetie. A friend."

"Oh."

Her face fell.

Eileen, standing by the door, lowered her head. Cain picked up the receiver.

"Something's come up."

"So I heard. I should let you go."

He'd handled that poorly. "I guess that . . ." he began, trying to choose the right words until he realized the line was dead. He turned to see Eileen watching him closely, and wondered how long it would be before Harris Euston knew everything that had just happened.

"The girl's had a bite to eat, sir, begging your pardon. Wasn't sure when you'd be arriving, so I figured it was safer that way."

"Thanks, Eileen. And how was the park?"

"Oh, just fine, sir." Eileen looked down at the floor. Then she and Olivia exchanged glances like two people caught in the act. Cain guessed Eileen must have done something indulgent—let the girl eat too many sweets, maybe. No big deal, so he let it pass.

"Can I have dessert now?" Olivia asked. "Some bread with butter and sugar on it?"

"Only if you wash your hands first." So much for his initial theory about sweets. Olivia and Eileen again exchanged glances, and he was about to probe deeper when he noticed his daughter was wearing a round white disk on a lanyard, with her name and grade written in block letters.

"What's that you're wearing?"

"It's an ID tag, sir," Eileen said. "All the schoolchildren have them now, in case there's some sort of . . . *disturbance* due to the war."

Olivia walked to the bread box in the kitchen. Eileen stepped closer and lowered her voice.

"They do air raid drills and make them hide under their desks, sir. I think it scared her half to death. But I'm sure you'll hear soon enough. Tomorrow then, sir? Bright and early again?"

"Not as bright and early as this morning, thank goodness. The regular time."

"Very well, sir."

And off she went, with at least an hour's worth of bus and subway rides before she made it home. Say what he would about Euston, Eileen was indispensible.

He and Olivia sat on the couch with her plate of sugary buttered bread and a glass of milk.

"Good?"

"Mmm-hmm," spoken through a mouthful.

"Tell me about your first day at school."

She shrugged.

"Not much to tell."

"What are the other kids like?"

She shrugged again. No words this time. For a few seconds she seemed lost in thought.

"I need to know something," she said.

"Okay. Ask away."

"Can U-boats shoot at us if they come ashore? Benny Stern said they could. He also said they could unload sabby tars, and send them all over the city."

"U-boats can't get close enough to shore to shoot at us here, honey. And I think he was talking about *saboteurs*, but I wouldn't worry about them, either. It's from a French word. The first saboteur was some worker who threw his wooden shoe—his *sabot*—into a machine at his factory, to make it break."

"So I could wreck a whole factory with my sandals?"

"Or even your tap shoes. Then they might think Shirley Temple did it."

He'd hoped for a laugh, but got a frown.

"I outgrew those shoes, and nobody talks about her anymore, Daddy. She's fourteen."

"Oh, I see. All grown up."

Olivia nodded, and maybe she was right. With a war on, fourteen was pretty old, for her and all her classmates. Make it to eighteen and you might even be bound for Europe or the Pacific, at least if you were a boy.

"I'm full," she said. The milk was gone, but half the bread remained. "You want the rest?"

"No, thanks. Not my kind of dessert."

"To each his own, said the lady as she kissed the cow."

Her words took him aback. It was an old expression of Clovis's.

"Haven't heard that one in a while," he said, hoping for a response. Instead, she averted her eyes like she'd been caught in a lie. Then she yawned and leaned against him, and soon was either asleep or pretending to be—a dodge he knew from his own childhood.

Let her rest. Maybe it would ease her mind before she climbed into bed. These worries of war could rob you of more than sleep. And now she was channeling favorite sayings of her mother, as if seeking refuge in happier times of the past. He nudged her gently.

"Time to put on your PJs, sweetie."

She opened her eyes and nodded. He went to the kitchen to put away her plate, then he tucked her in. After switching off the light he went to the refrigerator for a beer. He supposed he should scramble an egg for dinner, but he didn't have the energy. Mostly what he needed was companionship, and he again eyed the phone before dismissing the idea.

He took the beer to the living room, undressed, and sat at the foot of the unfolded bed with the windows open, listening to the sounds of a Chelsea night. Exhausted as he was, he knew he wouldn't be able to sleep for hours.

# 23

......................

"SERGEANT CAIN, IS THAT YOU?"

The man's voice, muddied by the sediment of sleep, seemed to reach Cain from the bottom of the Hudson.

"Wake up, sleepyhead."

It was first light. He was standing barefoot, and the Bakelite receiver of the telephone was somehow in his right hand. That told him that the phone must have been ringing, and that he must have walked to the kitchen to answer it.

"Come again?" Cain rasped.

"Time to get up, asshole." Spoken like a cop, cocksure and in charge. Cain heard laughter in the background, the toot of a boat.

"Who is this?" His head began to clear.

"Your girlfriend's in need, Sergeant Cain. Says she wants it bad. Up here in Harlem, no less. But not to worry, no brown sugar. Purely the white stuff, just the way you Southern boys like it."

He was about to hang up when the voice snapped back at him, all business this time. "It's Larsen from the two-five, asshole. Get up here before she scrams."

"Where? Who?"

Cain fumbled for his notebook from the pocket of his jacket, which was draped across a chair.

"Out at the end of a hundred thirty-seventh."

"Which end?"

"Harlem River, right off Madison Ave. Check your fucking map, farm boy. Nowhere near your jurisdiction, but since you're so in love with poaching why stop now?"

The line clicked.

"Shit."

He grabbed his pants, started looking for his shoes. Not a stitch of clothing that didn't need cleaning, but at this hour who the hell would notice? Olivia was still asleep, thank goodness. He phoned Eileen, waking her up and feeling bad about it. She promised to be there as soon as possible, but he couldn't just leave Olivia by herself, without even a doorman to guard the way for the next two hours.

Cain wondered what Larsen could have meant by referring to his "girlfriend." Surely not Beryl? He fought down a panicky feeling that something had gone wrong, and then he dialed her number. It took a dozen rings before anyone picked up, and then a few minutes more before Beryl came to the phone.

"Woodrow? Is everything all right?"

"I was worried about you. I'll explain later. In the meantime, do you think it would be at all possible for you to come by here, quick as you can? I've been called away to something, and Miss Eileen won't be here for at least an hour to look after Olivia, or even longer, and—"

"Give me fifteen minutes."

It took her closer to twenty, but in the meantime Cain shaved, got dressed, and made a cup of coffee. After Beryl arrived, he knelt by Olivia's bed and touched her shoulder.

"Sweetie?"

Her eyes opened.

"I have to go somewhere this morning. I've called Miss Eileen and she'll be here in a while. But in the meantime Miss Beryl, my friend you met the other night, will look after you, okay?"

"Okay." Her eyes were wide open now, her voice uncertain.

"You can go back to sleep if you want."

"What's happened?"

"I'm not sure. I'll find out when I get there."

"Is it the Germans?"

"No, no, sweetie. Just police business. Nothing for you to worry about."

"Okay."

She sat up, not looking so sure about things. He knew from her eyes that she wouldn't be going back to sleep. He probably shouldn't have disturbed her, but the thought of her waking up unexpectedly with only a stranger for company had been too troubling.

Beryl had poured a cup of coffee.

"Eileen should be here in less than an hour," he said. "Thanks for doing this."

She smiled.

"Happy to help. You surprise me. I would've thought that, well . . ."

"That I'd have been too embarrassed to ask you? Too much of a prude?"

"Well, yes."

"I'm a fast learner. Give me time."

She reached up, stroked his cheek.

"You look worn out."

"I'll nap on the subway."

"Is it serious?"

"Guess I'll find out when I get there."

He checked for his shield. Then for his notebook, and lastly for his gun.


Harlem was yet another new frontier for Cain, a place that until now he'd only read about in the papers or heard about from other cops, who never had much good to say. "Nothing but niggers," from Maloney, predictably enough, although the newspapers weren't a whole lot better.

*New York's city of Negroes!*

He'd spotted that line in the *Daily News*, and descriptions in the *Times* weren't much different. Both papers reported on the doings in Harlem as if it were a foreign country, and most dispatches told of exotic crimes or quaint local customs.

Coming up out of the subway, he saw that the sidewalks were

already crowded with men and women on their way to work. The voices were unexpectedly pleasing to his ear, with Southern locutions here and there. Close his eyes and he'd almost feel at home. The door of a breakfast joint opened to his right, unleashing the smell of bacon and warm toast.

He boarded a crowded eastbound bus, finding a seat toward the middle. On board it was warm, people fanning themselves with newspapers. Half the windows were jammed brokenly in the shut position, as if the bus company had taken the worst of its fleet and sent it here. His was the only white face. No one seemed to mind his presence, but everyone had taken notice.

Horton was a town where whites tended to reveal their social standing, and at least some of their politics, by the words they used to describe dark-skinned people. "Nigger" rolled freely off the tongues of those at the bottom, like Tom Strayhorn, the drunk who'd killed Rob. But even among the would-be gentry, who generally preferred "colored" or the standard-issue "Negro," a host of far less salubrious terms, as Danziger might have said, often came into play. Cain's grandmother had always said "niggra," no doubt thinking it to be quite acceptable. A jolly uncle, one of his favorites, went back and forth between "nig nog" and "jigaboo," depending on his mood. Cain himself was one of those Southerners who figured that an educated white man would never stoop to such usages, partly out of respect, but partly as well to indicate his place among the enlightened, a university man. In New York he'd given it no thought at all until now, seated on this bus, where his own social standing was beside the point. And that's when the thought occurred to him that many of these passengers—or at least many of the ones with the South still in their vowels—had come here specifically to escape places like Horton, and people like him. It was humbling, a little shaming. He glanced behind him, caught a probing gaze from an older man, and then turned back toward the front.

At the next stop a white cop in uniform boarded, and there was a noticeable change in the atmosphere. A few men stared openly, almost defiantly. Others looked away—out the window, or down at the floor. The cop didn't take a seat, pointedly avoiding one that a woman up front had opened for him by moving aside. He stood near the door, gripping a rail with his left hand while keeping a hand firmly atop his billy. His face broadcast an attitude somewhere between "I dare you" and "Who gives a fuck?"

The cop caught Cain's eye and nodded. Cain nodded back before realizing what he was doing, complicit now in this weird dynamic. He reddened under the collar, feeling like he'd betrayed his fellow passengers. Someone nearby made a remark he couldn't quite hear, and there was muffled laughter, the nodding of a few heads.

"Yes, yes," an older man said, drawing a glare from the uniform, who, mercifully, got off at the next stop. Cain relaxed a bit, but spent the rest of the ride staring out the window, and when he exited he felt their eyes on him, the man who'd shown his true allegiance. Another small way in which this city had turned out to be a lot like home.

At the end of 137th, he spotted a circle of uniformed cops down by the wharves, gathered like mourners around something on the ground. One of them saw him approaching and nodded to the others, who parted to open up a view of a woman's bare legs, bent slightly at the knees. Her glossy black slip was ripped along the thigh. There was something familiar about the translucent whiteness of her skin. As he moved closer he swallowed a lump in his throat when he saw that it was Angela Feinman, her head twisted at such a terrible angle that he knew right away that her neck was broken. He stopped, exhaled deeply, and collected himself.

The other cops smirked. A plainclothesman approached on his right.

"Are you Cain?"

He nodded.

"'Bout time, lover boy. She's been asking for you since sun-up."

The plainclothesman handed him a folded scrap of paper. Cain saw it was the page he'd torn from his notebook a few days ago at the theater, with his scribbled name and address.

"You must be Larsen."

"*Detective Sergeant* Larsen."

Cain squatted by the body, not wanting to touch, but wishing he could comfort her. A desolate sense of loneliness loomed about the cold, white body, her eyes staring at nothing. There was a purple bruise on her forehead, another on her left arm. No bullet holes, as far as he could tell, and no cigarette burns. Just the terrible wrenching of her neck.

A few flecks of encrusted blood caught his eye on the skin above her right breast. There was a small, fresh cut, probably from a knife, in the shape of an *L*, the mark of the Silver Shirts. Left as a calling card, perhaps. It looked as if one of their missing Germans was still alive and well, unless there were more of these fellows out there than he and Danziger had bargained for.

"Any idea who did this?" he asked Larsen.

"We were thinking you might know, seeing as how your name and number were stuffed in her garter, like it was her most valued possession." That got a few laughs from their audience. "What do you know about that cut mark? I'm thinking it's intentional."

"Probably. It's the sign of a Nazi group, the Silver Shirts. I'll give you some names."

"You could start by telling me hers."

"Angela Feinman. Worked at a theater at Third and 96th. Next of kin's a brother, Joel, who owns the place."

Larsen nodded to a uniform, who headed off to a radio patrol car to call it in.

They made him wait around until Joel arrived, which was fine with Cain because he had questions to ask. Larsen softened up after Cain gave him the names for Dieter and Gerhard, the two missing Germans, and the detective's mood improved further when Cain told him about the possible connection to the earlier murders of Werner Hansch and Klaus Schaller. If his disclosure meant that the cases would now be handed off to the Borough Homicide Bureau, then so be it. Obviously he hadn't been up to the job by himself, or even with Danziger's help, and Angela Feinman had paid for his inability to close it. He told Larsen the gist of his earlier conversation with Angela at the theater.

"And you've been working both those homicides?"

"Hansch, anyway. Schaller officially belongs to the one-nine."

"Surprised they haven't kicked it up to Borough."

"Probably will now. My captain will dance a jig."

"That bad, huh? Sounds just like mine. Here comes her brother. How 'bout I give you a few minutes alone with him?"

"That would be great. Thanks."

Joel Feinman, bald and unshaven and wearing a gray suit that was too tight around his massive shoulders, advanced up 137th like a man facing a firing squad. Cain intercepted him before he could reach the body.

"I've confirmed that it's your sister, in case you don't want to look."

"I want to see her," he said. "I'm her brother, for fuck's sake."

Feinman knelt next to Angela, covering his face with his right hand as his body sagged. He heaved out a sob and wiped his eyes, nearly losing his balance. Everyone gave him room, no more laughter, the uniforms turning their backs and lighting cigarettes. Their smoke caught on a breeze and blew toward the river. Joel stayed next to her a few minutes longer, touching Angela's shoulders and then her face. When he finally stood his lapels were wet with tears.

He walked straight over to Cain.

"Who found her?"

"You'll have to ask Detective Larsen. I spoke with her a few days ago, at the theater. That's why they called me here, she still had my number. Sounded like a pretty rough clientele you've got there. You think this had anything to do with her job?"

"Fucking Nazis. She loved making a buck off of 'em." He paused, shook his head. "Okay, so did I. But this . . ." He shook his head, took out a handkerchief and blew his nose. "Stupid fucks."

"Tell me something. Your English, well, it's a whole lot better than hers, if you don't mind me saying."

"She didn't come over until a few years ago. Barely got outta there, you wanna know the truth. I thought I'd saved her life." He shook his head. "Those *Dummkopfs* in the cheap seats thought her name was Sabine. Sabine Heinz, like the fucking ketchup. Just Aryan enough to fool them."

That solved the little mystery of Werner Hansch and his crude tattoo. No wonder she hadn't wanted to talk about Sabine.

"Did you know a customer named Werner Hansch?"

Feinman shook his head. Impossible to say if he was telling the truth.

"What about Klaus Schaller?"

He looked up abruptly.

"The guy who got shot? Five blocks away?"

"Five blocks from where?"

"From my house. It was in the papers."

"Yeah, him. Hansch is dead, too. That also made the papers, but not with his name. He had 'Sabine' tattooed on his arm. They fished him out of the Hudson a few days before Schaller was shot. That's when I asked your sister about him, before we even knew his name. She probably figured out who it was when I mentioned the tattoo, but she didn't let on."

Feinman puffed out his cheeks and exhaled loudly. He wiped his eyes with his handkerchief and then stuffed it in his pocket.

"She might have mentioned him once, this Werner creep. But she never told me he was dead. I didn't like the way she led them on."

"Maybe she shouldn't have been working there at all."

He looked up, suddenly furious. "Between the needle and the booze, I was the only person who'd hire her! Without the theater she would've been on the goddamn street, and without me she would've still been stuck in Berlin!"

"Admirable, but beside the point. Tell me about Lutz Lorenz."

That backed him down right away. Feinman looked at the ground and shook his head.

"Don't know the name."

"Angela said he fixed your ownership papers. For you and some guy named . . ." Cain flipped back through his notebook. "Albie Schreiber. To make it look like the real owner was Gerd Schultz."

"She said a lot of stuff that didn't make sense."

"Yeah, well. Maybe the DA's fraud squad would like to have a look at those papers."

"Hey, man. Those Bundist assholes would rip me to shreds if that ever came out."

"Like they did your sister, you mean? Your kind of help doesn't exactly seem to be making the world safe for democracy." It was harsh, but provocation seemed to be the only way to get anything out of him.

Feinman backed down. He again blew his nose and shook his head.

"What do you want to know about Lorenz?"

"He's disappeared."

"So I heard, but that's all I know. I hear the Feds took him."

"Feds? What about maybe some guy from the DA's office, named Gurfein?"

"The rackets guy?" Feinman frowned. "Why would he be in it with a bunch of guys from Immigration?"

"Immigration?"

"That's what I hear. And Lorenz is a citizen, so go figure. People say they think he's some kind of enemy of the state, like a spy or something. They're even saying he might get, what do you call it? *Denaturalized.* Then deported. Last I heard, they'd moved his whole family right out into the harbor, to Ellis Island."

"Where all the immigrants come in?"

"Used to. Now it's where Uncle Sam runs 'em out of the country. And if that's where they took Lorenz, then he's probably been ticketed for deportation. They've been rounding up quite a few krauts up my way. Guys with too many pictures of Hitler on the wall, or maybe with a shortwave set in the basement. That kind of shit."

Cain wrote it down. Then he scribbled his name and number on a page, which he tore out and gave to Feinman, just like with Angela. He placed a hand on Feinman's shoulder.

"I'm sorry about your sister. I wish she'd leveled with me."

"And what, you would've helped her? You fucks have never lifted a finger for any of us. You just figure all us mugs up in Yorkville can fight it out among ourselves, like the Chinks down in Chinatown. Or all the poor fuckers in Harlem."

He tossed Cain's number aside and walked away. Larsen took off after him. A gust caught Cain's scrap of paper and blew it out onto the Harlem River, where it began floating away on the outgoing tide.

Cain lit a cigarette and watched until it was out of sight.

# 24

·····················

CAIN WAS IN A BLEAK MOOD for the rest of the day. He tried phoning Danziger, but couldn't reach him. Then he called Beryl and invited her to dinner, hoping it would lift his gloom. They took Olivia with them and walked to a diner, one with booths so they wouldn't have to sit all in a row at the counter.

Olivia's presence meant Cain couldn't go into much detail about the events of that morning, which was just as well. Every time he shut his eyes he saw the cold whiteness of Angela Feinman's corpse, bare to the salty breeze, the tiny *L* gouged into her skin.

"Have you seen Danziger lately?" Beryl asked.

"We made kind of a house call together yesterday."

"Who's Danziger?" Olivia asked.

She was observing them closely, as if trying to determine how important Beryl was to her father. This dinner was becoming a more complicated enterprise than he'd bargained for.

"Olivia hasn't met him?" Beryl said.

"No. Although he seems to know all about her, even from the first time I met him. Including how she got her name."

"From that play, you mean?" Olivia said.

"Yes, sweetie." Then, in answer to Beryl's questioning gaze, "Shakespeare. *Twelfth Night*. Clovis liked it, because in the play Olivia is beautiful, of noble birth, and has plenty of suitors."

Olivia frowned, either because they were talking about her or because he had mentioned her mother's name in the presence of this other woman who hadn't yet earned the privilege. Or maybe, based on what she said next, it was because he still hadn't answered her question.

"I *said*, 'Who's Danziger?'"

"A man I'm working with. He's very smart and very mysterious. Miss Beryl knows him, too, and sometimes she calls him Sascha. But she won't tell me all that much about him."

Cain smiled to show he was joking, but he wasn't sure Beryl took it that way.

"Why won't you tell my daddy about Mr. Danziger?"

"Because my uncle likes me to keep my mouth shut about his friends, and Mr. Danziger is his friend." She turned toward Cain and searched his eyes. He searched back. They held the pose long enough to annoy Olivia, who sighed and began slurping through her straw at the dregs of her milkshake.

"Sweetie, that's impolite."

"He still has you at a disadvantage, doesn't he?" Beryl asked. "By knowing more about you than you do about him."

Cain told her about the police file, yet to be exhumed from the Hall of Records. She didn't seem at all surprised to learn of the demise of Alexander Dalitz.

"Damon Runyon wrote about him once. I do know that, from Uncle Fedya."

"*The* Damon Runyon? About Danziger?"

"About Alexander Dalitz. I've never seen it, but Uncle Fedya swears it was a whole column, not just a mention. He probably still has a copy somewhere, but I doubt he'd show me, now that I'm sleeping with the enemy." She blushed, and glanced at Olivia. "Figuratively speaking, of course."

"What does 'figuratively' mean?" Olivia asked.

"It means you shouldn't take what she just said literally."

"About what?"

"It's not important."

Olivia frowned, well aware that adults only said that when you'd missed something important.

"You mean about Damon Runyon?" she said. "Who is he?"

"A famous writer. He's got a column in the newspaper. Most of the people he writes about are really interesting, but not always in a good way."

"Like saboteurs?"

"No, not like that. And Mr. Danziger is a good man, and is helping Daddy. I'd just like to know more about what he used to do, a long time ago." He wondered how long it might take him to find the column at the public library.

"He sounds like one of those people who knows your business better than his own business," Olivia said.

"That's a very good way of putting it," Beryl said.

Cain was less impressed. The words were another favorite expression of Clovis's—the second time in as many days that Olivia had quoted her mother. He wondered if she was doing it to make a point. Letting him know that he was still a husband, for example, or that she still had a mom, absent or not. Or maybe, like him, his daughter was thinking about Clovis more now that she was living in her mother's old city.

"If he used to be bad, wouldn't he still be bad?"

Good question. Cain had no answer, so Beryl gave it a try.

"Unless he really wasn't so bad to begin with, but did bad things for good reasons."

Olivia frowned. "That sounds like something Benny would say in my class at school."

"I do know he worked as an interpreter for a while," Beryl said. "On Ellis Island, for the government."

"You're kidding," Cain said. "Did you hear that from your uncle?"

She nodded. "Some rabbi got him the job, when he was only sixteen."

He realized she meant a real rabbi, not a political hack.

"Who was the rabbi?"

"Rabbi Kaufman. Quite famous in his day. A do-gooder trying to keep all his promising young Hebrew scholars out of trouble, to hear Uncle Fedya tell it."

"I'm guessing he was unsuccessful."

"Not with Uncle Fedya. The rabbi got a storefront law firm on Delancey to take him on as a gofer. He stayed for thirty years. Sascha wasn't as lucky. Apparently he was fired his first week on the job."

"As an interpreter? You'd think he would've been great at it."

"I think it had something to do with lying on his application."

"About his age?"

"About being fluent in Turkish and Greek."

Cain laughed.

"Well, imagine that. Sascha Danziger, not being completely honest about himself. Ellis Island, though. Too bad he doesn't still work there."

"Why?"

"There's someone out there who both of us need to see. Detained, or so I've heard. Apparently they're using the place now for sending people *out* of the country."

"Yes. Enemy aliens. Even though some of them have been living here harmlessly for years. People we work with have ended up there."

"Have you been there?"

"A few times. There's a charity boat that goes once a week. They deliver books and magazines, letters, clothing. You'd be surprised. There are probably six hundred people out there, living in a big barracks with nowhere to go."

"Could they take me? Could you?" She frowned, so he retreated a bit. "Not as a cop. Or not *officially* as a cop. I'd be out of my jurisdiction anyway." The frown deepened. Her usual reflexive reaction against authority, he supposed. Olivia didn't seem to approve, either. She, too, could sense when one friend was attempting to use another. But this was important, and for a moment he considered employing Beryl's earlier line about doing bad things for good reasons. Then he looked at Beryl's face and decided against it.

"Forget it," he said. "What's for dessert?"

This coaxed a smile out of Olivia, and they moved on to a discussion of whether pie was better with or without ice cream. They opted for the former, and polished it off like pigeons attacking a crust of bread.

Coffee arrived. The waitress cleared their dishes and brought the check.

"My treat," Cain said. "You hardly ate a thing. Well, except for that slice of pie."

Beryl's expression turned solemn. She leaned across the table.

"This trip to Ellis Island—would Sascha be going with you?"

"Of course. I'd need him for language alone. German, in case you're wondering."

She sipped her coffee and thought it over.

"The next boat is tomorrow. It's short notice, but if I made a few calls I might be able to get us aboard. Do you think you can reach Sascha?"

"Yes."

"Because if he doesn't go, then you're not going."

"Scout's honor."

She held his gaze before nodding. Then she reached for the check. "In that case, I'll pay my own way. I won't be bought, you know. I'm not a police informer."

Cain would've smiled, except she was serious. With mixed emotions, he nodded and began totaling their shares.

# 25

......................

I HAD EXPECTED A LARGER BOAT, something solid and sea-worthy, but this so-called ferry more closely resembled a tugboat in shape and size, and as I stepped aboard it rocked slightly, which brought back a myriad of fears and hesitations.

"You okay?" Mr. Cain asked, sounding more like a New Yorker than he ever had. "You don't look okay."

"It has been a long while since I last put to sea."

"To sea? We're crossing the harbor. It'll take fifteen minutes, tops. Look, you can see where we're going, right over your shoulder."

I knew the view he was referring to. The long red rooftop of the Great Hall. The four domed towers with their spires and elaborate brickwork, looming above the island like minarets. Even from our point of departure at the Battery you could see all of it clearly in the morning sunlight, although it was already etched into my memory as solidly as the carvings upon a marble memorial. Less from the last time I'd gone there than from the first, forty years ago, when it had all been brand-new and I was a mere boy, flanked protectively by my parents, Solomon and Anna. We first cast our eyes upon this prospect as we stood upon the open deck of an oceangoing steamship, eagerly awaiting our arrival upon the shores of the United States.

The crew cast off the lines, and the diesel fumes blew toward us with a roar of the engines. The boat surged out into the harbor. I lurched toward the rail, holding on to steady myself.

"Maybe you should sit down," Mr. Cain said. Beryl had boarded ahead of us and was showing our Red Cross permission forms to the crew.

"No. Let us go forward. We will stand at the stern."

"The bow, I think you mean."

"Yes. The bow. I am not a nautical man."

And with good reason, although it was not a reason I wished to elucidate to Mr. Cain, or even to Beryl, now or ever.

I initiated our trip to the bow because I had decided to lay siege to my anxieties by confronting them head-on. We stood at the rail, where the spray heaved up at us from the bouncing hull. Hull—I do know that word. Then, in an act of defiance against my emotions, I turned my face toward our destination just as Mr. Cain addressed me again.

"Something I should tell you before Beryl joins us," he said.

"Yes?"

"Our two missing Germans might not be lying as low as we thought. I think one of them might have killed Hansch's Sabine. Except that wasn't her real name. It was Angela Feinman."

"The young lady from the movie house?"

Cain nodded.

"How horrifying. Perhaps they discovered she was a Jew."

"Or maybe they blamed her for what happened to Hansch, and then Schaller."

"Either would be sufficient grounds for their sort. But how do you know it was them?"

"I don't. But whoever did it marked her up with a knife. They carved one of those little *L*s just above her right breast."

I shuddered at the thought of it, and then nodded.

"Another good reason to find them as soon as possible," I said. "Perhaps Lorenz will know their whereabouts."

I tried to turn my attention to the task at hand, although I certainly drew no comfort from the sight facing me from across the water.

As our benefactor for this excursion, Beryl was officially represent-ing her employer, the American Red Cross. Also aboard were min-ions of the National Council of Jewish Women, the Daughters of the American Revolution, the Woman's Christian Temperance Union, and the YWCA. This cadre of charities had filled the cargo area with boxes of mail, books, and hand-me-down clothing for use by the marooned inhabitants of the island.

Beryl had already given us our marching orders for how to behave once we went ashore.

"Stick with me if you hope to succeed," she said. "They're pretty strict about access, but I know a few tricks that might help give you a little more freedom of movement."

I sensed in her demeanor an eagerness to tweak the noses of the federal authorities who ran the island. I suppose that is her way of rationalizing lending assistance to a police investigation. Having done so, she was now caught up in the spirit of our enterprise, and seemed intent on helping us locate and then interview Lutz Lorenz in as much privacy as possible.

She had suggested that once we arrived she should act as our inter-mediary. Her very sound reasoning was that a policeman asking for Mr. Lorenz might send him scurrying for the nearest bolthole. Mr. Cain thought that was a splendid idea, although it is clear to me that he would agree to almost any suggestion of Beryl's, such is his level of enchantment. It was fortunate that Fedya was not present to see the two of them exchanging admiring glances.

She soon joined us at the rail as the spray continued to blow into our faces.

"Are you all right, Sascha?" She could read the discomfort in my eyes.

"Fine," I said, nodding with what I hoped was a mien of steely resolve.

"I don't think he likes boats," Mr. Cain said.

"I'm guessing it's more than that," she said. "This must bring back a lot of memories. You first came here, when, around the turn of the century?"

I eyed them closely. There were some things I could comfortably reveal, and others I could not. Fortunately, the tale of my arrival was among the former.

"It was 1902. They had just reopened the Great Hall, after the old one burned to the ground. There were probably three hundred people out on the decks that day. Everyone was exhausted by our crossing, but exhilarated by our arrival. My father put me up on his shoulders while my mother held my right hand."

As I spoke, the Statue of Liberty loomed closer on our left. Not nearly as close as it had been on that day of my arrival, when our ship had approached from the open waters of the Atlantic, but close enough to stir some long-dormant emotions. Judging from what Mr. Cain said next, he'd seen me glancing at it.

"It must have been thrilling to see her for the first time. After coming all that way, I mean. Thrilling for everybody."

I saw in the glitter of his eyes his love for his country, and I was pleased for him. Still, I owed him the truth—on this matter, at least. So I offered it. "I found her to be terrifying."

"The Statue of Liberty?" He looked crestfallen. "I thought everyone was supposed to be overjoyed?"

"My parents were. My father lifted me as high as he could, to see above the crowd. That is when the fear began to grow inside of me. She was too stern, too forbidding. Look at her closely, Mr. Cain, and see her as a child might, standing guard with those blank, pitiless eyes. And her torch, raised like a weapon."

Mr. Cain did as I asked, but I knew he didn't see it. Even Beryl looked perplexed, although she nodded politely, as if to humor me.

"When we passed directly in front of her, I began to cry. I was sure she was about to reach out with her torch and set our ship aflame. I screamed for my father to put me down."

Mr. Cain laughed.

"My father laughed also. He was so happy that day that he wept tears of joy. But when my mother saw my face she became very quiet. Even then, I think she knew."

"Knew what?" Beryl asked.

"That my fear was an omen."

"An omen?"

A long pause. The hull boomed beneath our feet, sending a sheet of spray, higher than the others, into our faces like a slap from a barber after a shave. Beryl and Mr. Cain exchanged puzzled glances.

"That is a story for another day," I said, averting my eyes from Lady Liberty's, which were still as unfeeling as ever. "Look! On the island. You can see them coming out into the yard."

A line of bedraggled-looking people in dark clothing spilled out of a doorway onto the open ground between the front of the Great Hall and the harbor. There was no grass, only a barren tract of pounded gray soil. A high chain link fence blocked them from the water, but their view of Manhattan was unobstructed. A group of young men ran to one end and began kicking a ball between them. To the side, another cluster of people huddled in almost formal poses, and as we drew closer I saw that they were Japanese. Now I heard a smattering of Italian on the wind, lively and expressive, from a knot of three men gesturing with their hands. A language that will forever make my heart fill. There was German, too, low and bristling with its stout consonants.

"Do you see him?" Cain asked, from over my right shoulder.

I realized he was asking about Lorenz. I scanned the crowds, which were still trickling onto the grounds for their afternoon promenade.

"No. I suppose he might still be indoors."

"I asked about him among some of the others," Beryl said, nodding toward the representatives of the other charities. "Apparently he has a bit of a reputation. A cardsharp, an operator. And that's after only a few days on the island."

"Yes, that sounds like Lutz."

By then the boat had begun turning into the mouth of the long slip that bisects the island. My view of the building and grounds was almost exactly as it had been in 1902. A tremor coursed up my back. This was one reason I was never able to stomach working here in those later years when a kindly rabbi landed me a job. Three days was all I could bear. Then I stopped coming. I told the rabbi that I had argued with a supervisor. For my friends, I concocted a far more colorful version, saying I'd lied on my application, claiming fluency in Turkish.

Perhaps if the rabbi had found me employment elsewhere I might have stayed the course he had charted for me, thus avoiding all that happened later—the good as well as the bad. But once we have made our appointments with fate, I suppose it is impossible to weasel out of them. Maybe that is why I am returning now, to begin attending to unfinished business that has awaited me for far too long.

The boat eased toward its place at the wharf, and the crew stood ready to toss the lines ashore. My heart fluttered. I saw that Mr. Cain was again watching me carefully, in the manner of a scientist studying a specimen. He had enjoyed the boat ride, I could tell. He was relieved to be momentarily free of Manhattan, with its crowds and its close smells and its rising warmth which, all too soon, will gave way to the soft-tar furnace of summer. He may even have been wishing his daughter were here, to make an outing of our crossing.

But for me it was all memories, a ship of ghosts. Even now, silent hosts were filing past me, smelling of their weeks at sea, of the tattered world they'd left behind.

The boat bumped the wharf. We had arrived.

# 26

................

BERYL HERDED THEM TOWARD THE STERN.

"If we're to stick to our cover, first we'll have to earn our keep. Give me some help with these boxes."

"Sure," Cain said, eager to please. Danziger was slower to respond. To Cain he looked more ashen and worn than at any time since they'd met. At first he ascribed it to seasickness, but now he believed Beryl was right. Memories were to blame, and not just the specter of Lady Liberty. Cain wondered what must have happened here, but didn't feel it was his business to ask.

They hefted two boxes apiece and headed for the gangplank, where the other passengers were already going ashore.

"The crew will bring the rest," she said. "Set them down over there, where you see the other ones."

"It is the same spot where they unloaded our steamer trunks and carpet bags," Danziger said, his gaze a blank. He saw Cain watching him and looked away. From the dock they could see only part of the grounds at the front of the building, but there was still no sign of Lorenz.

"Follow me," Beryl said.

They moved toward a doorway on the left side of the main building, then up some marble steps through a double door. Inside, bored-looking men and women sat at desks with in-baskets, blotters, and rubber stamps—the very picture of officious obstruction. But they seemed to know Beryl, and waved her through. One of them even smiled.

"These two are with me," she said, smiling back.

They passed through a second set of doors and found themselves barricaded from the rest of the room by two long tables of stained pine that formed a giant L. Chairs on both sides faced each other across a low partition that ran down the length of the tables.

"This is the visiting area," Beryl said.

On the near side, several chairs were already occupied by waiting visitors. Cain noticed soldiers lurking here and there. He didn't like the idea of being overheard.

"If you want to play it safe, we could ask a guard to find Lorenz. But I'm allowed upstairs, and maybe they'll let you come with me. If so, you can try to pick him out from the crowd."

"I am not entirely sure I will recognize him," Danziger said. "I have not laid eyes upon him in many a year. But if he is already as notorious as you imply, we can always inquire of others."

"Then let's go," Beryl said.

She moved quickly. At the top of the stairs the doors opened onto a huge room with a soaring rooftop and a buzz of voices. By then, Danziger's breathing was labored, and he looked stunned.

"You need a rest?" Cain asked.

"How appropriate that you should ask. These steps were the first test of health for all new arrivals. My mother was feeling weak, but she made it without faltering. There was an inspector seated just there, off to the side, eyeing everyone for signs of illness. We learned this only later, of course. If he selected you, you were marched straight off to the doctors, perhaps never to return. I remember clearly what he said as we passed, because he spoke in very bad German: 'Get upstairs, cattle. You will soon have a nice little pen!'"

Beryl took him gently by the arm and led him forward. Cain wondered if her ancestors had also arrived here. He had no idea when his own family had come to America or where they'd landed, beyond a hazy knowledge that they'd settled in rural North Carolina in the late eighteenth century.

They moved deeper into the room, Cain expecting to be shouted down at any moment by one of the guards. Tables, chairs, and couches were clustered here and there. Perhaps thirty or forty people were scattered around the cavernous hall at this hour, since almost everyone else was outdoors. Six children, all of them younger than Olivia, shrieked with glee as they weaved through the tables at one end, playing tag. Older men sat smoking as they read newspapers and magazines. A few women were sewing, or talking in small groups. At the far end, two round tables were filled with men playing cards. Smoke rose from their cigarettes like the effluent of a small factory.

"I think that might be him," Danziger said. "At the card tables, the one on the left. See the fellow who looks like he's holding court?"

Cain saw right away who he meant. Lutz Lorenz had an air of command, or perhaps confidence was the better word. Even from here you couldn't miss his knowing expression, the deft movements as he dealt the cards. He struck Cain as one of those enviable men who could walk into a party, or a tavern, and within minutes look right at home, with a hostess or bartender already at his beck and call, and the respectful attention of his peers.

"They are hanging on his every word," Danziger said.

"He's also got the biggest pile of chips. Probably bluffing them right and left."

"His father's son." Danziger smiled.

"Would you like me to approach him for you?" Beryl asked. "He looks like the type who might easily become suspicious."

"We should approach him together," Danziger said. "But you speak first. If he is like his father, a feminine face will appeal to his greatest weakness."

As they drew nearer, Cain heard low voices in German and saw the men sliding chips toward a pile in the center. Lorenz said something that made the others laugh. When he saw the approaching trio he frowned, put down his cards, and spoke in perfect English.

"The lady is welcome to observe us. As for the two gentlemen, I am afraid that it is too late to deal anyone else into the game, and I don't wish you to stand there looking at our cards. So, if you please . . ."

Cain and Beryl hesitated, but Danziger continued past them until he was standing behind Lorenz's right shoulder. It left Lorenz little choice about what to do next, unless he wished to have Danziger looming over him like a bird of prey.

Lorenz scraped back his chair and stood. His look of easy congeniality was gone. The blue of his eyes turned colder. He gave no sign of recognizing Danziger, although their foreheads were only inches apart. No one said a word. The click of one chip against another was as jarring as if someone had cleared his throat.

"Look at me closely, Lutz," Danziger said calmly. Lorenz furrowed his brow. Something had registered, but his eyes said he wasn't quite ready to believe it.

"It is me, Lutz. Max Dalitz."

Lorenz's mouth opened and shut without any words emerging. Then it opened again.

"How . . . ?"

"With your father's help. But that is for another time. What is important now is that I owe him a debt of gratitude, so I have come to assist you in matters that only I will know how to handle. Am I making myself clear?"

"Let's go somewhere with a little more privacy."

He turned toward the others, who had put down their cards and were staring. It was clear they weren't accustomed to seeing Lutz Lorenz in any situation in which he was uncomfortable.

"Gentlemen . . ." he said. Then he corrected himself: "Meine Herren . . ."

The rest of his words were a stream of German. Lorenz tossed his cards onto the table and left his chips. The men nodded but said little, seemingly in awe of the entire episode. Cain, Danziger, Beryl, and Lorenz crossed the room to a space where three folding chairs faced each other in a tight circle. The only neighbor was an older woman on a couch, working at an elaborate piece of embroidery in a shaft of filtered sunlight. She looked up, frowning when she saw Lorenz. She gathered up her sewing, tutted under her breath, and departed hastily. Danziger watched with interest.

Beryl touched Cain's arm.

"I will leave you to your business," she whispered. "I'll keep an eye out for anyone who takes too much of an interest."

"Thanks."

"Good luck."

The men took their seats. Danziger spoke first. "You seem to have acquired quite a reputation, Lutz, for someone who has been here for such a short time."

"In this place you either make an immediate impression or you're swallowed whole by blanket disregard." He surveyed the room, shaking his head. "It's that or turn into a monk. The wakeup bell at six twenty, breakfast fifty minutes later. Germans and Italians at one end, Japs at the other. Exercise at eight for those who want it. Lunch at noon, more exercise at three, supper at five fifteen, lights out at ten. And just when you're beginning to really sleep, the bell rings again."

"And poker all day long?"

He shrugged.

"What do your new neighbors make of your politics?"

Lorenz snorted, shrugging again. "Stooges for Hitler, all of them. Fools and blowhards. But I never speak of that, or even the Fatherland. I deal with them on more pragmatic terms. We live by a capitalist culture here, and I've been able to bring certain assets to the table."

"In order to comport yourself in this manner, I gather you must have been able to smuggle in quite a bit of cash?"

Lorenz smiled, but said nothing.

"Where is your family?"

Lorenz lowered his head, the first sign that his cocksure attitude was an act.

"I won't discuss them. They're back on the mainland, somewhere far from Yorkville. It was never them they wanted, anyway. Just me."

"Who, exactly, wanted you, Lutz?"

He looked away and shook his head.

"All right, then. We know it was Gurfein's doing, even if Immigration brought you here."

Lorenz narrowed his eyes.

"Who's this other fellow with you? What's his business here?"

Danziger and Cain exchanged glances. They'd discussed earlier whether to tell Lorenz that Cain was a cop, but they'd never reached a decision. Cain sensed that now might be the right time to come clean.

"I'm a cop," he said. "A detective, nothing to do with Gurfein. If anything, I've got him in my sights. Plus a few other mugs, in the matter of a couple murders of some people you knew. Werner Hansch and Klaus Schaller."

Lorenz lowered his head and placed his hands on his knees. He was close enough for Cain to smell, and the scent was familiar—that of a jailed man, as if confinement itself was something that got under your skin and emerged in your sweat. When Lorenz finally looked up, he was a shade paler.

"That could have been me, out there in the river. I'll at least give Gurfein that, that he didn't stoop to anything as low as burning me full of cigarette holes, or shooting me in the face. For that alone I suppose I owe him my silence."

"Was it Gurfein's people who knocked them off?"

Lorenz shook his head.

"Is that a no?"

"I cannot, *will* not, say anything more."

He folded his arms. Cain looked to Danziger, who touched Lorenz's knee and leaned closer, speaking in the manner of an old confidant.

"Come, Lutz. You are acquainted with how these things work. I am sure that Mr. Gurfein, whatever his role in these affairs, intends to do well by you if at all possible. No doubt he was the one who arranged for the relocation of your family." Lorenz looked up, but didn't nod. "But we also know that he cannot possibly keep their whereabouts a secret forever. And if others wish you to do their bidding, that is how they will choose to apply leverage, no matter how long you remain here. Yes?"

"As if you could do anything about it."

"We could, in fact. Why else do you think we came? Why else would I be attempting to repay your father for all that he once did for me? And when that day comes, when those people go looking for your wife, your mother, your children, you will want to avail yourself of every asset at your disposal. As for Mr. Gurfein, yes, of course you will still want his allegiance. But we both know how short the memories of those kinds of people can be. It is his job to keep you and your loved ones safe, but not his avocation, not his solemn vow. And who is to say how long he will remain in his job? It is the government, Lutz. Men come and men go. Will his replacement have the same allegiance, the same sense of loyalty? Your friends, however—your oldest friends, in particular—those are forever, Lutz. As you know."

Lorenz uncrossed his arms. He picked at a piece of lint on his trousers and looked at Danziger.

"They first came to me four months ago. In December, a week or so after Pearl."

"Who did, Lutz?" Danziger asked. "Who came to you?"

"Please!" His eyes flared. "I have to tell this in my own way."

"Of course. As you wish."

Cain offered a Lucky. Lorenz nodded and took it, but waved away the offer of a match and pulled a gleaming Zippo from his pocket. Seeing Cain's impressed reaction, he said, "I won it yesterday, from those idiots at the table. Their poker is even worse than their politics."

He lit it, inhaled luxuriously, and flicked ashes onto the marble floor.

"They were Italian, to answer your question. And there was only one of them. He did not offer a name, but he fit the type. His suit, his hat, the bulge in his jacket, the way he talked. A goombah of the first order. And in case I was not already convinced, he made sure I knew by paying in cash, a big bag of it. In exchange, all I had to do was provide him with the names of four trustworthy German workers. And keep my mouth shut, of course."

"That's all?" Cain said.

"No. That's never all, is it, Sascha?"

Danziger showed no reaction. Lorenz continued: "They did not want just any Germans. They asked that these men be sympathetic to the current regime in Berlin. They said they only needed me as a procurer. They assured me that for any further involvement they would find a more prominent sponsor from the community in Yorkville. Someone a bit more prosperous, and who shared their backward politics."

"A Nazi, then," Danziger said. "Or perhaps a Bundist."

Lorenz nodded, took another drag.

"To assist with my recruitment, I was told to explain to these four men that they would be given union cards and provided with lucrative employment on a waterfront sector on the West Side."

"What union?" Cain asked.

Lorenz glared at him, and flicked ashes toward his knees. "The longshoremen. I don't know which local. I suggested that, to further insulate both of us, they use fake names on their union cards. The Italian liked that idea very much. He took it to his superiors, and when he came back they had even provided him with the names. Strange choices, but so be it."

"Strange how?" Danziger said.

"German poets and writers. I had the idea that someone was trying to show how smart he was. How educated. Or maybe it was just for a laugh. Heinrich Heine for Werner Hansch. Friedrich Schiller for Klaus Schaller. Wolfgang Goethe for the third one, Dieter Göllner. Thomas Mann for the fourth, Gerhard Muntz."

"Spell those last two," Cain said. "The real names—I've got the writers."

The question made Lorenz smile and turn toward Danziger.

"Nice to see you're working with a more educated class of people," he said. "No wonder you decided to—"

"Enough!" Danziger said. "There is no need to cover old ground."

Lorenz tilted his head and looked back and forth between Danziger and Cain. He smiled as the dynamics of the relationship dawned on him.

"You really have no idea about this man, do you?" he asked Cain.

"Some."

Lorenz chuckled, smoke puffing from his nostrils.

"It might behoove the both of you to know that the Feds have posted undercover men among the population here. Rats and snitches. Their German is excellent. They're not so hard to spot for someone like me, so I play it cool when I have to. But for you two? You can bet that by the end of the day their bosses will know you've been here, and who you came to see. One of them is watching even as we speak."

Cain decided not to rise to the bait by looking around; neither did Danziger. Even if true, there was nothing they could do about it now.

"You said they were going to find an official sponsor for these men," Danziger said. "Another German with Bundist leanings. Did you help them with that choice?"

Lorenz shook his head. "They didn't ask, and I didn't volunteer. I wanted as little to do with them as possible. I never even heard his name."

"Never heard it, or never knew it?" Cain asked.

Lorenz took another drag on his cigarette.

"And who was this Italian?" Danziger asked.

"I told you. He never offered his name."

"Not the errand boy. His boss. Who was he working for?"

"Do you think an errand boy would have been fool enough to tell me?"

"Of course not. But you would not have been fool enough to proceed without finding out."

Lorenz went a little pale. He shook his head and leaned down to stub out his cigarette on the floor. Danziger waited for more, but Lorenz again crossed his arms.

"Okay, then," Cain said. "What were these four Germans supposed to do?"

"No one told me, and I didn't ask. Supposedly their sponsor was going to be in on it, but I'm not even sure of that. That was the last I heard of it."

"Until Hansch and Schaller turned up dead."

"Yes."

"Why'd they round you up?"

"You don't know?" He looked truly puzzled. "Isn't that why you're here, with the same damn questions, the same damn accusations? As if I knew all along what they'd been hired for? It's like I said to that asshole Gurfein. All I knew about any of that business was what I read in the papers, like everybody else. Some dumb mick or whoever it was with a blowtorch. One spark and the whole damn ship goes up like a Roman candle."

"Ship?" Cain looked at Danziger, who wrinkled his brow.

"The *Normandie*, you stupid fucks. At Pier 88."

Cain felt like he'd had the wind knocked out of him, and had to take a deep breath. He lowered his voice and leaned closer, elbows on his knees.

"You're saying these men of yours were hired for sabotage?"

"They were not *my* men!" Lorenz said, almost hissing the answer to keep his voice down. "And I told you, I was not aware of why they were hired! I was the middleman, nothing more. I made a few calls, took care of some paperwork, and stepped out of the picture. I kept my head down and my mouth shut. And if one of those four lugs really did do it, then it's not on me, you can be damn sure of that. It's like I told Gurfein. Ask the Italian, if you can find him. Although if you've got any brains, you'll never want to."

"Luciano?" Danziger asked. "Is it Lucky?"

"He's in prison," Lorenz said, shaking his head. "He's miles from all this." Then, narrowing his eyes: "Unless you know something I don't."

"So if not Lucky, then who?"

"I told you, I *don't know*! So stop asking!"

Cain saw the fear in his eyes. The man knew the name, all right, but he'd never tell them, and maybe not even Gurfein. Which made Cain wonder if that was why Lorenz was here, being held in exile until he talked, until he gave up the names. If so, then Lorenz had decided that silence and confinement were safer options, at least for now.

The stakes were bigger than ever. The murders of a couple of small-bore Germans, important to almost no one, now felt like part of something important enough to draw the attention of all kinds of people, including the unlikely gathering that Danziger had seen around the breakfast table at Longchamps.

No one said a word. It was as if the gravity of the matter had silenced them all, a silence that was then broken by the sound of footsteps approaching briskly from behind. Lorenz looked up in surprise.

"Sascha! Woodrow!" Beryl had rejoined them from her outpost, and she nodded over her shoulder toward two men in uniform who were headed their way. One wore an officer's stripes.

"All right, you two," the officer said. "Time for you to leave the island. I'm not quite sure how you were able to take advantage of this young woman's trust, or exactly what you intended to accomplish here this afternoon, but I'm going to insist that both of you be thoroughly searched. You will then be escorted to the ferry dock for immediate departure."

Danziger and Cain stood. Beryl, head down, stood behind the soldiers with her hands behind her back. Lorenz wore a guilty smile. He lit another Lucky. Cain saw now that he had the pack.

After a vigorous frisk—and, thank goodness, they let Cain keep his notebook after he showed his shield—the two soldiers marched them toward the exit, with Beryl sheepishly bringing up the rear. People all over the Great Hall stared. A few of the card-playing Germans looked quite amused.

Cain was embarrassed. Danziger, however, seemed curiously unmoved. In fact, his most evident emotion seemed to be relief, as if he couldn't wait to get away from it all.

They boarded the boat and were escorted to seats in the cabin. A soldier remained on guard at the gangplank until the crew cast off. The engines roared, and within seconds they were easing back into the harbor.

"This is bigger than we thought," Cain said, staring straight ahead.

"Or as big as I feared," Danziger answered.

"But where's the FBI in all this? If this was a sabotage investigation, they'd be in this up to their elbows. Instead it's the rackets guy from the DA's office—on his own, for all we know—plus some Navy guy operating way out of bounds at the Astor, and a few hoods representing the worst of the worst, or what's left of it."

Danziger nodded. "It is wartime," he said. "I have seen it before, in 1918. People in high places stop paying attention to many things that interested them so keenly during peacetime. This, in turn, creates opportunities for those with fertile imaginations."

"Opportunities for mischief, you mean."

"The sort of mischief in which men end up facedown in the Hudson."

Cain looked out across the water, wondering who else might be bobbing just below the surface. The Manhattan skyline was straight ahead. Lady Liberty kept watch from their right. He glanced in her direction, wondering if he would ever again view her in quite the same way.

Then he looked at Danziger. The older man was gazing dead ahead, as if he didn't dare look back. His eyes shone. He hadn't put his hat on, and his white hair blew in all directions.

He looked terrified.

# 27

........................

"YOU'RE AN HOUR LATE, CAIN."

Captain Mulhearn was on the warpath, and he hadn't even opened his morning papers. Everything that Lorenz had told them about the sabotage plot was still whirling in Cain's mind, but he could already sense he was about to be sidetracked.

"I was out checking a lead in the Hansch case."

"Yeah, well. Borough Homicide wants a look at that whole package, so don't get too comfortable. We had two break-ins last night up on 39th, and the precinct squad's already got its hands full at the scene. They'll be needing your help on the paperwork."

Another punishment detail, plain and simple.

"Oh, and speaking of paperwork, somebody fucked up the UF-9 on that bunco artist you busted, Kannerman."

"That wasn't even my collar."

"But it was your tip on the address, and now some prosecutor downtown has a bug up his ass about how it was handled. He wants you to come straighten it out. Here. You're meeting him at noon."

Mulhearn handed him a scribbled note. There was a name, Ben Revis, plus an address on Bleecker Street. Between that and the break-ins, he'd be lucky to get back to the Hansch case by late afternoon. He could only hope Danziger would make progress on the union side of things, checking for the literary aliases Lorenz gave them. He also had to hope the Borough Homicide detectives didn't come take the file while he was gone. If word got out about the *Normandie* connection, he might even lose the case to the Feds. And given the nature of federal involvement so far—the detention of Lorenz on Ellis Island where he was practically unreachable, the peripheral and perhaps unauthorized role of some officer from Naval Intelligence—Cain suspected the Feds might be more preoccupied with sweeping the whole thing under a rug. Now if he only knew why.

The mention of the botched UF-9, however, did give him a pretext to go back down to the 95 Room, where he hoped to get another few minutes to poke around. Piled among his messages was yet another call from Linwood Archer, and the sooner he could get Archer off his back, the more time he'd have for the case of the Germans.

He rushed downstairs at a minute after eleven. Officers Steele and Rose had already left for their regular break. Cain looked both ways and was reaching into his pocket for the key when Maloney's voice called out from behind.

"Hey, asshole, What are you doing lurking around here like some kind of ghost?"

Cain, heart jumping, let go of the key and withdrew his hand from his pocket.

"I need a UF-9 from the other day, but these lazy fucks aren't here," he said.

"They're never here at this hour, nimrod, which you damn well ought to know." Maloney got right up in his face. "And maybe you ought to just stay the fuck away from here, unless you want to go for another ride, and this time it won't be to your rabbi's supper club."

Cain pushed past him and headed for the exit. He needed air and some time to think. The paperwork on the break-ins could wait, although he supposed the noon meeting with the prosecutor, Ben Revis, couldn't. He walked off his jitters by heading up 30th. Passing the Royal, he saw Officers Steele and Rose, sharing a laugh as they lazed over the day's *Racing Form* and their usual coffee and Danish. Too much to do, and too many assholes in his way to get it done.

...........

Cain had calmed down by the time he arrived at the address on Bleecker Street, which turned out to be a restaurant just off Sixth Avenue, a quiet place called Nino's with mahogany booths running down either side of a tiled center aisle. At least now he could grab a bite to eat.

He stood just inside the entrance, looking from table to table. He was a few minutes early, so maybe Revis hadn't arrived. A well-dressed man with a proprietorial air strolled briskly toward him, as if intent on protecting his regulars from this clueless newcomer.

"I'm here to meet Mr. Revis."

A frown of puzzlement, followed quickly by a smile of recognition. "Ah, yes." He handed Cain a menu. "This way, sir."

He escorted Cain to a booth on the left in the back, next to the swinging doors for the kitchen. Two men were seated. The one facing the front, mostly hidden by a *New York Times*, was visible only from the eyebrows up—a huge, bulging forehead with dark hair, flecked with gray. A column of cigarette smoke rose above his newspaper. The fellow on the opposite side was also smoking, elbows on the table. On his plate were a few scraps of pasta. Cain didn't recognize him, but he perked up as soon as he saw Cain, and knocked sharply on the table.

"He's here, boss."

The other man calmly folded his *Times* and stood in greeting, hand extended. The face was vaguely familiar. He was about five-nine, with a little extra weight around the middle. High arching eyebrows gave him an aspect of surprise, and he wore a crisp, professional-looking suit, nothing flashy.

"Ben Revis?" Cain asked as they shook hands.

The man smiled congenially.

"Frank Hogan, actually, the district attorney. Ben, how 'bout making some room for our guest."

The other man, presumably Revis, got up and stepped aside. Cain reluctantly slid into the booth, already feeling duped.

"Sorry about using Ben's name," Hogan said. "Whenever I use my own in setting up these little meetings, the captains get ants in their pants and start making phone calls. By the time lunch is over, half the cops in the city are gossiping about what I'm up to, usually without even a grain of truth." He gestured toward a menu. "Please, have some chow while you're here. On me. The spaghetti with clams is first rate."

A waiter appeared.

"I've eaten," Cain said, shoving away the menu even as his stomach growled.

Hogan smiled. "Suit yourself."

"Is this really about Kannerman?"

"Interesting case, and a nice collar. Also a bit of a small fry, don't you think?"

"That was my impression, sir."

"Please. Call me Frank."

Hogan's tone was cordial. He had a relaxed, patrician air about him that put you at ease even as it made you wonder what he was up to, and Cain already had his suspicions. Juries probably loved him.

"So was there some other matter you wanted to discuss, then?"

Hogan looked up abruptly as someone loomed up over Cain's right shoulder. Cain turned and saw Murray Gurfein. Stocky, clipped mustache, hooded eyes—the whole package—plus a scowl that could've curdled milk.

"Have a seat, Murray. We were just getting started."

Was it Cain's imagination, or had the guy to his right moved a few inches closer, practically squeezing him against the wall? A couple seated on the other side of the room got up to leave. They were now the only remaining customers. Gurfein slid in next to Hogan.

"Murray, would you like to begin?"

"You do the honors, sir. Maybe he'll actually listen if it comes from the top."

"Apologies for my assistant's peremptory tone, Sergeant Cain."

"Call me Woodrow." He said it pointedly, figuring he ought to show them that he wasn't a pushover.

"Very good." Hogan's smile didn't waver. "The problem, Woodrow, is that we're told you've been tampering with a material witness in a very sensitive ongoing investigation."

"Are we still talking about Kannerman?"

"You know who we mean. And we'd like you to cease and desist. No more excursions out into the harbor. No more inquiries, official or otherwise, into any and all matters pertaining to that conversation. And certainly no further trips to the Hotel Astor."

The last remark caught him off guard, although he supposed it wasn't all that surprising that someone in the intelligence business would keep track of people who were keeping track of him.

"Why?"

Hogan looked at Gurfein, who took it from there.

"Maybe because we already have matters well in hand."

"So well in hand that two men and one woman are dead, and at least two more fellows are probably in danger. Not that they don't necessarily deserve it. Then there's the guy who, as far as I can tell, you've put on ice. Treating him like an enemy alien even though he's a citizen of the United States."

Hogan chimed in: "You might check the law books for a federal statute passed by Congress in 1909," he said. "It sets out a clear procedure for denaturalization. We're operating completely within the bounds of law."

He gave Cain a few seconds to digest that before continuing.

"His being 'on ice,' as you so colorfully put it, is a matter of keeping him out of harm's way. In case you didn't notice, other branches of our government have placed men on the premises to ensure that no one's personal well-being is at risk."

"So he said. I presume that's who told you I was out there."

Hogan smiled and picked up his coffee cup. "They're very efficient fellows, for the most part."

"Lorenz thinks this whole thing is all about the *Normandie*. Some kind of sabotage plot."

This stopped Hogan cold. His smile vanished, and he set the cup in its saucer with a rattle, his first sign of less than total composure. Then he exchanged glances with Gurfein. Neither man was able to hide his surprise.

"He actually said that?" Hogan said.

"Yes."

Hogan slowly shook his head. "He's been misinformed."

"About what?"

"Everything."

"Then what is this all about?"

Gurfein leaned across the table like a mastiff eager to take a bite out of his neck. "It's a matter of national defense. Way above your pay grade, detective." His eyes bulged, hooded or not.

Cain stared right back, his temper rising.

"Is it also above my pay grade for me to ask why you've been meeting with the likes of Meyer Lansky and some lawyer who works for Lucky Luciano?"

Hogan's look of shock told Cain that he should've kept his mouth shut.

"See?" Gurfein said to Hogan. "I told you. He knows way too much. Him and the old guy, both of 'em."

Maybe Cain had watched too many movies, but he was well aware of what could happen to people who knew too much, especially when seated among the powerful in an otherwise empty Italian restaurant in New York. Then he reminded himself that these guys were law enforcers, not law breakers. Unless, of course, they were crooked, and so was Haffenden, working off-the-books deals at his private office.

Hogan was staring at him with an air of deep disappointment. Cain speculated for a second on whether he might be able to shove Revis out of the booth and make his escape. Not likely, he decided, or not without bloodshed. Gurfein and Hogan exchanged grim glances and then zeroed in on him.

"Woodrow," Hogan said, his tone chilly, "those are the kinds of questions that, under the present circumstances, can be very dangerous for a whole lot of people."

"Me included?"

"Everyone included. This is bigger than you, bigger than me, and bigger than a few small murders. It's bigger than everyone in this city." He leaned forward, the big forehead thrusting toward Cain like a bowling ball. "I urge you to not proceed with this matter a single step further."

"And what happens if it gets kicked up to borough level?"

"Let us worry about that. And not for my sake, not in the least. Do this for the sake of your country."

Another appeal to his patriotism, just like with Lanza. Either it was genuine or it was a convenient dodge. And whatever Hogan and the others were up to, at least some of the participants were willing to kill to keep it under wraps. But rubbing out a few illiterate Germans, or even a sadly addicted young woman, was one thing. Killing a cop would be quite another. So at least he had that going for him.

"What if I choose instead to keep doing my job?"

Hogan sighed, sat up straight, and looked away, while putting his hands on the table. Gurfein leaned into the breach.

"We've been doing our homework, too, Mr. Cain. For example, we understand you're a Valentine man." He tacked on a smile, and not a friendly one.

"Where'd you get that idea?"

"Am I wrong?"

Cain shrugged, trying to act like it didn't bother him. "I'm a cop. We're all Valentine men."

Hogan deftly took up the thread, calmly intoning his words as if he were the voice of reason. "Gentlemen, I'm sure we're all after the same thing here. Justice for the murdered, no matter their nation of origin, and the strongest possible defense for our country in a time of war. And at this point there's no reason we can't still have them both, provided you cooperate."

"By doing nothing, you mean."

"Woodrow, when I was in law school I worked a lot of different summer jobs in a lot of different places. I was a steamfitter, a Pullman conductor. I even kept books for a mining company in Guatemala, and, believe me, along the way I've come across any number of punks and tough customers. But let me say this about that breed of man. I have yet to find a tough guy in whom there is not some good. Meaning, lest I need to be more explicit, that even those people who you and I may oppose on most days of any given week might at other times be capable of acting for the public good, if you're willing to let them. Am I getting through to you?"

There it was again. A wave of the flag, in hopes that Cain would simply pledge his allegiance and look the other way.

"Tell you what," Gurfein added, as if sensing Hogan hadn't closed the deal. "You do as we ask, and when this is over I'll happily give you enough dirt on crooked cops in the 14th to keep your commissioner happy until you're ready to retire."

Smart move. Finally, a genuine incentive was on the table. It also told Cain that they truly *did* know he was a Valentine man, in the most secretive sense of the term. Wonderful. Further evidence that everyone he'd been dealing with had eyes all over the city. And if these guys knew about his arrangement with Archer and the commissioner, who else did?

"It's okay," Gurfein said, reading his face. "Your secret is safe with us. Provided that ours is safe with you."

So there it was, the stick behind the carrot. Keep nosing around, and your name will be mud in every precinct. And Cain knew where that led.

"You've given me a lot to think about. But right now I'm due back at the station house."

No one answered, and no one budged, and for a moment he wondered if they planned to hold him in place until he gave in. Finally, after a few seconds of silence, Hogan nodded to Revis, who slid out of the booth without a word.

Cain stood, feeling a little shaky. "Gentlemen," he said.

There were no answering farewells, no parting smiles. No one even nodded. He turned and walked out of the restaurant, feeling their eyes on his back all the way to the sidewalk.

This time Cain didn't calm down. The more he mulled over what had just happened, the angrier he got, because the bottom line was that Hogan and Gurfein wanted to bury everything, and they wanted his help in doing it. And if he refused, they'd rat him out to the likes of Mulhearn and Maloney. Unless . . .

Unless he beat them to the punch, by finishing his work in the 95 Room and turning over the goods to Valentine before they could derail his investigation. Then maybe he could secure the commissioner's backing in going forward with the case of the Germans, even if it led to the federal cover-up of a sabotage plot against the *Normandie*. Hogan and Gurfein had no idea how much progress he'd already made in digging out evidence of corruption in the 14th precinct, and when he returned to the squad room he set his sights on getting more.

First, he dutifully and quietly handled his paperwork, plus every other chore Mulhearn had dumped in his lap. Then, a little more than half an hour before the shift change, he went back downstairs to the 95 Room, where, true to further in-house gossip, Officers Steele and Rose had knocked off for the day well ahead of schedule.

Cain turned the key, slipped back inside, relocked the door, and switched on the light. He again got down to business. It turned out to be one of the most productive half hours of his day. Next time Linwood Archer called, Cain would have an earful for him.

# 28

............

*DANZIGER*

IN THE PAST HOUR I received a most alarming communication. My telephone rang, and upon answering I was hailed by a rough and taunting male voice, unfamiliar to me. The caller asked to speak to Alexander Dalitz.

"There is no such occupant at this address," I replied.

"You sure, pal?"

"Beyond all doubt, sir."

"Yeah? Well if you see him, let him know I'm looking for him."

"Who is this?"

The man did not answer before disengaging.

I climbed to the rooftop of my building, and there, among the pigeons and the soot and the detritus of time, I scanned the streets below for anyone suspicious, anyone eyeing or approaching my doorway. I saw nothing out of the ordinary, but knew that, henceforth, and for the first time in many years, I could no longer consider this location to be either safe or secure. In some fundamental way, the new life I had chosen for myself so long ago was nearing its end. The question, then, is whether it will end in violence or, like the previous one, regeneration.

Although it is small consolation in light of such a jarring interlude,

I do have progress to report on the matter of our investigation. Only this morning I was able to acquire new and interesting information concerning the four German laborers hired by Lutz Lorenz. Armed anew with their pseudonyms—Heinrich Heine, Friedrich Schiller, Wolfgang Goethe, and Thomas Mann—I ascertained through reliable connections with the Longshoremen's Union that four gentlemen using those names obtained union cards last December with a local on the Hudson waterfront. Listed on those cards were their last known addresses, which have in turn led me to additional new information, some of it quite alarming.

Intending to pass along these findings to Mr. Cain as soon as possible, I telephoned him a few moments ago in order to arrange a rendezvous. I chose the place of our meeting with care, partly out of the belief that my home is no longer either safe or suitable. Instead, I selected a more public venue, where we will enjoy the anonymity of the crowd. I expected Mr. Cain to object, or at least to question me further with regard to motive. But he agreed without hesitation, and in his ready acquiescence I detected a state of perturbation as advanced as my own.

"Are you well?" I asked. "What has upset you?"

"Nothing," he said, but I was not convinced. He then stated curtly that he would see me soon, and hung up.

Perhaps he was tired. I had telephoned at the end of his shift, and he may have been upset at the prospect of prolonging his workday. Then another thought struck me. Perhaps he, too, has been given reason to feel threatened, so much so that he did not feel free to express his true feelings while seated in his place of employment.

This thought disturbed me greatly, especially now that Mr. Cain's daughter has joined him in New York. It prompted me to revisit my vow from the previous morning, when I resolved to become a more watchful presence. It is obvious to me now that I cannot hope to accomplish this duty on my own. Yet, I do have an idea of who might be best positioned to help me: Beryl Blum, of course. Perhaps she can serve as my eyes and ears on certain occasions when I can be neither present nor in touch. And so, Fedya's protestations and objections notwithstanding, I decided to do all within my power to promote their liaison, amorous and otherwise. Partly, of course, for the sake of their happiness. But partly as well for their greater safety in each other's company.

So there we are, then—two wary and perturbed men on their separate ways to the location I chose for our rendezvous: a bench at the north end of Tompkins Square Park, favored environ of rabble-rousers, holy men on soapboxes, and children at play, with enough motion and noise to cloak our every word and deed. I confess also to an ulterior motive in choosing this location. You will discern it soon enough.

I will not wear my usual ensemble of clothing, seeing as how it no longer seems to offer its previous protections. This is yet another way in which I have begun adapting to the new circumstances of my once tranquil life here on Rivington Street. So, off I go, flushed from cover like a startled quail, in the awareness that from here on out I had best keep taking steps forward if I am to outpace those who now pursue me.

# 29

....................

CAIN ALMOST MISSED DANZIGER on his first circuit through the upper end the park. The man looked different—clothes, hair, the works. Not younger, exactly, but more polished, and Cain wondered at the transformation.

"Nice coat," he said, taking a seat beside him on the bench.

"Camel's hair," Danziger said.

"Tan. New color for you."

"Not really."

Cain detected the smell of mothballs. Not new, then. It just hadn't been worn in a while. As if you'd need any coat at all on a day this warm and beautiful. But without a coat perhaps he wouldn't be Danziger.

"Combed your hair, too. And the wool hat's gone. It even looks like you used a razor. Sort of. What do you call that style of beard you're growing, now that you've shaved the rest?"

"A Van Dyke."

Danziger stroked his newly smooth cheeks, as if to confirm it for himself. Cain noticed a small nick or two, marked with a styptic pencil.

"Usually I leave such duties to a barber," Danziger said, as if to explain the imperfections.

"You sounded a little shaken when you called."

"As did you."

Cain nodded. Each man waited for the other to speak, which led to several seconds of silence.

"You first," Cain said.

Danziger told him about the caller asking for Alexander Dalitz.

"I guess that explains the shave and the wardrobe."

"And our meeting place. Although there is a lesson for you here as well."

"A lesson?"

"It is staring at you from nearby."

Cain looked around, but noticed only pigeons and children. A nanny pushed a baby carriage past a small marble fountain.

"I must be missing it."

"We will proceed to that momentarily. Besides, I believe it is now your turn for explanations."

Cain told Danziger about the meeting with Hogan. Danziger reacted at first with shock. Then he frowned and shook his head. "I understand why they would want to keep an eye on Lorenz. But his patriotic defense of those other disreputable scoundrels makes no sense at all."

"Unless he's crooked."

"Remember that I told you Lanza was under indictment? Well, Hogan is still pursuing the charges—quite aggressively, I am told, possibly even with wiretaps in place. That would mean he knows all about any calls made by Haffenden to Lanza. Why, then, in speaking to you, would he cover for such people?"

"Could this all be for Luciano's benefit?"

"No. His prison sentence remains in full force. No motions of any sort have been filed on his behalf. Although, just as I heard at Longchamps, there *is* talk that he will soon be moved. But to Great Meadow prison, not Sing Sing."

"It's closer to the city?"

"Yes, but not anywhere nearly as close as Sing Sing. Great Meadow is up by Albany. Any visitor would still have to stay overnight, so it is not as if Mr. Luciano got his entire wish. Yet, now our district attorney, our supposed beacon against the darkness of organized crime, suggests that you should leave these fine gentlemen in peace, and, in doing so, drop your present inquiries."

"And with three murders still unsolved. While offering no plausible reason."

Danziger shook his head.

"You said you've been busy?" Cain said.

"Quite. Many contacts. Many inquiries. Any single one of them might have triggered the phone call asking for Alexander Dalitz, but I do have progress to report. I have acquired new and interesting information concerning our four literary Germans."

He told Cain about the union cards obtained under the fake names of Heine, Schiller, Goethe, and Mann, all of them on the same day in December, issued by a longshoremen's local on the Hudson.

"Bingo."

"Yes. And from those cards I obtained their last known domiciles."

Danziger told him the addresses for the two remaining Germans—Goethe's for Dieter Göllner, and Mann's for Gerhard Muntz. Cain wrote them down, while Danziger watched.

"May I borrow that notebook of yours for a moment?"

"Sure."

"Your pencil as well."

"Okay."

Danziger crossed out the address for Dieter Göllner.

"He's moved?" Cain said.

"He is dead. Beaten to death in a waterfront bar two days ago, by three men who ran out and have not been seen since."

Cain let that sink in, and frowned at the implications. "That makes Hogan's request to back off look even worse. Now it's four murders, which he probably knew by the time he was talking to me."

"And, soon enough, five. Not that Gerhard Muntz has been foolish enough to remain at his old address. His landlord reports that he left a week ago, three days behind on his rent."

"Days?"

"His place of residence was a flophouse, the Comet Hotel, on the Bowery. Thirty cents a night."

"Why would Hogan look the other way? If you believe what Lorenz told us, these four krauts were in the middle of a sabotage plot, with some mob guys running the show. Hogan should want to round up every last one of them for interrogation and intelligence. Haffenden, too. Instead, it's like they're throwing these guys to the wolves, then calling it an act of patriotism when somebody hunts them down. Never mind that a young woman got killed along the way."

"I do not know what to make of it, other than it seems to be making our lives more difficult and dangerous than they need to be."

"Sounds like you'd prefer to drop it."

Danziger turned toward him, scowling. "Absolutely not. Are you suggesting that course of action for yourself?"

"I hadn't been. Now I'm beginning to wonder. Cops up here, it seems like they've been going along to get along for ages. Not just the ones getting rich off bribes, or in some politician's pocket. I mean the everyday guys, like me. Every time I turn around it feels like I have to make another trade-off, just to keep going. And is that really all that different from what I used to do? Look at me. I came up here on a sellout to my father-in-law, after a failure under pressure. Maybe that's the way it'll always be."

Danziger narrowed his eyes. "Perhaps. First, I think it is time for you to learn why I called you to this location. Indulge me for a second. Look in that direction once again, and tell me what you see."

Cain obliged him. "Same as before. Kids and pigeons. Plus that raving lunatic of a preacher over there. Although on any given Sunday in Horton I could find you two or three who'd give him a run for his money."

"What about statuary?"

"You mean that little slab of marble over there, with the curved top?"

"Yes. Tell me about it."

"Well, there's a fountain in the front with some kind of carving. People's faces, it looks like, with an inscription."

"Can you read the words?"

"Not from here."

"Then, please." He gestured with his hands. "Go and have a look, and report back to me."

Cain, feeling this was getting rather strange, walked over. He expected to find a profound message or quotation, or perhaps the name of a famous New Yorker that would tie in to some sort of parable. Instead there was only a relief carving of two children in profile, gazing heavenward. Just beneath them was a marble lion's head, spitting water into a basin. On the side of the slab, which was barely more than a foot wide, was an inscription reading "They were Earth's purest children, young and fair." That was all.

He went back to the bench and recited the words.

"Like something you'd see on a tombstone," he added.

"It is a memorial," Danziger said, "although I doubt that even one-tenth of the people in this park could tell you what it represents."

"But you can."

"Yes. And since you have expressed such a keen and abiding interest in my past—the real me, as you seem to regard it—then here is your chance. You are looking at a relic of the event that ended my child-hood, in the year 1904. The biggest loss of life this city has ever seen. More than one thousand people, all perishing on a single morning in June. Among them, Solomon and Anna Dalitz."

"Your mom and dad?"

"On June fifteenth. The day I became an orphan."

"A *thousand* people? What the hell? Did some big building go up in smoke?"

"A ship. The *General Slocum*, during a pleasure cruise. Death by fire and then by water, a spectacle more horrible than the *Normandie*, right out in the East River, while thousands of people watched from both banks. I survived only when someone on shore pulled me from the water with a rake, just as the currents were sweeping me away."

"My God. And this monument is all that remains?"

"Dedicated to the children. There were so many that day, and women, too. Most of the fathers were working. Almost the entire congregation of St. Mark's Evangelical Church—you know them as Lutherans—was on board."

"Lutherans? But you—"

"My father kept their books. That was his business, bookkeeping. And for St. Mark's he did such a good job of cleaning up the mess left behind by his gentile predecessor that the Reverend Haas, a truly fine man, asked my father if he would like to bring his whole family along."

"No good deed goes unpunished."

"Yes. The nature of fate. We were overjoyed to receive the invitation to such a festive event. A day on the water, with food, a brass band. The perfect family outing. I was required to bathe the night before. My mother spent hours getting dressed. A corset, a flannel petticoat, a skirt and a shirtwaist—everything that would later become saturated with the waters of the East River and drag her to the bottom. Alas, that was the case with many women and girls. I wore knickerbockers and a jacket, my finest. My father, his suit and tie.

"We boarded on a beautiful summer morning. The band was already playing Christian hymns, and I was set free to roam the decks with two nickels in my pocket—one for a tongue sandwich, one for a slice of pie. It was the heart of Kleindeutschland, gathered on one happy ship."

"Little Germany? But I thought that Yorkville—?"

"Yorkville came later. In fact, if not for this terrible day, Yorkville might never have happened. Those brownshirt parades from a few years ago would have marched instead up Third Avenue, from Houston Street to Fourteenth."

"You said there was a fire?"

Danziger nodded, gazing vacantly, his eyes off in some other time and place.

"It started near the engine room. Straw and gasoline, or some such combination. I am not so clear on details. They were in all the papers, but I've never had the stomach to read them. I remember only the thick black smoke, and then flames, rising from nowhere, sweeping the deck toward us like a wave. And the screams, of course. I was eating, and could not find my mother or father. I never saw them again."

He paused, sagging noticeably before collecting himself.

"People began jumping overboard. Some ran for the lifejackets, but in fourteen years they had never been used, and the cork inside had turned to dust. The lifeboats had been repainted so many times without removal that they had become stuck to the sides of the boat."

"My God."

"Yes. We were quite helpless, all of us, and as the fire spread people rushed to the side of the deck nearest the shore. Of course, that caused the ship to list violently, throwing one and all against the rail. And when the rail gave way, I fell into the river, a long way down. And as I was falling—and I am quite sure of this—that is when I heard my mother's voice, calling out my name. I landed in the water, sinking and then surfacing. I looked up for her on the lower deck above me, but all I could see was people burning, people jumping. There was a beautiful young woman with her hair on fire. All around me in the water, people were gasping for breath, trying to stay afloat. I saw men just ahead, standing in the shallows of North Brother Island, trying to pull people to safety. Then the current swept me under. A woman just behind me pulled me to the surface and pushed me forward. I grabbed for a rake, barely holding on, and was pulled ashore. The woman who saved me was swept away. I heard her screams and then saw her passing as she sank beneath the surface, another poor soul dragged to her death by her wet wardrobe. For days I heard those screams in my head, whenever it was quiet."

Danziger went silent, his eyes misting. Cain remembered their trip to Ellis Island, and his description of the menacing Lady Liberty, raising her torch on high.

"An omen, you said. About the Statue of Liberty."

"Yes."

"No wonder you looked so shaky the other day."

"It never departs you, that sense of foreboding. That day was the end of Kleindeutschland, its moment of doom. A thousand gone, and many who remained simply lost heart. People began to move away to other parts of the city. Many went to Yorkville, both gentile and Jew, although some Jews instead chose the Upper West Side, a division that grew wider over time. And now, through the correspondences of my clients, I see this same sort of disaster taking place on an even larger scale, in city after city of the Old World where I was born. Entire communities, disappearing in clouds of smoke."

He looked at Cain, his eyes imploring.

"So you see? As their interpreter, as their archivist, I am the keeper of all that remains. I took on this role—writing and reading letters—as an expediency, as a means to a humble income. But in these past few years I have come to see it as a trust, an obligation, to all those who are vanishing from our midst."

Cain saw now that Danziger was telling this story for posterity. Not only for the sake of the people he served, but also for his own legacy, in case he should disappear.

"Don't worry," Cain said. "I won't quit on you."

"Simply agreeing to continue is not enough. You also must not waver. Do so, and I shall be lost. And all that I harbor within my house will be lost with me, the dead and the living alike."

"I'm with you. I won't waver. But we need a way forward. Preferably one that will attract as little attention as possible."

"I believe I may have found one. A means of finding our fourth German."

"Gerhard Muntz?"

"I was able to ascertain that, of the four, he alone was from Bavaria. That told me he was far more likely to be Catholic than the others. And for the Catholics of this city, there is one place where the down-and-out—and, yes, those who are too frightened to show themselves by day—are known to gather during the day's smallest hours. A worker's mass, held especially for those with nocturnal employment. It takes place every Sunday at two thirty in the morning, at St. Andrew's, near Chambers Street. A location, I might add, that is quite convenient to the Bowery."

"Sounds like a shot in the dark."

"Be that as it may, I believe that this shot may have already struck the bull's-eye, if I use the idiom correctly."

"You've found him?"

"An assistant rector, a contact of mine at St. Andrew's. He reports the recent and regular Sunday presence of a shy and lonely man who goes only by the name of Gerhard."

"Our Gerhard?"

"Perhaps yes. Perhaps no. Monsignor Cashin, who presides at

St. Andrew's, told my contact that he believes this Gerhard lives in a flophouse."

"Then why not just check the flophouses? Starting tomorrow morning, if you want, when everyone's still asleep."

"Do you have any idea what you are asking? Have you not been to the Bowery?"

"We're talking about, what, five or six places?"

Danziger threw up his hands, as if the number might be infinite.

"Dozens. Scores, even. From the top of my own head I can name at least eight. The Alabama, the Marathon, the Crystal, the Owl, the White House, the Grand Windsor, the Palace, the Newport. On and on, each with a clientele that pays by the night, moving on to some other bed if he feels the least bit threatened or uneasy, as our Gerhard certainly must. Seek him door to door and we shall only scare him deeper into hiding. We must wait for Sunday. Or, rather, for very late this Saturday night. We will attend the worker's mass."

"And if he doesn't show?"

"Then we will try again the following Sunday."

"By then he'll be dead. Or I'll be off the case. If I haven't been yanked already, once Hogan makes a few phone calls. Even if he shows, how will we recognize him?"

"The father, my contact, has promised to point him out. Gerhard always takes communion. The father will signal when he comes to the altar to receive the host."

"Worth a try. I doubt even Mulhearn will care what I'm up to on a Saturday night." Then he frowned. "Olivia. I can't just leave her."

"Then you must plan for her safekeeping."

"It'll be asking a lot of Eileen, but I guess she'll have to."

"Make your arrangements, then, and meet me at the church at two thirty. I will arrive early, and sit near the front on the left."

Danziger stood, wavered a bit, and took a moment to steady himself. Even with the shave and the nicer clothes, he once again looked old. This time his eyes were the giveaway—the blue now tinted by a somber grayness, a squint of effort. Then he turned and strolled off into the park, brushing his right hand against the marble memorial in passing.

By the time Cain got home it was nearly dark. Pete the night door-man informed him that Olivia and Eileen were again at the park. As he climbed the stairway he thought he smelled cigarette smoke, and he unlocked the door to see Linwood Archer seated by an open window with a huge revolver in his lap.

"Shut it slowly behind you and don't move," Archer said.

"How'd you get in?"

"You've been ducking me, Cain. Figured a house call was in order."

"Fine. I've got something for you."

Cain reached inside his overcoat, which prompted Archer to raise the revolver until it was aimed at Cain's chest.

"No, no," Archer said. "Take your hand out of the pocket nice and slow, and drop it to your side. We'll do this my way."

Through the open window they could hear a neighbor's radio. Once again, the voice of Red Barber provided the play-by-play.

*"Runners on the corners with nobody out. Newsom looks like a lost ball in tall grass out there on the mound."*

"Nice," Archer said as he stood, his finger on the trigger. "Don't even need your own radio to hear the bums. But what if you're a Yan-kees fan? I hate the fucking Dodgers." Reaching behind him with his free hand, Archer shut the window while keeping the gun trained on Cain's chest.

"That's better. Besides, wouldn't want to disturb your neighbors with any excessive noise."

Cain took a slow step backwards toward the door.

"Hold your horses, Cain. Go into the kitchen and sit down."

He did as he was asked, taking care not to make any sudden moves. Archer followed.

"What's this I hear about you paying the DA a visit this afternoon?"

News traveled fast, and through unlikely channels. Cain wondered if this was Gurfein's idea of a nasty joke.

"Hogan wanted to hear about a case," Cain said. "Some con artist named Kannerman."

"Not what I heard."

"Yeah? Then what did you hear?"

"This and that." He waggled the gun back and forth. Cain sensed Archer was bluffing, and was fishing for more information. "The commish doesn't like to learn about this kind of thing from a third party, Cain. It tells him that Hogan knows more about what's going on with your work than he does. How long you spend in his office?"

He was about to say that the meeting hadn't been in Hogan's office. Then he decided he liked the idea that Archer didn't have his facts straight. It meant there were probably other gaps in his knowledge, maybe even big ones.

"Not long. And you'll be pleased to know he was in a mood to help. He said pretty soon he might hand over all kinds of dirt on crooked cops in the fourteenth."

"How soon is pretty soon?"

"What if I told you it doesn't matter?"

Archer narrowed his eyes. "What do you mean?"

"Well, if you'll kindly let me reach inside my coat for a second, I'll show you."

"Okay, but no funny business."

Archer held the gun steady while Cain pulled out eleven arrest reports that he'd stolen that evening from the binders for March and April in the 95 Room. All were cases that had been checkmarked in the arrest record ledger for special handling. And, rather than just writing down the names and then waiting for the reports—and, thus, the evidence of the scheme—to disappear, he'd decided to steal the reports. The names listed on them showed which subjects had undue influence inside the precinct. In addition, the cops participating in the scheme had become so stupidly brazen that they'd left several attached notes, which included phone numbers listed for collection purposes. Cain was pleased to discover that for two of the notes he recognized the handwriting, because it was the same as on the note Maloney had left on Cain's desk the other day with his returned sidearm, after he'd been shanghaied to his lunch with Harris Euston.

He explained it all to Archer, who nodded, seemingly impressed, even raising his eyebrows when Cain told him about the Murder, Inc. connection on one of the gambling arrests.

What Cain didn't tell Archer was that he'd also recognized one of the phone numbers which appeared on two of the notes discussing collection. He'd seen the same number several other times recently, on phone messages left for him at the office by Harris Euston's secretary at Willett & Reed. Cain had already logged the names of the two suspects from the attached reports, figuring they'd turn out to be law clients of Euston's. Archer and Valentine would figure out the connection soon enough, he supposed.

"If you want to see who's already made payments to get their cases wiped clean," he told Archer, "all you've got to do is check the old arrest record for erased check marks next to the names. I saw at least twenty-five of them. One of them was that bookie, Ericson. And Valentine was right. It all started in January."

Archer shook his head. "What a bunch of stupid fucks, leaving a trail like that."

"You're talking about guys in their late thirties and forties who still haven't made sergeant. Are you really that surprised?"

"Not where money's involved. Ericson. The commish will like that. He'll like all of this shit." He flipped through a couple of the arrest reports. "But some of these names . . . Art Wheeler? Herman Keller? Frankie Disch? Who the fuck are these guys?"

"You tell me. You guys are supposed to be the experts on that old Tammany crowd."

From the hallway came the sudden sound of footsteps and cheerful voices headed up the stairs. Olivia was home. Archer smiled again. He leaned over and stubbed out his cigarette on the kitchen table—slowly, so that it left a round black dot that looked just like the ones on Werner Hansch.

"Not to worry," Archer said. "I'll go the way I came."

He crossed the room to the window, threw open the sash, and climbed out onto the fire escape.

"You should try locking your windows, Cain. Crime around here, it's pretty appalling."

# 30

......................

EILEEN O'CASEY WAS ALREADY more than an hour late when the phone rang. Cain answered in a state of nervous anticipation. It was indeed Eileen.

"I'm sorry, sir, but I can't make it tonight."

"What do you mean 'can't'? You *have* to!"

"It's beyond my control sir. It's . . . It's a family emergency."

"What kind of emergency?"

"I'm sorry, sir. If it was within my power, I'd be there. You know I would. But it isn't possible."

"Maybe I can help. Or I could bring Olivia to you. There's still time, so just tell me what—"

"No, sir. It's not possible, sir." She was rushing her words, completely flustered. "I'll be there first thing Monday. Goodbye, sir."

And with that she was gone, meaning Cain was now in need of a babysitter at twenty minutes before midnight. His scheduled rendezvous with Danziger at St. Andrew's Church, where they hoped to catch the elusive Gerhard Muntz, was less than two hours away.

If he were back in Horton, he would've just called on his neighbors. The Turners to the left, or the Whitcombs to the right. Either would have happily taken in his daughter at any hour of the day. Here, no such luck. His failure, he supposed. Neighbors lived above, below, and to every side of them here, yet he didn't know a single one beyond a nod or hello in the hallway. How else could so many people be lonely on an island of millions?

He tried Beryl's number with only a faint hope of success. He and Olivia had eaten dinner with her earlier, but from there she was going to look after her uncle Fedya for the rest of the evening, and would probably be staying for the night. Cain had no idea how to reach the man. Danziger might know, but he had stopped answering his phone after dark ever since taking the anonymous call asking for Max Dalitz.

Not long before two a.m., when it was time to leave, he stood in Olivia's doorway watching her sleep. He had decided to lock the doors and windows and write a note, in case she woke up while he was gone. But at this hour there wasn't even a doorman on duty, meaning anyone might come up the stairway unimpeded. He couldn't help but remember Archer, sitting by his open window with a smirk on his face and a gun in his lap.

Okay, then. Think this through. His destination was a church, a place of worship, located only a few blocks south of police headquarters. They would be among worshippers and holy men, with candlelight and hushed voices. If Gerhard showed up, he'd be coming for solace, not violence. How bad could it possibly be? He crouched by the bed, kissed Olivia's forehead, and tousled her hair.

"Sweetie, I'm sorry. You have to wake up."

"Why is it dark? Is it morning time?"

"No, sweetie. Still nighttime, it's very late. But Miss Eileen couldn't come, so you'll have to go with me."

"Go where?"

"We're going to church."

"Now?"

"To a Catholic mass, so it will be kind of different. It's a service for people who have to work really late, and I have to talk to somebody there, so get dressed. C'mon, we have to hurry."

She yawned and sat up. Then, in the trusting way of children, she climbed from bed and began dressing just as he'd asked. Her eyes got wide for a second.

"Catholic? Like the ones Grandpa talks about? Will they be taking their orders from the pope?"

"Miss Eileen's Catholic, sweetie. They're just like you and me. It'll sound kind of different. The hymns and prayers, mostly. They'll probably do some speaking in Latin."

Or so he assumed. Cain didn't really know. In Horton there hadn't been a single Catholic church, although Raleigh had a few. She nodded and pulled a shirt over her head. Five minutes later they were out the door.

"It's different out here this time of night," she said, wide awake now. "It's all quieter."

Spookier, too, although he knew she would never say it. Even the smells were different. The piney scent of sawdust from the West Side Lumber Company was stronger now that the noise and exhaust of traffic was mostly gone. There were no cooking smells, and no one was hanging out the wash, or playing stickball. Only a few windows were illuminated.

The subways were still open, running on wartime hours. Cain was surprised by the number of riders, and by how many of them seemed to be traveling to and from jobs. The war machine, he supposed, noticeably more vigorous than even a few months ago. Aircraft factories and shipyards were now operating around the clock, plus all the businesses that supported them, fed them, cleaned for them, and so on.

"Look!" Olivia said, gazing out the window of their car. "They're racing us!"

She always liked it when a train pulled even on a parallel track, the subway cars swaying and rumbling as they competed for a few seconds. Cain stared at the riders in the other car, mirror images of the ones in their own—reading papers, dozing off, staring at their feet.

"They're going to beat us!" she said, as their own train began to decelerate, brakes shrieking.

"That's an express. It always wins."

Cain's eyes locked onto the face of a woman across the way. His reaction was disbelief, until Olivia spoke up.

"That lady looks like Mommy!"

It *was* Mommy. Or seemed to be, although she was in profile, and partly in shadow. Then she turned to face them, and the illusion vanished. Not Clovis.

"I don't think it was her," Olivia said. "That's not her coat. Or the kind of hat she wears."

"Right you are," Cain said, although neither of those observations had occurred to him. Olivia had a better memory than he did.

The other train zoomed forward before descending into a deeper tunnel. Disappearing with it was the woman who was almost Clovis. Neither Olivia nor he spoke, and when he glanced at her she looked down at the floor. Cain felt like the rushing train had sucked the air right out of his lungs. They pulled into the next station, the platform again surprisingly crowded. He didn't fully regain his composure until the train reached Chambers Street.

"Okay, sweetie. Here's where we get off. We've got a bit of a walk ahead. Four or five blocks, so stay close."

The streets here were quiet, too, and even more imposing. Taller buildings with darker windows, deeper shadows.

"This is like the time we went looking for owls, when the moon was full," Olivia said. She held on tight to his hand.

"You're right. It's kind of the same thing. Anybody who's standing up there in a window can see us but we can't see them. Just like an owl, way up in a tree."

"Do you think people are watching us?"

Not the most reassuring question at this hour, but he was the idiot who had brought it up.

"Oh, probably not. I think everybody's sleeping, don't you?"

She nodded but squeezed his hand. His palms were sweaty, and he was sure she noticed.

A block later they heard the first faint strains of an organ, gothic and foreboding, as they turned left onto Centre Street. They were only about seven blocks south of police headquarters, but at this hour it seemed a world away. The music grew louder as they headed up a narrow passage between the looming Municipal Office Building on the left and the U.S. Courthouse on the right. A sinner, passing through the eye of the needle, Cain thought, tapping into memories from a distant summer at Vacation Bible School.

Other late-arriving worshippers approached from the right, climbing grimy marble steps to the open door. Cain and Olivia followed them in, and were greeted by an impressive sight. Stained glass windows glowed from high on both sides, above a balcony that spanned three sides of the church. The congregation, standing for a hymn, was mostly dressed for work. There were factory workers in coveralls, waitresses in uniform, and, here and there, tattered down-and-outers who'd drifted in from the Bowery. The air smelled of incense, candle wax, and body odor. Up front, a priest in white and gold vestments sang along with his flock.

A biblical verse in huge lettering caught Cain's eye from the right side of the altar: "A New Commandment I give unto you. That you love one another as I have loved you."

A worthy sentiment, ignored in wartime on a global scale.

Olivia tugged on his hand. "When do we sit down?" she whispered.

"When everybody else does. I'm looking for someone."

The hymn ended. Everyone knelt at their seats as the priest began a prayer. Cain bowed his head until it was over.

"What's that thing they're doing with their hands?" Olivia asked.

"Making the sign of the cross."

She frowned, then figured it out. "Like they're drawing it on their chests?"

"Yes. I see him. Let's go. He's over on the left, so we'll go up that aisle."

"The old man who's looking back at us?"

"Yes. That's Mr. Danziger."

"The one you said was mysterious?"

"Shhh!"

They slid down the wooden pew, settling in to Danziger's left. Olivia, who'd managed to scoot in ahead of Cain, sat between them. Not the optimum arrangement, but if anything Danziger seemed pleased after having initially reacted with surprise—perhaps even alarm. He smiled benevolently at her. Then he looked across at Cain, the smile gone, and mouthed the words "He is risen."

So, then. Gerhard was here. And before the hour was up, they would try to intercept him, right here in the church—all of it happening in full view of his daughter, unless Cain could spirit her away first to a place of greater safety.

The priest began to speak, and throughout the church every face but Cain's turned toward the front. He instead scanned the back of the pew in front of them until he found what he was seeking. He reached across Olivia for the Bible. He set the book in his lap and placed his right hand atop the black leather cover. And then Cain, who hadn't set foot in a church for nearly a year, closed his eyes and silently began to pray.

..........

## 31

## DANZIGER

AT FIRST I WAS APPALLED. How could he bring her to this place of danger? Church or not, we were about to pursue a man on a death list, someone who might himself be willing to kill. Had Mr. Cain lost his mind? Or had he merely lost his housekeeper, and thus, temporarily, his better judgment?

Turning farther for a better view, I then saw her face, her innocence, as they walked up the aisle toward me, and immediately I revised my assessment. I chose instead to interpret her presence—carelessly engineered or not—as an omen, a sign: We would be protected here.

When they reached my pew she darted in front of her father and, then, as if to function as an intermediary, sat between us. She turned her face toward mine. It struck me at that moment that she had come to this city at an age only a few years older than I when I first arrived, and so I fully understood all of the questions in her eyes. Yet, I also saw trust, and this melted my heart.

I smiled, and she did not look away, which probably required some courage on her part, because mine is not a welcoming face.

"Here," I said, handing her a hymnal. "In case you want to sing along. They post the page numbers of the songs up there on that board. The next one will be three twenty-seven."

"Thank you."

None of us seemed interested in listening to the priest. Olivia thumbed through the hymnal. Cain, I saw now, was actually praying, mouthing words with his eyes shut, and holding on to a holy book as if it alone might save him. So perhaps he *did* realize the risk he was taking. And with that thought I realized the true nature of what the girl was about to witness.

Cognizant or not, she would see a condemned man led closer to the scaffold. Because surely word of our actions here tonight would travel from this building on the lips of other denizens of the Bowery, many of whom were ever eager to profit from any special knowledge. For all we knew, this would be Gerhard's final night of freedom, of life itself.

As you well know, I am not a religious man. But in the way of many who have forsaken faith, I am often fascinated by the dogmas and rituals of believers. And, here, under this high arched ceiling, surrounded by symbols of the Christian God, it occurred to me that for us Gerhard would be the lamb of god. His blood, shed upon our altar of truth. As the congregation began to pray, I shut my eyes, receded into my thoughts, and asked some element of the cosmos—whether it be "God" or some other entity altogether—to grant us forgiveness for the sequence of deeds we were about to set in motion.

I opened my eyes to see Olivia looking at me, and could tell that somehow she knew and approved.

Then it was time for communion. We kept our seats, officially unworthy of the sacrament. Thirty or so people came and went from the altar. Several were dressed in the rags of flophouse poverty. We watched with keen interest, but the father dispensing the sacrament did not once look our way.

The next six communicants took their places before him. The fourth man from the left was a pale fellow with unkempt blond hair and a three-day beard. He took the wafer and sipped the wine. The father looked up, turned his head briefly in our direction, and nodded crisply.

"So that's the one," Cain whispered to my left. "And do we think this is *our* Gerhard?"

"Yes. I do. He has the look of the hunted. We should be prepared to move quickly."

"Who's Gerhard?" Olivia asked.

"The man we need to speak with," I said, as gently as I could. "And when we do, it would probably be best for you to wait here, maybe with one of the priests, until we are finished."

She looked to her father. Cain nodded, sealing the arrangement.

"Okay," she said, taking on a solemn air.

I am certain she could tell from our manner that this was a serious business, the affairs of a policeman and a stranger. Wise girl.

# 32

........................

CAIN WATCHED GERHARD RETURN to his pew, relaxing only when the man sat down and opened a Bible. The organ played until the last communicant was seated. Then the congregation rose for a hymn. Olivia, consulting the board, flipped to the correct page. She and everyone else began to sing—except for Gerhard, who dropped to his knees and bowed his head. His lips began moving at an almost frantic pace.

"Prayer," Danziger muttered. "Last refuge of the scoundrel."

Olivia's mouth dropped open in surprise.

"Is that true, Daddy?"

Cain was about to answer no, and then paused as he recalled his own desperate behavior from a few minutes ago.

"Sometimes," he whispered. "People take refuge behind a lot of things." Like patriotism, he thought, thinking of Hogan and Lanza.

"How can you tell when they're doing it to hide?"

"I'm not sure, sweetie. I'm still figuring that out."

The song ended. Then came the offering. Cain dropped some change into the plate. Danziger gave nothing, which seemed to either scandalize or impress Olivia. Even Gerhard put in a coin. Soon afterward the service ended. The lights came up, and the congregants began spilling into the aisles.

"Stay here," Cain said to Olivia. "Don't move, and don't speak to anyone unless it's a priest. Okay?"

"Okay." She frowned sulkily, but Cain couldn't think of an alternative.

He slipped into the aisle, Danziger right behind him, and they walked quickly toward the back.

"The father knows that we wish to speak to Gerhard," Danziger spoke into his ear. "He has promised us the use of a room, the sacristy. He has agreed to intercede on our behalf, if necessary. All he asks is that there be no trouble, no disturbance."

They were now within a few feet of Gerhard, who was unaware of their approach and seemed to be in no hurry. Danziger sidled up on his left. Cain scooted around him toward the doorway, to cut off his avenue of escape.

"Gerhard?" Danziger called gently. Then he said something in German.

The man froze, and his mouth opened in alarm. He raised his hands into a protective position and wavered like a man caught in a strong gust of wind. For a few seconds he seemed on the verge of collapse. He was pale and underfed, and for a moment Cain almost pitied him.

Gerhard bolted forward, but not before Danziger's right hand flashed out with impressive quickness and locked on to his forearm. Danziger whispered into his ear. Gerhard's eyes sought out the young father, who nodded reassuringly. Then the German sagged and blew out a deep breath, as if in surrender. Danziger called out to Cain in a low voice above the hubbub of the departing worshippers. "He will speak with us. Come. The sacristy is this way."

The three of them walked single-file toward an alcove to the right, with the father bringing up the rear. The sacristy was a quiet room with dark wood paneling, a modest desk strewn with notes, and a large bloody crucifix high on the wall. At the end was an open closet where vestments of various sizes and colors hung in a long row, smelling of incense.

Gerhard stood behind a folding chair, holding on to the back as if he wasn't yet ready to sit, or surrender. Cain slowly walked toward him. Maybe it was his imagination, but in the time it had taken them to reach the sacristy Gerhard seemed to have reconsidered his options. His eyes darted toward Danziger, and then toward the door.

"Gerhard Muntz?" Cain said, looking him in the eye.

Gerhard's eyes widened. He backed away from the chair and pulled a knife from his pants pocket. Cain heard the father gasp behind him.

"Ask him if that's what he used to kill Sabine," Cain said, keeping his hands ready for anything while Danziger relayed the question in German. The father also spoke in German, trying to calm the man, but Gerhard shook his head and said only "Nein! Es war nicht mich! Es war Dieter!"

"He says Dieter Göllner did it."

"So I gathered. Tell him Göllner is dead. And he will be, too, unless he lets us help him."

Danziger spoke rapidly, in a soothing tone. Gerhard uttered a low moan when he heard the news, and a tremor seemed to go through him. He shook his head and lowered the knife. He looked up at Cain briefly and put away the knife. Then he came forward a step and sank into the chair with a deep sigh.

Danziger addressed the priest. "I believe we now have matters sufficiently under control, Father. Thank you for your assistance."

The father looked from man to man with an expression of uncertainty, but he seemed to take the cue for his exit.

"Very well, then. I will be outside if you need me. Unless you intend to make an arrest, please do not harry him for longer than is necessary. He is a child of God."

"Of course, Father."

They waited until they could no longer hear his departing footsteps. Gerhard was now scrutinizing Cain, but when he spoke it was to Danziger.

"Ist er ein Polizist?"

"He asked if you're a cop." Then, to Gerhard, "Ja."

Gerhard folded his arms and stared at the floor.

"Dann werde ich nicht sprechen!"

"I doubt that needed a translation," Danziger said wearily.

"He says he won't talk? Fine. We'll wait him out."

"I am not sure how patient the father will be with us."

Then, as if someone had injected him with a tranquilizer, Gerhard unfolded his arms and leaned forward, his eyes softening. He was staring toward the door. Cain turned to see Olivia stepping across the threshold.

"Sweetie, I told you to wait!"

"They started turning off the lights. I was scared, and I saw where you'd gone, so . . ." She caught Gerhard's gaze, and for a moment she stared right back. Gerhard muttered sidelong to Danziger in German. Danziger, keeping his voice low, answered. The young priest entered the room behind Olivia.

"My apologies for allowing this interruption! I was dealing with parishioners." He turned toward Cain. "She is your daughter?"

"Yes." Cain felt like an explanation was in order. "I, uh—"

"Would you like me to look after her until your work is completed?"

"Please. That would be kind of you."

The priest offered his hand to Olivia. She frowned but took it. With her other hand she waved goodbye to the beleaguered Gerhard, who beamed as beatifically as if he had just watched an angel alight in the rafters. Once she was gone, he tilted his head as if to reappraise Cain, and asked another question. Danziger answered in the gentlest of tones. Gerhard nodded and spoke again.

"What's he saying?" Cain asked.

"He wanted to know if she was your daughter. I said yes. Then he quoted a line of scripture. Something about various animals coexisting, ending with 'And a child shall lead them.'"

"It's from Isaiah," Cain said.

Gerhard spoke again. A look of weary calm had descended on his features.

"He says, yes, the book of Isaiah. He says you may ask him whatever you like."

Cain shook his head in wonderment. "Let's start with how he got involved in all this. Lutz Lorenz and the four of them, and whatever it was they were trying to accomplish."

Gerhard nodded when Danziger relayed the question. He spoke in a monotone, as calmly and flatly as if he were reading from a printed statement, pausing only when Danziger stopped him with an upraised hand in order to translate for Cain, who took notes throughout. His account was frank, precise, and blessedly simple, and matched Lorenz's version almost exactly.

In December, not long after Pearl Harbor, Lorenz approached the four Germans with an offer of employment. If they accepted, they would be issued union cards, and someone else would meet them the following day at the Jaegerhaus, a Yorkville beer hall. They accepted. The next day, a nameless German businessman—or so they guessed from his expensive suit and coolly efficient manner—met them in a back room at the Jaegerhaus, and presented them with an enticing offer: Agree to help the Fatherland by making a strike upon the enemy, and you will be richly rewarded, now and later. At that time they knew only that the goal was to burn or sink a ship currently in harbor. The man promised to relay further instructions.

They quickly received their first installment of money, which bolstered their confidence. They also got their union cards, all on the same day. Two of them—Hansch and Schaller—then secured jobs with a maritime construction company which was working aboard the *Normandie*, the French luxury liner which was being retrofitted for use as an American troop ship. This, they were told, was to be their target, with further instructions to follow. But before either man could report to the job site they awakened to headlines announcing that the *Normandie* had burned and foundered.

Figuring that other operatives may have succeeded ahead of them, they awaited a new assignment. But weeks passed without further word. More to the point, they never received the promised second payment. With no name or contact information for the German businessman who was their intermediary, they contacted Lorenz. He wanted nothing further to do with them, but agreed to relay word of their concerns. Lorenz hadn't mentioned this second contact, but Cain wasn't surprised. Such an admission would have further implicated him in the *Normandie* plot.

The German intermediary relayed word through Lorenz that he would meet them again at the Jaegerhaus, where he instructed them to sit tight, and promised they would be paid soon. He told them they were never to seek to contact him again. For any further inquiries they should get in touch with a Mr. D'Amico, on Saratoga Avenue in Brooklyn, where he could supposedly be found after seven o'clock on any weekday evening.

At this point Cain held up his hand to stop them.

"Does he have an exact address?"

Danziger asked, and Gerhard nodded and spoke again.

"Not the street number," Danziger said, "but it was a store at Saratoga and Livonia, right by the elevated IRT. The awning out front had the words 'candy,' 'soda,' and 'cigars' across the front."

"Got it."

Gerhard continued his account. The Germans wondered why Italians had become involved, but concluded that if the two countries were battlefield allies in Europe, then why shouldn't they also be working together behind enemy lines in this country?

Another week passed without action, so they delegated Werner Hansch to present their grievances to Mr. D'Amico in Brooklyn. Gerhard accompanied Hansch on the IRT to the Saratoga Avenue stop, and then waited for him in a bar down the street. After nearly an hour, when Hansch still hadn't returned, Gerhard walked to the address himself, keeping his eye on the entrance as he lingered at a newsstand across the street. At nine o'clock, a prosperous-looking man emerged, smoking a cigar and talking loudly. Two apparent underlings followed, with Hansch between them. He looked bruised and frightened, and his clothes were in disarray. A gleaming black Packard pulled to the curb, and the men climbed in, shoving Hansch into the back seat. It pulled away and drove out of sight.

By this time, the man running the newsstand had taken note of Gerhard's interest in the doings at the store. Danziger translated the exchange.

"Better not let them catch you watching," the man said, "unless you want to end up at the bottom of the East River."

"Wait a minute," Cain said, holding up a hand. "I thought he only spoke German. How'd he know what the newsstand guy was saying?"

Gerhard smiled for the first time.

"An excellent question," Danziger said. "How *did* you know, Gerhard?"

"My speaking English, it is very bad. Hearing it?" He waggled a hand. "Sometime okay." He then addressed Danziger in a burst of German.

"He says he comprehends a general sense of what people are saying. Also, the news vendor's English wasn't much better than his. He said the fellow then told him the name of the man he'd seen with Werner Hansch."

"The one who was in charge?"

Danziger asked.

"Ja," Gerhard said. "The Mad Hatter."

Danziger's eyes widened. "You are quite sure of this?" he asked slowly. "The Mad Hatter?"

"Ja."

Cain caught Danziger's eye, but the older man frowned and tersely shook his head, as if to say that now wasn't the right time.

"Okay, then," Cain said. "What happened next?"

Danziger relayed Gerhard's answer as the words came tumbling out.

"That was the last time Gerhard saw Werner Hansch. Later he heard the news. Hansch was dead; his body had been found in the river. Then he and Göllner heard Schaller had been shot, so they both went into hiding. He said that Göllner blamed Sabine for giving them away, and vowed to kill her. But he says they did not see each other again. Gerhard moves every few days to a new flophouse. For the last two nights he has been staying in the Sunshine Hotel on the Bowery. He is careful. He mostly keeps to his room, except on Sundays, when he comes here to pray. He said for a while he went to the Church of the Transfiguration on Mott Street, but he did not like going to Chinatown. Too many neon signs for chop suey. Too many Chinese."

"That's very Aryan of him."

"He says he likes the words of Monsignor Cashin. They comfort him. Or did until we came along."

Gerhard spoke again, and Danziger replied. His answer prompted Gerhard to moan and bow his head.

"He asked how Göllner was killed. I told him he was beaten to death, and that no one has been arrested."

Gerhard raised his head and spoke rapidly.

"He said we must help him. He has helped us, and now we must do the same."

Gerhard's eyes pleaded. Cain looked at Danziger.

"Tell him we'd like to help but that it won't be easy. We must also be careful. Right now there is nowhere safe to take him. Coming with us would only expose him further."

Gerhard listened to the answer and shook his head. He began digging money out of his pocket—a few crumpled ones, a scatter of coins which clattered to the stone floor.

"He says he can get more if we will take him."

"No, Gerhard. It is not a matter of money."

"Information, then. He says he can tell us more. But we must help."

"Tell him we will try. But only, *only* if he tells us everything he knows."

Gerhard nodded quickly. He leaned forward. Then he told his last tale while Danziger translated simultaneously. Cain listened carefully and kept taking notes.

"The German businessman," Danziger said. "The intermediary. Gerhard says that after their last meeting at the Jaegerhaus he followed the man out to the street, and heard him give an address as he got into a taxi. Gerhard then went there himself. Not in a taxi, he couldn't afford it, so he went on the subway. It was an office on Wall Street."

"A bank?" Cain said. "Some investment house?"

"Please, let him continue!" said Danziger.

Gerhard again took up the thread.

"Not a bank, he says. An older building, a smaller one with only one business inside. He waited maybe half an hour and saw the man come out and hail another cab. He did not hear the address this time, so he went inside. There was a reception desk, with a woman behind it. She asked him what he wanted, and Gerhard asked for an appointment. But his English was not very good, and when he would not give his name or say who he wanted to see, she told him to come back later or to telephone first. So he left, but not before he was able to look at the visitor's ledger, where he saw the man's name. It was Herman Keller."

"Keller?"

"Yes. First name, Herman."

It was somehow familiar, yet just out of reach.

"What was the address on Wall Street?"

"He says you do not need the number, because the woman, this receptionist, she gave him a business card so he could telephone later."

"Does he still have it?"

Gerhard nodded, and reached into his pocket. He looked at them for a few seconds and then handed it to Cain. Black letters on a cream background, with a phone number and a Wall Street address. In the middle, a logo for Willett & Reed.

"Lawyers," Cain said, his voice hoarse. "Herman Keller was seeing his lawyer."

Cain now remembered why Keller's name was familiar. It was on one of the arrest reports earmarked for special handling in the 95 Room. Some minor vice charge, like gambling, and now he knew what connection Keller must have used to make sure the charge went away—Harris Euston, his lawyer, the man with all those friends in the 14th precinct. And when the four Germans hired for the sabotage scheme had threatened to become unruly, Keller had probably gone to Euston for help on that, too.

Cain's mouth was dry, and his hands were clammy.

"You know this firm?" Danziger asked.

Cain nodded and looked away. For a moment he was worried he might vomit.

"He says there is one more thing," Danziger said. "About this man Keller."

Gerhard spoke again while Danziger translated.

"He says that a fellow who worked at the Jaegerhaus told them that this Keller was known as some sort of money man."

"Like a banker?" Cain asked. "Is that what he means?"

Danziger relayed the question. Gerhard shook his head.

"No. Not a banker. He says Keller was raising foreign currency for the Fatherland, a scheme asking people in Yorkville to buy Reichsmarks with dollars. With foreign currency, Herr Hitler would still be able to buy goods and supplies on the world market despite the embargoes on commerce in Reichsmarks. Keller was fronting for some American bank, which didn't wish its name to be associated with what was happening. This is apparently why Keller was chosen as their intermediary, because he was known as a good soldier for the cause."

Chase: that was Cain's guess on the name of the bank. It would be yet another reason Keller used Harris Euston as his lawyer. In fact, maybe Chase was the client who'd introduced the two men.

"I've heard about that scheme, in some of the Yorkville gossip around the station house," Cain said. "It was back before we got into the war. Groups of thugs, going door to door to make collections. Extorting money from people who still had family in Germany. What else does he know?"

"He says that is all. He says now we must help him."

Cain shook his head, marveling at the implications, and wondering how deeply Euston was enmeshed, wittingly or not.

"Tell him I need to speak with you in private," Cain said. "Tell him we must also speak to the father if we are to arrange for his safekeeping."

Danziger relayed the message.

"He wants our reassurance that we will not leave him."

"Tell him we'll be right outside. We will send the father for him when it is time. Until then he will be safer staying here."

Gerhard nodded when Danziger finished.

"Ja. Ich verstehe."

"He understands."

Cain followed Danziger back into the sanctuary. There they retreated to an altar off to one side, where a console table was covered with votive candles, and everything smelled of warm wax.

"This Willett & Reed. It is your father-in-law's legal firm, is it not?"

"It is. Harris Euston, and he's an asshole with connections. But I'd never pegged him as a traitor."

"I doubt Keller would have revealed any word of the sabotage plot to an American."

"Then why would Keller have gone to see him?"

"Because he was under duress, and Euston was already his lawyer.

I suspect their working relationship has more to do with money. The banking scheme, perhaps."

"As if that makes it any better, raising spending money for Hitler. But, yeah, that's what I'm thinking, too."

"And if Herman Keller was fronting for a bank, well, money always makes its own allegiances, greater to some than those of country or king, especially if, as you said, it was happening before our country entered the war."

"But Germany was already in it, and anybody with a brain could see what they were doing."

"And you think that would taint matters for someone such as your father-in-law? Or for an American bank, even? Both Chase and their middlemen like Keller would stand to make a great deal in commissions from these transactions. Shady or not, this should hardly come as a surprise. Let me tell you of something that happened in this city two summers ago, just after the Wehrmacht marched into Paris. There was a dinner party at the Waldorf-Astoria. The guest of honor was a representative of the German foreign ministry. His hosts were executives for General Motors, Ford, and several oil companies. They shook hands and toasted the dawn of a new age of free trade. This was not a secret. It was in all of the newspapers. Money was their common ideology, not National Socialism. They would never dare to break bread together now, of course, but I doubt they have simply set aside all ambitions for future trade. And are these not the very sorts of people your father-in-law is paid to represent?"

"That's exactly what I intend to find out."

"How?"

"I'll confront him. Ask him face to face. At least now I know the real reason he had me to lunch. Even then he was asking me to keep him up to speed on the Hansch case."

"When was this?"

"Right after that story hit the *Daily News*. It was at his club."

"What did you tell him?"

"Not a damn thing. But he's got his spies. Maloney, Mulhearn. By now he probably knows plenty about where I've been going, what I've been up to. About you, too, maybe."

"And you've told him nothing? You're sure of that?"

"Positive." He paused. "Except . . ."

"Yes?"

"Lutz Lorenz. I mentioned his name. Euston said he had a few helpful contacts in Yorkville, so I bounced Lutz Lorenz's name off him. Claimed he'd never heard of him."

Danziger shook his head. "Another reason to watch your back. And hers."

Cain turned and saw Olivia near the front of the sanctuary, talking animatedly with the young priest, who seemed charmed, nodding as she spoke.

"He'd never do anything to hurt his granddaughter."

"But the Mad Hatter would."

"You know who that is?"

"You would, too, if you had been reading the papers a few months before your arrival. Albert Anastasia. One of the biggest murderers this side of the Atlantic. They have a name for his little enterprise at that candy store in Brooklyn."

"I know. Murder, Inc. Even some of those people have friends in the station house. But I thought most of them had been locked up?"

"Most have. The Mad Hatter has even been put on trial. Yet, whenever Albert Anastasia goes on trial, witnesses begin to disappear, or go silent, and inevitably he is freed. At least now we know why Lutz Lorenz would not reveal his name. In his shoes, I would have also remained silent. Lutz would like to survive this war. Mentioning the name of Albert Anastasia would be a sure way of guaranteeing he won't."

"Especially when he's already taken care of at least three of the men Lorenz hired. Cleaning up the evidence of his plans, I guess."

"What I don't understand is why he was involved in a sabotage plot."

"Well he *is* Italian."

Danziger shook his head. "It is not so easy as that. The Mafiosi despise Mussolini. Il Duce has been merciless in hunting down their brethren in Sicily."

"Extortion, then?"

"Perhaps. How, then, to explain the involvement of all the others.

Not Luciano, or Lansky. But Gurfein? Haffenden? Whatever we do next, we should not act in haste. We need time to plan, to deliberate."

"You do the thinking. I'll go see Harris Euston."

"If you must. But you should also consider her welfare." He nodded toward Olivia.

"I do. Every single day. And, yes, I know I shouldn't have brought her along. So let's get out of here."

"And what of Gerhard?"

Cain shook his head. "I don't see any possible way of helping him. Not without tipping off all the wrong people about what we're up to."

"I can only agree. And there is no escaping that he is a filthy Nazi who would gladly send me to the grave. Yet I cannot help but pity him. But as you say, it is not possible."

They walked over to Olivia. Cain thanked the father for his help.

"Has our guest departed?" the priest asked.

Cain and Danziger exchanged glances.

"He remains in the sacristy," Danziger said. "At the moment he is somewhat upset. It would probably be best to give him a few more moments alone. In the meantime, would it be all right if we were to exit that way?" He pointed toward a door off to the side at the front of the church. "Some rather dubious-looking people harassed the girl on our way in, and we'd prefer to exit by a different route."

Danziger winked at Olivia, who held her tongue.

"Of course," the father answered. "I will show you out."

Back on the street they walked two blocks in silence before pausing to make sure that Gerhard wasn't in pursuit.

"Neatly done," Cain said.

"I suppose we should not be so proud of our deceit," Danziger said.

"Were you able to help that man?" Olivia asked. Cain looked to Danziger.

"We did what we could," the older man said. "We did what we could."

"What's he afraid of?" she asked.

Danziger knelt so that they were eye to eye.

"The world, young lady. A world of his own making, I am sorry to say. I believe he described his situation best when he spoke the words of your holy book. 'The wolf shall dwell with the lamb.' For a while, he was the wolf. Now, at least in his own mind, he is the lamb."

"Which one are we?"

"A very sharp question, my dear. The kind that only a father should answer."

Danziger stood, nodded a farewell, and turned to go. They watched until he rounded the corner. Olivia was still awaiting an answer. Cain hadn't yet decided what to say, but he knew one thing for sure. He certainly didn't feel like the wolf.

# 33

...................

NOW IT WAS HARRIS EUSTON who wouldn't return a phone call.

On Sunday, Cain left three messages with the doorman at Euston's apartment building on the Upper East Side. By nine thirty Monday morning he had already tried the number at Willett & Reed five times. Each time he got a polite but curt assurance from a secretary that Mr. Euston would call back at his earliest convenience.

He had no better luck in reaching Herman Keller, whose phone had been disconnected, and whose office on 86th Street was locked and seemingly deserted. Presumably the man had gone into hiding. Maybe he, too, was now fearing Anastasia's wrath. Briefly he considered phoning Chase National Bank, just to rattle a few cages, but he had no idea who to ask for or even what questions to ask, and decided that at this point it would create more trouble than it was worth.

Between phone calls, Cain handled more busywork for Mulhearn. When no one else was listening he managed to squeeze in a request to the Bureau of Criminal Identification for their files on Albert Anastasia. A clerk promised they'd be delivered to the station house by noon the following day, meaning that by then everyone in the 14th precinct would know about it.

On his final attempt to reach Euston, shortly after five p.m., Cain told the secretary, "Tell him that if he doesn't answer then I'll be calling on him at home tonight. You'll tell him that, won't you?"

"Certainly, sir. But I do know that Mr. Euston has plans for this evening, an important charity event, so he may not be available until quite late. Perhaps it would be better if you phoned here tomorrow morning. I'm sure he'll respond at his earliest convenience."

"I'm sure he will. Maybe even before the end of the war."

Cain slammed the receiver down. Important event, my ass, he thought. But it gave him an idea.

All sorts of local socialites seemed to be holding charity fundraisers associated with the war effort, and in recent weeks he'd seen notices of them several times a week in the society pages of the newspapers. A few times he'd spotted Willett & Reed among the sponsors.

He retrieved Mulhearn's copy of the Sunday *New York Times*, and within ten minutes he found what he was looking for in a short article headlined "Fete to Aid Children's Fund." Euston's law firm was listed among the organizers for the black-tie event, which would be held at the Park Avenue home of a Mrs. Gordon Eglinton Stewart, to raise money to help feed and clothe British children orphaned by German bombing raids. There was even a minor celebrity scheduled to appear, the story said, noting, "At the event, Lady Ashfield will tell of her work in the evacuation of British children."

Jolly good, Cain thought, wondering how Lady Ashfield would react if she knew that one of her American sponsors was up to his neck in legal dealings with a sponsor of Nazi saboteurs. Probably not with a stiff upper lip.

In hopes of achieving maximum impact upon arrival, Cain waited until an hour after the event had begun before he showed up at the apartment building, where a doorman attired as grandly as a nineteenth-century general waved him into a lobby with a marble floor, a chandelier, and pink marble columns. Off to the side, a string quartet played a Bach concerto. A large desk stood between the entrance and the elevators. Manning it was another garishly clad satrap holding a clipboard.

"I'm here for Mrs. Gordon Eglinton Stewart's soiree," Cain said, relishing every syllable.

"Your name, please?"

"Woodrow Cain."

The man checked the sheet on his clipboard, scanning it twice and then nodding as if confirming what he'd suspected all along.

"I'm sorry, sir, but you're not on the guest list. And were you aware that the event was black-tie?"

"I don't care if it's buck naked. Just tell me the floor."

"Sir, you're *not invited*. If I have to, I'll telephone the police."

Cain took out his shield. "They've just arrived. Tell me the floor, please, unless you'd prefer I called in a few uniforms. We can always go floor by floor until we find the place."

"Twenty-two," the man said, going a little pale. "But, sir, you do realize this is a *charity* event?"

"I'll make sure to drop a dime in the plate on the way out."

Mrs. Gordon Eglinton Stewart, or perhaps her husband, must have been filthy rich. They owned the entire twenty-second floor. The elevator opened onto a small alcove with a rather grand-looking door dead ahead. Cain could already hear conversation, laughter, and the clinking of glasses.

He knocked. It opened instantly. Inside he was greeted by some sort of valet who was taking coats. The man looked askance at Cain's rumpled suit, and seemed on the verge of commenting when Cain again flashed his shield and said, "Don't mind me. This shouldn't take more than a few minutes."

Cain drew a few stares as he crossed the room, but hardly noticed as he surveyed the opulence of his surroundings, not to mention the spectacular view of the city through the huge windows along the front. Further doorways opened to either side—the one to the left onto a dining room and then, beyond it, some sort of parlor. To the right was a library. There must have been close to a hundred people here, scattered through the apartment. The women were dressed grandly, most of them in white or black evening gowns. Every man except him was in black tie. He had thought earlier that his workaday suit would make him feel empowered, or perhaps boldly revolutionary among the privileged. He realized now that he only felt belittled and all too noticeable. The moment of swagger he'd experienced while lording it over the deskman was gone. He wished Beryl were here. He was betting she wouldn't be at all intimidated by this setup, and at the very least she'd be able to buck him up for the task ahead.

With that in mind he straightened his tie, took a deep breath, and quickly scanned the room for Euston, hoping to find him before anyone else asked him to leave. There he was, in the dining room.

Cain set out toward a long table brimming with appetizing food. An attendant stood ready to carve slices from a rib roast, and there were silver platters of orange and black caviar. He doubted any children of Britain would be eating as well tonight as the esteemed Lady Ashfield, whom he now saw on the far side of the room, standing out from the others with a regal bearing and a very proper accent.

Euston looked up just as Cain was approaching. Surprise registered in his eyes, but only for an instant. He spoke before Cain could open his mouth.

"Well, aren't you the fish out of water, Woodrow. Let me guess. You forgot your invitation."

"Actually I've got one right here." Cain again flashed his shield.

Euston moved up in his face. "Ah, the all-purpose pass for steerage. If you're on police business then we'd better take this outside." He sneered as he spoke, as if they were standing in a school hallway and preparing to mix it up. Maybe they were.

Cain barely resisted the urge to bump Euston's chest. But he didn't back down, not even when Euston dug his fingers into Cain's left forearm and attempted to steer him toward the door.

"Indoors works just fine for me, Euston. In fact, I'd like a drink first, and I'm going to let you get it for me. Unless you'd like me to tell the good Lady Ashfield all about your recent adventures with your friends up in Yorkville?"

Euston released his grip and, glowering, went straight to the bar in the sitting room, where a stout black man in a white dinner jacket presided over a full range of offerings. Euston turned with an inquiring glance. Cain mouthed the word "Bourbon."

The host, like the Union League Club, hadn't scrimped on supplies. It was the best bourbon Kentucky had to offer, and it came in a glass of beveled crystal. Cain liked the way the first swallow smoldered as it settled into his belly. Euston, who'd been holding a drink earlier, was now empty-handed.

"What about you?" Cain asked. "Where's your invitation?"

"Mrs. Stewart is a longtime client. She's second cousin to a Vanderbilt, once removed."

"Does that even count?"

"Come on, let's go." Euston again took Cain's arm, more gently this time. "Let's do this with a little dignity, at least."

Cain relented, if only because people had begun to stare. They went back out into the small alcove, where Euston shut the door behind them.

"Tell me about your client over in Yorkville," Cain said, "the one who moves in the same circles as Lutz Lorenz. You remember Lorenz, don't you? That guy whose name didn't ring a bell at lunch the other day?"

"We have lots of clients in all parts of this city, Woodrow, so I'm afraid I have no idea what you're talking about."

"The one who likes hanging out in beer halls with Bundists. Does that help?"

"You're foaming at the mouth, Woodrow. So I happen to represent a few German-Americans. I represent Italian-Americans as well. Do you know that the authorities even arrested Joe DiMaggio's father the other day, for pity's sake? And does anyone truly believe *he's* a threat to our country? Yet now I suppose you intend to tar and feather me, or perhaps the good name of Willett & Reed, simply because some of our clients happen to be of German heritage? Is that your game?"

"Okay, you had your chance. Herman Keller. Does that one ring a bell?"

Euston flinched. Now he looked like he wished he'd brought his drink. He lowered his head and spoke into his chest. "Mr. Keller is no longer a client."

"Was that still the case when you were fixing his gambling charge with the boys in the 95 Room last month? What's the going rate for that, by the way? And I'm guessing you already knew Keller's connection to Werner Hansch, that fellow we fished out of the Hudson. That's why you were so eager for updates on the case when we lunched at your club. Lorenz was in on their arrangement, too, although I gather he's in some sort of protective custody now. Am I beginning to refresh your memory?"

But by then Euston had recovered from the initial shock and had begun to collect himself. He straightened and came right back at Cain, raising his voice.

"As you no doubt are aware, Woodrow, anything that previously took place between Mr. Keller and me is strictly protected, even and *especially* from the likes of you, by the sanctity of attorney-client privilege. So don't even try."

"Which of your big banking clients are you protecting with this bullshit, Euston? Chase? That's my guess. They were using Keller to front this Reichsmarks-to-dollars thing, weren't they? Hitler needed an international bankroll, and they were happy to help him collect it, as long as they got to make a killing on the commissions."

Euston went red in the face. "All right, then," he said. "If attorney-client privilege doesn't do the trick, how about a few personal considerations? With only the slightest exertion, Woodrow, I could break you in this town. Break you right back to Horton, where nobody will ever trust you again. Break you so badly that you'd even lose that fine daughter of yours."

"And who'd take care of her then, you?"

"What makes you think I haven't already made arrangements? What makes you think you'll retain custody even if you manage to hang on here by your fingernails?"

Cain backed him against the wall. "You know what really breaks a man these days, Euston? Striking it rich by cutting deals with the enemy, and then having the news spread all over town. The way I see it, you and your clients are up to your eyeballs with a bunch of kraut saboteurs. So you want to break me? Try it. And if you like the *Daily News* so much, maybe you'll enjoy landing on their front page. One of those big screamer headlines. *Hitler's Park Avenue Lawyer.* I bet that would sell a ton of papers, even in this building, don't you think?"

Euston seemed on the verge of throwing a punch when the door opened and a middle-aged man stepped into the hallway.

"Harris? I heard shouting, is everything all right?"

Cain flashed his shield and stepped briskly toward him. "Get the hell back inside until I'm through here. This man's a disgrace to you and me and everybody in that room."

The man blanched as white as his starched shirt, and he quickly retreated before shutting the door behind him.

"You'll pay for that as well, Woodrow."

"Good. Maybe I'll send the bill to Lady Ashfield. Go ahead. Start slinging mud right now, if you want, and we'll see whose name comes out dirtiest. But let me tell you one more thing that ought to sober you up. If shame doesn't move you, fine, I can work with that. How about fear?"

"You're threatening me?"

"Not me. Wouldn't dream of it. But how about the guy who seems to be single-handedly trying to clean up the mess that your client and his friends have made? Albert Anastasia. The Mad Hatter. Kills whoever he wants, and if he ever got word that you're part of the mess, then I wouldn't like your chances for tea with Lady Ashfield anytime soon."

Euston opened his mouth, but no sound emerged. He backed up a step, looking like someone had knocked the wind out of him, and his next words emerged in a hoarse whisper.

"Now be reasonable, Woodrow." He again took hold of Cain's arm, but this time in the manner of a supplicant, seeking mercy. "Whatever you think of me, I'm family. Right now I'm a big part of what's supporting you and Olivia, and I'm all that Clovis has left. Love her or hate her, she's still the mother of your child."

"Then give me something. If you want me to keep your name out of it, fine. Cover your ass to hell and back, and Chase Bank's, too. But where is Keller? Where is he hiding? Where has he gone?"

Euston exhaled loudly and lowered his head. "Jersey. Across the river."

Cain got out his notebook, wedging it beneath his glass of bourbon. "Where in Jersey?"

"Edison."

"I need an address."

Euston nodded. "Hand me that, plus your pencil."

Cain gave him the notebook and Euston began to write.

"If there's a phone number, give me that as well."

"There isn't. It's bare-bones, practically an empty apartment. Not even a man on the door."

"You'd think with all those Reichsmarks and dollars Chase could have at least afforded a bodyguard."

Euston opened his mouth to speak, then seemed to think better of it. He handed back the notebook and pencil. Then he crossed his arms and sighed loudly.

"I will stand by anything and everything we have done on his behalf," he finally said. "Our actions at the time were perfectly legal, and we've adhered to the highest professional standards throughout."

"And at a nice hourly rate, I'm sure. Next time you speak to him, you might advise him to cooperate fully when the authorities come knocking. Understood?"

"I told you, he's no longer a client."

"Right. Now he's just a tenant." Cain handed Euston the crystal cocktail glass, which was still half full of bourbon. "Here. You need it more than I do."

He turned and pushed the button for the elevator. Behind him, he heard the door opening to the party, a spill of laughter and conversation, with a woman's voice rising above it in a refined British accent. Lady Ashfield giving a speech, something bland about hands across the water. She spoke Hitler's name just as the door shut.

He wondered what Euston would tell his buddies about the interruption. He was even more curious about what Herman Keller would have to say. The elevator opened. Cain stepped aboard feeling like he'd just faced down a bully. But he had also stirred things up, quite violently, and by the time he was strolling past the doorman downstairs he was already wondering if he'd made a huge mistake.

# 34

..................

HERMAN KELLER WAS NOWHERE to be found. Or so said the police in Edison, New Jersey, who grudgingly checked the address Euston had written down, only to report back that no one had answered their knock on the door.

Maybe he was hiding inside. Maybe Euston had faked the address, or warned off Keller, who had taken off to points unknown. Cain told the desk sergeant in Edison that it might be worth forcing entry on the next try, but short of a search warrant or something more solid he realized that wasn't likely. Nor did Cain have time to cross the river to see for himself. Captain Mulhearn had seen to that by loading him up with fresh paperwork.

At eleven a.m. Cain also gave up on those chores when a clerk from the Bureau of Criminal Identification arrived at his desk with a box-ful of files on Albert Anastasia. It was quite a haul—arrest records, charge sheets, eyewitness reports, and plenty of lurid newspaper sto-ries. Paper-clipped to a rap sheet on top was a two-year-old mug shot. Anastasia stared up at him with an "I dare you" face—intense dark eyes, a small crooked mouth, strong chin, puffy cheeks, and a broad nose that looked like it might have been broken a few times. Black wavy hair, combed straight back from a high forehead, and piled into a high ridge on the left. Reading the particulars, Cain saw that Anastasia was thirty-nine, meaning he probably still had plenty of fight in him.

"What you got there?" It was Simmons, munching on a sandwich. "Nothing much."

Cain closed the box. Mulhearn stood only a few desks away, inching closer by the minute. The last thing he needed was to have everyone start poking their noses in. Loose lips sink ships, and his was already taking on water. He hefted the box, carried it downstairs to an empty interview room, and began to read.

Anastasia had come to New York at seventeen on a freighter from Italy with three brothers. He took a job as a longshoreman on the Brooklyn waterfront, and within two years he had killed a man, for which he was convicted and sentenced to death. That's where his story should have ended. Instead, he won a new trial on a technicality, and by then all four witnesses had disappeared. It would become a recurring pattern, right up through last November.

In 1928 a second murder charge in Brooklyn was dropped when the witnesses vanished or clammed up. In 1931 Anastasia was named as a participant in the killing of Joe "The Boss" Masseria, which had cleared the way for the ascent of Charles "Lucky" Luciano, the very man whose attorney was now meeting with Murray Gurfein and Meyer Lansky. No one was charged. A year later Anastasia was booked for killing a man with an ice pick. No witnesses, charge dropped. The following year brought another murder charge, also dropped for the same reason.

In the mid-thirties, cops and mobsters began calling Anastasia and his pals Murder, Inc. It was an industrial-strength subsidiary of the mob, a specialty shop for which no lethal assignment was too difficult. Cain took note of its purported hangout: Midnight Rose's, a candy store on Saratoga Avenue in Brooklyn. The very place where Gerhard had watched Werner Hansch disappear into the back seat of a Packard. He also noted several references to an associate, Clarence Cohen, the fellow whose recent gambling charge had been erased in the 14th precinct, thanks to the boys in the 95 Room. He shook his head and flipped to the next page.

Anastasia's most notorious work had come during the past several years. In 1939 he arranged the murders of a rival union official and an upstart union activist. Both cases made big headlines. But his boldest stroke had occurred only five months ago, a few weeks before Pearl Harbor, when Anastasia took notice of mob guy Abe Reles. Reles was cooperating with government prosecutors in cases against Anastasia and others. The authorities, understandably worried for Reles's safety, stashed him on the sixth floor of a Coney Island hotel and posted armed guards at the door. Reles was then found dead on a rooftop a floor below his room's open window. The latest theory was that Anastasia had offered a $100,000 reward for the deed. The press wasted no time in coming up with a nickname for Reles: "The canary who could sing, but couldn't fly."

Cain toted up the body count. Eight in all, plus dozens of other cases in which Murder, Inc. was implicated, not to mention the three dead Germans, with a fourth now living on borrowed time in some flophouse on the Bowery. He sighed and put everything back into the box.

But he also took note of one thing Anastasia *hadn't* yet done. He had never killed a cop. A small matter, perhaps, unless you were a cop. It gave Cain a measure of comfort as he contemplated how aggressively to pursue his case. It was Danziger who'd need protection. And any witnesses, of course. Gerhard, Lorenz, and probably Herman Keller as well.

What he still couldn't figure was why Anastasia would have involved himself in a plot to burn the *Normandie*. Yes, he had been born in Italy. But, as Danziger had said, mob guys despised Mussolini.

Cain resealed the box for delivery back to the Bureau of Criminal Identification. Just as he returned to his desk, Mulhearn dropped off yet another case for him to work on. At the next desk over, Yuri Zharkov smiled ruefully.

"Look on the bright side," Zharkov said. "It's time for lunch, and you look like you could use a break."

"I could use about ten of 'em."

"There's a Russian joint not far from here. My treat, if you're interested. The food's top notch and the vodka's homemade. A shot or two might change your whole outlook."

Cain was tempted.

"What I really need to do is head uptown. Or even over to Jersey, if only I could swing a car for the afternoon."

"Just so happens I can take care of that as well. I've got use of a radio car for the rest of the day. And, well, maybe after lunch . . . ?"

"Now that you put it that way, a little borscht and vodka would really hit the spot. But how'd you manage a car?"

"Let's just say Mulhearn owes me. Which means he won't make a peep even if he sees you walking out the door with me. When we're done, I'll run you across the river."

"Lead the way."

The patrol car was parked right out front, a '41 Plymouth with a black body and a white roof.

"Nice wheels."

"Only the best when your captain wants you to keep your mouth shut."

"Care to say what you've got on him?"

"Then it wouldn't be a secret."

Cain laughed, but wondered what Zharkov might be willing to hush up in exchange for a few favors. Zharkov drove uptown. They got hung up in heavy traffic near Times Square before Zharkov invoked a little policeman's privilege by blaring the siren to clear a path. Half a block later he turned up an alley behind a row of stout buildings along Broadway.

"Where the hell's this Russian place?"

"Dead ahead."

Zharkov braked sharply and pulled alongside a loading dock where laundry carts were piled with sheets and towels. Four men in cheap suits and fedoras came sprinting out an open cargo bay and hopped down into the alley, surrounding the car. Zharkov kept his hands on the wheel and his foot on the brake, even as one of the men opened the passenger door.

"What the hell, Yuri?"

Cain reached for his sidearm, but Zharkov beat him to it.

"It's for your own good."

Hands grabbed Cain and pulled him into the alley.

"Is that what you say to all of them?" he asked.

Zharkov wouldn't look at him. He just waited for the door to close and drove away.

Two men had Cain by the arms, one on either side. The other two walked in front and behind. He tried once to wiggle free, but couldn't shake their grip. But they didn't hit him, didn't threaten him. Nor did they look particularly like mob guys. They were clean-shaven and had short haircuts, and their suits looked straight off the rack, like the kind you might buy on a government salary.

"Is this some kind of shakedown?"

"Relax, fella. Right now you're safer than Fort Knox."

They hauled him up the steps of the loading dock and took him down a hallway and through a big kitchen, where men in white smocks were washing dishes. They came out the other side into a corridor where a service elevator stood with its doors open, ready to roll. They went up a floor, to the mezzanine, and when the doors opened Cain saw that they were in the Hotel Astor. They rounded a corner and he knew exactly where he was: just outside the offices of the Executives Association of Greater New York, where Naval Intelligence officer "Red" Haffenden presided over whatever private operation he'd cooked up with his mob buddies. Doomed or not, Cain at least felt like he was on the verge of learning something.

They entered an office where a neatly dressed middle-aged woman sat behind a desk. She stood and knocked on the door of an adjoining room before sticking her head inside.

"He's here, sir. They have him."

"Thank you, Elizabeth," a man answered. "Bring him in. And please hold all calls."

"Yes, sir."

She turned and nodded. The two men marched Cain forward, although by now his curiosity was piqued enough that he would have gone voluntarily. He entered a narrow room with a long table where six men were seated. The man who presumably was Haffenden stood from a chair at the far end. He wore a full dress Navy uniform with a star and three stripes on each sleeve. Murray Gurfein and his boss, DA Frank Hogan, were seated on the right side, opposite three men on the left whom Cain didn't recognize, although he was pretty sure that Socks Lanza was the third one down.

"Detective Sergeant Cain, I'm Lieutenant Commander Haffenden, U.S. Naval Intelligence, although I believe you already knew that. All the more reason we need to confer with you. Be seated."

Cain sat at the opposite end. His escorts left the room.

"I believe you're already acquainted with Mr. Hogan and Mr. Gurfein, correct?"

"Yes, sir."

Cain felt like he'd been called before a military tribunal, with Haffenden preparing to present evidence. Beneath the table he wiped sweaty palms on his trousers.

"The first of these gentlemen to my right is Mr. Joseph Lanza. I understand you attempted to visit him under some sort of cockamamie fake name."

A frowning Lanza nodded to drive home the point.

"To Mr. Lanza's right is Mr. Moses Polakoff, who is here this afternoon on behalf of his client, Mr. Charles Luciano."

"Soon to be residing at Great Meadows prison, correct?" Cain couldn't resist. If they were going to muzzle him, strong-arm him, or worse, he at least wanted to get in a few shots. Haffenden waited a beat, as if controlling his temper.

"He is. Although that is privileged information, Detective Cain, and it would be best for all concerned if you were not to repeat it outside this room. In fact, this is probably a good time to remind you that everything you'll be hearing is privileged information. Top secret. We'll be asking you to sign an FBI confidentiality agreement once we're done. On second thought, let's take care of that now, shall we, Frank?"

Hogan nodded, and Gurfein slid forward a legal-sized page of small print on an FBI letterhead, with his full name typed beneath a blank line for his signature.

"Should I even bother to read it?"

"Only if you want to waste our time," Hogan said. "It's boilerplate."

Cain nodded. The man to his immediate left, an exquisitely dressed fellow sitting on what Cain already thought of as the mob side of the table, offered him the use of a sleek and expensive-looking fountain pen. He had big ears, dark eyebrows, and intense narrow-set eyes that seemed to take your measure in an instant.

"Thank you," Cain said. "I don't believe we've been introduced."

"I'm sure Red will correct that oversight shortly. First things first."

Cain took the pen, warm from its resting place inside the man's shirt pocket, and signed the document. The scratching of the nib against paper was the only sound in the room. Cain started to hand back the pen. Then, thinking better of it, he dropped it into his pocket. This drew an enigmatic smile from the pen's owner. Gurfein took the document and handed it to Hogan, who locked it in a briefcase.

"Let's hope the rest of our business this afternoon proceeds as smoothly," Haffenden said. "Now I'd like you to meet Mr. Meyer Lansky, whose pen you just stole."

The others laughed uncomfortably. Cain managed a weak smile, which seemed to please Lansky a great deal. Cain met his gaze and tried not to waver. The Little Man, that's what Danziger had called him. Maybe Cain would've recognized him if everyone had been standing.

"Very well," Haffenden said. "Let's get down to business."

Lanza took the opportunity to glare at Cain once again. Lansky merely nodded, which somehow bothered him more. Hogan and Gurfein were preoccupied with their notes, and Polakoff was already glancing at his watch.

"Detective Cain, we've invited you here today—"

"*Invited* me, sir?"

This drew another round of uneasy laughter, but Haffenden wasn't amused.

"Let's not get hung up on logistics," he said. "You're here by whatever means because your work has become a nuisance and, frankly, a danger to an ongoing operation vital to our national security, a highly sensitive intelligence arrangement involving the cooperation of every man in this room, and quite a few of their associates."

"Criminal associates, you mean."

"Call them what you will, but in this instance they are acting legally and with the full consent of local and federal authorities."

"Doing what?"

"Finally, a relevant question. They are acting as our eyes and ears, sir, all along the waterfront. From Manhattan to Brooklyn and on over to Jersey, at every shipyard and loading dock, and aboard every fishing smack. When they're out on the water, they're watching for submarines, or for anyone aiding and abetting them. They're listening for signs of treason, or sabotage, or any loose talk that might tip the enemy to our shipping schedules. Call it unorthodox, I'm fine with that. But these people have power with the unions and clout on the wharves, and for the duration of this war I'm happy and even honored to have them on our side. Agreed, gentlemen?"

Everyone nodded or said yes, although to Cain's eye Gurfein and Hogan didn't look particularly comfortable about it. Whatever else he thought of the arrangement, Cain easily saw its logic. Truckers, fishermen, retailers, and shipping companies had long ago learned that if you wanted to do business on the waterfront, then you had to work with the mob. Perhaps it stood to reason that, with a war on, the government would be just as pragmatic. But at what price? Businessmen paid cash. He wondered what the government was offering. Legal considerations, perhaps, or why else would Hogan and Gurfein be involved?

"What do they get out of it?" Cain asked. "And did you plan on maybe letting the cops know?"

Haffenden frowned and hesitated. Hogan spoke up.

"I can answer part of that. Neither Mr. Luciano nor Mr. Lanza here have been given any special legal considerations whatsoever. Mr. Lanza remains under indictment by my office, and Mr. Luciano's prison sentence remains in force. Mr. Lansky will attest to that, I'm sure. He is currently acting as the liaison between Mr. Luciano and my office. And since you brought it up, Mr. Luciano's move to Great Meadows is a simple matter of convenience. Whenever we need to meet him—or rather, whenever Mr. Lansky needs to meet him on our behalf—he can now do so in roughly half the time. But we have made no promises of leniency, nor will we."

"As for the police," Haffenden said, "to this point we've kept Commissioner Valentine out of the loop for his own damn good. La

Guardia as well. But apparently now we're going to have to tell them *something*, largely because of you."

Cain had been debating whether to take his lesson quietly, or, since this might be his only opportunity, to try to get all the answers he could, even if it meant asking dangerous questions. He decided to opt for the latter, and his first question was a doozy.

"You say you've made no special considerations. Does that apply as well to the associates of these men who've been murdering German laborers? Three of them, so far, with the probable involvement of Albert Anastasia. Who, as far as I can tell, has been trying to cover up a plot to burn the *Normandie*, a plot which seems to have succeeded pretty damn well."

Haffenden sighed and slowly shook his head, as if he'd just heard the ravings of a lunatic. Hogan's reaction was far more interesting: a startled glance at Gurfein, who frowned and spread his hands, pleading ignorance. Lansky looked down at the table, his expression stony.

Haffenden turned to Hogan.

"Frank, please tell Detective Cain the full results once again of the select investigation of the fire on the *Normandie*, will you?"

Hogan nodded solemnly and produced a thick file. He plucked a sheet from inside.

"It was an accident, open and shut. This is not merely my opinion, Mr. Cain. It's the firm conclusion of a panel of experts from several walks of life, convened especially for this purpose. Believe me, these were people who *wanted* to find evidence of espionage if there was any to be found. There's nothing we would have liked better than to pin this on some foreign bogeyman. If you need further convincing, I can arrange for your access to the entire file—every eyewitness account, every expert analysis. I might even be able to arrange for you to speak to the stupid and careless welder who started the whole thing, because God knows he won't be busy with gainful employment anytime soon."

"No need," Cain said. "But if that's true, why have three men been killed? And why is Anastasia involved?"

Hogan lowered his eyes. He looked uncomfortable, the way he probably looked in a courtroom when a defense attorney blindsided him with new information. He jabbed a finger at Cain and raised his voice.

"Mr. Anastasia has nothing to do with this arrangement. If he's a participant in any way, shape, or form, then it is certainly not under our auspices!"

A strong remark, but the lawyerly wording left the door open to complicity by others in the room. Haffenden scowled as if the whole thing were preposterous, or maybe he was upset because Cain had introduced a note of discord to his collegial atmosphere. Lansky continued to look down at the table, no longer smiling. Cain turned toward him.

"Mr. Lansky, is that your understanding as well?"

Lansky looked up abruptly, narrowing his eyes into a gaze so penetrating that Cain almost wished he hadn't asked.

"I concur with everything Mr. Hogan just said. And I'll have you know that I, too, am a patriot, sir, as is every man at this table."

"Well spoken, Meyer," Haffenden said, sounding entirely too chummy for Cain's taste. Hogan and Gurfein were both fiddling with papers.

Lansky, emboldened, continued. "As for whoever might be running around murdering scrappy little Germans with swastikas sewn into their underwear, well . . . ?" He threw up his hands. "It's not as if those fellows get along all that well among themselves."

"Detective Cain," Haffenden said, "if we haven't sufficiently satisfied your curiosity, then you had better speak up now, because the last thing we want is for you to leave this meeting thinking you can simply resume business as before."

"You've answered some questions, obviously. But all of them? No."

"In that case, I believe it's time for our other special guest." He turned toward Gurfein. "Murray, bring him in."

Gurfein returned seconds later with a stout fellow in a gray suit. Cain was guessing he was yet another government lawyer. The man stood behind Hogan's chair.

"Thank you, Murray." Haffenden said. "This is Mr. Lawrence Albright, the U.S. Attorney for North Carolina. Mr. Albright, at taxpayer expense, has come all the way up here from Raleigh on an overnight train, and at very short notice. He tells us that he is in the process of deciding whether to take a new look at a case involving the shooting death of a former colleague of yours, Officer Robert Vance, due to certain irregularities that have come to light in recent weeks."

"Irregularities?" Cain felt his voice fading even as the word left his mouth.

Albright turned to face him, somewhat awkwardly perhaps, although he managed to spout his few scripted lines as if he really believed them.

"Yes, sir. Irregularities. Due to new information, some of it from a member of Mr. Vance's family."

"His brother James, you mean, who'd say or do anything to get back at me. I understand his grief, believe me. I share it. But he's become a bit unhinged, as you may have noticed."

"Be that as it may . . ." Albright paused to clear his throat. "We're currently considering whether to reopen the investigation with regard to possible federal charges."

"I see."

"I'm sure you do," Haffenden said. "And I'm sure you would prefer to put that matter to rest, just as we would prefer that your intrusive inquiry proceed no further. So do we have an understanding, Mr. Cain?"

He knew when he was whipped. "Yes. I believe we do."

"Outstanding. And by the way, since you're not the only one who's been creating problems, it might behoove you to learn a little more about your co-conspirator, Mr. Danziger. Turns out there is all sorts of readily available information, most of which we were able to discover thanks to your own initial inquiry. So we do have you to thank for that, I suppose. Frank, could you please give him that last item?"

Hogan reached beneath the table and produced a fat, dog-eared folder. He slid it across the table, and Cain's heart sank as he saw the name on the outer edge: Dalitz, Alexander. It was the police file that he'd requested from the Hall of Records. The word "CLOSED" was stamped in red on the outer flap. Below was a handwritten notation in black ink: *"Subject deceased. File closed, Dec. 4, 1928."*

So here it was, then. Everything about Danziger's past, filed under his true identity. And now, thanks to his own curiosity, everyone in the room knew about Sascha Dalitz's disappearing act, and his subsequent resurrection. He'd given them Danziger, served him up as conveniently as a Thanksgiving turkey, and this was their way of letting him know it.

"We've made our own copies," Haffenden said, "so feel free to keep that for as long as you like. As a bonus, we even threw in a nice little story, written long ago by America's favorite scribe of the streets. It's right there on the top."

Cain opened the folder just long enough to see the pages of a magazine story from 1920, written by Damon Runyon. So it was true, then. Danziger had even briefly been famous, or perhaps notorious was the better word. And now maybe he was about to be notorious again, in a way he never would have wanted. Cain felt sick to his stomach.

"You're free to go," Haffenden said.

He stood, saying nothing. He was a little weak in the knees, and he must have looked quite forlorn, because even in their moment of triumph none of the other men would look him in the eye. Except Lansky, who leaned toward him across the table, smiling enigmatically. He beckoned Cain closer, and Cain obliged. Lansky cupped a hand to his mouth and whispered, the words brushing Cain's ear like the wings of a moth: "Give my personal regards to Sascha. Tell him it has been far too long."

Turning to face him, Cain barely controlled a shudder as Lansky smiled again. Then he left the room, passing through the outer office like a sleepwalker. No escorts followed him. He stepped down the hallway toward the front of the building. The doors of an elevator opened as if by request.

"Which way, sir?" a uniformed operator asked brightly.

"Down," Cain said as he stepped aboard. "Ground floor. Straight to the bottom."

# 35

............

ZHARKOV WAS WAITING FOR HIM in the hotel lobby, hat in hand. He looked a bit sheepish.

"Thought you might need a ride back," he said.

Cain considered walking past him without a word, but Zharkov looked so eager to make amends that he nodded and said, "Guess we're not going to Jersey, huh?"

The patrol car was double-parked on Broadway, a brazen move which drew a few grumbles as they climbed in. Cain said nothing as Zharkov pulled away from the curb. He looked down at the folder in his lap. He opened it, glanced at the Damon Runyon story, and then turned to the pages below, a smattering of arrest reports and eyewitness accounts.

"What you got there?" Zharkov asked.

"The file for Sascha Dalitz."

"So they know?" He sounded upset.

"So do you, from the sound of it."

Zharkov shrugged. He didn't look happy.

Cain looked back at the file. The first thing that jumped out at him were the aliases—aka Sascha, Webster, The Dictionary. So, then. Even the thugs and mobsters had been impressed by his manner of speaking, or perhaps by his command of so many tongues.

Slowly and silently, Cain began to read, skimming pages while

Zharkov sat quietly at the wheel, stalled in Broadway traffic. Not that either of them was in a hurry.

The documented crimes began early, at the age of sixteen, but they were petty and infrequent—minor involvement in sidewalk crap games, or running numbers. And as Danziger—or Dalitz—entered his twenties there was practically nothing more. The real news at this point in his life were peripheral mentions, copied into the file from witness statements and charging documents for other suspects charged in far more serious cases involving extortion, assault, murder—crimes for which Dalitz either had been questioned or had turned up as part of the scenery, the background noise. There were a few pages from the NYPD's "modus operandi" file as well, which, when combined with the rest, built a skeletal portrait of an ambitious young man up to his neck in the mobster lifestyle, a workaday regular in the entourage of the kingpin of his era, Arnold Rothstein, aka The Brain.

But it was the Runyon piece that gave the portrait its flesh and blood, albeit without once mentioning Dalitz by name. It was not a newspaper column, as Beryl's uncle Fedya had thought, but a short story from *Collier's* magazine, in which Runyon described a quiet young man on the cusp of thirty who was known to his fellows as The Dictionary. Runyon set the scene by describing the characters gathered at a Broadway restaurant called Mindy's, which of course was a stand-in for Lindy's. Rothstein appeared simply as The Brain.

*One evening along about eight o'clock I am eating at Mindy's Restaurant when in walks The Brain and all his boys. It is that lonely hour when the hustlers and horseplayers have all gone home with their torn markers and glum faces, scuffling off into a night that is as cold as a blonde's heart.*

One of Rothstein's "boys," as it turned out, was The Dictionary. Runyon, the street poet who by all accounts was still hanging out with the likes of Jack Dempsey and Al Capone—or had been, until Capone went to prison—offered a brief close-up of The Dictionary, who he described as keeping to himself more than the others, even while attracting the attention of The Brain whenever an important question arose.

*For even though the boys are chatty tonight, and their gab sounds very dreamy, sometimes very pipe-dreamy, the real action is playing out as if in a back room of some road house off the Pelham Parkway. I learn this just by sitting in my chair without once making it squeak, which allows me to watch the one boy among them who speaks like a man with an education, like even maybe he should be covered in Ivy. He measures his every word, and never acts at all giddy or excited even when he sees, as we all do, the Brain hand a C-note to Mindy.*

The piece went on in that vein for a few paragraphs more, painting The Dictionary as a sort of oracle who The Brain consulted from time to time whenever the room got quiet. The story then veered off into a lengthy description of a colorful event in which two of The Brain's other minions played the most prominent roles. By the time you reached the meat of the action, Dalitz, or The Dictionary, had fallen by the wayside. In fact, he had exited Mindy's altogether, and for Cain the most intriguing sentence of the story was Runyon's passing description of The Dictionary's early departure.

*The boys all smile because he leaves on the arm of a doll called Maria who is black haired and built well from the ground up, with one of those heartbreaker faces that says there will soon be tears. And you can bet five to six that they won't be hers, because if there is anything apt to cause trouble it is dolls.*

Maria. Cain wondered if it was yet another pseudonym from Runyon, or the real thing? Maybe she had merely been a passing fancy. But the image stuck with him.

He put the story aside and thumbed back through the other pages toward the end. It was all disturbing, he supposed, although not as much of a punch to the gut as he would've guessed. What had Cain expected, after all? Something pretty much like this. For the moment he was far more troubled by having alerted everyone else, Lansky included, to Sascha's new existence as a harmless old letter writer named Danziger.

Then he turned to the final page, and there was the punch to the gut. It was an incident report for a murder, citing a body that had been pulled from the East River on a cold morning in late November of 1928. The naked corpse was bloated from its prolonged soak, and had been severely disfigured by deep knife wounds to the face and chest. Those circumstances made identification difficult, and the body sat for six days on a slab at the city mortuary before an enterprising young beat cop was able to make a positive identification, finally settling the matter to the satisfaction of the medical examiner and the principal investigator.

The dead man, the cop said, was Alexander "Sascha" Dalitz, age thirty-eight. The policeman attested to this fact in a sworn statement, which he signed with a flourish: Patrolman Yuri Zharkov, of the 7th precinct.

Cain was unable to withhold a gasp. He abruptly shut the file and looked out through the windshield. They were stopped at a red light at Broadway and 35th.

"So it was you," he said to Zharkov.

"The guy who gave him his new skin?"

"Yeah."

Zharkov nodded.

"Who was it really? The body, I mean."

Zharkov shrugged. "Who knows? Some nobody. The gangs were going at each other pretty good right then. Everybody was fighting over Rothstein's old turf, so it wasn't exactly a big deal for some stiff to turn up nobody had ever heard of."

"I suppose it was his idea. Danziger's, I mean."

"It's a long story. I'm sure Sascha could tell it better."

"Oh, I'm quite sure of that." Cain's tone was sarcastic enough to draw a look from Zharkov, who then turned back toward the traffic.

"If you're waiting for me to act ashamed then you're going to be waiting a long damn time."

"What did you get out of the deal?"

"A friend worth saving."

"That's all?"

"Like I said. Ask Sascha. Or Danziger, or whatever the fuck you want to call him. But only if you're ready to be the guy who saves him this time around. If all those guys know, then he's pretty fucked. You're aware of that, I hope."

"Well aware. Considering everything I just learned back at the Astor, I'm pretty sure me and him both are fucked. Especially as long as no one seems inclined to do anything about the Mad Hatter."

Zharkov frowned darkly. His hands tightened on the steering wheel. "Anastasia's involved in this?"

"Has been all along, apparently. Just not in any sort of officially sanctioned role."

Zharkov whistled and shook his head. "Shit. Poor Sascha."

"Yeah," Cain said without much emotion. "Poor Sascha."

He glanced down at the file, with all its evidence of Danziger's misspent youth and beyond, all the way up to age thirty-eight.

"How 'bout if you take me on home? Not sure I can stand another whole afternoon of Mulhearn."

"I'll cover for you."

"I'm sure you will. You're good at that."

Zharkov might have winced, but he didn't speak. Cain entered his apartment building in a bit of a daze, which is probably why he didn't pick up on it right away when the day doorman, Tom, began to gush about how Cain must really be coming up in the world, a real man of means, based on the posh treatment his family was getting these days.

"Ain't that right, sir?"

Cain turned at the base of the stairwell. Tom was grinning ear to ear.

"What was that, Tom?"

"I mean, driving around in limos. Or practically limos, from what I could see. Living in the lap of luxury. At least, that's pretty much how everybody else on the block must have seen it."

"Back up a second. Who are we talking about here?"

"Why, your little Olivia! And Miss Eileen. Less than an hour ago, climbing into that big black Packard like they owned half of Macy's or something."

Cain's backbone went rigid.

"Say that again. Olivia got into a black Packard? Going where?"

"Straight to the Plaza for tea and crumpets for all I know, Mr. Cain. You mean to tell me you didn't know about this? We all figured you was putting on airs!"

"Who took them? Who made them get in?"

"Made them, sir?" Tom's smile disappeared.

"Did they get in on their own, or was somebody forcing them? Who the hell was in that car, Tom?"

Cain's fear was contagious. Tom was now blinking rapidly as he racked his brain for details of what he'd witnessed less than an hour ago.

"I dunno, sir. It all happened so fast, and so smooth. If I'd have thought something bad was going down I sure as hell would've done something. Do you think—?"

"I don't know what to think. But I need to find them."

Cain pushed back through the door and onto the sidewalk. He ran toward the street, looking left and right for the patrol car so he could flag down Zharkov. But the patrol car was gone. Cain was in a panic, out of breath and out of ideas.

All he could think of was the black Packard that Gerhard had watched pulling up to the curb on Saratoga Avenue, just before Werner Hansch and Albert Anastasia climbed in.

# 36

........................

## DANZIGER

IN APRIL 1917, SHORTLY BEFORE my twenty-sixth birthday, I
tried to become a soldier in the United States Army. The world was at
war and I wished to do my part. I meant to "beat back the Hun," as the
placards said, even though by birth I *was* a Hun. I saw it as my chance
to prove that I was at last fully American, and with my mother and
father long gone there was no one to object. Or so I thought.

Out of professional courtesy I decided to notify my boss of my
intentions, the very man of genius and largesse who had utilized my
talents to date, and, by doing so, had turned me into a somewhat polished man of means.

It was early evening by the time I steeled myself for this task. He sat
in his usual booth at Lindy's, dapper as ever in a pressed suit, starched
shirt, and his almost dainty bow tie. I detected the scent of his aftershave as he welcomed me into what passed for his office. I must have
been more nervous about it than I wanted to let on, because I remember trying to strike a casual pose by leaning against the coatrack. I
cleared my throat and broke the news.

"I am going to enlist."

"Enlist?"

"For the war."

"You already *have* enlisted," he said, gesturing grandly with his right arm to encompass the room and all his minions and petitioners, gathered under one roof as they did each and every night. It was, in that sense, very much like a corporate headquarters.

"With the draft board, I mean."

"I know what you mean. But you're needed here, Sascha. For this war, which will still be going long after the one in Europe has ended."

I eyed him closely. The intensity of his resolve was written in the steady coolness of his eyes. He was practically daring me to blink. Then, as it became clear that I wouldn't, he rose slowly and placed a hand on my shoulder. Under other circumstances it might have felt protective, but at the moment it seemed only as if he were driving home the message that he would never willingly release his hold. For the first time since we had met, I was genuinely frightened by the man.

Yet, I could not resist raising at least the possibility of a challenge to his authority.

"And if I sign up anyway?"

"Well, you know what becomes of deserters, don't you? In anyone's army, theirs or ours."

I nodded, hoping that he would see that I had exhausted the limits of my resistance, and therefore needed no further explanation. Apparently he was not convinced, because he then elucidated further by miming the shape of a pistol with his right hand. He held this pose briefly before snapping down his thumb like a firing hammer.

"Bang," he said.

Then he smiled, so that we could pretend it was a joke, even though we both knew it wasn't.

So, I stayed home in New York, and continued to fight in that other war which only occasionally made the newspapers, issuing its casualty reports in ones and twos. I suppose you might say I worked in the intelligence corps, a role which fortunately did not often lend itself to criminal charges or grand jury proceedings.

That alarming moment of candor made me realize that there would never be any safe exit from this world unless I was willing to take extraordinary measures. It was then that I first began to contemplate what those measures might entail, even though I would not come up with a satisfactory answer for another eleven and a half years.

Now, having heard the terrible name of Anastasia in association with this scheme that Mr. Cain and I have stumbled upon, I realize that those extraordinary measures, which once seemed foolproof, were almost certainly insufficient. And with the world once again in conflict I fully expect in the days to come to be called back into active duty in that other, lesser war, the one closer to home, the one in which service is always compulsory. Except this time my charge as a soldier will be to protect Mr. Cain and his daughter. Having drawn them into the line of fire, I must vow to act more out of concern for their safety than my own.

Such were my thoughts as I rounded the corner onto Rivington Street and saw, to my horror, that the windows and doors for house number 174 were pouring black smoke into the gray skies above. A crowd stood outside, clamoring, alarmed, mouths open. A long truck of the fire brigade had arrived, and men in red helmets were smashing forward with axes and hoses. I thought of all those lives trapped inside, in their snug holes and crevices, spirits which now seemed to be rising from the windows with each bellow of smoke.

I cried out loudly and ran. Reaching a cordon of neighbors, I shoved them aside, desperate for entry, until my progress was halted by a pair of rough hands that seized me from behind and threw me backward to the ground. I looked up expecting to see an overzealous fireman, but instead beheld two grinning men in fedoras and dark pinstripe suits who began kicking me with the toes of their lace-up Italian shoes.

"It burns, and you're gone, chump!" the one on the right said as his toe hammered my rib cage.

I rolled onto my stomach just as a blow from the other direction glanced off my head. I already felt light-headed, trying to fend off their kicks with my arms at my sides even as their blows drummed my ribs and my back. I heard shouting, some sort of commotion in the crowd beyond, and then the noise went fuzzy and the world grew dim. That was when the kicking suddenly stopped, leaving my ears ringing and my body in agony, but my consciousness intact. Slowly, painfully,

I raised myself onto my knees. Then a hand came down to help me, pulling me unsteadily to my feet.

It was Yuri Zharkov, I saw now, although my eyes were swimming. A police patrol car, its door open and the engine still running, was pulled to the edge of the crowd at a violent angle. Half the people were still watching the fire, and half were watching me. Another policeman, arriving on foot, held one of the thugs at gunpoint. The other had presumably made his escape.

"You okay, Sascha?"

Zharkov looked back and forth between me and the thug, who had a nasty welt in his forehead with an imprint of the grain of Zharkov's gun stock. The thug was swaying on his feet, even woozier than me.

"I think so." I patted myself to check for anything broken.

"Here," Zharkov said, handing me a handkerchief. "Your nose is bloody."

I tasted salt and wiped at my face. The handkerchief came away red, so I held it again to my nostrils and squeezed.

"You need to find a bolthole and stay in it," Zharkov said.

"You expect there will be more of them?"

"Your secret's out. *Our* secret. Cain, everybody, they all know it. Hogan, Lansky, everybody. I'll make do, you know how that works, but you are well and truly fucked."

"Yes," I said, taking it all in. A gust of smoke blew through us, acrid and stinking of burned paper, suddenly reminding me of why moments ago I had been in such a panic.

"My letters!" I exclaimed, turning. But as I did so, a shower of sparks blew toward us and the gasping crowd surged back. We heard the crash and splintering roar of falling timbers. The roof was collapsing. The house was caving in on itself. *My* house. My neighborhood nerve center, with all its memories, its archival importance, turning to ashes before my eyes.

I sank to my knees. I saw no way forward, no way of moving anywhere at all. And for a moment or two I contemplated how I might most easily finish what the two thugs had begun. Drown myself, shoot myself, jump off a bridge. Into the East River, perhaps, to join my mother and father.

Then I shuddered and drew a few deep breaths to clear my head of smoke and fear and pain. I stood, regaining my balance more easily than I would have thought possible. Zharkov told me to get into the patrol car. His words came to me muted and wavery, as if we were both underwater.

However dimly, I now realized that one course still remained open to me—a dark and slender path leading back into the past. Just as I'd suspected, just as I'd feared, I had become a soldier again, called back to duty in the only war I had ever known.

"Get in," Zharkov said again, taking me by the arm. "We have to find someplace where you'll be safe for a while."

"Yes," I said, nodding.

I was eager to get moving, eager to tend to my wounds. It was time to re-enlist.

# 37

...................

CAIN'S PANIC MOVED INTO its second hour.

He had already phoned Danziger three times and Beryl twice. No answer at the former, but he had finally reached Beryl, who vowed to be there as fast as she could. In desperation for any possible help he had even tried to reach Harris Euston, but all he got was his father-in-law's secretary, who curtly took a message and told him that her boss was gone for the day, even though it was only three p.m.

Finally he tried phoning Zharkov at the station house, but neither the detective nor the patrol car had returned, and for the moment both were unreachable by radio.

Briefly he toyed with the idea of asking Mulhearn to sound the alarm, or put out an APB for his daughter. But he knew from experience that they fielded missing person calls like this all the time, and never did a damn thing until at least forty-eight hours had passed. And for all he knew, Mulhearn, or Maloney, or another of his corrupt colleagues from the 14th precinct was in on the whole thing, so what was the use?

Going stir-crazy as he paced the floor of the small kitchen, Cain grabbed his keys, ran down the stairs, and headed for the street. Tom the doorman bounded to his feet, following Cain onto the sidewalk.

"Any luck, sir?"

"No," he called over his shoulder. "Not a sign."

He had no plan, no leads, no ideas, and at first all he could think to do was circle the block, if only to burn off nervous energy. He then expanded his orbit by a block in each direction, on the slim hope of stumbling onto Olivia and Eileen in some park or school playground, or on the stoop of a beneficent friend or neighbor who would turn out to be the person who'd generously sent the limo, although Cain knew that didn't make a damn bit of sense.

Misery seemed to be everywhere he looked. A young woman emerged from a store in tears; a beggar fell to his knees at the curb, pants torn, ranting about a spilled cup of coffee; the old grocer Aldo from around the corner, usually so cheerful, stood morosely in his doorway, head down. On Seventh Avenue, Cain looked up at the sky hoping to see a hopeful expanse of blue, but instead felt hemmed in by the tall buildings, windows reflecting sunlight so sharply that it hurt his eyes. Omens and portents, all of them bad.

He stopped to collect himself and was immediately bumped into from behind.

"Move it, bud!"

This wasn't bustle, or vibrancy. It was a stampede before an ill wind. He resumed his progress, such as it was, and as he returned to the apartment building he saw Tom galloping toward him.

"They're here, sir! All in one piece!"

Cain stopped, momentarily overwhelmed by relief, blood pounding between his ears. He stooped over, pressed his hands to his knees, and then straightened as he drew a deep breath, tasting spring.

"Thank you, Tom. Are they upstairs?"

"Yes, sir. I'm sorry to have upset you, sir."

"No, Tom, it's fine." He heaved out another deep breath. "All's well that ends well."

He came through the door to find them both in the kitchen, Olivia seated at the table with a glass of water, and Eileen beside her with a look of concern, still holding her purse, as if she expected to be asked to leave immediately.

"Mr. Cain," she said. "My apologies, sir. We just—"

"Where were you? Oh, Olivia, come here."

He reached her before she could even climb out of the chair, and he pulled her into the air with a fierce hug. If anything she seemed baffled, but she kissed him on the cheek. He gently set her back down and turned to Eileen.

"Who was in the limo?" he asked. "The big Packard that came and picked you up?"

Eileen lowered her head. "I am so sorry, sir. I have been a deceitful woman. But I cannot do it no more, sir, no matter how much he pays me."

"Who?"

She winced and averted her eyes. "Mr. Euston, sir."

Cain was about to ask more, but she rushed onward in another burst of confession.

"I knew I'd reached my limit, sir, when the girl told me about what happened last Saturday night, after I called in saying there was a family emergency, like he'd asked me."

"Euston *asked* you to do that?"

She nodded rapidly.

"And on Monday morning, when this poor girl told me about all the places she'd been that night, and everything that she had seen." Eileen shook her head. "Well, sir, not that I don't wish for her to spend more time in the house of the Lord. But, glory be, Mr. Cain, with all of those people of the night? You couldn't burn enough incense to hide the stench of their mortal sin. The ladies alone. And when she told me the story of that poor man . . ."

"The German? You know about him? Tell me, when you last talked to Mr. Euston, did you tell him about the German?"

She lowered her face, and didn't look up as she answered. "Only in the most general way, sir. Just as I'm telling you now. It wasn't as if the poor girl gave me chapter and verse."

Cain stood there marveling at his father-in-law's manipulative powers, at all of his conduits for information. And no wonder, with clients like Herman Keller and Chase Bank to cover for. Poor old Gerhard. Even a knave like him seemed to deserve a little pity in the face of such formidable opposition. And this certainly explained why Euston had been so willing to pay for all of Eileen's extended hours—except on Sunday, of course, when Euston must have realized Cain was still working the case in his off hours, so he had acted accordingly to try to stop him.

"Where did you go this afternoon, then, in Euston's limo?"

This was Eileen's worst moment yet. She twisted the handles of her purse. For a moment he thought she would cry.

"I don't blame *you*, Eileen," he said softly. "Just tell me what happened."

"It's the girl's mother, sir. He sends the car with her in it, and we climb in for a visit, for a ride."

"A visit? With *Clovis*?"

The mention of the name almost crumpled Eileen. She answered with a nod.

"How many times has this happened? How many times have you taken Olivia to see her behind my back?"

Eileen began to shake with sobs.

"Daddy, it's all right." It was Olivia, who lowered her head when he looked her way. Then she slowly looked up at him, her face imploring him for mercy. He realized then that he was quivering with anger, so he took another deep breath and blew the air out his cheeks.

"I was going to tell, you," Olivia said, suddenly looking quite grown up. She paused. "Not right away, but someday." A girl with her secrets. All those earlier trips to the park. "It's just been a few times. We drive around mostly. Or stop for ice cream and stuff. She asks about you."

Cain dropped into a crouch and again enfolded his daughter in his arms.

"I'm not mad at you, sweetheart. I just need to know what you're doing, who you're seeing." He steeled himself for his next words, not sure he could say them without a tinge of bitterness. "It's okay if you see your mama. But just tell me about it next time. Preferably beforehand, okay?"

"Okay."

"Now why don't you go to your room and get washed up for dinner. Maybe we'll go out, all right?"

"All right."

His anger began building again almost the moment she departed—not at Eileen, or at Clovis, but at Euston, whose long-range plan now seemed clearer than ever. Give Cain a job to lure him and Olivia to New York. Then secretly reunite the girl with her mother, and as soon as Clovis was healthy or stable enough, snatch Olivia away from him with Eileen's assistance. In the meantime he'd use Cain all he could to find out more information from inside the 14th precinct. Then the Hansch case had come along, giving even greater urgency to Cain's role as a conduit, a tool. A bonus return on Euston's investment.

Although that part of the man's scheme had backfired, because Cain had now dug up enough dirt about Euston to stay his hand with regard to Olivia.

Provided no one killed Cain first. Because now he had the likes of Hogan and Haffenden bearing down on him with threats of prosecution or, at the very least, further embarrassment, over the shooting in Horton. Plus Lansky, Lanza, and, worst of all, Anastasia, who seemed to be acting beyond everyone's control. Even if Haffenden's intent was truly to secure the waterfront, at minimum the naval officer had been duped about the Mad Hatter's doings. Lansky himself had implied as much, with his gestures if not his words.

How do you fight back against those kinds of forces? Cain didn't yet have an answer.

"Is it all right if I go now, sir?" Eileen asked as meekly as a girl of nineteen.

"Yes, Eileen. You may go. And I hope you'll be returning in the morning."

"Of course, sir."

She bustled away before he could change his mind. Cain stood in the kitchen, worried and discouraged, trying to come up with any plausible means to keep the investigation going. His thoughts were interrupted by a tentative knock at the door.

"Christ!" he muttered. Eileen must have forgotten something.

Instead it was the night doorman, Pete, who must have just come on duty.

"Pardon, sir, but you have visitors, and considering the shape one of 'em is in I thought it was best to bring them up straightaway."

The door opened wider to reveal Danziger, bruised and bleeding and smelling of smoke, with a shaken Beryl at his side, helping to support him. He was stooped beneath the weight of a dingy sack, a pillowcase bulging with papers which Cain now saw were letters and envelopes, folded and crumpled in a slapdash pile.

"What's happened? Bring them in, Pete. Danziger, are you all right?"

He and Beryl led Danziger to the couch, where the older man collapsed. He let his makeshift sack fall to the floor, where it slumped sideways and spilled a pile of letters onto the floor. Mixed among them, Cain saw, was the small photo of the young black-haired woman that he had seen atop Danziger's desk. Cain was now pretty sure he knew who it was. Among the letters that were showing, many were yellowed, with faded ink and foreign stamps. Lives, he thought. Scattered on his floor as if rescued from disaster.

Danziger followed his gaze.

"It is all that remains," he said, patting the sack as if to reassure himself. His voice was hoarse with exhaustion, his blue eyes almost spectral. "I am fortunate in the extreme to have even this much. A neighbor, who is also a client, ran inside the moment he saw smoke, or else it would all be gone. Of course, some he could not save. A third of it, perhaps. Maybe more. Gone. Like smoke up a chimney."

"Your whole place burned?"

"To the ground."

"But how did you . . . ? You're bleeding, and—"

"A pair of thugs, almost certainly dispatched by the Mad Hatter. They took hold of me as I tried to get through the crowd. They beat me, right there in front of everyone, and I have no doubt they would have finished the job if Yuri Zharkov had not arrived."

"In the patrol car?"

"Yes. He told me of your lunch appointment, and of your newest archival acquisition. Even the Runyon story, he said. So now you know. Now you have seen it. The life of Sascha."

Cain glanced at Beryl, who had settled onto the couch at Danziger's side. She frowned with concern.

"You can stay here if you like," Cain told the old man. It seemed more important right now to offer assurance than to pry deeper into his past. Explanations could wait. He fetched a blanket, and Beryl put it around Danziger's shoulders. Then he got a glass of water. The older man drank and nodded in gratitude.

"I thank you for your generous offer," Danziger said, "but it will not be safe for me here. It is one of the first places they will seek me. Fedya will know where I can hide. That is where I have come from, courtesy of this sweet young woman."

"Fedya called me right after you did," Beryl explained. "I'm glad to see Olivia's all right."

"False alarm," Cain said.

"The girl?" Danziger said, eyes shining with sudden alarm.

"She's fine," Cain said. "See?"

Olivia, looking a little bewildered by the scene, waved to him from the kitchen doorway. Danziger smiled and relaxed back into the cushions.

"I've led you right back into the middle of everything," Cain said.

"I have gone of my own accord. It was I who sought you out. Even then I probably knew where it would lead." He looked off toward an empty corner of the room. "Perhaps that is why I did it."

"But we can't stop now. Not completely. You should lay low, but I've been thinking about what I can still do, and—"

Danziger's hand shot out and gripped Cain's forearm. His blue eyes glowed with vitality. He may have been drawing upon his last and deepest reserves, but he was not yet beaten.

"That is the very thing you must *not* do. Later, perhaps, when we are thinking more clearly. For now, you have your girl to think of, and you are yet so young. Please, Beryl, make a call now to your uncle, to see if he has completed the arrangements for my lodging."

Beryl did so, and kept it brief. Cain heard the anxiety in her voice. Mostly she nodded while Fedya talked.

"You should eat," Cain said to Danziger. "All of us should. Olivia and me were about to go out."

Danziger shook his head. "Go, then, the two of you. I should not be out and about with you. I would not put her at risk in that way. I have put far too many innocents at risk in this life of mine, as by now you must be aware."

"Sort of."

"Yes. Police records are always incomplete. The bones only. Perhaps after you have eaten, I can offer you the flesh and blood."

"You don't have to, you know. You don't owe me that."

"I do, especially if I am to ask one last favor of you."

And so, an hour later, after Beryl ventured out for sandwiches from a diner, the three of them ate while Danziger watched from the couch, the blanket still around his shoulders. After washing up, Cain sent Olivia off to her room, and Beryl left for her uncle's.

Danziger shed the blanket and joined Cain in the kitchen, where the two men sat at the table with two bottles of beer. Danziger then began to talk of things that he had not discussed in ages.

# 38

·····················

DANZIGER TOOK A LONG SWIG OF BEER, his Adam's apple bobbing with every swallow. Then he sighed, as if suitably fortified for the task ahead.

"May I?" he asked, tilting the bottle toward the file folder across the table.

Cain slid it toward him, and Danziger opened the flap. He picked up the Runyon story, curling at the edges, and he slowly broke into a smile of deep fondness. Then he shook his head.

"It shames me to say it now, but the day this edition of *Collier's* first went on sale was one of the greatest of my life. Or so I believed at the time. I clearly remember the morning. I had received advance notice of the story's contents from a writer friend in the Village, who knew very well the identity of The Dictionary. I rose at dawn in anticipation. I practically beat the delivery truck to the newsstand, and I didn't even wait to take it home. I stood there reading it on the sidewalk, pigeons strutting at my feet. My reaction was quite vain, quite proud, and quite stupid."

He set down the beer.

"There is no fool like a young fool, especially one who believes he has arrived because suddenly he is notorious and has money in his pocket. I was also convinced, at least for a day or two, that I need never worry again about having a conscience. Folly and consequence. Engage in the former, and the latter will surely follow."

Cain had already told him about his summons to the meeting at the Hotel Astor, with its unlikely cast of characters—so similar to the one at Longchamps—and the even more unlikely scheme that was afoot to secure the New York waterfront.

"Wartime," Danziger said. "It breeds such creative alliances, yes? Hitler and Stalin, at least for a while. And now, Lansky and Luciano are breaking bread with Frank Hogan and the United States Navy."

"The lion shall lie down with the lamb," Cain said.

"Yes. Although I doubt Gerhard would take any comfort from this current manifestation. As long as Hogan and Haffenden remain willing to overlook the occasional excesses of their new friends, those friends will hunt until their quarry is dead."

"There was one last thing," Cain said. He hesitated.

"Yes?"

"Lansky, right before I left. He whispered in my ear, so that no one else would hear. He sent his personal regards to Sascha, and said to tell you that it had been far too long. He was smiling, but I wouldn't call it friendly."

"I feared that would be his response."

"You knew him then?"

"I was there at the birth, you might say. Of his career, I mean. And we did not part on the best of terms. You will understand when I have finished."

Sascha then seemed to shiver. He swallowed more of his beer. A few minutes later, the bottle was half empty as he again took up his tale.

"I might have easily avoided this sort of life, of course. All of it: The disappearing act and, before, my descent into perdition, my apprenticeship among dangerous people. Even after losing my parents, I was well cared for. The good Reverend Haas saw to that after the *General Slocum* calamity. I was lodged with caring neighbors. Jews, of course— the reverend was not that magnanimous. I stayed in school. I had all the books I ever wanted. Responsible adults were concerned for my welfare."

"Beryl said something about a rabbi."

"Rabbi Kaufmann, yes. He became a presence when I began to

discover the attractions of the streets. If I had heeded his counsel, I suppose that I might have taken up a respectable profession or trade. I might even have read for the law. But the competition was fierce, I must tell you. Stroll down Second Avenue, and how could a boy not be dazzled? Crap games in which, with a modicum of intelligence and mathematical cunning, you could instantly become wealthier. Whiskey and women—for a price, of course, but available all the same. Joints and hangouts offering all the action a boy could ever ask for. Tischler's on Rivington, Max Himmel's on Delancey. And there were so many easy ways for a boy like me to make pocket money from the macks and the gun molls."

"Like what?"

"Running numbers, delivering a parcel here and there. For a while I was just an errand boy, until they learned I was also good at finding out things."

"Such as?"

"Anything. Names, addresses, people's daily habits."

"Information. Just like on your card."

"Well, it's true. It is what I have always excelled at. Along with the languages, of course. But even then I was not a fool about it. I knew the temptations. I saw the dangers. Left to my own devices, I am confident I would have followed Rabbi Kaufmann's guidance. But I was led astray."

"By who?"

"Not who. What. It was love. Love for a woman who is not at all to be blamed, because she, too, would have chosen the straight and narrow path for me."

Cain wrinkled his brow.

"Then how—?"

"Her brother, Angelo. She was Italian, you see. Her family lived two blocks over. Upright people, all of them except Angelo. When I saw her at a dance, I knew I would have to impress him if I were ever to stand a chance at an introduction. So for a while—too long of a while—I did as he asked, and took orders from whoever he said, and I was happy to do so because it was leading me closer to her.

"I knew as well that I would have to learn her language, all of it, and not just the few rough terms I had acquired for my dealings on the street. I was happy to do this as well, because her language was a thing of beauty. Italian is like the lyrics to a love song. All of those vowels, rolling around like lovers in a bedchamber. Compared to it, German stumbles along like a defeated army in retreat, a dirgelike procession of consonants down a stony lane.

"And it worked! She liked me! Loved me, even, in spite of what I was up to with her brother. Her father did not share her feelings, of course, but sometimes at that age a father's disapproval only adds to a young man's charm. I became forbidden fruit of the sweetest variety. I was living in a dream of the best sort."

Danziger paused for a moment, his eyes staring off toward something Cain would never see.

"Maria?" Cain asked.

Danziger's body jolted as if he'd been struck. His eyes flamed with accusation.

"Runyon mentioned her name in the story."

"Ah." He relaxed instantly. "Of course. Yes. Another reason I was so fond of that tale, although even he surmised correctly that tears were ahead."

"It didn't last?"

"Unless you count the first nine years."

"*Nine?*"

"Nine years in which she would never give her hand in marriage. Her father would not consent, not as long as I was a filthy companion of her disreputable brother and all of those terrible people he worked for. By then, of course, it was impossible for me to leave that sort of work. The Brain made that painfully clear to me. So I tried to earn my way financially into her father's graces. Yet, even after I moved into a fine new home in a far better neighborhood—up on the fringes of Yorkville, in fact—he would not relent. Still, she stayed loyal to me, or tried. But not long after the story in *Collier's* I sank so deeply into my own delusions that she moved away. Quite literally. Over to Queens, parting with a request that I not see her again. In my hubris, and even in my heartache, I insisted that I was not wounded. I assured her that I would soon find someone better. An idiocy, of course, but understandable because by then I had been in thrall to another for far too long, a devotion that had nothing to do with love."

"Arnold Rothstein."

"The Brain. My talents came to his attention fairly early. He was only eight years my senior, but seemed well advanced beyond the rest of us in both wisdom and sophistication. He was the up-and-coming force of our time—in those circles, anyway. So I did as he asked, whenever he asked it. And it was my ruin, as Maria could plainly see."

Cain nodded at the file folder.

"Your arrest record was pretty thin."

"Mine were not the sort of assignments which tended to land a man in jail. At first I was simply a finger man."

"Finger man?"

"I knew how to find people who didn't wish to be found, usually those who were behind on their payments to Mr. Rothstein. He told me it was quite harmless, of course. He said it was like working for a bank, being a loan officer who went after welshers and deadbeats. I would hang around Lindy's, waiting for a name.

"Then one night he saw Maria, or, more to the point, saw me speaking to her in her own tongue. And with my fine and fluent Italian—I was overly proud of my accent, I must admit—I soon became an asset of another sort, by being able to find out what certain rivals were up to. A careful listener in all the right places. A spy, if you will.

"When necessary, I also functioned as a liaison for important meetings. Mr. Rothstein knew that whenever his Italian associates wanted to speak to each other in their own language I would not miss a trick."

"It all sounds so normal. Almost like you were working for J. P. Morgan."

"That is what I wanted to believe as well. Mr. Rothstein knew this. Because one evening he sent me out with two men who had been supplied with one of the names and addresses I had found for them. He told me to accompany them in order to witness the fruits of my labors. I was somewhat puzzled by the request, but I went without protest.

"It was a man, I soon learned, who was not simply behind on his payments. He had defaulted altogether. He had been redlined, as a bank officer would say. They stood me in the room and made me watch as they beat him. Quite thoroughly, with saps and a hammer. Then they bound him, forcing me to tie the knots while he squirmed and whimpered. We placed him in the trunk of a large Chevrolet and drove him to a dock on the Harlem River, where we put him aboard a boat. Cement shoes, you have heard this term, yes?"

"Yes." Cain said.

Danziger's eyes looked dead, his face a blank. "Well, we made him a pair, then and there on the deck of the boat, in a galvanized washtub. I was charged with stirring water into the mixture. All the while this man watched me with his red eyes and his whimpers. I helped lift him overboard, and stood at the rail as he sank. His hair, trailing like sea-weed. So many bubbles. I shall never forget."

The room was silent a few seconds. Cain got up to peek around the corner to make sure Olivia wasn't listening. He heard her soft and steady breathing from her bedroom doorway. When he sat back at the table, Danziger had his head in his hands.

"Why did they do that?" Cain asked.

Danziger lowered his hands. He was pale, drained.

"To let me know that I was eternally theirs. A fact which Mr. Roth-stein reminded me of not so much later, when I considered enlisting in the Army. So by the time Mr. Runyon met me on that night in 1920, I had hardened myself, and I had insinuated myself ever deeper into the organization. I was a planner, a thinker. I needn't dirty my hands anymore from that point forward, but certainly I was aware of what my talents helped bring about in the dark regions beyond my sight. Maria read this in my eyes, and that is why she finally gave up on me. A few years later I heard she had married a grocer, a man who sold citrus fruits in Queens. I never heard his name. I never went looking for her address. I could not bear to."

"How'd you get out? I know you faked your own death, but that was eight years after the Runyon piece."

"It took that long for me to see an opening for my escape. It came the night Mr. Rothstein was killed. Everyone was at Lindy's. A call came in, a little after ten. Mr. Lindy, he was not fond of having his telephone line tied up in this way, but what could he do? I watched as Mr. Rothstein took the phone. He got out his black book and nodded as he spoke. When he hung up he gave me the high sign, and motioned me to the door. I followed him outside, where he told me he was going to meet George McManus at the Park Central Hotel. I was puzzled, because Mr. McManus was a gambler of small consequence. The Brain handed me his gun for safekeeping until he returned. 'I'll be right back,' he said. Those were his last words to me.

"The rest I learned from the newspapers. He arrived at room three forty-nine and was shot. A day or so later he died of his wounds. No one was ever convicted for the shooting, although that should not surprise you if you have read any stories about Mr. Anastasia."

"Some kind of fix?"

"Yes. Some kind of fix. But by the time of the trial I was preoccupied by my own fix. From the moment The Brain died I knew there would be a war of succession. Even at his funeral people were already speaking of it."

"The last time you rode in a taxi?"

Danziger smiled ruefully.

"Yes. Because from that point forward I began living more modestly, more carefully. As the killing began I awaited my moment, and it arrived quickly, well before the trial, even. I received word that one of the fallen, a poor mack of no account named Whitey Mendel, had been knifed in the face and dropped into the river. His corpse had turned up, but the police had not yet identified it. This was my chance. But to succeed I needed an accomplice, one who could not be chosen from any of the usual interested parties."

"Yuri Zharkov."

"A fine beat cop. He knew when to pry, and when to look away."

"He was on the take."

"No, no, no. You still do not see. As a cop in our neighborhood in those days you could either make yourself an ineffective nuisance by trying to stop every petty act, or, if you were wise, choose larger targets and work in concert with the neighbors to bring them down. He chose the latter, and in exchange for his assistance I helped him in return."

"You ratted on someone?"

"On three men in particular. All of them deserving, and all of them by now deceased, thank goodness. It was a boost to his career, and to the city's law-abiding residents."

"So Zharkov made detective and you got a new life."

"Yes."

"Who else knew?"

"The elder Lorenz, Lutz's father, who arranged my paperwork. And Fedya, my oldest friend. Plus a handful of others whose help I needed in various ways. Mostly they are dead now. Only four people today know me as Sascha, and one of them, Beryl, knows little of its significance."

"Five now, counting Lansky."

"Yes, there is him as well, plus everyone else in that room today at the Astor."

"Okay, but here's what I still don't get. When a man escapes his past, he usually runs from it, the further the better. But you went right back to the old neighborhood, almost like you *wanted* them to find you. Hell, you'd been there at Lindy's practically every night, standing at the right hand of God himself where everybody could see you. Yet when Mr. Big dies you figure you can just vanish into the woodwork?"

"Let me correct you on several points. I certainly did not want to be found, nor was I daring them to do so. Moving to Rivington Street was a form of camouflage they did not expect. It is called hiding in plain sight. And by the time I returned I was a different person, with new documents and a new face. A surgeon in the Catskills accomplished that. A nose job, I believe it is called now, plus more.

"I asked that he make me look ten years older, which astonished him because it was the opposite of what all his other customers wanted. But he did what he could to oblige me. The mere whisper of a mark became an indentation. He moved flesh from one place to another to make my neck sag like a turkey's, well ahead of its time. I purchased gray coloring and applied it to my hair, which cooperated by exploding in all directions. I grew a beard, which I did not shave even once until three years ago, when I deemed that enough time had passed to allow for some harmless nostalgia, in the form of my monthly breakfast at Longchamps."

"So much for harmless."

"No one is infallible, and my biggest asset all along was the nature of what I had done before. You said I stood at the right hand of God? Perhaps. But who really bothers to watch who is at God's side as long as God himself is there to be gazed upon? Yes, I drew the eye of Mr. Runyon, only because it was his job to observe, to notice. To others in my profession—to almost everyone, in fact, except Mr. Rothstein—I was a nothing, a cipher. I worked at the center yet existed on the fringe. Close to the throne, but a mere whisperer in the royal ear, neither seen nor heard in any real sense except by the one man who mattered, The Brain. And once he died it was all the easier for me to disappear and never be missed. It might have been flawless but for a single complication."

"Lansky?"

Danziger nodded.

"In the matter of those three men I fed to Zharkov, one of them turned out to be a protégé, alas, of Mr. Lansky's."

"I see."

"No. You do not see. Meyer Lansky is a man incapable of forgetting. He is also the one man who could have ever possibly recognized me, changes and all, beard or no beard. So when I saw him walk into Longchamps, I was very careful to hide behind my newspaper."

"You said you were there at his birth, professionally speaking."

"It was 1922. Mr. Rothstein asked me to arrange a table for two for a noon business lunch at the Park Central Hotel. He said he was meeting a hungry and ambitious young man, a fellow who had as good a head for numbers as I did for words. At one point, around three that afternoon, the maître d' telephoned me to say that Mr. Rothstein wished for me to bring him some papers. When I arrived he introduced me to this short, brash fellow, twenty years old and dressed ridiculously in an overly large suit. It was Meyer Lansky."

"Three o'clock, on a noon reservation? Lansky must have made quite an impression."

"That is safe to say. Their lunch lasted six hours."

"Okay, then. Point taken. He's dangerous, particularly to you. But our more immediate problem is Anastasia."

"Of course. But from what you have told me he is a problem for *everyone*, Lansky included, and I am guessing that others will deal with him before we will ever have to. It is another reason for us to wait."

"To *wait*? He's already gotten to three of the Germans. If we wait he'll also get Gerhard, and there goes the last of our evidence. And who's to say he won't come after us?"

Danziger shook his head impatiently. "Listen to me! It is Lansky who had a hand in this as well. Not in these sloppy murders in the aftermath, perhaps, but certainly in the larger scheme—the *Normandie* plot—before any deal was ever made with Hogan, or with the Navy. Do you not see this?"

"The *Normandie* was an accident. I doubt even Hogan or Haffenden would try to fake that investigation."

"Of course it was an accident, a most fortuitous one which accomplished exactly what Mr. Lansky hoped for, by scaring the United States Navy enough to bring Haffenden and Hogan to grovel at his feet. But that left these four restive Germans still to be accounted for, out there on the docks, loose with their union cards and their letters home. Four men still awaiting orders and, more important, awaiting payment. So Anastasia took care of them. Not in the manner Lansky would have recommended, because it was far too sloppy. But I assure you, Lansky's hand is evident in all that has occurred."

"There's no proof. Not from Lorenz, not from Gerhard, not from anybody."

"The proof is in the design, Mr. Cain. The proof is in the details."

"I'm not seeing it."

Danziger pounded the table in exasperation, and then sagged in his chair. He took a few seconds to collect himself, and then put both hands flat on the table.

"Tell me, then," he said, "those clever names that were chosen for our four Germans—Heine, Schiller, Goethe, and Mann—are those the choices, do you think, of a stupid and uneducated killer like Anastasia? Or even of an unimaginative dollar snatcher like Herman Keller?"

Cain shrugged, but had no rebuttal.

"Let me tell you what Mr. Lansky is like when it comes to books and thinking. He is proud, he is vainglorious, and he is insecure because he never went to university. Within an hour of meeting you he will tell you that he can recite all of Shakespeare's *Merchant of Venice* from memory. He is intelligent, yes, but what he wishes most to impress upon you is that he is brilliant. And no matter how much he wishes to portray Anastasia as some wild man who acted completely on his own, it is not believable. Do you not see this?"

"Maybe you're right. But for now he's still not the biggest danger. And even after what they threatened me with at the Astor, there are still certain things that I can do as a policeman that—"

"Please! No more talk of action, and no more talk of Anastasia! He is a killer, yes. But even he operates under certain rules, and one of those is that you do not kill a policeman. Not even a policeman who is meddlesome and has become a terrible nuisance. If this rule did not exist you would already be quite dead, trust me. Anastasia will be dealt with by his own people. Let them do so! And in good time we can decide how to best deal with Lansky."

Cain wasn't ready to buy it. "Lansky isn't the guy who's been burning people with cigarettes, or dropping them into the river."

Danziger shook his head and sighed, but this time he did not shout. He leaned across the table and spoke in a quiet but determined voice. "Let me tell you a story of the last time I saw Meyer Lansky. The Little Man, face to face. He had brokered a deal for us, and Mr. Rothstein put me in charge of ensuring that all sides met their obligations. Lansky knew this, and one night outside of Lindy's he walked up to me on the sidewalk and put his hands upon my face, one to either side, and he began to squeeze. He felt deeply of my bones and muscles, like a sculptor trying to imprint a memory. He turned my jaw one way and then another. Then he pulled my head down to meet his own—eyes to eyes, nose to nose. I smelled his peppermint breath, the spice of his aftershave. He waited for a few seconds longer, and then he smiled in a most unpleasant manner."

"Yes. I've seen that smile."

"Then you know how vulnerable it makes you feel. He spoke to me, whispering, probably just as he did to you at the Astor."

Cain felt a shiver, remembering.

"He said, 'Treasure this moment, Sascha. Imprint it on your memory. Because I do not forget, and I do not let go. Even when you think I am gone, I will be there always, Sascha.'"

Cain nodded, unsure how to respond. He swallowed more beer and offered Danziger another, but the older man declined.

"So let us agree then, shall we?"

"Agree on what?"

"Agree that for the time being we shall both lay low. Yes?"

"Okay."

"And that we will no longer speak of foolish acts, and that you will put these ideas of further action far from your mind until we are able to meet again. Yes?"

Cain nodded.

"Promise me."

"I promise."

Danziger held his gaze, as if watching for any sign of falseness.

"Good," he said finally. "I will have that next beer, then. As shall you."

Cain pried off the caps of two more bottles. He handed one to Danziger, who raised it in a toast.

"To sanity, then. Sanity and caution, while we await our moment."

Cain clinked his bottle to Danziger's, and over the next several minutes they finished several more while they waited for Beryl and Fedya to arrive. Danziger said nothing further about his past. Cain, as if to show how faithfully he was already abiding by his promise, said nothing further about any plans or stratagems.

But he did not stop thinking about them.

# 39

........................

CAIN DID NOT LAY LOW.

After Danziger left with Fedya and Beryl he barely sat still and hardly slept, mostly because he kept going over everything in his head. By morning he was exhausted. He was also elated, convinced that he had come up with a fresh way forward.

Promise or no promise, doing nothing wasn't an option. He was a cop, for Chrissakes, and Hogan and Gurfein were prosecutors. And he was betting that during the meeting at the Astor both of them would've asked plenty of questions about the issues he'd raised if they hadn't been so intent on presenting a united front with Haffenden, who, to Cain, seemed far too willing to go along with whatever script the mob guys wanted. There was no mistaking the flicker of doubt that had passed between the DA and his deputy when Cain mentioned the three murders linked to Anastasia, and he saw that now as an opening.

A private meeting with the two men might actually get some results. But what he needed first was stronger evidence. An official statement from Gerhard might do it. Better still, why not give them Gerhard himself? That would solve two problems at once: convincing Hogan and Gurfein that they had been duped, and protecting his best remaining eyewitness. A rackets investigator like Gurfein was probably well practiced in keeping witnesses out of harm's way. And who knows? With Gerhard in hand, maybe they could even persuade Lorenz to open up.

First he needed to find Gerhard before Anastasia did, which meant a trip to the Bowery and its skid row of flophouses and rummy bars, the so-called "mile of misery" that stretched from 4th Street down to Chatham Square, home to tens of thousands of down-and-outers who paid thirty cents a night for a bed.

It wouldn't be easy. Gerhard's last known residence was the Sunshine Hotel, but by now he had probably moved on, which left scores of possibilities. Each would be best explored after dark, when Cain was off duty, and free of Mulhearn and all his busywork. The lone advantage of Eileen's complicity with his father-in-law was that she was now so guilt-ridden that he would have no trouble persuading her to work enough extra hours to cover for him at home.

Danziger could not be a part of this, of course. He needed to keep the older man out of harm's way, and mob guys would now see Danziger as one of their own, a fallen figure who was fair game. Cain, however, would be protected by his status as a cop. They could threaten him or even rough him up, but they wouldn't kill him. Even Danziger had said it. Or so Cain kept telling himself as he rode the subway downtown an hour after sunset.

The Bowery ran beneath the Third Avenue El, and it only took a block or two to get the flavor of the place. Doorways smelled of urine and stale beer. Most of the people on the street were men, hard-luck cases with weathered, stubbly faces and floppy hats slouched low on their foreheads. A few stumbled; others shuffled. To his right, Cain passed three men seated in a row along the curb, passing a half-empty bottle of cheap rye from hand to hand while they laughed and talked. A downtown train clattered overhead, casting them in deeper shadow.

At the next corner, a sidewalk preacher thrust a handbill toward him. Cain took a look at the drawing on the front—a drunk in a gutter, with empties at his feet. On the back was the same fellow, cleaned up and gazing heavenward into a ray of godly sunshine, a Bible tucked under his arm.

"No thanks," Cain said, handing it back.

He checked first at the Sunshine, passing through a sad little downstairs bar to climb an echoing stairwell to the second-floor lobby. The white tile floor smelled like a sour mop. Two men seated in beat-up chairs stared vacantly out the streaked front windows. A third fellow sat on a couch, smoking a sloppily rolled cigarette and reading a *Herald-Tribune* from the previous Sunday.

Cain crossed the floor to the caged reception cubicle, where the attendant looked up from a copy of the *Racing Form* and frowned. Cain flashed his shield, which made no noticeable impression.

"I'm looking for a German guy who would've been staying here a few nights ago. Named Gerhard, although he might've been calling himself something else."

The guy reading the *Herald-Tribune* flipped to another page but tilted his head, eavesdropping. The attendant opened a beaten-up looking ledger, flipped it back a page or two and ran a forefinger down the side.

"He was in five-oh-five. Stayed two nights. Took off yesterday."

"Know where he went?"

"Beats me."

"Maybe I'll take a look upstairs."

"Suit yourself, flatfoot."

Cain turned toward the stairwell to find the guy with the *Herald-Tribune* blocking his way, an eager glint in his eyes.

"You asking about the kraut? Sorry G?"

"That's what they called him?"

"Sorriest man I ever seen. A toes-up goddamn nuisance who wouldn't lift a finger for nobody. Had him some money, too. Not much but enough, and wouldn't share a dime of it, which don't sit well when you're plinging dawn to dusk just to get three squares and a flop."

"What's your name?"

"Ace Andy."

A nickname, but it would do for now.

"Any idea where he went?"

"Let's get something straight. I don't normally make nice with bulls. But Sorry G, he could use some manners."

"Okay. Nice talking to you."

Cain turned to go, figuring that would get him talking, and it did. Ace Andy bustled up on his right.

"I can tell you where he likes to eat, and his dinner time's in about half an hour. You could set your clock by it."

"You eat with him a lot?

The guy laughed, wheezing.

"You bulls. It ain't like that at all. I was his runner, yeah?"

"Runner?"

"Got stuff for him. He didn't like going out on the streets, so he paid for special deliveries, a nickel a pop."

"Thought you said he was a skinflint?"

"Hey, I was working for my keep. Waited on him hand and foot."

"For what kind of stuff. Narcotics?"

Ace Andy wheezed again, face crinkling.

"He was clean. Just a basket case, that's all. Didn't even touch the sauce except for a beer now and then."

"And you'd bring those for him?"

"I got every motherfucking thing for him, like I was his goddamn valet. His runner, that's what I'm telling you. Got his morning paper, his coffee, his lunch, his dinner. And along about now he always wanted the same thing, at seven on the dot."

"Night after night, huh?"

"You bet.

"And you know this from what, two whole days?"

Ace Andy frowned and waved him off.

"Fine. You don't want it, I don't need to be seen sucking up to a bull anyway."

"Suit yourself." Cain again turned to go. Ace Andy again followed, and sidled past him to block the doorway.

"Okay, then," Cain said. "Tell me what you know."

"Just like that, free of charge? You think I'm the Salvation Army?"

He handed the guy a nickel, who dropped it in his pocket and laughed.

"Down payment, but not even close to the balance due. Way I see it, you're probably half the reason he skipped without telling anybody, meaning you've already cost me two bits a day, right there."

Cain held out a quarter, and the guy shook his head. He pulled out his wallet and forked over a dollar.

"Here's four days' pay," Cain said. "You better be worth it or I can always run you in."

"Yeah, well, what you didn't know was that I've been running for him ten days in a row. Or had been till you scared him off."

"You've been moving whenever he does?"

"The White House, the Comet, the Crystal, the Providence. And now, nothing. Steady source of income, gone just like that. And he trusted me, or did until you spooked him."

The idea that skittish Gerhard had ever put his faith in the likes of Ace Andy made Cain question the man's judgment, but he supposed that you took your allies as they came, mercenary or not.

"What else did he do?"

"Church on Sundays, up at St. Andrew's, too damn early even for me. Not much else. Went to the pictures once a week. He liked the Venice, over on Park Row, 'cause they opened at eight and he could stay most of the day. You get a double feature, a newsreel, a cartoon, and a short. Then maybe a cop serial, all for a dime. An even better deal when you sit through it twice. I don't think he was watching much, though." Ace Andy grinned crookedly. "Making the bald man cry, you ask me."

"The bald man?"

"Beating his bologna." Andy moved his fist up and down so Cain wouldn't miss the point a second time.

"Right."

Andy wheezed with laughter.

"Okay, so where does he like to eat?"

"I'll take you there. It's extra, though."

"Had a feeling you'd say that."

"You want to get all huffy, I'll just give you the name, and you can go all by your lonesome. But I know his order, and I know the other runners, 'cause it won't be him coming to pick up the food."

Cain gave him a quarter. Andy nodded.

They walked to the block between Grand and Hester, to a joint called the Blossom Restaurant, where the entire steamed-up window was covered in a scrawl of white lettering listing every item on the menu.

"Pig's trotters and cabbage for a dime, that's what he gets. With buttermilk. Guy ought to be along any minute."

Five minutes later, and right on schedule, Ace Andy perked up as a fellow rounded the corner with his hands in his pockets, looking a bit lean and hungry. They watched him enter the Blossom.

"Easy Zeke," Andy said. "He runs from the Victoria House. Those krauts, they're creatures of habit, huh? All that *ordnung*. Must be what keeps 'em going, yeah?"

"Yeah."

Cain was about to pay the guy a final dime to keep his mouth shut and scram so he could follow the runner alone, and then a complication occurred to him.

"So I take it you speak some German."

Andy shrugged.

"Ein bisschen, aber genug. Means 'a little but enough.'"

And that's when it hit him. Trust hadn't been the issue for Gerhard with Andy. Language was. Which was why Cain still needed Andy's help.

They headed for the Victoria House to wait for Zeke and settled in on a couch in the lobby, which was drearily similar to the one at the Sunshine except the windows were smaller and the attendant's booth had a block-lettered sign saying ROOMS WITH ELECTRIC LIGHTS, 30C.

Zeke came up the steps a few minutes later, carrying a brown paper bag with dark blotches of grease. He climbed past the lobby toward a higher floor, and they got up to follow him. They heard him exit on the fourth-floor landing, and reached it just in time to see Zeke going into a room six doors down a narrow hallway. A few seconds later he came back out, flipping a nickel in the air like he'd just hit the daily double at Aqueduct.

Cain opened the door into a cramped room with a camp bed and a bare bulb hanging by a cord from the ceiling. Gerhard, shirtless, was hunched in a chair by the window, already gorging himself, hands greasy. He looked up in alarm and stood quickly, the food spilling everywhere. He tried to reach the door but Cain grabbed him, barely holding on to the grease-slicked wrists.

"Tell him it's okay!" Cain shouted to Andy. "I'm here to help him!"

Gerhard either gave up or understood enough to calm down. Cain coaxed him back into the chair, where he stared forlornly at his spilled dinner on the scuffed floor. The room looked like a jail cell. Maybe six feet wide and ten feet long. The walls didn't even reach the ceiling, and the proprietor had put chicken wire across the top from one end of the place to another, in order to keep the tenants from climbing over the partitions into the rooms of their neighbors.

Cain figured that everyone on the fourth floor must have heard the commotion, because he could easily hear Gerhard's neighbors coughing, laughing, and mumbling to themselves. The whole place smelled of sweat, piss, fear, and exhaustion, plus the greasy stink of Gerhard's pig's feet and cabbage. If anything, the man looked more baffled and forlorn than he had at the church, although now his hair was clipped in a buzz cut.

"You got a haircut," Cain said. "Good idea."

"You can get 'em for free at the barber college at Chatham Square," Andy answered.

"Tell him what I said!" Cain snapped. "In German!"

Andy obliged, although he couldn't resist adding at the end, in English, "This'll cost more, right?"

Cain handed him another quarter and told him to shut the hell up and do as he was told. Andy nodded and for a split second looked almost chastened.

"Tell him I didn't forget. That I wasn't trying to shake him the other day." Even though that's exactly what he *had* been doing. "I needed time to figure out where to take him next, to keep him safe."

Andy took a while to finish that one, and Gerhard frowned, giving Cain the idea that Andy's German wasn't the greatest. Finally Gerhard nodded and asked a question.

"He says—uhh, hold on a minute."

Andy spoke German again, trying to zero in on Gerhard's meaning. Gerhard replied with a hint of exasperation.

"He asks where you can go that's safe."

"Tell him I'm going to take him there right now. That he and I will wait a few minutes while he finishes his food, and then we'll go, and he will be safe."

This time Andy must have done reasonably well. Gerhard nodded and began picking up the spilled dinner, grabbing the pig's foot and scooping the cabbage with the palm of his left hand. He heaped everything atop the flattened bag.

"Okay," Cain said to Andy. "Time for you to take off."

Andy stood uncertainly, and then hesitated by the door like a bellhop hoping for a tip.

"I said scram!" Cain shouted. Andy left, shutting the door behind him. After that there was nothing to say.

Gerhard ate quickly, and then licked his fingers. He went down the hall and washed up in the common bathroom. Cain decided they should wait another ten minutes, explaining to Gerhard with hand signals and basic English, which he seemed to understand. Cain hoped this would be enough time for Andy to lose interest and be on his way. The last thing they needed was someone else tagging along, or demanding further pay to keep his mouth shut.

Cain's plan was to put Gerhard up for the night in a more secure and respectable place, a small hotel he'd picked out on Seventh Avenue, much further uptown. He'd show his shield and, if necessary, have a uniform drop by a few times to make sure everything was okay. It wasn't perfect, but for one night only it would probably be safe enough. Then, first thing in the morning, he'd march Gerhard over to Gurfein's office and hope that somebody there spoke enough German to take an official statement.

After that, it would be out of his hands. Either the DA would do the right thing, or he'd let Anastasia slide. That, too, was imperfect, but for the moment it was the best plan he could come up with.

When they got downstairs the lobby was empty and no one was in the cage. It gave Cain a bad feeling as their footsteps echoed on the floor tiles. He slid a hand inside his jacket, feeling the stock of his Colt, and he was on the verge of telling Gerhard to turn around so they could wait a while longer when two guys emerged from a rear hallway with guns drawn. They wore dark pinstriped suits and white fedoras, and their pistols looked big enough to blow you to kingdom come.

"Take your hand out of the cookie jar," the first one said, aiming at Cain's chest. "Real slow like. Then put your hands on your head."

Cain did as he was told, trying to keep his cool in hopes that Gerhard wouldn't panic and get them both shot. The German looked worried, his eyes wild, brow creased. He'd already raised his hands into position to fend off any blows.

The first guy strolled up, casual as you please, and reached inside Cain's jacket to remove the Colt. The second thug broke into a grin.

"Nice work, flatfoot," he said. "We'll take the kraut off your hands now. Good to finally get something out of all those tax dollars we spend on all you boys in blue."

"As if you guys pay taxes."

"Tell him he's coming with us, how 'bout it."

"You tell him. I don't speak German."

"Hey kraut!" The first guy shoved the gun underneath Gerhard's chin. He reached into Gerhard's pocket and pulled out a knife. "That's much better. You're coming with us!"

Gerhard glared at Cain, as if to say thanks for nothing. He bowed his head and walked out of the building with the first guy behind him, pressing a gun barrel to his back. The second guy lowered his gun and walked up beside Cain.

"Let's take it outside."

A big dark car was idling at the curb. A Plymouth Road King, not a Packard. The first thug and another guy were putting Gerhard in the back while a third fellow watched from a perch near the hood. He, too, was armed. The thug next to Cain spoke again.

"So who's your shadow?"

"Shadow?"

"Your little friend out there. If he's your guardian angel, better give him a whistle before he does something stupid."

"I don't know what you're talking about. You mean Ace Andy, the bum?"

"Don't get wise. He's been with you for this whole tour, up one block and down the other, like you had him on a string."

Cain looked in both directions, noticing nothing beyond a few bums, and all of them had their eyes averted, scrupulously avoiding this bit of unpleasantness outside the Victoria House. All except for Ace Andy, who stood just across the street with a wry look on his face and a fresh greenback in his right hand. So, then, outbid in the end, by these guys who'd probably picked up his trail the moment he hit the Bowery.

But who was this shadow they were talking about? Cain wondered again about the odd recurring feeling he'd had lately, a sense of being watched, or even stalked. Archer? Not after what Cain had given him. But the thought gave him an idea. Feeble, but an idea nonetheless.

"Probably a cop," Cain said. "I'd asked for some backup."

The thug chuckled and got out a toothpick, which he used to begin working at something stuck between his molars.

"This guy ain't no cop, I can tell you that. Way too wet behind the ears. But he's steady. Hey, Bingo!" He shouted to the guy posted by the hood of the car. "What happened to our little ghost back there?"

"Scrammed. Guess he didn't like your looks."

"So there goes your backup," the thug said. He tossed the toothpick to the curb.

The Plymouth revved its engine. The lookout stepped away and the car smoothly glided toward the next corner and turned out of sight. Poor Gerhard. And poor Cain, who'd just lost his last hope for making a case to Hogan. His shoulders sagged. At least he'd gotten the tag number on the Plymouth. In the morning maybe he'd write the whole thing up, start to finish, and drop it off at Hogan's office, just in case. Then he could figure out how to best protect Danziger. For now, Anastasia had beaten them.

"Well, nice meeting you," Cain said, "but I better get my gun back from your friend over there." He stepped toward the curb only to have the thug wheel on him and get right up in his face. The big gun was back in full view.

"Where you think *you're* going, pal? Me and Bingo, we're still waiting for your ride. So hold your horses."

"*My* ride?" His voice was a little weak. "For what?"

"The boss would like to express his gratitude. Now how 'bout shutting it until we're in Brooklyn."

Cain did as he was told. For the moment, he was out of ideas, even feeble ones.

# 40

................

THE DIFFERENCE BETWEEN looking at Albert Anastasia's mug shot and seeing him in the flesh was, to Cain, like the difference between seeing a tiger at the zoo and meeting up with one in the wild. The former is tame, or at least caged, its primal instincts held in check for your idle observation. The latter is a force of nature, eyes gleaming, muscles poised, ready to pounce and devour.

"So you're the flatfoot I been hearing about," Anastasia said, voice a little raspy, eyes aglow. He walked slowly toward Cain in measured footsteps, as if worried about scaring off his prey.

Cain swallowed with some difficulty, unable for the moment to come up with a suitable reply other than "Yep."

"Shame," Anastasia said, shaking his head slowly. "Real shame about that."

They were in the back room at Midnight Rose's, the very place Gerhard had scouted on Saratoga Avenue. Cain knew this not only by the address, but also from the awning out front, printed with the words "candy," "soda," and "cigars," like Gerhard had said. Except Gerhard, by now, was probably settling into the silt on the bottom of some river.

Cain had tried to keep calm on the way over, mostly by repeating to himself, in the manner of a Catholic praying the rosary, Danziger's maxim about the mob's unbreakable rule, the one that forbade killing a cop. Because it created too much trouble, too much grief with other cops, too much scrutiny from prosecutors. It was too sloppy altogether, and never worth the aggravation. Right?

By the time he got out of the car—a black Packard, no less—he'd decided to approach this confrontation like a business meeting. Seek the best possible deal by using whatever leverage remained at his disposal. But, of course, Gerhard had been his biggest asset, and Cain was still trying to come up with a fresh approach when Anastasia emerged from the back.

He wore baggy gray flannel pants, a wrinkled white shirt with the sleeves rolled to the elbows, black suspenders, and a yellow necktie, sloppily knotted. His combed-back hair, as advertised, was wavy and shoved higher on one side. The biggest surprise was his aura of casual menace, a sense that he approached the most brutally violent acts with the indifference of a man smashing a bug, or prying loose a dead mouse from a trap—an almost blasé attitude that seemed to lurk at the back of his eyes. Or maybe Cain had read too many press clippings while going through the man's file. The words "Murder, Inc." flitted around his brain like a bat trapped in a closet. It was just business to this guy, and as with any business he probably grew bored from time to time—an idea which only compounded Cain's anxiety.

"You've been causing an awful lot of trouble for me," Anastasia said. "But we're all done with that now."

"Okay." Was he offering a way out? At that moment Cain realized that maybe he did have something to offer. His cooperation, of course. A cop's surrender. Craven and submissive and completely unworthy, yet redeemable in full for one human life if the offer was accepted.

" 'Okay'? Whadda you mean with the 'okay'? We ain't here to bargain. This thing's done."

Cain wet his lips and swallowed, or else he might not have been able to utter a word.

"Don't you guys have a rule against killing cops?"

"Rule?" Anastasia grinned widely. He stuffed his hands in his pockets and rocked back on his heels, playing to his audience. "Hey, you fellas remember that last rule we heard about? What was it, Bingo?"

"Never kill a mob boss."

"Yeah. Never kill a mob boss. Maybe our guest here could ask Joe 'The Boss' Masseria what became of that one."

Cain knew the answer from the file: Anastasia and three others had shot Masseria dead at a Coney Island restaurant.

So that was that. Somehow, by knowing that his fate was now inevitable, Cain was able to, if not relax, then at least marshal his wits, even though all his wits gave him in return was a snappy comeback.

"I'll make sure and ask him if I bump into him a few minutes from now."

Anastasia laughed, pulling his hands out of his pockets and clapping them sharply. So, then. Not bored after all, Cain thought, or at least not bored by this job. Glad to have helped brighten your workday, sir. He wished he had his gun back. Point the barrel right at his open mouth. Shatter the teeth and blow a hole through the back of his neck. The goons would shoot him immediately, but at least he'd have the pleasure of recompense.

Instead, his only recourse was to stand there in silence, thugs to either side. Anastasia stepped back across the room while rubbing his hands together in apparent relish. He plucked a gray suit coat off the back of a chair and spoke to one and all: "Okay, gents. What do you say we all go for a spin?"

Yet another unwanted ride in a stranger's car. It seemed to be the only way Cain got around anymore.

Out at the curb, the black Packard stood waiting. Cain thought of it now as a hearse, a prop for some movie shot on a gray film set where the street lamps were misted over. Except in reality it was a fine April evening, a little chilly maybe but with the stars out—one of the few benefits of the dim-out—and a rising three-quarter moon suitable for lovers and children alike.

Anastasia sat up front, Cain in the back with beefy escorts to either side. The boss rolled down his window.

"What'll it be tonight, sir?" the driver asked. "East River or the Hudson?"

"I was thinking maybe the Harlem."

They crossed through Brooklyn and headed up into Queens. Along the way, shoppers were still out on the neighborhood streets with their sacks and baskets. Cain looked up a cross street and saw kids playing beneath a dimmed street lamp, one last game of hopscotch before mom called them to bed. The guy named Bingo spoke up.

"Hey, Cain. Look at it this way. You'll be immortal. Up on the wall of the fallen. At the cop bars down on Centre maybe they'll even name a drink for you."

"The Cain Cocktail," Anastasia said. "A shot and a splash."

They all had a nice laugh and settled back into silence. To Cain it was surreal. A jolly old time with men seated to either side, everyone in a suit, with a crisp breeze pouring in through the window, as if they were headed for a night on the town.

Traffic was light, another perk of wartime. They crossed the Queensboro Bridge back into Manhattan and headed up East River Drive. They exited and rolled down to a wharf, only a few blocks from where Angela Feinman's body had been found. The driver cut the headlights as they rolled onto cobbles.

"Just doing our part for the dim-out," the driver said, laughing at his own joke.

"Shut up and drive!" Anastasia said. "I'm not paying you to laugh." Becoming testy now that it was almost time to get to work.

Cain looked straight ahead. Deep shadows. An approaching shimmer of black water along an abandoned stretch of wharf. He thought back to that first night on the job, down by the Hudson, and he imagined writing his own name onto that list of victims in his notebook: *Woodrow Cain, 34, white, gunshot.* Although he supposed the real cause was stupidity, or not knowing when to quit.

They parked and opened the doors. Cain got out with them. The thugs again flanked him, holding his arms. He kept expecting to panic, to cry, to piss his pants. But all he felt was disbelief, a simmering anger. Anastasia led the way toward the water, turning his back on them. That was when Cain tried to lunge away from them, twisting both arms and kicking out with his feet. But the goons held tight, grunting and laboring without complaint. Fully accustomed to this type of resistance, probably. All in a day's work.

They walked him onto the wharf and turned him so that his back was to the water. He looked up at the staved-in windows of an empty warehouse, a blank stare from every opening.

Anastasia chambered bullets into a huge revolver and slowly raised the barrel. The men holding his arms leaned away from him, which made Anastasia smile.

"That's right, gents. Keep your suits clean." He aimed at Cain's nose and stepped closer. They heard tires bouncing on cobbles, a big car by the sound of it. Then a tunnel of headlights swerved around the near corner and illuminated them all. Cain's hopes soared and then collapsed as he saw it wasn't a cop. Anastasia turned his gun toward the car. One of his thugs reached into a coat pocket and pulled out a revolver.

The car switched off its headlights. An Olds 98, long and black. The passenger door opened, and a shadowy figure stepped out onto a crunch of broken glass.

"Fine night, gentlemen. But not for this sort of thing."

Anastasia frowned and lowered his gun.

"This is none of your business, Stu."

"Never said it was. But the Little Man says otherwise. Sorry, Albert. This one doesn't belong to you."

So the cavalry had arrived, courtesy of Meyer Lansky. But why? Was this a reprieve or a temporary stay of execution, merely to allow for a change of venue, a different executioner? Somehow he'd gotten caught up in the middle of a mob tussle, a tug-of-war in which his arms were likely to be pulled off. And while that didn't exactly sound promising, without it he'd be dead by now.

Anastasia raised his gun and again pointed it at Cain's face.

"Yeah, well. We'll just see about that."

"You know the score, Albert. Don't be stupid."

Anastasia seemed to quiver with anger as he aimed, the trigger finger moving but not yet squeezing. With the possibility of hope now on the horizon, Cain lost his composure, breaking into a sweat. A bead crawled down his spine like a caterpillar. Another rolled to the tip of his nose, as if to provide Anastasia with a target.

"Goddamn it!" Anastasia again lowered the gun. "Then take him, you asshole kike! Get him the fuck outta my sight!"

"He'll work it out with you, Albert." Stu was walking toward them now, cool as you please. He wasn't even carrying a gun. "You know he always does."

Anastasia waved him off and stalked back toward the Packard, refusing to watch the handover. And then, just like that, the two thugs let go. Stu took Cain's left arm as gently as an usher at a wedding and steered him toward the waiting Olds. Cain barely breathed until the doors were shut and he was seated in the back, alone this time. Then he exhaled deeply and wiped the sweat from his nose.

Stu slid in up front, next to the driver.

"Next stop, Curtis. You know the way."

Yet another strange ride in another strange car. Cain wondered if he'd ever go for a ride in New York that was his own idea, and not somebody else's.

They drove off into the night, with Cain still in one piece, and still very much alive.

# 41

........................

CAIN WAS SO OVERCOME with relief that it was several minutes before he spoke.

"Where are you taking me?"

"Keep quiet, how 'bout it."

Hardly reassuring, but by now they were on Fifth Avenue, headed toward Midtown along the east side of Central Park. The location made him feel relatively safe, almost cheerful. So did the Olds, which felt more like a family car than a mob wagon. There was a Felix the Cat doll down on the floor to his right. He'd already dug out a school pencil, well chewed, from the seat to his left. Kids rode in this car with their mom and dad. Surely it wouldn't be used to run death errands like Anastasia's Packard.

Just as he was starting to feel better about things they turned right into the park at 72nd, and the darkness was complete. Okay then, maybe not so good. He now envisioned being garroted beneath the trees, followed by a midnight burial on the fringes of the Ramble, or the Sheep's Meadow, one of those big fields that Olivia liked so much. His bones would be discovered years later by a puzzled landscaper, or maybe never.

They drove deeper into the park, the car slowing. But the driver was just being careful on a curve. Weaving past dense foliage, they topped a slight rise. At this point they were past the halfway mark through the park, and he began to take hope. At least now they were heading back to civilization, and looming above the treetops just ahead were the twin towers of a grand apartment building, which even in the dim-out was lit as brightly as a birthday cake. After everything Cain had been through in the past hour, it looked like an oasis across the sands.

"What's that building up ahead, the one that looks like a castle?"

"Funny you should ask. That's the Majestic."

"Well named."

"Ain't it, though."

They emerged from the park, crossed Central Park West and braked at the curb alongside the Majestic. Stu turned and slung his arm across the back of the seat.

"You were way out of your league back there."

"I got that idea."

"You're way out of your league here, too. But who knows? Play your cards right and you should at least get out of it with your skin."

"I take it I'm here to see Lansky."

"*Mister* Lansky. Third floor. You're expected."

Cain slid left across the seat and unlatched the door. Then he hesitated.

"I guess he wouldn't like it too much if I decided to not show up."

Stu shrugged. "Your choice. Him or Albert."

"That's an easy one."

Cain got out, waltzed through the entrance, and gave his name to the doorman, who directed him to the elevators.

"Apartment three-oh-one, sir."

Lansky answered the door himself. He *was* a little man, not an inch over five feet, which hadn't been apparent around the table at the Astor. Cain had to suppress his astonishment. The last thing he wanted to do was get off on the wrong foot, and he was nervous enough as it was.

Once again Lansky was sharply dressed in clothes that looked prosperous, with creases in all the right places even at this hour of the day.

"Come in, Cain. We've got the place to ourselves tonight, so make yourself at home."

It was a comfortable room, large by Manhattan standards, with plush-looking wallpaper, a big Oriental rug, and a long couch facing two love seats and a wing chair. Off to one side was a grand piano. But the real draw was the row of big windows across the front, which looked out onto a moonlit view of the treetops of Central Park. Cain strolled over for a look.

"The view is what makes the place," Lansky said. "Drink?" He stood by a cart loaded with bottles and crystal decanters. Cain was about to say no when he realized how badly he needed one.

"Bourbon, straight up."

Lansky poured a whiskey for himself and brought the drinks over. He made a short speech before handing Cain the glass.

"You're a pretty sharp 'tec, Cain, but you're not exactly a fast learner. So I've brought you here in hopes of imparting a little education, since our lesson the other day didn't seem to make a dent. I like to think we'll be able to speak frankly, man to man. But if you intend to run home when we're done and scribble everything into that notebook of yours, well, then I might as well have Stu take you back to Midnight Rose's. So, whadda you say?"

"We'll keep it man to man, and nothing goes on paper."

"Swell. Like I say to my associates: Trust your memory, and keep your business in your hat."

He handed over the drink, and as he did so their eyes locked. Lansky's gaze was sharp, probing, and Cain now saw how the Little Man made up for his unimposing stature. Even in the studied informality of the moment, his eyes told you that there were wheels in his head that never stopped turning. He was calculating angles, laying plans, anticipating the next question, arranging the next dodge.

Cain realized how badly he had overreacted during the drive over here, thinking he might be murdered in Central Park. Not Lansky's style at all, nor would he ever be a shot and a splash kind of guy. Lansky could pull off whatever he needed without even giving an order. He'd just make a suggestion to somebody, who'd make a suggestion to somebody else. Then one day you wouldn't show up for work, and your seat would remain empty at the dinner table. Gone without a trace, except for a few well-placed rumors about how you'd crossed the wrong guy, or maybe absconded with the kitty from the commissioner's favorite charity. In fact, for all anyone knew you might still be out there, spending the loose change. That's how Lansky would do it—excuse me: *Mister* Lansky.

That unsettling train of thought probably explained why Cain flinched noticeably when Lansky made a sudden move to shut the window blinds.

Lansky, taking notice, straightened and then smiled.

"Now, see? That's the nature of power in this town. I make even a suggestion of a threatening move, and you're halfway to the floor." He slapped Cain on the shoulder. "Perception. It's something you can't buy with all the money on Wall Street. The very thing that allows Charlie Luciano to still call the shots from inside a prison cell. A few symbolic gestures might be needed once in a while, but otherwise nothing even the slightest bit illegal has to be done. Then who comes calling in our nation's hour of need? No less than the United States Navy."

He squeezed Cain's shoulder before letting go. He nodded toward the couch.

"Whadda you say we sit down?"

"Sure."

Cain was relieved to discover that his voice was still working. He sat at one end of the couch. Lansky settled into the wing chair, with arm rests that made it look like a cushiony throne. Cain's eyes were drawn to a family photo on a side table. Lansky's wife with their two young sons and an infant daughter, everybody smiling and in their best clothes. Lansky followed his gaze.

"You got a kid, too, I hear. A girl, right?"

Not the sort of information he wanted the Little Man to know, but that was probably why Lansky brought it up.

"Yes."

"It's the best part of living, having a family. Having a wife? Well . . ." He waggled a hand, his little joke about infidelity, or maybe a nod to Cain's recent history.

"So let's get down to business. As I'm sure you know, you've made a lot of people unhappy."

"That's been made pretty clear to me."

"And I know you're probably thinking, hey, these mugs are really getting away with something. Am I right?"

"One of them is."

Lansky nodded.

"Yes, he is. As you've seen for yourself, Albert is a man of excesses. Far too often he strikes out on his own, and thinks he's a damn genius for doing so. But that's Albert, not us. Which is why we will deal with Albert in our own time, in our own way. So, you see, if you and that old Jew keep poking around you're going to fuck this up for everybody."

"Then why didn't you let Albert kill me? Not that I'm ungrateful."

"Because the only thing that would fuck this up even more would be if he killed the very cop who'd just been asking the DA about him. That would have sunk this thing for sure, and right now, I've gotta tell you, it's a real good thing. And I don't just mean for Charlie and me. It's a real good thing for this country."

"If you say so."

"Don't you get smart with me!"

Lansky leaned across the space between them, jabbed a finger against Cain's chest and left it there. This was the pivot point of the night, Cain sensed, the moment at which Lansky would begin making demands, and Cain would either pass the test by capitulating or fail miserably by standing up to him. The worst kind of choice, in other words, pitting his life against his honor. Or so he thought.

To his everlasting surprise he instead got a lecture, a plea, plus a wave or two of the flag. What's more, the performance felt oddly sincere, as if the Little Man wanted earnestly for Cain to believe that, at least this once, he really was doing the best of deeds for the best of motives.

"There is one reason only that I'm in on this deal, Cain, and it's very simple. I am a patriot, helping my country. Don't smile, don't even think about it, unless you want your face knocked through those windows."

"Okay." Cain didn't move a muscle. Lansky's finger was still pressed firmly against his chest. Finally he removed it, and settled back into the chair.

"Tell me something. Do you know how I used to spend my weekends around here back in the thirties?"

"No."

"Busting heads at Nazi rallies, all over town. You ever heard of Nathan Perlman? Used to be in Congress, now he's a judge?"

"No." Cain had been rendered almost speechless. He could hardly believe the pleading tone of Lansky's voice, as if the man's soul were on trial and he was delivering the closing argument for his own defense.

"Well, he came to me personally back in thirty-five and said, 'We Jews have to start demonstrating a little more militancy.' A judge, mind you, so I took him at his word. And one night Walter Winchell calls—he lives in this building, you know—and he tips me off to a rally of a bunch of Bundists up in Yorkville. Well, I get on the horn to as many of my pals as I can. There were only fifteen of us, but let me tell you, by the end of the night those brownshirts were calling the cops to help *them* get out of there alive."

Lansky's face was beaming.

"And you know what I did last year, even before Pearl Harbor ever happened?"

"I don't."

"Signed up with my local draft board. Told 'em I'd do anything. You can check. It's all in writing. Knew they'd say I was too old for soldiering, so I said I'd work in a machine shop, like when I was a kid. Run a lathe, a drill press, whatever they needed! Of course they never got back to me. But then, you see, *then* I get word from Lanza that this Haffenden guy is trying to put together some deal for the waterfront, so of course I get on board. *Of course!* Because it's my chance to do something!

"Now, is Charlie thinking this way? Hell, I don't know. Maybe Charlie sees a way out of the joint, 'cause that's Charlie. I do know he hates that asshole Mussolini, whose cops rounded up half the wise guys in Sicily, bad blood all around. But he's in this for the full ride, even if he gets nothing out of the deal. Lanza, too. All our guys. As for Albert, well, we knew we had a problem as soon as we heard what he'd been up to."

"The plot, you mean. To burn the *Normandie*."

Lansky shook his head in exasperation. "Dumbass figured he'd be doing Charlie a favor. Make it look like a bunch of German zealots had done it, to scare everybody into begging for Charlie's help. Then the damn thing burns anyway, and Haffenden's people come looking for us, and things start moving in the right direction. So when we hear what Albert's been up to, Charlie about blows a gasket, and tells him to clean up his fucking mess before he ruins it for everybody. And, Albert being Albert, he just makes a bigger mess, which brought you into it."

"And now you want me out of it."

"Of your own accord, and for the good of your country."

"What about Albert?"

"Like I said."

"You said you'd deal with him. I need something better than that."

"Or what, you'll haul him in?" Lansky laughed aloud. "Like I said, Cain. You're not a fast learner, although you are persuasive, so I'll tell you one thing, and one thing only about where this is headed. But it sure as hell had better not leave this room, because right now even Albert doesn't know it's coming."

"Okay."

"Albert, he's practically forty. Only two months younger than me, in fact. Nonetheless, I have it on the best of authority that Albert will soon be enlisting in the United States Army. They're going to make a soldier out of him. They'll post him somewhere well beyond the city. He'll be training soldiers to be military longshoremen. That will take him off the streets and out of that candy store. He'll live in a barracks and take orders. And you can take that to the bank."

Cain was astounded. What's more, he believed it. Murder, Inc. goes to war. The final swipe of the mop to clean up Anastasia's mess, once and for all, so that the bizarre waterfront security alliance of mob guys, prosecutors, and the Navy could march onward without further distraction. It was just strange enough to be true.

"Then do we have an understanding, Detective Cain?"

"Maybe."

Lansky raised his eyebrows and opened his mouth. For the first time tonight, he was the one who seemed astounded.

"Just one other thing," Cain said. "The old Jew, Danziger. Or Sascha, as you know him. I want him left alone."

Lansky frowned and tilted his head.

"You don't exactly have much leverage, you know."

"I could go to the DA tomorrow, tell him everything you just admitted to me, not to mention tell him all about my little ride to the Harlem River."

"Not if you value your life."

"You just said bumping me off would fuck up everything."

"Sure, if you did it Albert's way." Lansky smiled, the wheels turning again behind his eyes.

"But it's not my life we're talking about. It's Sascha's."

Cain had no more cards to play, and he supposed Lansky knew it. Lansky scrutinized him for a while longer and then smiled wryly.

"You know, Cain, the way I see it, it's probably good business if I can find some way to ingratiate myself with one of New York's finest. 'Cause you never know what dividends that might pay somewhere down the road. Right?"

Cain couldn't bring himself to say yes to that kind of mortgage on his future, so instead he nodded and smiled uncomfortably, which seemed to amuse Lansky a great deal. What had Cain really expected? To be able to walk out of here clean as a whistle? He would be lucky if he walked out at all.

"In that case," Lansky said, "I have something for you. Something to give Sascha. Come with me a second."

They stood and crossed the room, walking past the piano to a wood-paneled study with wall-to-wall bookshelves. Lansky opened a desk drawer and retrieved a black book. Now *that* would probably have lots of interesting reading. He also got out an envelope and a sheet of paper, and began rooting through the top drawer of the desk, presumably in search of a pen or pencil. That's when Cain remembered what he still had in his trouser pocket.

"Allow me," he said, producing the fountain pen that he'd pocketed at the Astor.

Lansky smiled and stared at Cain for an extra second or two.

"Never let it be said that you're short of chutzpah, Cain. Are you familiar with that word?"

"No, sir."

"That does not surprise me. One moment, then."

He opened the black book in a way that Cain couldn't see the contents. He eyed the page for a second, put away the book, and began writing. It took only seconds. He capped the pen, stuck it back into the desk with a wink at Cain, and then folded the paper, which he slipped into the envelope. With a lick of his tongue, he sealed it and handed it over.

"For Sascha. A down payment on his continued silence. In fact, if I'm not mistaken it may well suffice for all future installments. Listen to me! Just thinking about the guy, and I start talking the way he does." He shook his head, as if marveling. "The fucking Dictionary!"

Cain took the envelope. "May I ask what it is?"

"The thing Sascha has always liked best. Information."


Cain emerged into the night feeling like he'd attained an imperfect but defensible sort of justice, if only at the level of one friend looking out for another. The war would continue, of course—not just the larger one abroad, but the one here with its casualties on every front, some of them hidden forever. But he would have at least defended one small citadel, however compromised in his tactics.

The moon was rising over the park, and after everything he'd just endured he felt like a stroll. Maybe he'd even stop for a beer along the way. Kick back and collect his wits before heading home. Give Olivia a kiss goodnight, maybe talk about when she would next see her mother, and then he might make a date with Beryl. Tomorrow he'd alert Danziger and sound the all-clear. He was eager to see what was in Lansky's note.

He crossed the street to be as close as he could to the trees and flowers of the park, with their springtime perfume that was strong even in the chill. This wasn't bad at all, being alive like this. Then he stopped and turned, having experienced once again that odd fleeting sensation of a watchful presence at his back. Considering what had just transpired, he was frankly a little surprised to feel it again.

He looked toward the trees and down the sidewalk. Nothing. Just as he was about to be back on his way, a voice called out his name.

"Cain!"

A familiar voice, although he couldn't yet place it. He looked again, and still saw no one.

"Cain! Over here!"

The voice was calling from the trees, from perhaps ten feet inside the stone wall that bordered the park, where he now saw a familiar face emerge into the moonlight. A face from home. James Vance, Rob's younger brother. He was slowly raising his right arm, which Cain now saw held a pistol with a long barrel, rising like a periscope from the deep.

"These bullets are Rob's!" James shouted. "This gun is his! I'm finishing this for him!"

Even as Cain's muscles tensed for a leap to safety, he thought he also detected a second man, just emerging from the trees. But by the time that thought had registered he was throwing himself to the ground, the gun had already fired, and the bullet had found a target.

# 42

..................

*DANZIGER*

I HAVE LIVED A LONG LIFE—longer, anyway, than the numeric span of my years would imply. That is the first thought that drives my actions as I watch the desolate young man raise his gun into a firing position and take careful aim at Mr. Cain. A long life. Or long enough.

Besides, if I am ever to make good on my recently stated intention to act more out of concern for the safety of Mr. Cain and his daughter than for myself, then I had better move now or forever be branded as a fraud and a liar. The tragedy of this moment, the absolute *blunder* of it, is that I should have seen it coming. Instead, I underestimated the danger of this forlorn fellow, who on both occasions when I saw him before had looked so hopelessly lost and out of place that he seemed a mere zephyr, a bothersome bit of wind but nothing more. Now, too late, I see him as I should have. His is the bottomless grief of the untethered, of those who are capable of any action. I missed this because I was distracted and diverted by more familiar faces, marked by a more familiar brand of danger.

But there may yet be room for me to act. Because for men such as him it is never sufficient to simply fire a weapon and be gone. They must announce their presence, and enunciate their purpose. They must ritualize their vengeance. And that is what I see and hear him doing now as he calls out again to Mr. Cain. So perhaps there is time.

I have put myself into this position thanks in part to the assistance of friends. When Mr. Cain and I parted company the night before, I knew he would not keep his promise to lay low. It was clear in his eyes and his manner. He lied so that I would not act. So I lied as well, and made ready to assist him.

Mr. Cain is a restless man, prone to risk, so I knew he would act quickly. But he is not rash, he is not a fool, and I knew as well that he would wait until after dark. My own status as a hunted man made matters tricky, and I was not certain where Mr. Cain would venture first. So, I enlisted Fedya and Beryl as lookouts. Fedya in particular was excited to be included in such a seemingly dubious enterprise. Beryl acted only out of concern, although I took pains to ensure that her assignment was the more benign of the two.

I stationed Fedya at the newsstand on Saratoga Avenue, the very one where Gerhard had watched Hansch disappear into Anastasia's Packard. Beryl took up her post on a park bench across the street from Lansky's home, at the Majestic. Surely, one of these places would be Mr. Cain's eventual destination, whether of his own choosing or not, and when he arrived, my observer would notify me so that I could hurry to the scene.

And after that? I did not know. I did not even think about it all that much, perhaps because I did not wish to confront the possibility that I would be wholly inadequate to the task of helping him in the face of such formidable opposition.

Fedya being Fedya—a wonderful friend, but one who has never engaged in these kinds of activities—he soon grew bored and restless. Even though he paid for his right to his post by purchasing three newspapers and a magazine, he deserted after only an hour in order to fortify himself for further duty with a cup of coffee at an eatery around the corner. As luck would have it, Mr. Cain must have arrived shortly after Fedya's departure, because by the time Fedya returned the operator of the newsstand told him all about the excitement that had transpired in his absence. Fedya telephoned me sheepishly with the news, and for more than half an hour I paced the room, fearful that hope was lost.

Then Beryl telephoned with the news that Mr. Cain had miraculously arrived at the Majestic. I departed immediately, even hiring a taxi, and as soon as I arrived I dispatched her to retrieve the poor, distraught Fedya and put him to bed.

So here I am, then, lurching forward, my body moving with an alacrity I have not experienced in ages as the young man, James Vance, shouts his intentions and prepares to carry them out. Even as I do so, I realize somewhere deep within me that the man I used to be would not have been up to this task.

During the Great War—the *first* Great War, I suppose we should call it now—I often heard accounts of men my age calling for their mothers and crying like infants as they died in the trenches. They suffered their final agonies in a panic, dying poorly and pitifully, and I probably would have done the same.

But twenty-four years have passed, and with them a second lifetime. When the idea of death now intrudes upon my thoughts, I find to my surprise that I am calmly accepting, I am prepared. Perhaps it is because I have endured much and have survived more.

For once, then, let it be said of Danziger—or of Sascha: I will leave it to you to choose—that he acted on motives that were entirely selfless. Let it be said in five languages, if possible. And, if necessary, let it be said in memoriam. But do let it be said.

Consider that to be my final request as I cross the darkened sidewalk toward the space that separates the boy from Danziger. I plunge forward into the breach as the gun fires. I cry out, I know not in what language. American, I suppose.

The bullet strikes. The ground rushes up to greet me.

# 43

............................

FROM THE MOMENT HE REACHED Danziger's gurney at Bel-
levue, Cain resolved that he would splurge on a taxi for the old fellow's
funeral. But, please, he prayed, let that happen in some other year, and
by some other cause of death.

The gurney was parked in the emergency ward, not in the mortuary. That at least offered cause for hope, although matters were far
from settled. It was something of a snafu that Danziger was at Bellevue at all, so many blocks from the shooting. But ambulance drivers
apparently had their turf wars, too, so here they were. Nurses had just
wheeled the gurney out of an operating room. One of them hovered
nearby, her scrubs still bloody.

"You're not allowed here, sir."

"Police," he said, flashing his shield.

She probably would have ordered him out anyway if his eyes hadn't
looked so pleading. So instead she waited, a rare moment of grace in
such a bustling place, and she indulged him for a few seconds while he
surveyed the pale, thin, unconscious figure stretched out on the white
sheet. Danziger's mouth was agape, as if he might begin snoring at any
moment. His chest was stitched up like a cadaver's. Then time was up.

"I'm sorry, sir. Police or not, you can't stay. This is a recovery area."

"Okay then."

He touched the gurney but didn't dare touch Danziger—germs, a jinx, who knew what maladies he might visit upon the poor man? He went to the waiting room to begin his vigil.

Between all the mayhem in front of the Majestic and the reams of police work that followed it had taken him hours to get here. As soon as James Vance had seen what his shot had done—striking an old man instead of Cain—he'd stood dumbfounded as Cain rushed to Danziger's aid. Cain glanced up just in time to see Vance raise the gun a second time. Their eyes locked. Vance's were desolate. He then turned the gun on himself and placed the barrel in his mouth.

"James, no!"

The young man blew out the back of his head and crumpled to the ground, another member of the Vance family whose blood would forever weigh upon Cain's conscience.

Cain remained at Bellevue until dawn. Eileen, the family spy, still contrite in her duplicity, had gotten in touch long ago to ask if it was okay if Olivia spent the night at her mother's apartment on the Upper East Side. He supposed it was. If Clovis could handle being a mother again, then it was actually a relief. She might be just what the girl needed in the coming year. Even if they ended up parenting by subway, maybe they could make it work. Not for themselves—that was dead on the floor of the drunk's shack in Horton—but for Olivia.

Shortly after sunrise, a nudge awakened him. Creaky and sore from the chair, Cain looked up and saw the nurse from the night before. Her face was so filled with concern that panic rose up like something alive in his throat. She put a hand on his arm, as if to steady him, and spoke. "You're Mr. Danziger's friend, right?"

He nodded, too scared to speak.

"It looks like he's going to survive, but he might not be conscious for quite a while. Besides the bullet he also took a blow to the head when he hit the ground."

"A few more hours, you think?"

"More like days." She hesitated. "Maybe longer. I guess what I'm saying is that there's really no sense in you waiting. Maybe you could leave a number."

Cain nodded. Then he noticed for the first time that Beryl was seated to his left, as quiet as could be. She must have arrived during the night. They stood to leave. Only then did he begin learning of the measures Danziger had taken to protect him.

On their way out the door he felt inside his jacket for the envelope Lansky had given him. He thought about leaving it behind but felt responsible for protecting it, so he merely tapped it like a talisman. Then he took Beryl's hand and they strolled into the morning.

Danziger rejoined the world six weeks later. By that time he looked as if he were intent on assuming a third identity, so changed was he by his time in a coma. He was pale and bony. The nurses had shaved his beard and stubble, and had clipped his hair to military length. Only his eyes remained the same, still shining with that June vitality from the moment he reopened them.

"What am I supposed to call you now?" Cain asked.

Danziger smiled weakly, his eyes flickering with amusement. "That is up to you." The voice was raspy, but filled with warmth. His diction was impeccable as always, the accent still roaming across two continents. "Friend will do for now."

"Sounds about right. I've brought you some things."

"Yes?"

"Fresh news, for starters, from the United States Army."

"An invasion of Europe?"

"Sorry, no. This is from the home front. The newly enlisted Private Albert Anastasia has reported for duty at Fort Indiantown Gap, out toward the middle of Pennsylvania. He's got a bunk in a barracks, gets three squares a day, and says 'Yes, sir' about twenty times an hour. Who knows, maybe he'll learn to act like a human being."

"Doubtful."

"Probably. But I hear his wife is looking for a house in Jersey, for after the war. So there's that."

"And what of our other friend? Should I fear a visit in the night sometime soon?"

"Mr. Lansky continues to pursue a patriotic course of action, or so Hogan tells me."

"Hogan himself?"

"Gurfein joined the Army. Some intelligence outfit called the OSS. Maybe he couldn't stomach the idea of working hand in glove with all those goons he'd been trying to put in jail. As for whatever beef there was between Lansky and you, well, he says that's over now."

Danziger took a moment to digest that.

"You are sure of this? He gave his word?"

"He did. About five minutes before you saw me walk out of the Majestic."

"Then perhaps this time I can keep my current name. Or even go back to my old one."

Cain told Danziger what had become of their investigation. It no longer existed. The files for four unsolved murders had already been marked for storage in the cold case drawer. A fifth, the murder of Angela Feinman, had been established as the handiwork of the late Dieter Göllner.

"They didn't all get away, though. Hogan at least took an interest in Herman Keller, over some business deals he'd brokered that were a little too cozy with Germany. Seems he was in violation of some laws that only my father-in-law could understand."

"Laws which will mysteriously not be applied to Chase National Bank, or to the machinations of their favorite lawyer, correct?"

"Correct. I guess some people always have the muscle when they need it."

"Now and forevermore. And you, Mr. Cain? Do you remain employed?"

"One week suspension without pay, but that's over and done with."

Danziger raised an eyebrow.

"Not for anything we did. For losing my sidearm. Anastasia's guys never gave it back. Two weeks ago I got transferred to headquarters to work an internal investigation with Zharkov. There are some indictments pending on some of my former colleagues in the fourteenth precinct, and last week Hogan dropped some more dirt in through the transom, so it looks like we might be busy a while longer."

"A man of his word, after all."

"And from all I've heard, the waterfront operation actually seems to be working. Lanza put some Navy people aboard some of the fishing fleets. Just last week some mob guys out on Long Island helped round up a few saboteurs that the Germans had landed from a sub. Luciano moved to his new digs at Great Meadow prison last month, and it looks like Lansky will be visiting every week or two. Not that anyone really thinks they'll only be doing the country's business."

Danziger shook his head in apparent amazement.

"Oh, and one other thing about Lansky. He gave me this. For you." Cain held out the envelope, still sealed. "He called it a payment for your continued silence."

Danziger wrinkled his brow and, with some difficulty, reached out to take it. He struggled for a few seconds to tear it open, and then sighed in exasperation.

"Allow me," Cain said.

Cain retrieved a knife from Danziger's breakfast tray and slit open the envelope. He pulled out the folded sheet of paper and handed it over, and then moved around the bed so he could read over Danziger's shoulder. Having resisted the temptation to open it for all these weeks, he figured he'd earned the right.

Danziger unfolded the paper to reveal a few brief lines in Lansky's neat handwriting. There was a name, Maria Corazza, followed by an address in Queens, and then a single word, "Widowed."

"So is that . . . ?"

Danziger nodded. For a few seconds he seemed to be in disbelief. Then his eyes darted back and forth, as if he were watching a newsreel inside his head.

"She's the real reason you never left New York, isn't she? The whole reason you were willing to take the stupid risk of going back to your old neighborhood."

"The whole reason? No. But one of them. Foolish, of course."

"What about now?"

Danziger's eyes were swimming. For a moment he didn't speak. He blinked, but no tears fell. Then he drew a deep breath and smiled, still holding on tightly to the paper.

"Now," he said, "now I believe that I shall go on living for a while longer."

"Good plan," Cain said. "For both of us."

# AFTERWORD

......................

After finishing any novel which combines the real and the imagined, some readers inevitably ask how much of it was true. Quite a lot, in the case of this book, especially with regard to the unholy alliance that U.S. Naval Intelligence and District Attorney Frank Hogan cooked up with the Mafia to secure the New York waterfront against sabotage and enemy submarines.

It is also well established that the burning of the luxury liner *Normandie* was a major impetus to the arrangement. Even though a subsequent Navy inquiry established that the fire was an accident, that didn't stop several Mafia figures—Charles "Lucky" Luciano and Meyer Lansky, in particular—from claiming years later that mob hit man Albert Anastasia, a Luciano ally, had arranged the burning of the ship in hopes of engineering a better deal for his imprisoned boss. For me, their claims raised the possibility that, at the very least, a fellow as unpredictable as Anastasia might have indeed concocted such a plot, even if he never brought it to fruition.

The subplot involving Harris Euston, Herman Keller, and the scheme to raise capital for the German government by selling Reichsmarks for dollars is also rooted in fact, as described in Charles Higham's 1984 book, *Trading with the Enemy: An Exposé of the Nazi-American Money Plot.*

It's interesting to look at some of the well-documented particulars of the Navy-Mafia deal to see how they align with events in this novel. Naval Intelligence operatives at first tried to do the job themselves, but failed miserably when mob guys and their union allies easily saw through their cloak-and-dagger approach. Navy Captain Roscoe C. MacFall then decided that his intelligence people should enlist the help of the underworld, and his point man was Lieutenant Commander Charles R. "Red" Haffenden.

MacFall and Haffenden sought advice from DA Frank Hogan and his rackets investigator, Murray Gurfein, on how to best approach the Mafia. Gurfein suggested that the Navy contact Joseph "Socks" Lanza, because of his control over the Fulton Fish Market. Lanza agreed to do what he could, but soon discovered that many colleagues suspected a trap because Lanza was under indictment at the time. Lanza suggested that the only way to get everyone on board would be to obtain the blessing of mob boss Charles "Lucky" Luciano, who was serving a thirty- to fifty-year sentence at a state prison in remote Dannemora, New York. Gurfein telephoned Luciano's attorney, Moses Polakoff, who suggested Meyer Lansky as the best choice to approach Luciano on the government's behalf.

Lansky, as he tells Cain in chapter 41, was indeed patriotic about the war effort, and about opposing Hitler. He really did get into violent scrapes at Bundist rallies in New York in the 1930s, and he really did try to enlist in the Army at the age of thirty-nine. And, just as described in this book, he helped initiate the Navy's waterfront security deal with the Mafia by participating in a face-to-face meeting with Gurfein and Polakoff on a Saturday morning in April 1942, at the Longchamps Restaurant on 57th Street—the same breakfast meeting which Danziger witnesses in chapter 12.

Just as described here, the three men discussed moving Luciano to a more convenient location. Also as depicted in the book, the three men then continued their discussion by taking a taxi to the Hotel Astor, where they met Red Haffenden, who indeed had a suite of offices at the hotel under the auspices of the Executives Association of Greater New York. From then on, Haffenden used the Astor office as a sort of safe house for his increasingly frequent meetings with mob figures, although later he became so chummy that they began brazenly visiting him at Naval Intelligence offices in the federal building on Church Street.

State authorities did, in fact, move Luciano to a more convenient location at Great Meadow prison, and Lansky became a regular visitor as part of the deal. A wide array of other notorious mob figures soon joined the parade to Great Meadow under the auspices of the Navy arrangement. No one ever bothered to bug those meetings, and it has always been assumed that Luciano discussed matters well beyond his work for his country. Thus did the U.S. Navy make it easier for Luciano to keep running his criminal enterprises.

Although Hogan gave his blessing to the arrangement, he never lost his skepticism of some of the figures involved. He ordered a wiretap of Lanza's phone at the Meyers Hotel, and in one instance recorded Haffenden approving of activities that resulted in mob figures beating up a union official who was trying to organize a strike on the Brooklyn waterfront.

Other excesses were also overlooked or glossed over. As one historian has noted, there were approximately thirty unsolved murders on the New York waterfront between 1942 and 1950.

Gurfein, as mentioned in the book, did leave the DA's office not long after helping bring about the arrangement, to become an officer in the Office of Strategic Services, precursor to the CIA.

But the biggest lingering question mark concerns the role played by Anastasia, whose Murder, Inc. was known by then to be operating out of Midnight Rose's candy store in Brooklyn. If he had indeed pursued some sort of plot to burn the *Normandie*, as Luciano and Lansky later claimed, how would he have reacted if fate had preempted his plans with an accidental burning? That tantalizing possibility—and the current lack of a clear and convincing answer—drove much of my plot.

This, in turn, left me wondering whether Anastasia would have taken it upon himself to remove all traces of such a plot, in order to keep from jeopardizing the deal his boss had negotiated with the Navy. If so, how would Anastasia's associates have reacted to his possible excesses? The historical record provides the answer I eventually chose for my plot: In June of 1942, just as the Navy-Mafia arrangement was hitting its stride, and only a few months before Anastasia's fortieth birthday, the government accepted his enlistment into the U.S. Army, which promptly posted him to Fort Indiantown Gap, in Pennsylvania.

There is also a historical basis for the character of Danziger, at least as far as his occupation as a letter writer is concerned. My inspiration for him was a seven-paragraph description of "Alexandroff the Letter-Writing Man" in a 1932 book, *The Real New York*, by Helen Worden, an item which also appeared under her byline in the "Talk of the Town" section of the October 8 issue of *The New Yorker* that same year. Worden depicted a tall, broad-shouldered "Cossack" of indeterminate age who wrote letters for his illiterate and non-English-speaking neighbors of the Lower East Side from an office on East 4th Street. He spoke Russian, Polish, and German, charged fifty cents per letter, and wrote about five letters per day. All well and good, but this was the passage that intrigued me the most, with its rich well of possibility:

> *When Alexandroff isn't writing letters, he is answering questions. Across his window is inscribed, "Alexandroff—Information." . . . Through the thousands of letters he reads (his little shop is the local post office) he is closely linked with the current situation in the small towns of Europe . . . "Alexandroff is wise," the neighbors say. "He knows much."*

After reading that, how could I possibly resist?

# Acknowledgments

I would like to thank the following people for their invaluable assistance in the course of researching this book: Ellen Belcher, special collections librarian at John Jay College of Criminal Justice; Barry Moreno, librarian at the Ellis Island Immigration Museum; Professor Trevar Riley-Reid, librarian at City College of New York; the staff of the Municipal Archives of the City of New York's Department of Records (especially for their help in using the wonderful archive of photos taken by the city tax assessor of every property in the city in 1938–40); and the staffs of the New York City Public Library and of the archives of the New-York Historical Society.

In addition, the following books were of great assistance:

*The Luciano Project*, by Rodney Campbell

*Over Here!: New York City During World War II*, by Lorraine B. Diehl

*New York in the Forties, 162 photographs*, by Andreas Feininger

*The Rise and Fall of the Jewish Gangster in America*, by Albert Fried

*Helluva Town: The Story of New York City During World War II*, by Richard Goldstein

*The Last Testament of Lucky Luciano*, by Martin A. Gosch and Richard Hammer

*Flophouse: Life on the Bowery*, by David Isay, Stacy Abramson and Harvey Wang

## ACKNOWLEDGMENTS

*WWII & NYC*, by Kenneth T. Jackson

*The Big Bankroll: The Life and Times of Arnold Rothstein*, by
   Leo Katcher

*The Upperworld and the Underworld: Case Studies of Racketeering and
   Business Infiltrations in the United States*, by Robert J. Kelly

*A Treasury of Damon Runyon*, edited by Clark Kinnaird

*Little Man: Meyer Lansky and the Gangster Life*, by Robert Lacey

*Honest Cop: The Dramatic Life Story of Lewis J. Valentine*,
   by Lowell Limpus

*Up in the Old Hotel*, by Joseph Mitchell

*Manhattan '45*, by Jan Morris

*Mafia Allies*, by Tim Newark

*The Burning of the* General Slocum, by Claude Rust

*Broadway Boogie Woogie: Damon Runyon and the Making of New York
   City Culture*, by Daniel R. Schwarz

*My Mother and I*, a memoir by Elizabeth G. Stern

*Night Stick*, by Lewis J. Valentine

*The Real New York* (1932), by Helen Worden

I would also like to thank the Graduate Center of the City University
of New York's Center for Urban Research, for its wonderfully informative website, 1940snewyork.com.

ALSO BY

# DAN FESPERMAN

THE DOUBLE GAME

A few years before the fall of the Berlin Wall, spook-turned-novelist Edwin Lemaster reveals to up-and-coming journalist Bill Cage that he'd once considered spying for the enemy. For Cage, a fan who grew up as a Foreign Service brat in the very cities where Lemaster set his plots, the story creates a brief but embarrassing sensation. More than two decades later, Cage receives an anonymous note hinting that he should have dug deeper. Spiked with cryptic references to some of Cage and his father's favorite old spy novels, the note is the first piece of a puzzle that will lead Cage back to Vienna, Prague, and Budapest in search of the truth, even as he discovers that the ghosts of Lemaster's past eerily—and dangerously—still haunt the present. As the suspense steadily increases, decades of secrets begin to unravel.

Thriller

ALSO AVAILABLE

*Layover in Dubai*
*The Arms Maker of Berlin*
*The Prisoner of Guantánamo*
*The Warlord's Son*
*The Small Boat of Great Sorrows*

VINTAGE CRIME/BLACK LIZARD
Available wherever books are sold.
www.blacklizardcrime.com